PRAISE FOR

A GILDED GRAVE

"This well-crafted mystery is an absolute delight. Freydont has brought Gilded Age Newport to life with the skill of a historian and the insight of the keenest social observer. Deanna Randolph is my favorite new sleuth."

—Tasha Alexander, *New York Times* bestselling author of
The Counterfeit Heiress

"Evoking the luxurious and extravagant world of the Gilded Age, Newport heiress and feisty amateur sleuth Deanna Randolph is a force to be reckoned with in this lively mystery."

—Tessa Arlen, author of the Lady Montfort series

"Utterly captivating! Freydont skillfully combines the glittering excess of the Gilded Age and a believable upstairs-downstairs dynamic with a thrilling murder mystery. Readers will fall in love with this intrepid new sleuthing pair and the dashing young men they assist. A must read for fans of historical mystery."

—Anna Lee Huber, national bestselling author of
the Lady Darby Mysteries

"A wealth of secrets lies beneath the surface as spunky heiress Deanna Randolph and her maid Elspeth navigate the glittering waters of Gilded Age Newport's high society while working to catch a murderer. Charming and colorful characters, a richly detailed setting, and a compelling mystery make *A Gilded Grave* a thoroughly captivating read."

—Ashley Weaver, Edgar® Award–nominated author of
Murder at the Brightwell

A
GOLDEN
CAGE

Shelley
Freydont

BERKLEY PRIME CRIME, NEW YORK

An imprint of Penguin Random House LLC
375 Hudson Street, New York, New York 10014

This book is an original publication of Penguin Random House LLC.

Library of Congress Cataloging-in-Publication Data

Names: Freydont, Shelley, author.
Title: A golden cage / Shelley Freydont.
Description: Berkley Prime Crime trade paperback edition. I New York,
New York : Berkley Prime Crime, 2016. I Series: Newport gilded age
Identifiers: LCCN 2016002305 (print) I LCCN 2016006190 (ebook) I ISBN
9780425275856 (softcover) I ISBN 9780698165694 ()
Subjects: LCSH: Women detectives—Rhode Island—Fiction. I Upper class—Rhode
Island—Fiction. I Newport (R.I.)—Social life and customs—19th
century—Fiction. I BISAC: FICTION / Mystery & Detective / Historical. I
FICTION / Mystery & Detective / Women Sleuths. I GSAFD: Historical
fiction. I Mystery fiction.
Classification: LCC PS3556.R45 G65 2016 (print) I LCC PS3556.R45 (ebook) I
DDC 813/.54—dc23
LC record available at http://lccn.loc.gov/2016002305

PUBLISHING HISTORY
Berkley Prime Crime trade paperback edition / June 2016

PRINTED IN THE UNITED STATES OF AMERICA

10 9 8 7 6 5 4 3 2

Cover illustration by Aleta Rafton.
Cover design by Lesley Worrell.
Interior text design by Kelly Lipovich.

Penguin
Random
House

To my aunt, Mot.
A free spirit who led the way.

Chapter

1

Deanna Randolph tried not to stare, but it was the most remarkable thing she had ever seen. When she'd first learned that Maude Grantham was transporting an entire theater company to perform for her husband's birthday fete, Deanna hadn't known what to imagine.

The Granthams' "cottage" on Bellevue Avenue stood out like a sentinel of good taste against the more imaginative façades of the other "cottages" that were being built in Newport. But even its stalwart presence was a study in excess, if you asked Deanna.

Tonight it was the scene of festivity and color. Across the meticulously trimmed lawn, huge golden cages, trimmed with fairy lights, held birds of iridescent plumage. Exotic flowers cascaded down the bars and spilled onto the ground.

A red velvet carpet led across the lawn to a canopy and booths of entertainment. And at the back of the garden a theater—an actual theater—had been built for the occasion.

This was Deanna's first season, and though she'd attended many extravagant affairs, none came close to what she was seeing tonight.

Gwendolyn Manon, with whom Deanna was spending the summer, leaned closer. "My goodness, it looks like a combination of an Istanbul bazaar and Brighton Beach."

Deanna thought it was all those things and more.

"Close your mouth, my dear, and prepare to meet our hostess." Gwen nudged Deanna forward.

Deanna closed her mouth, but her eyes continued to drink in the spectacle. Such a play of lights against shadows. The huge August moon hung above the carnival atmosphere like a stage set. She didn't see how any actual play could surpass this scene. She'd love to paint it. She'd call it *Festive Lights on a Dark Summer's Night*.

Now that her mama had taken her sister, Adelaide, to Switzerland to cure her migraines, Deanna was enjoying many more freedoms, including painting objects that Mama wouldn't approve of at all. This was all thanks to Gran Gwen, who wasn't Deanna's grandmother but a friend of her father's and the grandmother of Joe Ballard, to whom Deanna was almost engaged the previous summer.

Gwen led her to a woman of robust proportions. Their hostess, Mrs. Samuel Grantham, stood in a circle of soft light that illuminated her champagne-colored ball gown with its sweep of train, covered in embroidered gold and silver stars. A firmament herself, and circled by her glittering guests.

"Maude." Gran Gwen offered her gloved hand for a brief return of pressure. "I believe you are acquainted with my guest, Deanna Randolph."

Maude Grantham turned slightly toward Deanna, and Deanna was momentarily blinded by the sparkle of the thick diamond choker that graced the lady's neck.

"Ah yes, George and Jeannette's girl. I'm surprised that her mother would leave her to stay with you, especially after that business last month."

Deanna held her chin high. At least murder had stopped all the gossip about why she and Joe Ballard had broken off their assumed engagement.

Mrs. Grantham sighed. "A detective. What will they do next, these modern girls?"

"There's no telling," Gran Gwen said with an air of agreement, but there was a malicious glint in her eye. "She was br-r-rilliant," Gran Gwen said, rolling her *r*'s in such an exaggerated fashion that it made Deanna want to laugh. It was daunting to be known for her "exploits," as her mother called them, rather than being sought after for her breeding, beauty, and monetary future.

Though if she had to choose . . .

"I suppose we can't expect less, considering the way that young Joseph has surprised us all, throwing off society to consort with . . ." She raised a desultory hand.

"The great unwashed?" Gwen supplied.

Maude cut her a look. "Why am I surprised? You've set such an outrageous example, but surely you could have stopped that nonsense if you had tried."

"Surely, I could have. But you know how indulgent we older folks can be. I'm surprised that you allowed Drusilla and Walter to have a theater constructed on your property and present a play."

"It was an indulgence, I know, but Drusilla so wanted to

please her father, and the Judge does love the theater. As long as it's on a decent subject."

Gran Gwen smiled and moved on.

Deanna gave a quick half curtsey and followed her.

"I'm sure the play will be very staid . . . and long . . . and boring," Gwen said as she nodded and smiled at people as they made their way across the lawn.

Deanna hoped not. She loved going to the theater. Something her own mama didn't totally approve of unless it was the opera or Shakespeare.

"Maude is becoming more of a stickler than her husband. She's always been a bit of a prude, and marrying the Judge didn't help. But now that Anthony Comstock with his asinine morality laws has got his talons into the Judge, not to mention that Parkhurst fellow, there's no bearing either of them. At least the Judge, moralistic bombast that he is, enjoys a good play, and the occasional glass of champagne.

"Ah, there are Joseph and his parents." Gwen took Deanna by the elbow and propelled her down the velvet walkway to where Laurette and Lionel Ballard were standing with Joe.

"Where have you all been?" Gwen asked. "I was beginning to think you weren't coming."

"Laurette received a telegram that of course must be answered," Lionel said, casting an amused but loving look to his wife, Joe's mother.

Laurette was Gran Gwen's daughter; and though they both shared the same fiery temperament, the two women couldn't have been more different in looks. Gwendolyn Henriette Laguerre Manon was large of name but diminutive in figure, petite and small boned; she nonetheless held the respect of all of Newport in spite of her less-than-orthodox life and loves. Her daughter Laurette was tall, willowy, with light brown hair and classic features. The story was that Lionel Ballard had met, fallen in love with, and proposed to her in the same night.

"Yes," Laurette said. "From Rosalie Deeks. Her daughter, Amabelle, left home, must be two years ago now, to become an actress. Evidently she is one of the players in tonight's performance."

"Ah," Gwen said. "And I imagine she wants you to convince the girl to go home?"

"Yes, but of course I will do no such thing. The theater is one of the few professions where a woman can earn as much money as a man. I will, however, look in on the girl. Perhaps invite her to stay with us while the company is in Newport. If that's all right with you, Mama."

Deanna noted that even Joe's mother, the actual mistress of the Ballard cottage, was still seeking the approval of her mother. Though Deanna expected in Laurette's case, it was more a show of respect than needing Gran Gwen's approval.

Laurette was an indefatigable worker for women's suffrage and children's welfare. She traveled widely to organize marches and workers' strikes. Lionel, whose family was one of the scions of old money, was a respected financier who dabbled in business, though "silently" in most cases. Joseph, their only son, and heir to the Ballard fortune, had surprised the entirety of society the summer before, by remaining in Newport full-time to live in the working-class Fifth Ward, where he could house and work on his inventions.

An eccentric but respected family by the sheer dint of Lionel's money and Gran Gwen's personality.

And into their lives, Deanna had come. Sometimes she couldn't believe her good fortune.

"I'm sure I don't care what the girl does," Gwen said.

"Nor I," Laurette agreed.

"In that case, my love," Lionel Ballard said, "shall we leave the topic and have our fortunes read? I see a gypsy tent among the arcades."

Laurette laughed and took his arm, a familiar gesture that might scandalize some of the more staid members of society, Deanna's mother included. But her mother was an ocean away. Deanna didn't even try to suppress her shiver of exhilaration.

"Are you cold, my dear?" Gran Gwen asked.

"No, ma'am, just excited," Deanna said as she watched the two Ballards enter the canopy and stop at a colorful tent before stepping inside.

"I suppose you'll want to have your fortune read, too?" Joe said, sounding jaded and worldly and bored.

"I don't think so," Deanna answered. Maybe it was better not to know. Anyway, fortune-tellers always told you that you would meet a tall, dark, handsome man, and she was standing next to one. That would be beyond embarrassing, since Joe had already rejected her as a potential wife. Not that she cared.

There was a whole world to experience out there, and she intended to experience all of it.

"Then, come. I'll win you a prize at the coconut shies booth. Grandmère?"

"You two run along. I see someone with whom I wish to speak." And before Joe could offer to accompany her, she swept away like a woman of many fewer years. Deanna and Joe both turned to see where she was going.

"Of course," Joe said. "Quentin Asher. Well, it won't be a dull evening."

How could it be? Deanna wondered, with a play and carnival games and dinner and dancing—and fireworks.

"What are coconut shies?" she asked as Joe escorted her beneath the bright red canopy toward the rows of colorful tents.

—⋘◉⋙—

Coconut shies turned out to be a game where each player was given three wooden balls to knock over a line of coconuts. Joe won a pretty gold and enamel box, which he presented to Deanna, but when she announced her intention to try for herself, he guided her away.

"Not tonight, but someday I'll take you to Coney Island and you can ride the carousel and throw balls at coconuts to your heart's —" He broke off. "There's Mother and Father. Let's join them."

Just as they reached them, a gong sounded, deep and reverberating through the night, announcing the performance was soon to begin. The four of them joined the other guests as they began to make their way toward the theater.

"It looks just like a real theater," Deanna said as soon as they entered. There was a raised stage with heavy curtains pulled across the proscenium. An orchestra was placed in front of the stage. Rows of chairs were arranged at comfortable intervals across the wide expanse of wooden floor which Deanna guessed would soon become the ballroom.

They were shown to four chairs by a footman, one of a dozen who were showing parties to their seats. Mrs. Grantham had surely hired extra for the occasion. Deanna looked around at the audience. Some of the finest families were there. Several

Vanderbilts, the Olneys, the Wetmores, a veritable who's who of Newport society.

Lionel leaned toward the others. "I talked to Walter Edgerton. The play's called *The Sphinx*. He says Maude had the good sense to have it cut down to one act. It only lasts an hour."

"Good," Joe said. "These chairs are about as comfortable as a second-class train car."

Deanna frowned at him. He'd joined them for dinner the night before with stories of watching the construction of the stage; he'd explained in detail the operating of the sets. As far as Joe was concerned, he'd seen the best the play had to offer. He couldn't care less about the acting or being swept up in the emotions of the characters.

It really was just like being at the theater, Deanna thought as the lights dimmed and everyone became silent.

"The lights are run from a large master board at the side of the stage," Joe whispered to Deanna. "They use—"

"Shh," Laurette warned.

Joe settled back to endure the play.

A door at the side of the stage opened and the conductor stepped through. Applause broke out as he climbed the podium, where he turned and bowed to the audience.

The music began, the curtain rose, and everyone's attention was focused on the stage. Before them stood a golden pyramid almost as large as the stage itself. Its large Sphinx head scrutinized them all as if from a far and exotic place.

"Impressive," Joe said under his breath. "I wonder . . ." He trailed off into silence before his mother had to warn him again.

Deanna knew he was wondering how they'd managed to construct such a massive structure in such a limited time. He'd probably sneak off sometime during the evening to get a closer look. Deanna just planned to enjoy the play.

Two rows of girls dressed in school uniforms entered, singing in chorus. According to the program, they were students from the P'teecha's Institute. On closer inspection, Deanna saw that though a few of them could be schoolgirls, others were long past their schoolgirl years.

They were interrupted by the entrance of a male chorus of approximately the same number as the girls', costumed as bedouins, spinning and leaping onto the stage. They were dressed in colorful robes and held scimitars over their heads, and they quickly subdued the girls with the power of their love.

Deanna peered more closely at the women on stage. "Which one is Amabelle?" she whispered to Laurette.

"I'm not sure. Maybe . . ." She lifted a finger toward one. "Or . . ." She shook her head. "We'll have to wait until the play is over to find out."

Deanna hoped that "we" meant Laurette was including her in the meeting. She'd never even been close to a real actor or actress. Her mama considered them unprincipled, immoral, and a few other things Deanna didn't remember.

Deanna thought they were fascinating. And to think actresses made just as much money as the men.

The play proceeded with a Professor Papyrus giving the schoolgirls a book that held the answers to the Sphinx's questions each one must answer in order to marry her bedouin.

Deanna wished they would make plays of some of the stories from the dime novels she and her maid, Elspeth, read together each night. They were much more exciting than most plays she'd seen. They told of dangerous adventures and female detectives who did a lot more than worry about marrying some bedouin.

She was startled from her wandering attention by a cymbal crash. Several members of the audience started. The orchestra swelled, and a panel that looked just like stone, rose, exposing a golden room inside the pyramid. Light shone from it like rays of the sun, glinting on the golden walls and pouring out onto the stage. And from this stepped Hathor, the embodiment of the great stone Sphinx, dressed in shining gold.

The goddess stretched her arms forward, and she seemed to rise from the floor.

"Hydraulic lift," Joe whispered.

Deanna ignored him. Hathor stepped out of the chamber and walked forward almost as if she were standing on air—not the wooden stage. The audience applauded her appreciatively.

The young girls returned, now dressed all in white for their weddings. Only, these wedding dresses looked more like the drapery one saw on Greek statues. They were made of some filmy see-through material, but were completely respectable since they were draped over a satin underdress.

One by one they answered the Sphinx's questions correctly. The action became a little tedious, and by the time the maids had married their bedouins and Professor Papyrus and Hathor had fallen in love, Deanna was thankful the play had been only an hour.

And then in the final chorus, the Sphinx broke apart, and the first young couple stepped back into the golden space. Before everyone's eyes, they rose up and out of sight. The second couple did the same and the next, until all had ascended in heavenly wedded bliss, and only the professor and Hathor remained on stage.

The orchestra swelled and the lights rose to reveal the couples standing above the audience, raining rose petals down on the solitary couple below them.

"How did they do that?" Deanna asked Joe.

"Some kind of wheel, probably a modified Ferris wheel. With platforms instead of baskets."

"But where did they go and how did they get all the way up there?"

"I imagine they stepped off the platforms and onto a catwalk that spans the stage. Hmmm." Joe leaned forward. "Interesting. Yes."

The curtain fell to enthusiastic applause, and thoughts turned to dinner being served on the terrazzo. But Joe just sat there looking at the closed curtain.

Deanna recognized that look. He was getting an idea.

"Did you enjoy the play?" Mr. Ballard asked her.

"Immensely. Though there could have been a little more adventure."

"A band of bedouins isn't enough for you?"

"He's teasing you, Deanna." Laurette gathered them up. "Lionel, you and Joseph go on up to supper. I must say hello to Rosalie's daughter, and then I'll join you. Deanna, would you like to come with me?"

Joe started to protest, but Laurette cut him short. "It's all well and good for you to turn your back on society and go off to do what interests you, but should not Deanna have the same choice?"

Joe's mouth tightened.

Laurette patted his arm. "Don't sulk. It's only a handful of actors in Mrs. Grantham's garden, not suffragettes on a hunger strike." And with a trill of laughter, she spirited Deanna away.

"Men," she said as soon as they'd rounded the back of the

theater. "You know I would never do anything to put you in harm's way. And if any of your mother's friends objects to your visit backstage, tell them I made you do it."

She led the way, humming one of the tunes from the show.

They passed a tent set up for dining.

"So society won't have to interact with the hoi polloi, though, mark my words they'll be sauntering down to get a close-up view before the night is over."

Ahead of them a wide wooden walkway ran between the back wall of the stage and a row of tents. They made their way down the path avoiding the large chunks of pyramid, which was being dismantled and carried into one of the tents. It had looked so real onstage, but now Deanna saw that it was made mostly of thin wood and cardboard.

There was a costume tent and an equipment tent, and two additional tents on the end.

"See? Separate dressing areas for males and females. Perfectly respectable."

As if to prove her wrong, a commotion burst out ahead of them, and a woman carrying a heavy bundle of gowns out of the women's changing tent backed out with a final battery of French. As she was turning to go, two beefy workers careered around the corner, carrying a length of footlights between them.

"Watch yer back."

The *costumière* let out a squeal. At the last second, they managed to slide past one another and detour around Laurette and Deanna so smoothly that if it had appeared onstage, a choreographer would have been employed to ensure there would be no mishap.

But once disaster had been evaded, the accusations and

insults blossomed into a bouquet of harsh words—with sneers
from the stagehands and fiery insults delivered in perfect French
from the wardrobe lady—catapulting over Deanna's head.

Laurette pulled Deanna aside. "Perhaps not totally respectable. But energetic. Yes, real energy. If it could only be reined
in and used for . . ."

Laurette's words trailed off as she saw a handsome middle-
aged man in an exquisite dressing gown striding toward them.
He was still wearing full makeup; his hair was parted in the
middle and winged back from a long face and patrician nose.

"*Mon Dieu*, if it isn't the lovely Laurette." He bowed low over
her hand, then still holding that hand, he looked up. "And
where is the honorable Lionel this evening?"

"Waiting for his dinner up at the terrazzo."

"But of course." He let go of her hand. "And how did you
enjoy our little show?"

"Well, actually—"

"Yes, a butchery of a play that wasn't that meaty to begin
with." He glanced at Deanna and tilted his head.

"Edwin. May I introduce my friend Deanna Randolph?
Deanna, Edwin Stevens, our star of the evening. And manager
of the acting troupe."

Deanna curtseyed, trying to take in this debonair, refined
gentleman who had just spent the last hour playing the ridic-
ulously comic Professor Papyrus. She wondered which one
was the real Edwin Stevens.

"Edwin. I've come to say hello to Amabelle Deeks. Is she
in the ladies' tent?"

Edwin's eyebrows winged slightly upward, making his
expression more humorous than he obviously intended. "She
is in the last tent with the other chorus ladies." He nodded

toward the end of the row of tents, moved closer to Laurette, and said so quietly that Deanna almost didn't hear him, "If she has a friend, that friend should take her away . . . now." He lifted his head. "Ah, Theo. I was just coming to talk to you. If you will pardon me, ladies. Delightful to see you again." He tipped his chin and strode away.

Deanna peered at Laurette in the uneven lighting of the backstage area, but she couldn't gauge her expression. She wondered how she knew Edwin Stevens, and if Mr. Ballard knew or minded.

"Yes, Deanna?"

Deanna blushed at what she had been wondering, and answered with the other thing on her mind. "Do you think he doesn't like your friend's daughter? Why would he say you should take her away?"

Laurette sighed. "You know these actors. Always onstage. I'm sure he was just being dramatic."

Deanna nodded but noticed that Laurette walked a little more quickly toward the last tent.

"Ladies?" Laurette called when they stood at the opening of the women's dressing room tent.

"Who is it?"

"A friend of Amabelle's."

There was silence, then a young woman opened the flap and peered out. She was blonde and pretty even with the dark kohl encircling her eyes and the rouged cheeks and her red-painted lips.

She pursed her lips into a pretty bow. "Mrs. Ballard. I suppose my mother sent you to beg me to come back to the fold."

"Oh, mainly just to see how you're doing," Laurette said

lightly, and swept past her into the tent. Amabelle looked sourly at Deanna and said, "I suppose you might as well come in, too."

Deanna entered but stood just inside the door, taking it all in. It was a tent, but there was a wooden floor and a long dressing table where several of the chorus sat taking off their makeup in front of a mirror outlined in lights.

Amabelle sat down at an empty chair and began to apply cold cream with a cotton pad. "Thank you for your trouble, but I'm very happy doing what I'm doing."

"Certainly," Laurette said. "I shall tell your mother so. Are you staying long in Newport?"

Amabelle looked in the mirror and spoke to Laurette's reflection. "The company will stay until tomorrow night's ferry, a morning off, and we'll arrive in New York in time to open again on Tuesday."

"And you're staying where?"

Amabelle eyed her suspiciously. "At a local boardinghouse."

Her expression said she was used to finer accommodations, and Deanna wondered where and how she lived when in the city. Then something on the dressing table caught her eye. A magazine.

Deanna stepped closer. "Is that *Beadle's Weekly*?"

Amabelle pulled the cotton away from her face and looked from Deanna to the magazine and back to Deanna.

"The latest issue. I brought it from the city. Do you read *Beadle's*?" she asked. "You look like someone who would consider it too trashy." She pursed her lips. "Not edifying for a young lady."

"You sound like my mother."

"Mine, too," Amabelle said. "And she lets you read them?"

"I hide them under my bed. I read them with my maid every night, but I haven't gotten the new issue yet."

"It's delicious," Amabelle said, warming slightly. "I'd loan it to you but I haven't finished it yet."

"Oh, I'll have to get a copy from the bookshop."

"And your mama—"

"Is in Switzerland with my sister."

"Lucky you. And you're staying with Mrs. Ballard?"

Deanna nodded. "Well, really with Gran Gwen, Gwendolyn Manon, Mrs. Ballard's mother. She stays in Newport for the full season. Laurette travels quite a bit."

"Ah. And what about her handsome son, what is his name?"

"Joe—seph."

"He's staying there also?"

Deanna wasn't sure she understood the look in Amabelle's eye.

"No. He lives . . . elsewhere."

Deanna glanced at Laurette, but she had wandered over to the other girls and was deep in conversation, probably talking to them about birth control or women's suffrage.

A man leaned into the tent opening. "Well, come on then. Chow's on." Behind him, several other male voices urged the girls to hurry up to dinner.

"We won't keep you," Laurette said as she returned to them. "But if you need anything or decide you might want to stay for a night and have your own bath, you're welcome at Bonheur. Just ask anyone the directions."

Amabelle nodded. "Thank you, but . . ."

"Amabelle, hurry up," called one of the girls as they bustled out of the tent.

"Yes, do," said the young man who held the flap open for

them, then stepped inside. He was very handsome, with longish blond hair and sparkling eyes, and was dressed in the plaid leisure suit that actors seemed to be fond of. Deanna blushed as their eyes met. She had admired his calves in his Egyptian wedding kilt.

"Excuse me," Amabelle said.

Laurette nodded and guided Deanna toward the door.

"Nice to have met you," Deanna said over her shoulder, just in time to see the young man move closer to Amabelle.

"You, too," Amabelle called. "You'll have to button me up, Charlie. Everyone seems to have left me." Then she giggled and the tent flap closed behind them.

Chapter

2

Deanna didn't break the silence as she and Laurette made their way to the terrace for dinner. It was obvious that Joe's mother was deep in thought, and Deanna wondered if she was worried about the vivacious Amabelle.

It had been a shock to see the backstage area. The magic and exoticism of the play seemed like a different world. The pyramid had become mere pieces of wood. The giant Sphinx head papier-mâché and plaster. Even the costumes so luminous and airy under the lights were mere piles of fabric in the costumer's arms.

With adventure novels, you merely came to the end. There was no seeing what happened next. The characters just disappeared, and you could imagine them off doing more daring deeds while you waited for the next installment. You didn't see them wiping cold cream on their faces and acting like everyone else.

Deanna didn't think she'd ever look at theater the same way again.

"The theater may be one of the few venues open to women, where they are as respected and well paid as men," Laurette said out of the silence. "Though not necessarily a place for someone brought up in the lap of luxury and as silly as Amabelle Deeks."

"Do you mean she is in danger of becoming a fallen woman?" Deanna ventured.

Laurette snapped her head around to look at her. "I think Amabelle has always been a somewhat flighty, shallow girl. Actors and actresses live by a different code than other people . . . well, maybe not all that different, but they live their lives fairly openly. I'm not sure Amabelle understands that difference."

She took Deanna's arm in hers. "But let's leave Amabelle to herself and to her Charlie. We have offered our hospitality. Our obligation is fulfilled. Now let us find the others. I'm quite famished."

As they reached the brick piazza, they were joined by Joe and his father.

Lionel offered his arm to his wife. "Gwen is sitting with Quentin Asher. I told her we would join them." They strode off together.

After a moment of hesitation, Joe offered Deanna his arm. She looked at it.

"Dee."

"Are you sure you want to be seen escorting me across the floor?"

"Haven't we gotten past that stupid engagement thing yet? I escorted you to the Wetmore ball the other night."

"And Olivia Merrick and that awful Ivy Bennett commented about it nonstop at the Casino the next day."

"Well, I can't leave you standing here. Grandmère will have my head."

Deanna pursed her lips and primly took his arm and allowed him to escort her to the table. "But if I hear anything about it at the next get-together, I'm going to be really mad."

"Well, be mad at them, not me."

Deanna cut him a sideways glance, but didn't comment. She wasn't angry with Joe, she just didn't understand what had happened.

This wasn't something she'd taken into consideration when she'd begged her father to let her stay with Gran Gwen while her mother took her sister to Switzerland.

Her father and Joe's had been the ones who made plans for Joe and Deanna to marry, but Joe had balked and left society to live in the working-class Fifth Ward.

Which was fine by her; he'd rarely attended social events, was even looked down on by some families. She hadn't worried about seeing him again. Now suddenly he seemed to be everywhere. Probably from some misplaced sense of gallantry. Or maybe because Lionel made him.

Either way, it was more humiliating than flattering. She was perfectly capable of taking care of herself. And there was always some young man willing to escort her.

Gwen was already seated next to Quentin Asher, whose name was often linked to Gran Gwen's, though surely any kind of possible involvement was in the past. They both must have been in their sixties, maybe even seventy.

He was still a very handsome man. Tall and straight, and not bent over at all. And he strode, not shuffled. He had thick white hair, sun-crinkled skin, and Deanna could imagine him at an earlier age, gracing the cover of one of her adventure stories.

He stood and offered Deanna a seat between himself and Herbert Stanhope, a friend of Joe's and someone of Deanna's own set.

"I thought you might like someone closer to your own age to entertain you," Mr. Asher said as she sat. "Though I'm more than willing to give young Stanhope a run for his money."

Deanna smiled. "I'm sure Herbert couldn't begin to keep up with you."

Mr. Asher broke into a charming smile. "I shall certainly try to stay apace."

Across the table, Joe's parents sat down together, breaking the usual form of sitting at separate tables. Lionel had been adamant. "I see my wife so infrequently that I insist on keeping her to myself when we are together."

Joe sat next to a young woman, who was introduced as Yvette Schermerhorn, a cousin of the Astors'. Deanna was surprised at the little spark of proprietary jealousy that she felt. Which was stupid. Joe didn't want her, and she didn't want him. Still . . .

As soon as they were seated and greetings exchanged, two footmen began to serve supper.

Champagne was served with the cold salmon and dill, and even though her mother was thousands of miles away, Deanna remembered her admonishment to drink and eat sparingly.

"We haven't seen so much of you lately, Herbert."

Herbert raised both eyebrows and put down his fork. He was the comic of their set. Slightly gawky, with carroty orange hair and a ready smile, he kept them in stitches with his antics and witticisms. But lately he'd been a bit removed from them, and had been attending fewer and fewer functions.

"Ah. I've been busy making preparations for my visit to the continent at the end of the season."

"Do you plan to stay long?"

"Yes. Perhaps. It depends."

Deanna laughed. "You haven't made up your mind yet?"

"That's it. Are you going to the regatta next week?"

"Oh, I imagine so."

"And I imagine you'd prefer to be sailing rather than watching."

"Well," Deanna said, "truthfully, I'm not that good of a sailor. Mama doesn't like us to be out in the sun too much."

"Ah yes, your mama. Have you heard from her? How is Adelaide doing?"

Conversation continued as it always did at dinner parties, keeping to innocuous subjects—even among Gran Gwen and the Ballards. As the last course was cleared away, Walter Edgerton, Judge Grantham's son-in-law, rose and quieted the guests.

"It is my great pleasure to fete a man most dear to me and all who know him. He has had a profound impact on interpreting the laws that make our society safe and wholesome. An inspiration to friends, family, and those of us in the jurisprudence professions. And for me personally, as mentor and professor, as well as the father of my beautiful wife. So I ask you all to raise your glasses to Judge Grantham."

"To Judge Grantham," was the response, though some toasted through tight lips.

"A man who is hand in glove with Anthony Comstock,"

Laurette said so loudly that Deanna was afraid she might have been overheard.

"Don't bite the hand that feeds you, my dear," Lionel Ballard said. "At least not until after dessert."

Deanna knew that Comstock was the purveyor of what constituted morality, much the same way that Mr. McAllister had dictated who was to be considered society's elite.

But she also knew that there was a big chasm between not being invited to a party and being thrown in jail for things Comstock considered immoral, even if they were done in the privacy of one's own home.

And from what she'd heard, there wasn't much that Mr. Comstock hadn't deemed immoral.

A dessert of meringue and crème anglaise and more champagne was served, and conversation turned to talk of the upcoming regatta and the next concert at the Casino theater.

It was afterward, when the women were entering the house to freshen up before the ball began, that Deanna saw Alva Vanderbilt ahead of them.

"Well, well," Gran Gwen said as they climbed the stairs to the ladies' withdrawing room. "I wonder who's guarding the prisoner?"

"What prisoner?" Deanna asked.

"They say she's got that poor child, Consuelo, locked in her room at Marble House. So afraid she is that she'll try to escape before they can marry her off to the duke."

"It's criminal," Laurette said.

"True. I personally see no reason to keep the destitute European aristocracy afloat on the back of American money."

"Poor Winnie Rutherford. They say he's heartbroken."

"I assume Winnie understands. It's just business as usual. And I mean that in the literal sense."

Maybe, Deanna thought. But she thought it was awful that Consuelo had to give up the man she really loved to marry some English lord she didn't even know.

"Why must Consuelo marry one man?" Deanna asked. "If she loves someone else?" But she knew the answer.

"Because she knows her duty, my dear."

Deanna and Joe's situation hadn't been that much different, though Joe wasn't royalty and Deanna's fortune wasn't anywhere near the Vanderbilts'. Their match had been orchestrated by their fathers, but at least they hadn't been officially engaged. Joe had been the one to break it off, but if he hadn't Deanna would have, duty or no duty. If you asked her, Consuelo should have spent more time reading dime novels than practicing the harp. Then she'd have some gumption.

When they came downstairs again they were directed to the lawn for a fireworks display. They'd just joined Lionel and Joe when, with a chorus of pops and whistles, Roman candles sent swords of color through the night air. Reds, greens, yellows, followed by a spray of white stars. One after another until the sky was filled with color. Just as they started to subside, three Catherine wheels whirled to life along the cliff walk. Only to be replaced by a giant scales of justice blazing against a background of real stars.

As the guests applauded, the orchestra began to play, and everyone retraced their steps over the lawn to where the theater had been transformed into a ballroom.

The orchestra had been moved to the front of the stage to allow extra room for dancing. To each side, the black proscenium curtain glittered with electric stars. And where the wedded couples had ascended into the clouds, golden birdcages and flowers appeared and reappeared in a continuous rotation.

It *was* like a Ferris wheel, Deanna thought. And amazing to see.

"Shall we?" Herbert Stanhope offered Deanna his hand and led her onto the dance floor.

As soon as the dance ended, Deanna was claimed for another, and another, and it was sometime later when she wondered what had happened to Amabelle and the other actors. Had they gone back to the boardinghouse where they were staying? They certainly hadn't been invited to mingle with the guests. Were they having a party of their own somewhere?

Deanna hardly saw Joe all night, though she imagined he was backstage talking to the stagehands about hydraulic lifts and such. The few times she did see him, he was always dancing. And when Deanna and the rest of his family climbed into the carriage well after two o'clock, and started for home, they had left Joe waltzing with Yvette Schermerhorn.

—◦◦◦)◦(◦◦◦—

D eanna went straight up to bed. As she opened the door to her bedroom, Elspeth appeared in the doorway to Deanna's dressing room, poking wisps of burnished copper hair behind her ear. She was smaller than Deanna, but strong. Tonight her cheeks were flushed from the heat, and one side of her face was creased from sleep. She stepped into the room, and, stifling a yawn, she took Deanna's wrap and purse.

"Did you have a good time?"

Deanna yawned. "Yes. There was a fair with games and things and Joe won me a little lacquer box. It's in my bag."

Elspeth opened the bag and took the box. "Hmmph. It's not

big enough to put anything much in, but pills, and you don't take any. But it's pretty, I guess." She put it on the dressing table.

"The play was kind of silly, except when the bedouins came in spinning to the music and holding their scimitars above their heads."

"That sounds exciting."

"It was, but then the girls just had to answer questions so they could get married. But I enjoyed the songs. Oh, and the fireworks. They were great. I'm sorry you missed them. Did you get home for a bit tonight?"

"Yes, miss. Orrin was there and we played with the little ones, but then Ma's been feeling a little down so I helped her with the wash."

"She isn't sick, is she?"

"No, miss, just tired. She really ought to get some help if she keeps taking in other people's clothes."

"Not you," Deanna said quickly, alarmed at the idea of losing her maid. Not only was Elspeth a good servant, she was also Deanna's best friend. Practically her only real friend since Cassie Woodruff had to move out West.

Gran Gwen assured her she'd make other friends, but most of the girls she knew were vapid and on the hunt for rich husbands or ones with a title, like poor Consuelo Vanderbilt.

"I'm not gonna go to be a washerwoman as long as I got a posh job like this."

Deanna stared at her. Deanna would hardly call being a lady's maid a posh job, but Deanna did suspect that she was a less demanding mistress than many of her peers.

She turned to let Elspeth unbutton her. "I met an actress tonight."

"Lord save us," Elspeth moaned. "First you go to a carney, then you're consorting with theater rabble." She ruined her stricture with a big grin. "What was she like?"

Deanna stepped out of her dress. It was one of her favorite purchases, a light yellow China silk embroidered with humming-birds. "She's not your typical actress, I don't think. She's about my age; she might even be younger, though I don't think anyone would hire her if she were younger than eighteen."

"Ha." Elspeth scooped the dress up and carried it to the dressing room, then came back with Deanna's nightgown. "Those theater companies even have children working for them."

"I know, but I think their mamas go with them. To be like their mama and their manager."

"So what's this girl's name?"

"Amabelle, and she's the daughter of one of Mrs. Ballard's friends. Evidently she ran away from home and her mother wants her to come back."

"Is she going back?"

"It doesn't seem likely, but guess what?"

"What?"

"She reads dime novels and she had the new issue of *Beadle's*."

"How did she get that already?"

"They probably get them in the city sooner than here. But first thing on Monday we're going down to the bookshop and see if it's come in."

Deanna sat down at the dressing table, and Elspeth began pulling the pins from her hair. It felt almost like being in her own home, living here at Bonheur. Her bedroom was larger than at Randolph House, but still cozy in the style of the older cottages, not the huge rooms of the new cottages. And unlike her papa, Mr. Ballard had installed electricity the year before so things were brighter here and the lamplight was easier to read by.

The dressing table was Louis XIV; the four-poster bed had at one time been canopied. The woodwork was dark but the walls had been papered in cornflowers and pink anemones. Sometimes she missed Mama and Papa and Adelaide, but mostly she loved staying at Bonheur.

While Elspeth brushed out Deanna's hair, Deanna reached for the latest tale of Loveday Brooke. It was lying on the table in plain view. She hadn't had to quickly stuff a story out of sight even once since she'd moved into Gran Gwen's.

She turned to the page where they'd left off.

"'Loveday did not linger here even to admire, but passed at once round the south corner of the house to the windows which she had ascertained, by a careless question to the butler, were those of Mr. Craven's study. Very cautiously she drew near them, for the blinds were up, the curtains drawn back. A side glance, however, relieved her apprehensions. . . .'"

—◦◦◦◉◦◦◦—

It was well after two o'clock when Joe thought to take leave of his host and hostess. He'd stayed longer than he'd intended. But he was actually having fun, and when he finally did think about calling it a night, he realized that his family had already left. And that he hadn't danced once with Deanna.

Which was just as well. Better not to encourage gossip. Though he'd been tempted. She was wearing a new dress that Grandmère had bought her from Worth's shop down at the Casino. It was in a style of which Deanna's mother would never approve. Actually she would probably be scandalized. The décolleté was cut lower than he'd ever seen Dee wear. But no lower than most of the girls—young ladies—there tonight. Grandmère had been right. Dee's mother was stifling her spirit, and she had begun to blossom during the last few weeks spent with Grandmère.

To blossom and to test her freedom. A dangerous thing with Dee. She'd always been fearless; now she was frightening. Last week he'd watched her arrive at the Casino in her brand-new tennis dress and proceed to wipe the court with a shocked, and later embarrassed, Cokey Featheringham. She was practicing her archery and had joined a ladies' cycling club with her newly purchased safety bicycle.

At least Grandmère had made her promise not to go swimming in the ocean by herself. The tides could be strong around the point of land on which Bonheur was built. Something he'd experienced personally only a few weeks before.

He took leave of his hosts and had started down the drive to walk home when he heard Vlady Howe hail him. Vlady was leaving with Herbert Stanhope, and Joe waited for them to catch up.

"Have your carriage tonight, Ballard?"

Joe shook his head. "I came in the family carriage, but they left earlier."

"I say, Dee was looking smashing tonight, wasn't she?" Herbert said. "I think you're a damn fool for not securing her when you had the chance."

"We decided we wouldn't suit."

Vlady laughed. "Some of us just aren't the marrying kind." He clapped Joe on the shoulder. "We're going down to Mersey's yacht for a little after-dinner entertainment. He's bringing in some of the chorus girls from the play tonight. There will be champagne and a breakfast. Why don't you come along?"

Joe really needed to get to bed. He had a lot of work to do tomorrow, but the thought of breakfast was tempting. He tried to remember if there were any eggs or bacon in his larder. "Well, maybe for a while."

"Great. We'll take my carriage." Vlady motioned to the footman, who relayed the message to one of the grooms, who went off to get Vlady's carriage. Within several minutes they were traveling across town to the Newport docks.

Jacob Mersey's yacht, the *Sophia*, was moored at the long wharf and was one of the largest yachts in the harbor. It was lit bow to stern with strings of lights. As the carriage drew up, a shout of raucous laughter rose above the piano music that meandered from the cabin into the night air.

Joe began to have second thoughts. He'd already enjoyed his share of champagne tonight, and he wanted a clear head for his work the next day. But he caught a waft of food and allowed himself to be trundled down the wharf and onto the gangplank.

They were ushered across the deck and into an immense cabin in paneled dark wood, furnished with overstuffed chairs and sofas. The air was thick with smoke and tobacco fumes. Gentlemen who had dropped their wives at home before continuing on to the after party had shed their ties and opened their waistcoats. Several prominent men stood talking as they smoked cigars and drank Mersey's excellent whiskey. Quite a few of their sons were also in attendance. Even Walter Edgerton had made an appearance, though Joe doubted if the Judge or his wife knew it.

Servants carried bottles of spirits through the room, sometimes pouring out a glass to one of the revelers, often leaving the entire bottle. There were quite a few young women in attendance who appeared to be actresses in the chorus of *The Sphinx*. They were garbed in white see-through fabric that floated around their bodies. During the play they'd worn an underdress of some shiny opaque material, but now the "gowns" were covering only skin.

A little after hours improvisation for extra money, Joe thought. He wondered if the costumer knew how her creations were being used tonight.

Jacob Mersey stood surrounded by two lovely girls dressed in see-through togas. One held his cigar and another his drink, giving his hands freedom to roam over their lush bodies and creep beneath the flimsy fabric.

Almost immediately, another one of the maidens sidled up to Vlady and spirited him away. He smiled back at his two companions and disappeared into the haze.

"Not really my thing," Herbert said as he and Joe took drinks from a tray. Seeing several friends, they made their way through the crowd.

Two of the actresses were hoisted onto the table and were dancing in slow, sinuous movements to the delight of anyone still on their feet.

One of the girls jumped from the table into a gentleman's arms, where he kissed her, fondled her, and set her back to dancing. Soon the two were joined by others, and the dance became a game of jumping into someone's arms, where the girls would be manhandled and set back on the table to go again or be taken off to a more private quarter.

Joe couldn't help but think of how his mother would disapprove. Not of the girls' morals, but of them being used as objects for the men's lust. He was pretty sure his father wouldn't be enjoying himself here.

One of the girls caught Joe's eye as she turned and raised her eyebrows. Joe minutely shook his head.

It wasn't that he was indifferent to her or any of the women. They were all quite lovely, but for them tonight wasn't necessarily about fun, and if they were looking to make an extra bit of cash, they should go after richer game than Joe.

The only delicacies Joe was interested in tonight were on the buffet table. He filled a plate with roast beef, ham, bread, and salad and went to find a quiet place to eat, preferably one less crowded and less smoky, though he had to peel another young nymph off his person, by promising her he would look for her shortly.

He stepped out of the cabin into the corridor of guest quarters, which he knew would lead to the foredeck. The hall was sometimes used for trysting, but more often the revelers managed to control themselves until they were behind locked doors.

He strolled out to the almost empty deck and sat down in an alcove on a comfortable couch to enjoy his meal. The night air was cool; beyond him the bay seemed quiet in comparison, though there were plenty of yachts and fishing boats moored there.

He ate until he was content, then finished the last bit of cheese off with a sip of champagne and stood. He was looking forward to his bed.

As he stepped back inside, he heard an argument coming from one of the guest compartments. He was sure he heard the name Belle. Were they arguing over the actress?

He slowed. After all, he was his mother's son, and if Amabelle or any of the women were in trouble, he might be forced to intercede. He listened more closely; the voices, both male, grew louder then suddenly cut off as a door opened. Joe hurried back the way he'd come. He'd just reached the deck again when the door slammed shut.

Seconds later, a young woman, one side of her toga sliding down her shoulder, ran toward him. "Help me, please!"

Joe pulled the girl onto the deck and pushed the door closed. They were standing in shadow and he couldn't see her face but he could feel her trembling against him. She wasn't wearing a corset or anything beneath that flimsy piece of fabric as far as he could tell.

When Joe was sure no one had followed them, he pulled her out into the light.

"Are you all right? How can I help you?"

Sobbing, the girl looked up at him with red, frightened eyes.

Joe cursed himself for letting Vlady talk him into coming. He looked more closely at the girl's face. She looked familiar. *Because they had met before.*

"Amabelle?"

Chapter
3

The girl pushed Joe away.

"How do you know my name?"

"I'm Joseph Ballard, we met last summer. My mother is Laurette Ballard, she's a friend of your mother's."

"Oh . . . at Saratoga . . . the races."

Joe nodded, relieved that she actually remembered him and he wouldn't have to go into lengthy explanations. He thought he should be getting her out of this environment before whoever was frightening her came looking for her.

She stood quietly chafing her bare arms. Joe tried not to notice the see-through fabric or the curvaceous body beneath it.

"You're cold. Would you like me to see you home? Where are you staying?"

"No—no—he would kill me."

Joe's face suffused with heat. "No, I mean—I could put you in a cab, pay for it of course, if you wanted to leave this place."

Amabelle shook her head. Her hair had partially come

loose and bright blonde ringlets bobbed around her face. She reminded Joe of a china doll, with high round cheeks, big round eyes fringed by long lashes, and a rosebud mouth.

Pretty, soft, and helpless-looking, though he imagined she would have to have some backbone to manage the life of an actress.

Voices brought him back to himself.

"I have to go," she whimpered and pulled away from him.

"If you need help, go to my mother at Bonheur."

A door closed. Joe stepped in front of the door to bar their way, but the footsteps receded. He opened the door just enough to see inside. The corridor was empty.

He turned back to tell Amabelle she was safe.

She was gone.

He hoped she would be all right. He didn't know if she'd heard him tell her to go to Bonheur or not.

He left soon after that. He didn't see Vlady or any of the other men his age, nor did he see Amabelle Decks again. His conscience clear, he set off down the cobbled street toward the Fifth Ward and the warehouse he called home.

Church bells, thought Deanna, and tried to force her unwilling eyes open. But surely it was too early for church. She pulled the satin comforter more tightly around her neck and turned over.

The bells rang again, followed by the sound of feet running outside her bedroom. Her eyes pried open. It was still dark. The sky was only a slightly lighter shade of ebony than when she'd gone to bed and Elspeth had turned out the lights.

Not church, but the doorbell. Her first thought was that

something had happened to her papa or Adelaide or her mother or Joe. She pushed the covers away and grabbed her robe, pulling it on as she ran across her room.

She opened her door to Gran Gwen and Laurette standing in the hallway. Mr. Ballard, a burgundy and green paisley dressing gown thrown over his nightshirt, was running for the stairs.

Laurette held out her hand to Deanna, who hurried over to stand with the other two women.

"Oh, for heaven's sake," Gran Gwen said. "It isn't a burglar, they never show such good manners, and I doubt if it is a marauding militia come to pull us out of our beds in the dead of night." She marched off down the hall.

Maybe not, Deanna thought, but a predawn caller could not bode well. Nevertheless, she and Laurette followed Gran Gwen down the stairs.

The Ballard butler, Carlisle, was just opening the front door when the three women reached the foyer. Mr. Ballard stood with one hand in his dressing gown pocket, and for a moment Deanna wondered if he was holding a pistol out of sight. She shook her head.

Too many dime novels, she told herself. Then changed her mind when she saw his hand tighten inside the pocket.

No great scuffle ensued, no attacks or shooting or low-down grappling. Nothing at all happened.

The two men just stood looking out the door. Then simultaneously, as if they'd awakened from a spell, Carlisle opened the door wider and Mr. Ballard stepped out onto the flagstones to usher in a diminutive figure wrapped in a gold cape, the hem of a diaphanous white gauze skirt swaying beneath the cape's hem.

It was a girl. She looked up and Laurette shot forward. "Oh my dear, are you hurt? What on earth is the matter?" She began unclasping the cloak from Amabelle Deeks's neck.

"I—I've done something. . . ." The girl swayed, then crumpled to the floor.

"Good heavens," Gwen said. "Someone call Minerva."

Carlisle moved quickly out of the foyer as Mr. Ballard scooped Amabelle into his arms and carried her into the back parlor. He gave his wife a quick look as he passed her. Laurette shrugged slightly. They seemed to know without saying a word just what the other was thinking.

Deanna followed the others into the parlor.

Amabelle Deeks lay on the settee, looking pale and vulnerable in spite of the exaggerated red of her lips. Almost like a nymph in her gauzy—and very revealing—white dress. Deanna raised an involuntary hand to her mouth; Laurette pulled a tapestry off the arm of a chair and spread it over the girl.

Minerva, Gran Gwen's maid of long-standing, swept into the room carrying a small silver tray holding an array of bottles, atomizers, and tiny pill boxes. Elspeth slipped in behind her, stopped while her eyes scanned the room, then rested on Deanna's face. Her relief was palpable.

"Come, Elspeth," Deanna said, "and see if you can be of some use to Minerva."

Deanna thought she'd given the order with authority, but Elspeth slowly let her eyes drift toward the ceiling before she stepped to Minerva's side. There was absolutely nothing Elspeth could do to help, and they both knew it.

Minerva was the consummate lady's maid, trained in Paris by Gran Gwen over twenty years before. Deanna had been hoping some of her aplomb would rub off on Elspeth while they were staying at Bonheur, but so far Minerva had managed to ignore the younger woman.

Of course, Elspeth was from Ireland via the Fifth Ward of Newport; her English was underscored by a thick Irish brogue. Minerva spoke impeccable English with a cultured French accent.

She was nice enough, helpful, never complained that Deanna knew about, but still she always made Deanna feel like a clumsy oaf whenever she was around. Deanna could only imagine what Elspeth must feel. Well, actually, she could do more than imagine. Elspeth could give as good as she got. Didn't care for maids who put on airs, even if the airs were real. And passed damning judgment on poor Minerva by saying that she bet she'd never had a sweetheart and wouldn't know what to do with one if she did.

She'd made Deanna blush, because the same might be said of Deanna.

Amabelle stirred, her eyelashes fluttered, and she awoke with a start. Minerva moved the salts from under her nose.

She reared back. "Where am I?"

Deanna caught another roll of Elspeth's eyes as the maid turned from the invalid.

Deanna had to look away to keep from smiling. Amabelle sounded just like one of those pitiful girls in the melodramas at the afternoon theater.

Laurette helped the girl to sit up.

"I'm sorry," she said. "But you said I could come here if . . ." Her lip trembled.

"And we're very glad to have you," Laurette continued for her in a tone of voice that Deanna could imagine she used when inspiring the suffragettes to walk one more mile. "But what has happened?"

Amabelle looked around the room and bowed her head.

"Good heavens, Laurette," Gran Gwen said. "It's nearly dawn. The girl is exhausted. You can ask your questions in the morning. Deanna, you and Elspeth take Miss Deeks to your room and find her something to sleep in. Minerva, have the rose guest room made up for our visitor."

Minerva curtseyed and smoothly left the room.

Laurette helped Amabelle from the settee. "Can you manage the stairs?" Laurette asked.

Deanna moved to her other side. "We'll help you. You can come to my room and you'll be right as rain." Besides, Deanna was dying of curiosity to find out why the runaway actress had now run away again and shown up at the door without her valise. Or even a hairbrush.

"Laurette," Gran Gwen said, "please come down when our guest has been safely bestowed with Deanna."

Laurette hesitated, then nodded slightly, and with Deanna's assistance helped Amabelle from the room. Deanna glanced at Gran Gwen, wondering what had just happened, and Gran Gwen returned her look with one so intent that Deanna knew she had just been given a command. The whole Ballard-Manon family were very good at giving silent orders. Now Deanna just needed to figure out what she was supposed to do.

Elspeth led the way and straightened the covers of the bed Deanna had just vacated, while Deanna and Laurette settled Amabelle in a slipper chair. Elspeth went into the dressing room to find her something to wear.

She'd barely gone before there was a light tap at the door.

For a tiny second no one moved, but since Elspeth was in the dressing room, Deanna answered it.

Minerva stepped just inside. "Madame, you're wanted downstairs. Miss Deanna, Madame said for you to call me when the young lady is ready to be shown to her chamber."

"Thank you, Minerva. Please tell my mother I'll be down shortly." Laurette stood until Minerva reluctantly left the room.

Deanna thought Minerva was showing just a bit too much attitude, but Laurette laughed. "Those two—you'd think Bonheur was their house instead of Lionel's. Though I suppose we're so infrequently here that it must feel that way.

"Well, it seems I must go see to *la grande maman*," Laurette said. "If you need anything more, just ask Deanna or Elspeth. And please feel free to stay as long as you like."

She smiled and left the room.

Amabelle relaxed as soon as the door closed. And so did Deanna. She knew what Gran Gwen wanted her to do.

"Is that old gorgon downstairs Mrs. Ballard's mother or mother-in-law?"

"Mother," Deanna said. "And she isn't a gorgon, she's just . . ." She searched for a word. "Majestic."

"Well, I'll give you that."

Deanna was confused by this sudden change in Amabelle. One minute she was a terrified child depending on the mercy of a family she barely knew. Now she acted like an ordinary guest who belonged there.

Which Deanna guessed she did. She came from a good family and was probably used to the opulence of her surroundings.

Then she shuddered violently, and Deanna felt contrite. She was obviously just trying to put on a strong front.

"Are you cold?"

Amabelle shook her head, but she was clutching the tapestry around her shoulders as if expecting a storm. It was a mild night and the windows in Deanna's room were open to let in the sea air.

"I can close the windows."

"No, please, leave them open. It's so calming to hear the sea. It's so beautiful here in Newport."

"Yes, it is," Deanna agreed.

"I wish I could stay here forever."

"But then you couldn't be an actress."

Amabelle smiled a little sadly. "True."

"It must be exciting to be an actress," Deanna said.

"I suppose, but it isn't easy. You have to work every night. And days, we have to rehearse, you know. It's long hours and you get tired."

"It sounds hard, but exciting to have freedom. To be in charge of your own life."

"I guess."

Deanna thought people who were lucky enough to have adventures should at least appreciate them. "So why don't you go home?"

She hadn't meant to speak so harshly, and when tears filled Amabelle's eyes she rushed to make amends.

"Amabelle, I didn't mean it that way. Won't they take you back? Mrs. Ballard said your mother asked her to make sure you were all right."

"I can't go back." She broke down into sobs. "I won't go back."

"Amabelle," Deanna said, alarmed.

Amabelle said something, but her hands were covering her face, and Deanna couldn't make out the words—word—it sounded like "hell."

"What?"

Amabelle looked up. "Belle. Call me Belle."

Deanna pulled a footstool up and sat facing her. "Belle. Is there any way in which we—I—can help you?"

Amabelle gave her a tentative smile. "I'm not sure anyone can help me."

"Well, we won't be able to help if we don't even know what's bothering you."

From the corner of her eye, Deanna saw Elspeth, carrying one of Deanna's white nightgowns, step out of the dressing room. She stopped, then melted back into the dressing room, where, Deanna didn't doubt for a second, she was all ears.

"It isn't me." Amabelle stood suddenly and walked to the table next to Deanna's bed. She picked up the copy of Loveday Brooke Deanna and Elspeth had been reading before bed.

"I liked this one," Amabelle said, beginning to recover. But I like Kate Goelet better."

"Me, too," Deanna agreed.

"Your mama lets you read them? And with your maid?"

"No. I have to hide them at home. . . . But not here."

"My mama would never let me have any fun."

Deanna bet she wasn't any stricter than her own mother was. Not only did she have to hide her reading material, but every idea, plan, opinion, or desire she ever had. Until her mother had been forced to take Deanna's sister to Switzerland for the cure.

Since coming to stay with Gran Gwen, she'd been part of conversations that her mother would never have allowed. Learning about things a young lady shouldn't know. Wore clothes she would consider unacceptable, like the new lighter, more comfortable tennis outfits and the scandalous bathing costumes.

She'd even bought a bicycle, against her mother's express wishes, though fortunately, the letter forbidding her to buy one had come too late. She'd even joined a bicycling club that met every Saturday afternoon. Cycling was all the rage among the more modern cottagers.

Now she was talking to a bona fide actress. Well, almost bona fide. And it was time she probed a little deeper into why Amabelle had come.

"Mrs. Ballard says that the theater is one of the only places that women earn as much as men."

Amabelle shrugged. "I guess. But being in the chorus doesn't pay all that well for either men or women."

"But if you work hard and—"

Belle sighed. "The leading actors have a better time. They get real parts and are courted by patrons, taken out to dinner. People send them gifts. They are treated with deference and get called great artistes. The chorus?" Amabelle shrugged again.

Deanna really hoped she had a better repertory of gestures if she planned longevity in the dramatic arts.

"Some people stay in the chorus their whole lives." Belle was beginning to sound like the vapid young ladies Deanna spent every afternoon with.

"But you get to dress up in costumes and pretend to be somebody else. And meet interesting people."

Amabelle had begun to relax, but now the blood rushed from her face and she gripped the tapestry in both hands.

Deanna shot a desperate look toward the dressing room. Amabelle looked like she might bolt, wearing nothing but a see-through gown that made Deanna blush for her.

Elspeth bustled into the room. "I bet there are all sorts of handsome young men in love with you," she said matter-of-factly as she pulled Amabelle to her feet and relieved her of the tapestry.

She only gripped it for a moment, then allowed Elspeth to pull off her costume and replace it with Deanna's nightdress.

"I—" She shot a look at Deanna. It was obvious that she was surprised at Elspeth's familiarity. "Yes, very handsome . . . and some not so." Amabelle turned to let Elspeth button up the front buttons. It was a gesture more natural than any of the others she'd made that night.

As soon as Elspeth closed the last button, Amabelle tried to hide a huge yawn behind the back of her hand.

"You're tired, miss," Elspeth said, dropping back into her role as maid. It occurred to Deanna that Elspeth might make a good actress, though she'd never suggest it. She needed Elspeth by her side.

Elspeth saw Amabelle to her room down the hall. She returned a few minutes later with a knowing, "There's a man involved."

Deanna, who was just drifting off to sleep, sat up. "Yes, I thought maybe that was the case. Did she tell you?"

"Didn't have to. Always is with actresses." And on that pronouncement, she tucked Deanna in and went off to seek her own rest.

When Deanna woke next, it was light outside and there was a bustle in the hallway. It must really be late. But when she turned to look at the clock, she saw that it was only six o'clock. She'd barely been asleep two hours.

She scooted back down under the covers and had just closed her eyes again when Elspeth burst into the room.

"Miss, miss! There's a body in the conservatory."

Chapter
4

Deanna's first thought was that whomever Amabelle was afraid of had found her and killed her. Then she had a worse thought. One of the Ballards? She threw back the covers and practically fell out of bed.

"Who is it?" she asked, groping for the sleeve of the robe that Elspeth held out for her while her feet slid into her slippers.

"I don't know, miss. A stranger. The parlor maid went in to clean and found him. Been screeching ever since. Not making no sense at all. Thought you'd want to come see."

A well-brought-up young lady would stay cringing and simpering in her bedroom, holding smelling salts to her nose, and would remain there until the excitement was over and the gossip had started.

Deanna was well brought up. Too well. But she had no intention of missing the excitement. And she bet neither did any of the Ballards.

She managed to get the second arm in her dressing gown. "Bring my salts," she ordered Elspeth.

Elspeth frowned at her.

"I do have some, don't I?"

"Yes, miss, but why?"

"Well, you need an excuse to come see, don't you?"

"Yes, miss." She rummaged in the dressing table drawer, snatched up the never-used bottle of smelling salts, and hurried after Deanna.

She met Gran Gwen and Laurette at the head of the stairs, Laurette was already dressed except for her hair, which was hanging down her back in long tresses. Gran Gwen was still in her nightclothes, covered by a heavy brocade caftan. They could hear Mr. Ballard's quiet yet authoritative voice ordering maids and footmen to clear the area.

"They're in the conservatory," Gran Gwen said. She immediately started down the stairs; Deanna, Laurette, and Elspeth followed quickly behind, Elspeth gripping Deanna's arm so tightly it was beginning to hurt.

They passed the parlor and the library. A group of servants were crowded around the conservatory door. Gran Gwen cleared her throat, and they quickly dispersed, leaving the entryway open.

But when she tried to enter, Carlisle, the Ballard butler, stepped in front of her. "Madame, I don't think you should come in."

"Thank you, Carlisle," Gran Gwen said, and walked right past him.

"Mrs. Ballard," Carlisle protested as Laurette followed her mother.

"It's all right, Carlisle. Has someone called for a doctor?"

"Yes, Madame, and also for the police."

"Ah." Laurette followed Gran Gwen into the room, and Deanna and Elspeth followed so close on her heels that Carlisle had no choice but to let them pass.

The conservatory air made Deanna shiver. The morning light was just beginning to seep into the room, and the chill of the marble-and-wood floor bit through the thin soles of Deanna's slippers.

Lionel Ballard knelt over a man, who lay on his back on the Turkestan carpet. Behind him, a marble statue of Aphrodite was flanked by two large needle palms.

The weak rays of the sun cast their fronds into high relief, accentuating their sharp edges. *Like daggers*, Deanna thought.

Two footmen stood off to the side, their expressions blank, but their eyes fixated on the recumbent man.

It looked just like an illustration for *Beadle's Weekly*. "The Body in the Conservatory." And it made the whole situation unreal.

But only for a second.

Deanna couldn't see who it was, but she knew who it wasn't. Not Joe, because Joe would never wear those plaid trousers, which—Deanna realized with a sickening jolt to her stomach—looked awfully familiar. *The kind of suit that actors favored.*

She glanced over to see if Laurette was thinking the same thing, but it was hard to tell, since Laurette was staring intently at her husband's back.

Deanna took a step forward; Elspeth's small hand clamped around her elbow, not to stop her, but to stay close. As one, all four women moved closer.

Mr. Ballard rose to his feet, leaving a full view of the man's face. A young face, a handsome face, except where the cheek had been crushed, blond hair—matted with blood.

Deanna brought her fist to her mouth. Elspeth's grasp was

so tight, Deanna was afraid her fingernails might draw blood. Gran Gwen sucked in a sharp breath. Only Laurette kept her presence of mind to take a closer look.

"My dear." Mr. Ballard reached for his wife.

But it seemed she barely heard. "The poor boy. It's that young man from the theater."

"Charlie," Deanna said, but her voice didn't sound like her own. "Charlie. We heard Belle call him Charlie."

"That's right," Laurette said. "But what on earth is he doing here?"

"Where is the girl?" Mr. Ballard asked. "How could she possibly sleep through this racket?"

The four women exchanged looks.

"I'll go see if she's still asleep," Deanna said. "Come, Elspeth."

They walked abreast to the door and across the landing and up the stairs. Then, seeing that no one was about, they took the hallway at a run.

The guest room was empty. Deanna's nightgown lay across the bed. But the cape, the gauze costume, and Amabelle's shoes were gone.

And so was Amabelle Deeks.

———⚬❯❮⚬———

Joe Ballard and his apprentice, Orrin, had just fired up the new centrifuge machine they were working on when there was a rap at the door to the warehouse.

"Must be Hiram," Joe said. "I wonder if they had any trouble last night?" He put down his wrench and went to answer the door.

Joe had hired Hiram Harkevy to oversee a corps of local men to guard the workshop at night or when Joe was away for more than a few hours. Like last evening.

There had been several break-ins and sabotage attempts on his inventions, which he hoped would soon revolutionize the refining and distribution of sugar. But the sugar industry was volatile, and some people would stop at nothing to gain an edge, even if it meant stealing Joe's machinery. Or destroying it.

His father and George Randolph had recently almost lost their sugar refining business. Fancy negotiating and a little underhanded coercion had saved it, but their major competitor, H. O. Havemeyer, who now owned the monopoly on sugar refining, was determined to buy them out or finish them off.

And Joe didn't intend on letting that happen.

He opened the front door and was surprised to see Will Hennessey. Joe felt a frisson of panic as he did every time he unexpectedly opened the door to Will, his friend from college, and now a sergeant of the Newport Police Department.

An unannounced visit from the police didn't bode well.

"Your family is fine," Will said before Joe even had time to ask. "And Deanna."

Joe stepped aside. "Come in. I think there's still some coffee."

"Thanks, but I'm on my way to Bonheur and thought you might want to come."

"Bonheur? I thought you said everything is fine."

"Your family is. But it seems they discovered a body in the conservatory."

Joe cocked an eyebrow. "A body . . . in the conservatory? Is this some kind of joke?"

"No. The maid went in to dust this morning, and a man was lying on the floor, evidently bludgeoned to death, though I won't know for sure until I see for myself and the medical examiner has examined the body. I thought you might want to come."

"Of course," Joe said, already removing his leather work apron. "You said a man. Is it anyone we know?"

"I don't believe so. But Carlisle called as soon as they found the body. We'll know more once we get there."

Joe, realizing he'd stopped to listen to Will's answer, yanked the apron over his head, threw it on a peg, and went to the back room to let Orrin know where he was going. Also to reassure his apprentice that all was well, since his sister, Elspeth, was Deanna's maid.

Joe didn't bother to wash, just unrolled his sleeves, grabbed a tie, and slipped into his jacket as he walked Will to the door.

"I'm on my bicycle. I thought it would be faster than waiting for the police van. They'll meet us there."

Joe nodded and rolled his own bicycle out to the street.

A minute later they were bouncing down the cobblestone street. After a teeth-rattling few minutes they hit the smoother macadam of Bellevue Avenue. Leaning into the shore breeze, the two men sped toward Bonheur at the tip of the island.

Joe had worked up a sweat by the time they turned into the drive to Bonheur. No official vehicles had arrived, so they drove around to the servants' entrance, parked their bicycles, and went inside.

They could have gone through the front door. Will would always be welcomed at the front door of any Ballard house, but it was easier and faster to swing through the kitchen.

They stopped in the hallway long enough to collect themselves, Will knocking the dust off his hat and Joe pushing his hair back with his fingers. Then they made a dignified entrance into the main hall.

It was empty, but Joe could see two footmen posted on either side of the double doors to the conservatory. They nodded simultaneously and stepped aside for Will and Joe to pass.

Joe's father and Carlisle were standing over the body.

Carlisle bowed. "I'm afraid you had to let yourself in, sir. The bell for some reason didn't sound."

"We came in through the kitchen," Joe said, and walked past him to where Will had knelt over the body. "Who is it?"

Lionel Ballard moved closer to Joe. "Evidently it's one of the actors from last night's play."

"What's he doing here?"

"Well, we weren't expecting him, if that's what you're asking," his father said in his driest manner.

"No, of course not." It had been a reflexive question.

Will stood. "Excuse me, sir, but if you could both step away from the deceased."

"Of course, Sergeant." Lionel moved Joe back. "We haven't let anyone touch the body."

"Thank you, sir. And the other members of the household?"

"They have already been here, identified the poor soul as an actor named Charlie, and are off searching the house for our houseguest."

"Houseguest, sir?"

"That Deeks girl who ran away from home, Amabelle. She showed up here in the middle of the night. Looking, I might add, like a frightened fox. I believe your mother invited her."

Joe hoped it had been his mother's invitation and not his that had brought her here.

"Not that we expected her to arrive unannounced and close to dawn. She wouldn't talk, at least not while I was around. Deanna took her off to her room to find night things, so if you want to know more, I'm afraid you'll have to ask Dee." He looked quickly over his shoulder, almost as if he expected Deanna's mother to be there to thwart him.

Joe knew just how he felt. The woman was a stickler and ruled Deanna and her sister, Adelaide, with an iron glove. Fortunately she was out of the country, and as far as Joe was concerned, she could stay there. Though she might do a better job of keeping Deanna out of trouble than he seemed to be doing.

"And now the damn girl has disappeared. We have the entire household looking for her."

Will had started a circuitous route around the room. He looked out the French doors that led out to the lawn. Checked the marble floor for footprints. Inspected the cushions of the wicker furniture, the tables, the baskets of exotic plants, searching for any clue that might lead to the reason for the man's death or who killed him and how. Besides the obvious: his face and head and been bashed in.

Joe and his father stood watching until Will came back to them and pulled out a black notebook and pencil.

He cleared his throat. "Did the dead man—"

"His name is Charlie," Lionel supplied. "My wife and Miss Deanna met him briefly backstage at the play."

"The play at . . ."

"For Judge Grantham's birthday party. His son-in-law and daughter brought in a troupe from Manhattan to perform."

Will nodded and continued to write.

The front bell rang, and Carlisle excused himself to answer it. He returned a few minutes later, accompanied by the medical examiner, the police photographer, and several other police officers, who looked nervous to be in the home of one of Newport's elite.

Will gave orders for the men to search the grounds.

"We've begun a search of the house," Lionel told him. "And sent the stableboys out to search the cliffs. Though in retrospect, I suppose we should have waited for your men. We were concerned for the girl and her safety. The cliffs here can be treacherous if you don't know them. Especially at night."

Carlisle stepped into the room.

"Yes, Carlisle?"

"Cook has prepared coffee and a light repast in the breakfast room if the sergeant would like to continue his questioning there. The ladies are already there."

"This is a little strange," Will confided to Joe as they walked toward the door.

"Well, at least Carlisle didn't call you Master William, like he used to."

"For which I'm truly thankful. This is uncomfortable enough." Will stopped to say a few words to the medical examiner and then accompanied Joe down the hall to the breakfast room.

Cook's light repast turned out to be warming dishes of eggs, tomatoes, ham, sausages, and a rack of toast surrounded by homemade jams and honey.

Joe filled his plate. Murder or no, he wasn't about to turn down Cook's breakfast.

Will turned down food, though he did accept a cup of coffee.

"There's no reason to stand on ceremony with us, Will," Laurette said.

"Yes, ma'am. It's just that it goes against protocol to break bread with those you're questioning. Even if they're not suspected of a crime," he added hastily.

Carlisle filled his cup. "Cook anticipated this. She asked if you would step round to the kitchen before you leave. She has packed you what seems to be a very substantial picnic lunch."

Will grinned, but quickly wiped it off his face. "Tell Cook I shall certainly stop in at the kitchen on my way out."

∞≫◄●►≪∞

Deanna couldn't repress the sigh that escaped as she listened to Will question the Ballards. They were acting so formal, as if they were strangers, and it was so stupid. Obviously none of them had killed that poor actor, Charlie.

But he was dead. Amabelle was out there somewhere, probably frightened, and surely hungry. If they would just put their heads together instead of acting like people in a play, they might be able to find her before something bad happened to her . . . if it hadn't already.

Was it Charlie she'd been running from? That didn't make sense. She'd been flirting with him when they'd left her backstage after the play. Maybe they'd quarreled. Had he overheard Laurette offer her a place to stay at Bonheur? Laurette had made the offer right before they left the tent and just as Charlie arrived. Or he might have just followed her there. Anyone could have followed her. She rather stuck out in that gold cape and diaphanous gown.

"Deanna!"

Deanna jumped and turned to frown at Joe, who had sat beside her at the table.

"Will has been trying to get your attention, but you seem to be off in—"

"Joseph, that will do," his mother said. Deanna blinked. She sometimes forgot that Laurette was Joe's mother. She seemed so young and vibrant; Deanna had even heard her laughing with her husband.

"I'm sorry, Will—Sergeant Hennessey," Deanna corrected herself. "What did you ask?"

"Mrs. Manon"—he glanced at Gran Gwen—"says you took Miss Deeks to your, uh, room, to um . . ."

He was blushing. Probably because of his reddish chestnut hair, but still . . . Will Hennessey was blushing over bedrooms. The mind boggled.

"I took her to my bedroom to find her something to sleep in since she arrived with only the clothes on her back." She glanced at him, but he was focused on the notebook. "A gold cape and a white gauze dress, probably a costume   you could see straight through it and she didn't have anything on underneath."

Laurette cast her a sideways look and quickly hid her face behind her napkin.

"Really, Dee," Joe said.

Really, Joe. You're getting to be such a prude.

"It's important to be accurate when giving details of a crime scene . . . isn't it, Sergeant Hennessey?"

Will cleared his throat. "Indeed. So you loaned her night-wear and did she go to her room then?"

"Not immediately. We talked a bit first."

Suddenly she had everyone's attention.

"About what?"

"Well . . ." Deanna was sure some of the things Belle had

told her she'd told in confidence, but did that count considering Charlie was dead and Belle was missing?

"Go ahead," Laurette said. "Whatever she said might help us find her."

If she wants to be found, thought Deanna. "I asked her about being an actress."

"Don't even think it," Joe said under his breath.

Deanna ignored him. "She said she liked it, but you had to be strong all the time."

"Did it sound like she was planning to go home?" Laurette asked, then put her fingers over her mouth. "I do beg your pardon, Sergeant."

"That's quite all right, Mrs. Ballard. Did it?"

"She said she couldn't go back."

"Did she say why?"

"No." Deanna pressed her fingers to her temples as if she could jar the memory of their conversation.

"Is something wrong, Dee? I mean, Miss Randolph," Will corrected.

"No. I just wish I could remember. It was late and I'd been awakened from sleep and I guess my observational skills weren't at their best. I'm sorry."

She could swear she heard Joe grinding his teeth. They needed to have a little talk if they were to keep from coming to blows.

"Oh, I asked her if there was anything we could do to help her. I mean, she seemed so distraught. But she said that she didn't think anyone could help her."

"Did she elaborate?"

Deanna shook her head. "Then we started talking about

the latest *Old Sleuth*." She'd been looking at her uneaten food, but looked up at Will. "She reads dime novels, too."

Will merely nodded.

"Elspeth said she bet there was a man involved." Deanna's voice wavered. "And I guess she was right."

The room had become so silent that Deanna could hear the search party outside the windows. "You don't think she killed Charlie, do you?"

Chapter

5

Deanna had known better than to ask that question. She knew Will wasn't at liberty to say even if he had formed an opinion. But as far as Deanna could see, Amabelle had either killed her friend then fled, or conspired with someone to kill him and had fled. Or she had seen who had killed him and was either dead at the villain's hand or had run, afraid that the murderer would be coming after her.

Any way you looked at it, it didn't look good for Amabelle.

"We won't be able to make any statements until we have further information," Will said, looking into the middle space between them.

He wouldn't even look at her. Because he didn't want her butting in or because he thought Amabelle was guilty?

"Does anyone have anything to add?"

Deanna had plenty to ask. Like had he noticed the heels of poor Charlie's shoes? Or the blades of newly cut grass on his trouser leg?

She could picture the scene in her mind. It was something she'd learned from her drawing lessons, out of necessity, because someone was always eating the fruit from her still lifes before she finished her picture. She knew she couldn't see anything that the photographer couldn't see. Still . . .

Deanna looked around the table. No one else had anything to say. Good. She couldn't wait to get away from this. As soon as she got upstairs, she'd make her own sketch of poor Charlie. She was about to ask to be excused when Joe said, "I suppose I do."

Joe rose from his seat and strode toward the window. "Mother wasn't the only one who offered her an invitation to Bonheur last night."

If Deanna thought it had been quiet before, the silence now was smothering. She tried not to look at Joe, standing at the window, his back to the room.

He had everyone's attention.

"How's this?" Mr. Ballard asked.

"When did you see Amabelle?" his mother asked. "I didn't think you remembered her. It's been a year or two since we've seen the Deekses."

"Son."

Deanna's head snapped back from Joe to his father, which was the only reason she saw Mr. Ballard's reaction, the minute quirk of the head, the lift of the eyebrow.

Joe turned slowly to face the room. Deanna swallowed. She hoped this wasn't going to turn into one of those things young ladies shouldn't know about.

Fortunately the gonging of the hall wall clock, and the subsequent echo of the other clocks throughout the room, prevented the conversation from continuing.

"Deanna?" Gran Gwen said once it was quiet again. "Aren't you meeting your cycling group this morning?"

Her cycling group. She'd forgotten all about it. But if she went, she wouldn't hear what Joe had to say, though from everyone's reaction, it might be better if she did leave. But would it be disrespectful to the dead to go and enjoy herself?

"Yes. You don't want to miss that," Laurette said, glancing at Joe.

Her better judgment told Deanna it would be smart to leave now that she had the chance. Curiosity told her to stand her ground. For once better judgment won out. If Joe had been carrying on in ways that weren't exactly proper, she didn't want to know.

She assuaged her curiosity by telling herself that Elspeth, who had been sent with the other servants to search the house for Amabelle, would be full of news from the search.

"I believe that's all I need from you at the moment. You've been most helpful."

Will was addressing Deanna, but he was looking somewhere past her shoulder. She had an overwhelming desire to turn and look, but she knew it was just a wall. Why wouldn't he look at her?

And suddenly she didn't feel like she could meet any of their eyes. She pushed her chair back and walked blindly to the door, which fortunately was opened by a footman as she approached. She didn't slow down as she left the room, didn't slow as she climbed the stairs. Didn't stop until she reached her room and shut the door firmly behind her.

"Miss, what is it?" asked Elspeth, hurrying in from the dressing room. "Did they find her? Is she dead? Was it awful?"

Deanna shook her head. "They haven't found her."

"Then what is it?"

"I—I think Joe may be involved in some way."

"Is the sergeant still down there?"

Deanna nodded.

"Is he questioning Mr. Joseph?"

Deanna shrugged and sank onto a chair.

"Well, if you're looking like that because you think Mr. Joseph bashed that man's head in, you need to take a tonic."

That forced a laugh from Deanna.

"That's better."

"No, I don't think he killed poor Charlie." She was thinking about something else entirely. *Oh, grow up, Deanna. Men do those things. Joe is a man, ergo* . . . "So did you find anything during the search?"

"Nothing," Elspeth said, obviously disappointed. "We looked high and low. Checked every window—and let me tell you, some of these footmen don't have brains for nothing. They looked at every window, even the ones with sheer drops to the ground. I coulda told them not to waste their time. But would they listen to a maid, even a lady's maid?"

"No they would not." Elspeth answered her own question before Deanna even opened her mouth.

"If you ask me, she walked right out the door. 'Cause while those pretty boys were hanging out the windows with their breeches' backside in full view, we maids were checking the linen for anything missing and anything that could have been made into an elopement rope."

"An elopement rope? She wouldn't have come here if she was planning to elope with Charlie—or anybody else—she just would have done it."

Elspeth fisted her hands and gave Deanna her most exasperated sigh. "That's just an expression. What I mean is, she didn't climb out of no window."

"Your grammar is slipping."

"Sorry, miss, but you can be very vexing," Elspeth said at her primmest.

Deanna sank onto her bed. "I know. It's just that I think Joe was doing something he shouldn't last night, because Gran Gwen reminded me that I had to meet the cycling club and that I should go change into my cycling outfit. Which I'm pretty sure was just a pretense for getting me out of the room while they found out what he did. And if the Ballards and Gran Gwen are trying to protect me, it must be something bad."

"Not Mr. Joseph."

"You don't even know what it was."

"I don't need to. Orrin says—"

"I thought we were going to dispense with things your brother says after his dead misses on some important issues not so long ago."

Elspeth's eyes rolled up into her lids until the blue irises disappeared. "Well, Mr. Joseph wouldn't do nothing illegal. And though I'm sure he enjoys his pleasures as much as the next man, if that's what you're thinking, he wouldn't be making up to any young unmarried girl, even if she was an actress."

"Then who would he—No, don't tell me what you think or what Orrin says. It's none of our business."

"Well, that's the first sensible thing you've said all morning. Now, get up off that chair and let's get you dressed so you won't be late for that club of yours."

———◦◦◦)◦(◦◦◦———

"Would you like your mother and grandmother to also leave?" Lionel asked Joe as soon as the door had closed behind Deanna.

"No, of course not. All I did was offer to help a girl. By sending her here, I might add, not taking her into my den of iniquity. Not that I even have one."

His father snorted. "Is that what you're afraid Deanna will think?"

"No. Shall I tell you what happened last night, or not?"

"Please," Will said.

"Please do," his mother said.

Joe sighed and sat down. He knew his mother wouldn't approve of Mersey's yacht party, not because she thought it was immoral, necessarily, but because the men who would be there would invariably take advantage of the women who were hired for the occasion. Not only would they use them but oftentimes abuse them as well.

"I ran into Vlady Howe as I was leaving the birthday fete last night. He and Herbert were going to drop by Jacob Mersey's yacht. I agreed to go with them."

He shot his mother and grandmother a serious look. "Mainly because I was hungry and Mersey always does a good spread. So we went; it was the usual, women and drinking and lots of noise. A number of the actresses were there.

"I went out on deck to find a quiet place to eat, and when I'd finished and was coming back inside, I passed a stateroom where voices were raised—angry voices. I slowed just to make sure no one was in trouble. But the door opened so I quickly went back outside, waiting for them to leave.

"As I stood there, a girl runs out saying, 'Help me,' and I recognized her. It was Amabelle Deeks, and I told her if she were in trouble, she should come here. Which evidently she did." Joe shrugged. "Then we heard one of the stateroom doors close and she ran off.

"I thought she would be safe, so I left."

Will turned a page in his notebook. Licked the end of his pencil. "And about this argument you overheard. Was it in connection with Miss Deeks?"

"I didn't hear, though I thought I heard one of them say 'bell.' When I saw Amabelle, I made the connection." Joe thought back. "It might be coincidental that she ran from the same corridor as the arguing men. There are maybe four guest rooms there. It might have been about her—or over her. Or something totally unrelated. I didn't hear any female voice."

"And did you know the owners of those voices?"

"Not that I noticed at the time."

"Do you think you would recognize the voices if you heard them again?"

"I might. Like I said, I wasn't paying that much attention, and they were muffled by the door."

"And did you look for her afterward?"

"No. I had just come to have some breakfast. I'd had it and I went home."

"Next time," his father interrupted, "you might do better to come to Bonheur for a home-cooked meal."

"Yes, sir. And I'm sorry if I brought the family into this mess. I was trying to help a young woman." He glanced at his mother. "I didn't think she would murder someone."

"You don't know that she murdered Charlie," Deanna said, striding into the room.

Joe did a double take. She was dressed in a tailored shirt and a skirt hemmed several inches above her ankles. A skirt that was actually divided, similar to trousers. The cycling club. He'd seen their costumes before, just not on Dee.

She stopped in the middle of the room. "You don't know that she murdered poor Charlie, or did you discover evidence while I was upstairs changing?" She cocked her head at him. She was upset that she'd been made to leave, regardless of how gently it was done.

"Did you?" she reiterated.

"No. And since when did a dead stranger become 'poor Charlie'?"

Gran Gwen threw up both hands. "*Pour l'amour du ciel.* You children are enough to make one tear one's hair. A girl is missing. A man is dead. Deanna may call him 'poor Charlie' if she so desires. It is time for Deanna to meet her group, and for Carlisle to bring me a sherry. Joseph, ring the bell."

Joe jumped to his feet and rang for the butler.

Lionel stood. "Ladies, have your sherry, though I must say—" A quick glance from his wife stilled his tongue. "Then, if you'll excuse us, Joseph, Will, and I will see Deanna off." He ushered Deanna out of the parlor. Will bowed to the ladies, and he and Joe followed.

"Whew," Lionel said once they were in the hallway. "Not the quiet weekend with my wife I envisioned. Now, my dear, where is your bicycle? Carlisle?"

The butler was suddenly at his elbow. "I've had it brought round to the front, sir."

"Excellent."

"Will there be anything else, sir?"

"The ladies want their sherry."

"I had anticipated that, sir," Carlisle said, as a footman carrying a tray with a decanter and two glasses arrived at the door to the parlor.

"And if I might say . . . Cook has asked that I remind Sergeant Hennessey to come round to the kitchen before he leaves."

"To do with the case?" Lionel asked.

"To do with his breakfast, sir."

"Bribing a police officer," Lionel quipped. "Cook's a deep one."

"I think this one incident can be overlooked, sir."

"Good man," Lionel said. "You see to the ladies. I'll see these three out and make sure Will gets his sandwiches."

Deanna went down the steps and took her bicycle from the footman.

"Do you think she needs help getting on?" Lionel asked.

"If you suggest it, you'll get your head bit off," Joe said.

The three of them watched wordlessly as Deanna maneuvered the bicycle onto the drive and glanced back at the three men, scowling like only Deanna could scowl.

"Maybe she'd prefer to get started without an audience," Lionel suggested.

The three of them turned back toward the house, but quickly looked back over their shoulders in time to see Deanna pedaling down the drive, wobbling slightly at first but steadying and gaining speed as she reached the avenue.

The three men expelled their breath.

Lionel went back into the house.

"So where will you go from here?" Joe asked Will.

"I'll check in at the station and write my report and make sure it is being attended to properly. Then I plan to talk to the theater company. But I'll also need to question the people who were on the yacht last night. Someone might have seen Miss Deeks after you left, maybe even saw her leave."

"Or followed her to Bonheur and killed Charlie and possibly her?"

Will shrugged. "It would help to know how Charlie fits into this and whether he followed her or accompanied her. How many of the theater people did you notice?"

"Several of the young women. At least I assumed they were from the theater. Girls from the chorus. Six or seven, most dressed the same way as, um, Deanna described."

"Planning to pick up a little extra cash between performances?"

Joe nodded. "Some of the actors might have been there, but since they weren't running around in Egyptian kilts, I wouldn't know. I was only there for an hour at the most."

"Hopefully one of the members of the troupe knows more, but if not, I'll have to question the other guests."

"The yacht guests or the party guests?"

Will swallowed. No one in the force wanted to deal with the cottagers. They wielded a lot of power, and even the highest officials thought twice about crossing them. That job had fallen to Will since he was well educated and grew up if not exactly one of their set, at least having been accepted by it. Until he'd joined the force, of course, then everything changed and they conveniently forgot that he had ever been a guest in their homes.

"Good luck with trying to get them to talk. They may not be afraid of the police, but they're petrified of their wives, and they won't take a chance of ending up in the gossip column of *Town Topics*."

"True. Sometimes I wonder why I was cursed with an aptitude for science."

"You mean you'd rather be knocking heads together down in the Fifth Ward than following forensic clues to a successful end."

"Something like that."

"You wouldn't be happy. Come on. I'll ride with you back to town."

They walked around to the kitchen door, where Cook handed Will a large basket filled with sandwiches, pickles, a pie, and a jar of tea. Will kissed her cheek.

"Get on with you, now. And don't you share that. You eat every bite yourself."

While Will secured the basket to his bicycle, Joe picked up his own bicycle.

"Going back to work?" Will asked.

"Yes, but first I'm going to follow Dee and make sure she gets to her group in one piece."

"What you really mean is you're going to make sure she goes cycling instead of deciding to search for Amabelle Deeks."

Joe grimaced. "Something like that, but afterward I could drop by the yacht, just to see who's still there nursing a pounding head and if anyone remembers anything about last night. That will save you the aggravation of dealing with them."

"Unofficially, of course," Will said.

"Of course." Joe grinned. "I think I might have left my hat there."

They rode north toward the town and parted on Thames Street, Will to the police station on Marlborough Street, and Joe to ride by the Washington Square, where the Newport Ladies' Cycling Club met.

He slowed to a stop when he saw the ladies and their bicycles gathered on the side of the street. There must have been ten or twelve of them. Joe even recognized a few.

As he watched, they climbed onto their bicycles and pedaled away in the opposite direction. Deanna, as one of the lesser-experienced riders, was positioned near the back of the group. Joe watched until they turned the corner and the last one disappeared from view. Satisfied, he turned his own bicycle in the direction of the wharves.

———◦◦◦)◦(◦◦◦———

Deanna had to concentrate to keep her handlebars steady. Between the rough street and the proximity of the other cyclists, it was a bit nerve-racking. She knew that, like every other skill, conquering cycling was merely a matter of practice. And she was already feeling more comfortable astride the contraption. The group moved at a sedate pace, navigating between pedestrians and carriages and handcarts. As soon as they passed the string of shops that lined the street, they would pick up speed until they came to the open road.

Two young women stood on the walk, waiting for the group to pass before crossing the street. One was tall with light brown hair, the other a blonde, slightly shorter and plumper than her companion. They were dressed for shopping and carried themselves well, but there was something about them that told Deanna they were not members of the cottagers. Deanna recognized them immediately as members of the acting troupe.

Their dresses were fashionable, but made of less-expensive cloth than their couture cousins. Their demeanor was polished, but learned. They weren't at all stilted, just seemed to be enjoying themselves as they leaned toward each other chatting. One thing gave them away. They were carrying their own packages.

Deanna was so intent on watching them that she nearly ran into another cyclist. She put on the brakes and stopped in the street. The other cyclists continued on their way.

The two actresses started across the street. Deanna slipped off her bicycle and rolled it over to walk next to them.

They both turned their heads to look at her but didn't slow down.

When they reached the other side, they would have gone on without acknowledging her, but she called out, "Please wait."

They kept walking and she hurried to catch up. "I just want to know if you've seen Amabelle."

They hesitated, then started walking again, ignoring her.

"Please," Deanna said, maneuvering her bicycle alongside them. She didn't want to give too much away. Will would have her head if she warned them about Charlie and the missing Amabelle, but she needed to know if the girl was all right. Deanna just hoped she didn't run into him before she could look for her.

"Have you seen Am—Belle today?"

They kept walking.

"I was supposed to meet her this morning but she didn't come." Deanna mentally crossed her fingers, but what was a little lie when Amabelle's life might be at stake?

One of the women stopped. "What would Belle be doing meeting you and in the morning, of all times? We're theater people. We work late and sleep late."

The taller of the two said, "Come on, Talia. Haven't we had enough of the rich slumming on us for one week?"

Talia, the plumper of the two, nodded, but said, "Belle is one of them, in case you forgot. Nice enough, though. We'll tell her you asked about her . . . when she wakes up."

The two women exchanged quick looks and began to walk faster.

"Would you mind if I came to see if she's awake?"

"Mrs. Calpini doesn't like the guests to have visitors, does she, Noreen? We'll give Belle the message."

"Please, it's really important."

The taller actress, Noreen, turned on Deanna. "Just what are you up to? Her mama didn't send you down to spy on her, did she? Belle said someone had come and tried to get her to leave the show last night."

"She told you that?" Deanna asked. Had Belle misinterpreted their visit? Laurette certainly didn't say anything close to that. She'd even wandered off to talk to the other girls and left Deanna and Belle together. Then the two of them had left for supper.

But who else would have tried to persuade her to leave the theater troupe and return home?

"I don't want her to go home," Deanna said. "I think she should do what she wants. I was just supposed to meet her."

"Aw, Noreen, let her come. Maybe Belle was supposed to meet her. She's always doing crazy stuff like that."

Noreen didn't look convinced, but she moved over and the two women allowed Deanna to walk along beside them. She wanted to ask what kinds of crazy things Belle did, but didn't want to press her luck. If she found Belle safely tucked in her own bed, well, then she'd decide what to do.

She was pretty sure Will would be questioning the actors about her whereabouts and about Charlie's movements the night before. She just had to make sure she was gone before he arrived.

She'd just see if Belle was there and then she'd leave.

Mrs. Calpini's boardinghouse was a gray clapboard house with a white front porch. The windows were open and white gauze curtains wafted in and out with the breeze, reminding Deanna of Amabelle's gauze hem, swaying beneath her cape the night before.

Deanna leaned her bicycle against the latticework alongside the house, then climbed the steps behind Talia and Noreen and stepped into a square foyer. The house was clean and neat though a bit shabby. A wardrobe mirror sat to one side, next to a hat and coatrack.

A cherrywood staircase climbed one wall. The wood was polished but the stair runner was faded and worn. Deanna could hear the sounds of a piano coming from the parlor, but Noreen and Talia didn't stop. Once they'd decided to bring Deanna with them, they seemed in a hurry to get it over with. They looked quickly around and motioned her to follow them upstairs.

They climbed all the way to the third floor, where they stopped in front of one of four doors.

Noreen knocked softly.

There was no answer.

"See, I told you. She's still sleeping."

"Please try again," Deanna said.

She knocked again. "Belle, Belle, you have a visitor."

Not getting an answer, she slowly turned the knob, opened the door just wide enough for her to stick her head in, then she opened it all the way.

"She isn't here."

"Oh," squeaked Talia as if she'd just seen a mouse. And from what Deanna knew about boardinghouses, she might have.

"She must have gone out," Noreen said, and started to close the door. Deanna slipped past her and forced her way into the room.

"Hey, what do you think you're doing?"

Deanna quickly looked around the small room, trying to see if anything looked unusual. But Belle's dressing table was neatly arranged; her clothes hung on pegs along the wall in lieu of a closet, which was probably reserved for the larger rooms.

"She's not here. Now you'd better go. We'll tell her you were looking for her."

Deanna nodded and went back to the landing just as a young man bolted up the stairs. "The police are here. They're looking for Amabelle, and they want everybody downstairs."

Talia and Noreen exchanged panicky looks, then turned on Deanna.

"Did you set us up?"

Deanna shook her head. And she would be in serious trouble if Will Hennessey caught her here. She instinctively started toward the stairs.

Noreen grabbed her and pulled her back. "You're not going down there."

"I'll be in such trouble if they find me here. I've got to get away."

"You're not going anywhere until we find out what's going on." She was gripping Deanna's arm so tightly that Deanna couldn't run. "Timothy. Hold on to her." She shoved Deanna toward him.

The actor grabbed her and held her in a tight embrace. Only it wasn't an embrace at all.

Noreen rushed to the far end of the hallway and opened a door. It was a linen closet. "Put her in there."

"Norie, what are you doing? Who is she? What if the police find her?"

"No," Deanna whispered. She was in such trouble.

"They won't. At least not until she answers to us." Noreen pushed Deanna inside. "One peep out of you and it's curtains. Understand?"

Deanna nodded. Noreen shut the door and Deanna was left in the dark. She heard a key in the lock. She was well and truly trapped. Now, if the actors just didn't give her presence away.

Chapter
6

Joe wheeled his bicycle down the wooden pier and leaned it against a pylon next to the *Sophia*, the scene of last night's carousing. If Joe knew anything about Newport after parties, at least a few men would still be partying or sleeping it off on the yacht this morning.

The crew had finished up its work of clearing any residual vice from the night before. Liquor bottles had been disposed of, food dumped overboard to feed the fish of Newport Harbor. The deck was swabbed, and the yacht gleamed innocently in the morning sun.

Joe nodded to the bosun, who was acting as a de facto sentry, but he merely nodded back and turned to look out to the bay. The man would no more think of stopping Joe than stopping the Judge himself, not that Judge Grantham would ever lower himself to such debauchery. Actually, Joe had been somewhat surprised to see Walter there the night before. It made him like the man more than he usually did.

Joe wasn't really shocked that Walter enjoyed a bit of fun. The Judge wouldn't begrudge him as long as he was discreet and did nothing to embarrass or humiliate his daughter. The Judge, according to Joe's grandmother, had been known to have a drink or two and enjoy not only the theater but a day at the races. The moral, the judicial, the capitalists, and even most of the reformers were known to turn a blind eye when the occasion called for it.

Lord, he is beginning to sound like his mother.

He shook off the thought and stepped into the darkened parlor cabin, which only a few short hours before had been rollicking with food, drink, and half-clad women. This morning only the stale odor of liquor and smoke gave evidence to the previous evening. That and the snoring that reverberated from various places in the darkened room.

Here and there he could see the dark shapes of gentlemen sleeping on chaises and in chairs, still dressed in evening wear. Mostly young bucks who would rouse themselves and stagger down to the corner pub to rub elbows with the hoi polloi long enough to have a wake-up drink before continuing on their way home.

He wouldn't get any information out of them—at least not for a while—and he doubted any of them would have much memory of the night's activities. He trod across the room, careful not to step on any recumbent forms that might lie in his path, and entered the hall that ran between the several guest rooms.

The doors were all closed. Either unoccupied and cleaned, or still in use. And Joe had no intention of disturbing anyone in flagrante.

He continued aft until he heard voices, then climbed out to

the deck, where a breakfast was in progress. Mersey was there, as well as several other men Joe recognized. Vlady Howe, Erik Dolan, who was visiting the Wetmores for the season, Frank Trumball, who spent his summers drifting between Saratoga and Newport, never staying long at either, and a couple of others.

"Ballard"—Mersey motioned him over—"looks like you actually made it home last night. What brings you back? Perkins, bring Ballard a cup of coffee and an eye opener." He leaned forward. "Good for what ails you. Even if nothing ails you." He laughed until he coughed.

Perkins—Mersey's "yacht boss," as Mersey called him, served as valet, butler, and all-round dogsbody, as far as Joe could tell from the few occasions he'd seen him—bowed and crossed to the coffee urn.

Joe didn't make a habit of associating with Mersey. There was nothing really wrong with him; he was just lazy, dissolute, and lived to be entertained. He was also quickly dissipating into illness.

"Why did you come back, Joe?" Erik asked.

"Thought I might have left my hat here."

"Well," Mersey said, "I'll get Perkins to have a look-see, once we clear out all the dead men, and he'll have one of the boys bring it round to you. Sit down and have some ham and eggs."

"Thanks," Joe said, and helped himself to another breakfast. One that he didn't want, but needed in order to have an excuse to stay.

"It was a pretty happy crowd last night," he said as Erik slid over to make room for him. Joe sat.

"Yeah, but it got even better after you left." Frank laughed. "I think."

Unfortunately, Joe never drank enough to forget the boring evenings spent at the soirees, fetes, balls, and dinners that Newport was addicted to. He hadn't planned on attending any of them this summer, but with Deanna here, he couldn't not go.

Though as it turned out, he didn't really need to go. His mother and Grandmère, for all their bluster, kept a watchful eye on her, and would never let any harm come to her if they could help it. Still . . .

"Brilliant of Edgerton to bring the theater to town for the Judge's birthday."

"Surprised he managed it. Mrs. Grantham was dead set against it. She's joined one of those women's groups that's always harping about something. Oh, not like the one your mother belongs to," Erik added quickly.

"I can assure you that my mother and Mrs. Grantham will never be members of the same club," Joe said.

"Thank God for that," Mersey said. "Between her and his wife, Drusilla, I don't know how poor Edgerton gets in even a bit of fun. Do you know they even balked at serving whiskey at the ball? As if a fellow could drink champagne all evening."

"I'd be giggling like a girl halfway through the night," Frank said. "No, give me a good aged whiskey to offset the bubbles."

"And the chorus girls were a nice touch," Joe added, apologizing silently to his mother.

"Very nice," Mersey agreed. "We were going to bring down a couple of those big birdcages, maybe have the girls show off some leg and their own exotic plumage."

Frank laughed. "But none of us could figure out what to do with the birds. Did you see those things? Huge and mean. Had to give the idea up."

"The girls did all right without it," Erik said.

"Indeed."

"There was one particular blonde," Joe began.

"Why, Ballard. Never knew you to slum down, in spite of the talk a while back."

Joe waved his hand dismissively in the air. He could imagine all the interpretations they might make of his gesture.

"But I know the one you mean," Frank Turnbull said. "Left early, well before first light. She must have found a good position. . . ."

The men laughed.

". . . If you know what I mean," he continued. "I didn't see her most of the evening, then she left early. I'm thinking that woman knows how to use what she's got."

"I wonder where she went," Joe said, noticed the others looking oddly at him, and hurriedly added, "Was there another party I missed last night?" He laughed, not very convincingly, he thought.

But they all joined in, and Joe used the opportunity to take his leave. He had no talent for this. How on earth did Will ever learn anything during an investigation?

⚬⚬⚬❈⚬⚬⚬

Deanna didn't think she could stand being stuck in the linen closet much longer. She was about to yell "Let me out" when her rational mind took over. She'd be in big trouble if the police found her here. And being found locked in a linen closet would be beyond humiliating.

Kate Goelet wouldn't be caught locked in a closet. She would figure out a way to free herself. Cad Metti, who was Elspeth's favorite female detective, would break the door down, but that would draw too much attention, and that's the last thing Deanna wanted.

She looked up from where she was seated on the floor. The closet was dark and fairly large, but the space was taken up with deep shelves holding sheets and towels, which didn't leave her much room for maneuvering.

Deanna considered the doorknob; it was worth a try. She pressed her ear to the door and, not hearing anything, she tried to turn it. It didn't budge.

She groped in her hair for a hairpin, and when she found one, she straightened it out and began to poke at the keyhole. But since she had no knowledge of how to pick a lock—none of the novels she read actually described the process—she had no success.

She tossed the hairpin aside and groped along the walls, pressing her palms to the plaster, like one of those mimes at the musical theater house, looking for she didn't know what: an extra key hanging by a nail in case someone got inadvertently locked in, which would be ridiculous. A light switch. She hadn't noticed if the boardinghouse was wired for electricity or still using gas. She cautioned herself to be more observant in the future.

All her exploring didn't uncover one thing that would help free her. Finally admitting defeat, she sat down on the floor again to wait for her captors to release her.

And while she waited she listened, but all she could hear was an occasional murmur, then a sudden outburst of anger that had her pressing her ear to the door. But try as she might she couldn't make out a single word.

She jumped when she heard steps on the stairs. Lots of steps. It was bound to be the police, come to search Amabelle's room.

And Deanna felt just a soupçon of annoyance that she hadn't gotten there first. Well, she'd gotten there, just hadn't had time to search.

She knew it was wrong, but she couldn't help it. Hadn't she helped bring a murderer to justice just a few weeks ago?

"Is this the room?"

Will's voice. Deanna shrunk back, making herself as small as possible in case he thought it necessary to search the linen closet.

She heard a door open. Will must have stepped inside, because she didn't hear anything else for several minutes. Deanna tried to breathe as quietly as possible, but to her ears each breath sounded like a hurricane. At last she heard the steps return, then go down the stairs, and she let her breath out in a thankful whoosh. Surely it wouldn't be long before they let her out.

But it seemed like forever before Deanna heard the key in the lock. She pushed to her feet, but unfortunately her foot had gone to sleep while she waited in the cramped space, and she fell back on her rear end—a term her mother would never allow her to use—and was sprawled ungracefully on the floor just as the door opened and four faces peered in, then down at her.

"Get up," said Noreen.

"My foot went to sleep."

"Oh, for crying out loud," said a second man who had joined the two actresses and the man who Deanna recognized as Timothy. "This is your dastardly spy?" He reached down and offered his hand.

Deanna took it and he hauled her to her feet.

"There now. Would you like to explain yourself?"

"Yes," Deanna said. "Are the police gone?"

"They left," Noreen said. "But I wouldn't put it past them

not to be lurking in the bushes waiting to catch us out in some-thing."

"Bring her back to your room, Gil. It's the most secluded."

"Not a good idea." He turned to Deanna. "I'm Gilpatrick Finley. You can call me Gil." He smiled at Deanna and gestured her to the back of the landing. "But really, the state of Rollie and my digs . . ."

"Out late," the other man explained. "Landlady hasn't had a chance to make the beds." He stuck out his hand. "Roland Gibbs at your service. My friends call me Rollie. Are you friend or foe?"

Deanna shook it. "Friend, I hope."

"That remains to be seen," Noreen said. "And I suggest we get out of this hallway and find out just what she's about." She huffed out an exasperated sigh. "We can use our room." She grabbed Deanna by the elbow and muscled her down the hall, where Talia opened the door at the far end. They all crammed into the room.

It was a small room, not much bigger than the linen closet—or a Bonheur bathroom. The wall was covered with cabbage rose wallpaper. Two twin beds were separated by an oval rag rug, and the room had one window that looked into the win-dows of the house next door. Beneath the window, a curved-front dresser and a washstand vied for space. On the far side of the bed an upholstered side chair was shoved into the corner.

Noreen squeezed between the bed and the wall to extricate the chair, and carried it to the center of the room. "Sit," she ordered Deanna.

"Prepare yourself for interrogation of the vilest kind," Gil said in sepulchral tones.

Deanna wasn't sure if he was kidding or trying to scare her.

She sat. Noreen stood before her, fists on her hips. She was pretty in an exotic-actress way, graceful and sure of herself. But she was also physically strong and spoke with such an edge of hardness and mistrust, so at odds with her looks, that Deanna wondered for a moment if she wasn't acting.

Actually, they all seemed to be acting. Facing her in a semicircle like judges at an inquisition. Only Talia kept glancing at the door as if she were afraid the police would raid the room and they would all be carted off to jail.

Or was it something more sinister than that?

Nonsense, Deanna told herself. She was falling under the allure of the actors and the stage. She had to admit it was energizing.

Noreen leaned over until her face was inches from Deanna's. "Now, why are you looking for Belle? What do you know? Why do—"

"Why don't you stop asking questions long enough for her to answer one?" Gil suggested, and smiled at Deanna.

Gil was a handsome man, fine figured, and Deanna thought she recognized him as the head bedouin in last night's play. Rollie, on the other hand, was medium height, slightly fleshy with dark red hair that was pomaded and combed back from a high forehead. Deanna definitely remembered him as the comic character of "This" and his silly song trying to convice the schoolgirls he was "This" and not "That."

"Thank you," Deanna said, trying to appear refined and confident. She didn't think she was fooling any of them. They could probably do upper-class snobbery better than she could.

She sighed. "I'm looking for Belle because I'm worried

about her." No need to say that she may be wanted for murder . . . yet. "Did the police have any idea of where she is?"

"No, that's what they wanted to know. Seems she's disappeared."

"They think she killed Ch-Ch—" Talia burst into tears.

Rollie put his arm around her. "Courage, *mon amie.*"

Deanna looked at both of them, still not sure if this was honest emotion or put on for her benefit.

Well, either way, she would listen and, if need be, would tell them enough to get them to trust her. Whatever she had to do to help Belle.

"She didn't kill Charlie," Noreen said. She narrowed her eyes at Deanna. "Did you know about Charlie?"

Deanna nodded. "I'm so sorry."

"Did you kill him?"

"No, of course not."

"Maybe you should just start at the beginning."

They sounded just like characters in one of Deanna's detective stories.

"Ama—Belle's mother is a friend of the people I'm staying with. She asked us to say hello. See how she was."

"Try to get her to come home," Talia said. "We heard all about her parents. And how stifling they were."

"We didn't come to coerce her to go back. I don't even know her parents. I didn't even meet Belle until last night."

"And she agreed to meet you today? Why?" Noreen asked.

"She didn't."

"Ha."

"Do you want to hear what I have to say and maybe help me find her before she gets hurt?"

Noreen made a sour face. "Or find her so they can send her to jail."

"Stop it!" Talia cried. "Charlie's dead and maybe Belle did kill him."

Deanna's heart hiccupped.

Gil grabbed Talia by the shoulders and yanked her to her feet. "You're getting hysterical. Pull yourself together and be quiet.

"Now, miss—I'm sorry. I didn't catch your name."

"Randolph, Deanna Randolph, but you can call me Deanna." Deanna gave him her most charming smile.

It must have worked, because Gil nodded slightly. "Deanna," he said, drawing out the syllables as if he were savoring them. Then he smiled. "We'll call you Dee."

Deanna took a breath. "Fine. My friends call me Dee."

At least they had until recently.

"Belle came to our house last night," Deanna continued. "It was very late and she woke the household. She seemed . . . distressed. I took her upstairs and gave her a nightgown and we talked a little about dime novels and what it was like to be an actress, and then my maid took her down to the guest room. It was nearly light by then."

Now Deanna hesitated. How much could she tell without impeding Will's investigation? He hadn't said anything about keeping the information secret. Of course, it probably didn't occur to him that she might run into Belle's colleagues and friends.

It certainly hadn't occurred to her.

"What did W—the police tell you?"

The four actors frowned at her. Finally Rollie said, "Just

that Charlie was dead." His voice wavered, and Talia slipped her hand into his. "And that they were looking for Belle," he continued.

"You must forgive our emotions," Noreen said.

Deanna thought Noreen was controlling hers to perfection. But the others seemed genuinely moved. *They're actors*, she reminded herself. But didn't actors have to feel more emotions than ordinary people in order to portray them so well? Still, it wouldn't do to drop her guard while around them.

"Later that morning a parlor maid discovered Charlie. He was lying on the floor of the conservatory." She watched her audience for the slightest hint of recognition. And got none.

"He'd been bludgeoned to death." She shouldn't have said it. She knew better than to divulge the details of a case and take the chance of tipping off the perpetrator, but she also knew the value of shock tactics. And her announcement certainly had shocked them.

Talia gasped a cry, Rollie covered his face with his hands, Gil turned to look out the window. Only Noreen stood unmoved, except that her face had drained of color, leaving her makeup looking like slashes of paint. "He was a beautiful man," she said quietly.

Was. Only now he was barely recognizable as the handsome, laughing young man who had taken Belle to dinner.

Gil turned from the window. "And they think Belle beat him? With what? She wouldn't. She couldn't. Charlie could have easily overpowered her."

"Did you tell this to the police?"

"Of course not. We're educated, sophisticated people, Miss Randolph. We understand more than most why the police look anywhere but the local elite for their miscreants. They'd happily blame one of us for this—we're outsiders, morally suspect, hated and feared and yet loved and idolized.

"We won't be cooperating with them or making it easy in any way to accuse one of our own."

"Or with you," Noreen added, frowning down at Deanna. "I ask you again. What's your interest?"

"I'm worried about her. The police don't—as far as I know—suspect her of murder, but I am concerned for her safety. How do we know that whoever killed Charlie didn't kill Belle or wants to and is looking for her as we speak?"

"Wait a minute," Gil said, striding across the room and coming to stand over Deanna. "The police knew his name was Charlie, but if they came straight here from the scene, how did they know?" He narrowed his eyes at Deanna, and the affably, slightly roguish man became a predator. He turned away, then came back, leaning over her. "They must have learned it from you. How did you know his name was Charlie if you just met Belle last night? Did she tell you about him?"

Deanna shook her head. "But I recognized him from when we were backstage. He'd come to take her to dinner. She called him Charlie."

"Charlie. Charles Withrop," Gil said.

"And he was more than a friend," Talia said. "He was her fiancé."

"Talia, that's enough." At last Noreen seemed to be losing her sangfroid.

"Noreen, at least listen to what she has to say." Rollie shot a hopeful look at Deanna. "If it can help catch Charlie's murderer and find Belle."

Noreen frowned. "If you're a spy for the coppers . . ."

"I'm not," Deanna said. At least she wasn't officially a spy.

But if she learned anything that could help catch the killer, she would be duty bound to tell. She started to say so, then held her piece.

"Then why are you interested in Belle?"

Deanna looked down at her hands, which she was glad to see sat quietly in her lap. Calm. At least on the outside. "I thought we might be friends."

Noreen cracked a laugh.

"Why?" Talia asked. "Belle isn't one of your class anymore. Why would you want to be friends?"

"I don't know," Deanna said. "Why do any two people become friends? Why are you and Noreen friends?"

"We work together," Noreen said. "You obviously don't have to work at all, and you certainly aren't an actress. How could you and Belle possibly have any common interests as friends and after knowing each other for not even a few hours?"

"But we do."

"And just what is that?"

"Like I told you, we both like dime novels," Deanna said, feeling embarrassed and for some reason sad.

"Well," Gil said. "I didn't think ladies read books for the masses."

"I do," Deanna said, beginning to get a little tired of their attitude.

A knock at the door made them all jump.

"Noreen, have you seen Rollie and Gil? Edwin wants to see us all downstairs."

"I'll go find them," Noreen called. "We'll be down in a minute." She waited until the footsteps receded. "You'll have to go now."

"But I—"

"Listen. If the police hold us in town until they find Belle, we'll lose a huge amount of income. Income none of us can afford to lose. But we can't discuss this now."

"And you can't stay here by yourself," Rollie said. "I'll escort you downstairs." He offered Deanna his arm. Reluctantly, she took it. She hadn't learned anything helpful except that this was a very loyal group, so loyal that they might withhold any useful information until it was too late to save Belle Deeks.

Rollie walked her down the stairs, put his finger to his lips at the bottom of the stairs, and motioned her to stay until he peeked into the parlor. Then he gestured for her to hurry to the door, which Deanna did. And before she knew it, she was back on her bicycle and pedaling toward . . .

She meant to head south, back to Bonheur, but at the next block she turned west. Joe had said he'd seen Belle at a yacht party. Maybe Belle had returned there today.

———◦◦◦❧◦◦◦———

Joe stepped out into the bright sunshine and walked down the gangplank to the pier. He took a couple of deep breaths in an attempt to drive the odor and sting of stale whiskey, eggs, and cigars from his person.

He made his way over to where several of the crew members were now standing on the pier, smoking hand-rolled cigarettes and passing around a bottle of Mersey's whiskey.

Joe nodded to them and slowed. But he could tell right away they weren't in a talkative mood. He'd do better to leave them to Will and the head-cracking dock patrol.

With a final look around he took his bike and rolled it across the wharf to the street.

Ahead of him a wooden crate leaned precariously against a shipbuilder's wall. Just as he reached it, it rattled, and Joe made a quick detour away; he was in no mood for rats or feral dogs at this time of day.

The figure that crawled out was neither rodent nor beast, but a man, ancient, by the looks of him. He slowly unfolded to his feet, where he stood at an angle that complemented the crate.

He was wearing filthy denim pants held up with a piece of rope and a torn and filthier wool sweater. He squinted at Joe, his nose stuck in the air like he smelled something bad. Most likely himself, because Joe could smell him from where he stood, a combination of stale beer and unwashed body.

The man stuck out his hand, bony fingers shook either with palsy or to urge Joe into giving him something. Joe reached in his pocket, found a coin, and withdrew his hand. He flashed it open just long enough for the old man to see it but not to grab it and run.

"Where do you live?" Joe asked.

"Useta have a room over the shipbuilder's."

"Don't have it anymore?"

"Naw. Got my palace right here." The old man gestured vaguely in the direction of the crate.

"So you were sleeping there last night?"

"Couldn't hardly sleep with all the gaiety going on down there. Kept me awake nearly to daybreak. How's a body to sleep with all that racket?"

He lifted an arm, then let it drop. "Over on them dem floating palaces. All sorts of carousing going on. Every end of week, always something goin' on at one or t'other of them. Women and liquor. Wouldn't even give a bit to a man in need."

"The one last night kept you awake all night?" Joe asked.

"Pretty much all night." The man beetled his eyes at Joe and thrust his chin out so far that Joe was afraid the rest of him would follow it, and he'd end up facedown on the walkway. "Say, why do you want to know? You ain't with the police, are you?"

Joe shook his head. "Looking for my sister."

"You oughta not let a young girl go all among those gentlemen." He spit out the last word, letting Joe know what he thought of those gentlemen. "She'll come to no good, if she ain't already. And don't expect them to take care of her. They don't feel beholden. They just use them and throw them away."

He started hobbling away. Joe went after him. "You see anyone fighting? Maybe over a woman?"

"Nope. Well, yep. Only he wasn't fighting over her; he was chasing her. Almost got her, too."

"Chasing her?"

"I'm feeling awfully parched, and I get real forgetful when I'm thirsty."

Joe shoved his hand into his pocket and brought out a second coin. Went through the same motions he had before. Flashed both coins and closed his fist around them.

The old man moved closer.

"Tell me about this man and the woman he was after."

"I could remember more if I had something to wet my whistle."

Joe shook his head and started to put the coins back in his pocket.

"Wait. I'm remembering now. Young fella. He wasn't on the yacht but was waiting outside. Not one of them. First, I thought he was waiting to roll one of them gentlemen when they staggered home, so I kept my eye on him."

To demand part of the take, Joe had no doubt.

"But he just sat there. Then this one young woman come out and he stops her. She pushes him away and runs off into the night. He yells after her, then he follows her. That's all I know."

"Can you describe them?"

The old man heaved a sigh that ended in a rattle of a cough. He grabbed the edge of the crate to steady himself. "Young. They was young. Just young."

He held out his hand. Joe dropped the coins into it. Then he reached into his pocket and pulled out a few more. "Have yourself something to eat."

The old man just looked at him.

"Food, man. Don't waste it all on drink."

"You one of them pro ho-pro ho—teetotalers?"

"Not me," Joe assured him.

The old man nodded. "Then, I thankee, sir." He pushed away from the crate. "The boy. He was a towhead." He peered over Joe's shoulder and his mouth dropped open. "Well, did you ever, now? What's the world a-coming to? Women on bicycles, pure craziness, next they'll want the vote. You mark my words."

Joe felt a second of sheer panic. He quelled it. It couldn't be Dee. He'd watched her cycle away with the other members of the club.

He turned around. It was Dee. She'd given him the slip. Joe gritted his teeth, waiting for her to see him, and wondered what she would do when she did.

The old man took the opportunity to shove the coins in his pocket and take off down the street.

Dee hadn't seen him, but she was definitely on her way to the pier.

Joe leaned his bike against the crate and crossed his arms.

She was so busy steering her bicycle over the wood planks that she didn't see him until she was almost upon him. She squeaked and barely managed to jump off her bike before she fell.

She stood on the wharf and scowled at him.

He loved that scowl. She'd used it since she was little—when her feelings were hurt, when she was disappointed, when she was frustrated, to get her way—but today Joe wasn't moved. "What are you doing here?"

"What are you?"

"You were supposed to be out with your cycling club."

"I was."

"Back so soon?"

She shrugged. She wasn't going to admit to him what she was up to. Though it was obvious to Joe. "Go home, Dee. This is no place for you."

"For a girl, you mean."

"A lady. Go home."

She rolled her eyes.

"Now, Dee."

"You go first."

"I'm not going—" But he knew he wasn't going to win this, and they would look ridiculous acting out this childish spat on the wharf.

"We'll both go," he said. He waited for her to get on her bike; she waited for him to get on his. Then they both rode south, arriving at Bonheur fifteen minutes later, not having said a word between them.

———∞◉∞———

Deanna handed her bicycle to one of the footmen and started up the front steps to Bonheur. Joe wasn't even going to see her inside. He just sat astride his bicycle, feet on the ground, arms crossed. He was mad at her. Not just annoyed, like he and Bob used to be when she pestered them to play with her, but really angry. They used to always give in . . . eventually. But Joe wasn't budging. She didn't understand what was happening to him.

He was the one getting to do what he wanted to do. He got to leave society, live in a drafty old warehouse, spending all day working on the things that fascinated him. But as soon as Deanna tried to do something interesting, he got all cross with her.

He was turning into a bully.

"The master and mistress are sailing. Madame Manon is taking tea in her room," Carlisle informed her once she was inside. "As she didn't expect you to return so soon."

Deanna supposed she would have to confess to Gran Gwen that she hadn't actually joined the group for long.

"Then I won't bother her. I'll have tea in my room, if you please."

"Certainly, miss. I shall inform Cook."

Deanna smiled and climbed the stairs. She imagined the blues of the water and sky, the white of the clouds, and the Ballards, not on the yacht that was moored at their private dock nearby, but on Lionel's sailboat. Laurette would be dressed in one of her light, airy dresses and a wide hat with a big bow tied under her chin. He would have his sleeves rolled up, and they'd work the sails together and laugh as the boat danced among the waves, sea spray covering them in a fine mist.

Happy on the Waves.

She stopped when she reached the landing, recollecting herself. This was no time to think about sailing or happiness. Amabelle Deeks was out there somewhere, afraid—but hopefully alive.

Chapter
7

Joe had spent a long, fruitless day, first with the murder, then with Dee. They'd parted badly. Well, to be truthful, he had left without even saying good-bye. He'd just been so angry with her for reasons that weren't altogether clear to him, but had something to do with the difficulties in which she seemed bound and determined to place herself. Situations that were dangerous and unseemly. But mainly dangerous.

He wasn't sure that she understood how dependent her good reputation was on society's opinion. He knew she didn't care a fig for society now. But one day she would. She'd marry some acceptable man—and probably the sooner the better. She'd settle down and become . . . It made his heart hurt a little to think of Dee as a staid, appropriate society lady. He'd hated watching her shrivel up under her mother's constant demanding oversight.

He preferred the vivacious, daring young girl he'd known for over half her life. He and Bob had made sure she came to no harm, though she did try their patience and their nerves often. Since Bob's death, Joe had watched over her alone. And at first he'd been delighted to see that vivacity blossom once again under the tutelage of his grandmother.

But it was dangerous to let it flourish. Deanna was eighteen, soon to be nineteen. She needed to take her place in society; for himself, he had no intention of going back.

He was feeling fairly glum when he and Orrin closed up for the night. So when Will showed up at his door, wearing civilian clothes and suggesting they go out for a beer, he'd been surprised but more than willing. It was something they didn't often do anymore, now that Will was in the police force.

He'd also been surprised when they didn't stop at the local pub but hailed a hack and drove back uptown to the White Horse Tavern.

The bar was located not far from the police station and was mostly filled with regulars and guests from the handful of nearby boardinghouses. It was not even midnight and yet most of its customers, shop owners, clerks, teachers, craftsmen, had gone home to bed so they could awaken early the next morning in time to attend one of the several churches in town.

Joe and Will didn't have the pub to themselves, but it was considerably emptier and quieter than the bars and pubs in the Fifth, where they would be packed and rowdy far into the next morning.

Nonetheless, Will led them to a table in an alcove near the front door, but well back in the shadows.

"It's not that I'm not enjoying the evening," Joe said as he looked around the half-filled room, "but are we on a surveillance?"

"Not really. I was told some of the actors came in here after the performance. I was hoping to talk to the barmaid or maybe have a chance to talk with the actors again. None of them would cooperate when I went to the boardinghouse where they're staying. I didn't even have anything to bribe—or threaten—them with. And at this point I would consider using threats to get some information."

They were interrupted by the appearance of the barmaid, a hefty woman who on first glance looked younger than she actually was.

"Evening, Sergeant."

Will nodded. "Peg."

"You here on business or pleasure?"

"For a beer and maybe a little information."

Peg pulled a rag from her shoulder and slapped it on the table.

It made Joe jump, but Will just sat there, leaning back in his chair, as Peg began to swab the table clean. When she was finished she slung the rag back over her shoulder and said, "A beer for you, and what's your good-looking friend gonna have?"

"Beer," Joe said, "Providing you're referring to me."

Peg let out a hearty laugh. "See anyone else here with even half a decent face? 'Cept the sergeant here, of course. Though I gotta say, some real lookers in here last night." Her eyes narrowed and her smile turned into a frown. "One of those boys was the man they found dead last night, weren't he?" She beetled her eyes at Will. "Which one?"

"The one they called Charlie. Charles Withrop."

"Charlie?" Peg tapped the dimple in her strong chin. "Charlie . . . Not that pretty blond boy? Him with the angel face?"

"I'm afraid so."

"Well, the devil take it all. I could name you fingerfuls of useless grunts that he coulda taken before that boy. Heard they found him up at one of the big houses."

"That would be my friend's house." Will gestured to Joe.

"Joe Ballard," Joe said, introducing himself. "And yes, he was found in the conservatory at my father's house."

"Joe Ballard. Ballard. Ain't you the one Orrin O'Laren's apprenticed to?"

"That's the one," Joe agreed.

"So Charlie was killed at your posh house. Huh." Peg shook her head. "Must be some powerful interesting gadgets down here to make you leave the comforts of home."

"They are to me."

Peg laughed almost silently. "If that don't beat all. I'll get your beers, gentlemen. If that ain't a kick in the pants."

"Buy yourself a pint, Peg," Will said. "And come have a seat with us. Joe can tell you about his inventions." He smirked at Joe.

Peg laughed uproariously at that. "Well, it's tempting, but I'm worried about my virtue." She grinned and rested her hand on the table and spoke in a lower voice. "And my life. I don't know nothing anyway. Just that while he was here, he seemed like a sweet boy, young like, but with an air about him, don't know what you'd call it. Like he'd . . . oh, I don't know, just not all sweetness."

"A violent streak?" Will asked, jumping on her statement.

"Oh no. I expect any violence done would be done to him, not the other way around. And it seems I would be right. Damn shame, though."

"When did he—"

Peg stopped him. "Not all at once, or my other customers will

think I'm buttering up the cops. I'll be back with your beers."
She left them, moving slowly and methodically, her head shaking in counterpoint to her hips.

"Do you think she knows something?" Joe said as soon as Peg moved out of hearing distance. "Maybe you're about to break the case."

"I doubt Peg knows more that she's just told us. But I'll keep at it. I'm under the gun to get this murder solved quickly."

"It's only been a day. Surely your superiors can be more patient than that."

"They can. The Judge can't."

"Judge Grantham? It's not like anyone can blame him for Charlie's murder. He wasn't killed on his property. If anything, they should be snubbing us, because he was found at Bonheur. Though I suspect that will start soon enough in some quarters."

"Well, my captain said the Judge demanded that we wrap this up immediately. He—get this—feels responsible for bringing that 'shady element' to town, though everyone knows the event was actually concocted by his daughter and son-in-law."

"He's probably afraid that being associated with them in any way might sully his reputation." Joe leaned back in his chair. "Thank God I don't have a profession that is dependent on what everyone thinks of me."

"I admit, I can see his point. Evidently he's been hearing a big case which is due to wrap up any day now. He only came to town long enough for his birthday celebration." Will grinned. "I guess he couldn't give up having his very own performance at home."

"Or he was afraid he would appear unsympathetic if he ignored his family on his special day. Monday will be soon enough for sentencing. What's the accused up for?"

"Dissemination of information on birth control. The court is asking for full sentencing and Judge Grantham will surely rule accordingly."

"Twelve years?"

Will shrugged. "The man's some half-wit who someone paid ten cents to hand out flyers."

"And for that he gets twelve years? That's criminal. Killers have gotten less."

"Killers have gotten off scot-free."

Peg returned, carrying two fairly clean mugs with foam oozing over their sides. She set them down on the table. "There you go, gentlemen."

"Peg," Will asked, "do you remember if they all left together?"

"Who?" asked Peg, seeming to have forgotten their conversation.

"The actors, last night, did they all leave together? Did Charlie leave with them or before them?"

"Why don't you ask them yourselves?"

"I already tried. They won't talk." Will picked up his glass.

"Well, try again." She hurried off.

Will sighed and took a drink of his beer.

"Well, if it's any consolation, you may have a second chance soon enough," Joe said. "If those aren't your actors coming through the door, I'll go get myself a pair of spectacles."

A group consisting of four men and two women entered the premises. They were chatting but not raucously so. Joe squinted through the uneven light to see if he recognized any of them from the yacht. Because it was beginning to seem to him that if Amabelle had left the yacht party and gone straight to Bonheur, chances were Charlie had followed her there, and if Charlie had, someone could have just as easily followed him.

Will ducked his head and looked at the door. "Damn. I wanted to question everyone else first."

"Then we should have come earlier. They didn't see you. They're moving to the other end of the room."

Joe didn't recognize any of them. It was impossible to tell about the women because of the hats they were wearing. And the men all looked like . . . actors. Joe hadn't been aware of any actors being at the yacht party, but he hadn't really been looking.

"So you questioned that lot already?"

"The ones I could see, yes. The troupe is spread out between two different places. Chorus—men and women at Mrs. Calpini's boardinghouse. She wasn't thrilled but she wasn't going to turn down cash. Most of the principal actors are staying at the Ocean House Hotel. A couple are staying with friends."

"And all are complaining. They're losing money by being kept here. But once I let them leave, there will be no way of discovering the murderer. The Judge is adamant about keeping them until they've been cleared or accused."

"That might never happen," Joe said. "Is the Judge willing to foot the bill for keeping them here? It's got to be costing them a pretty penny, renting rooms for the whole cast, not to mention the box office they'll lose."

"The Judge has higher things to worry about."

"Like sentencing some poor sod to twelve years?" Joe shivered. "No wonder he enjoys the theater. Something to take his mind off the sordid realities of life."

"True," Will said. "And there are some who would begrudge him that."

"Like his pal Comstock?"

"Nah, as long as a man keeps the footlights between himself

and the actresses, he's not a problem. And he's sure of the Judge's allegiance. But cross over that line . . . The man is indefatigable in his war against smut. When the Judge ceases to be useful, he won't think twice about feeding him to the hounds."

"All in the name of morality," said Joe. "Uh-oh, here comes one of the actors. I guess they saw us after all."

Will glanced over his beer mug. "Edwin Stevens, the company manager."

Stevens was above medium height, middle aged, handsome—it seemed to Joe that all the actors he'd ever seen were good-looking men. Stevens was dressed in a brown suit and was making his way toward their table. He had a trim figure, wavy dark hair, and eyebrows that flew up at the arch. The eyebrows gave him away. Joe wouldn't have recognized him otherwise.

"Professor Papyrus," Joe said, and half stood as the man reached the table.

As Joe had hoped, the greeting took him off his stride physically and emotionally. He stopped and turned to bow to Joe. Joe had known that stroking Mr. Edwin Stevens's vanity would throw him off long enough for Will to prepare to address him.

"Ah, you were perhaps in attendance at our little performance last night?"

Yes, before one of your chorus members was murdered, Joe thought. The man seemed totally unaffected by the death, and the actors whom he could hear laughing were certainly losing no sleep or jollification over "poor Charlie."

"Yes, and I enjoyed—"

"Thank you," he said, dismissing Joe. "Now, if I may, Sergeant. I am most saddened to interrupt your leisure time, but while you sit here drinking your beer, my actors are kept cooling their heels, losing their income, and forgetting their lines, while I, my dear sir, am losing my shirt paying for the accommodations." He lifted one of his flying eyebrows so high that Joe thought it might lift the man off the floor.

And Joe had been completely wrong about deflecting the man's attention from Will. He'd recovered himself way too quickly, probably from having to think on his feet onstage. Joe sat back and waited for him to have his say.

He stood over Will like a human colossus, though Will was the taller, stronger man.

"Are you any closer to finding the villain who did this dastardly deed?"

Joe listened, fascinated. He talked like a character in a play— or in one of Dee's dime novels. The thought of her deflated his spirits somewhat. At least she would be at the Rensselaers' dinner all night and under the eagle eye of his grandmother, though she would be more likely to enter into Deanna's schemes than try to dissuade her from them.

Though to give the old lady her due, she knew how a young girl needed to conduct herself in order to enter society. Once Dee was there, it would be a whole other kettle of fish.

"I have authorities that I must answer to," Will was saying. "The more your people cooperate, the sooner you will be allowed to return to the city."

"We have cooperated. I don't know what more we can do, unless it's to draw straws to decide which one of us will give up his life and confess so that the others may go back to work."

A muscle in Will's jaw tightened. He was trying to hold on to his patience. He wasn't easily riled, Joe knew, but this theater man was definitely pushing him to his limits.

If only someone would tell this Edwin Stevens that it was better to talk to Will, than to have their heads knocked together by a less sympathetic police officer, of which there were plenty. Most of the force still thought beating a suspect was the first and fastest way to a confession.

Which, Joe had to agree, was true. Unfortunately, they got a lot of confessions from innocent people just to stop the pain.

"Sir," Will said, giving Edwin Stevens his full attention. "I will find the person who did this and bring him to justice. No matter how long it takes. You may be assured of that. So please tell your people that if any of them remembers something, no matter how small, to bring it to me. Help me find the culprit so we can all get back to living our lives."

Stevens studied Will's face, glanced down at Will's hands, which were cradling his beer mug.

Taking the measure of the man, Joe thought.

"I'll tell them. Now, if we are to be stuck here, to whom do I speak in order to find a place to rehearse my players on the chance we are ever to get back to what we do?"

Will looked at Joe.

"Possibly the Casino theater? It may be available during the day, but it will be costly, I imagine."

"Like everything in Newport. Still, I thank you." Stevens reached into his inner jacket pocket and extracted a card. "My name and local address." He handed the card to Joe. "Good evening." He strode to the door and left the tavern.

"Did we just agree to find them a space to rehearse without guaranteeing they help us in return?" Will asked.

"I believe so," Joe said. "Perhaps this will soften their attitude toward cooperating."

"We can but hope." Will snorted. "God, listen to me. Two minutes around that spouter and he has me talking like someone out of a play."

"Another beer for you gentlemen?" Peg appeared like a stage effect in the space Stevens had just quitted.

"No thanks, Peg. I have to get back to the station. You, Joe?"

Joe frowned. "Yeah, Peg, I think I will have another." He pulled out his money clip and handed her enough for the drinks, including Will's. "Have another round sent over to the actors. Keep the change for yourself."

"Well, ain't you the big spender. Thanks." She stuffed the bills down her blouse, scooped up both mugs by two fingers, and started to walk away but then turned back. "I remember now, the women weren't here, and I don't think the man who just left was, but those three were: the two tall ones and the roly-poly one. They were with the man who got offed. Having a real set-to, they were."

Both Will and Joe sat up.

"Not like they was arguing, though, not like they were going to end up with their fists in each other's faces, more like they was trying to persuade him of something."

"Do you have any idea what it was about, Peg?" Will asked.

"Nah, I can't say. You'll have to ask them." Peg smiled at him, showing uneven teeth. "I'll get ya beer."

"What are you up to, Joe?"

"I think I'll go hobnob a bit. See if I can get any information out of them so we can get this group out of town before all of us are running around in tights yelling 'A horse, a horse, my kingdom for a horse.'"

Will laughed. "Shakespeare? I prefer something from Gilbert and Sullivan. But I take your point. This could get expensive all around."

"Yes," Joe agreed.

"Not to mention, this has 'potential Deanna escapade' written all over it."

"That, too."

As soon as Peg returned with Joe's beer, Will took his leave, and Joe wandered over to the other side of the room where the actors were just receiving their free beers.

Joe waited until they were served, then he sidled up to the table.

"Looking for a seat, sailor?" said the taller of the two women. She'd taken off her bonnet, revealing light brown hair. Classical features, nose, eyes, mouth, all proportioned to be perfect for the stage. And the way she was looking at him told Joe she was smart and pulling his leg.

"Is that a line from a play?"

She shrugged coyly.

One of the men rolled his eyes and looked away.

Joe pulled up a chair from a nearby table and sat down. "Sergeant Hennessey is as good a man as you'll find."

"If he's looking for a job," said one of the men, "he'll have to audition for the manager. You just missed him."

"Don't be impertinent, Gil," the actress who had spoken said. "I'm Noreen Adams. Coryphée and headed for stardom. And you would be . . . ?"

"Joe."

Their eyes met, there was a brief standoff, then she laughed, a throaty but not unpleasant sound.

"Come now, you'll have to do better than that."

"Joseph Ballard."

"Well, Mr. Ballard. What's your interest in our poor band of players?"

"He thinks one of us murdered Charlie."

"Rollie, stuff it."

"Gil, both you and Rollie stuff it, and let the man talk." Noreen laughed. This time it was a lighter, genuinely amused laughter. "I'm sorry, but this is so ridiculous. Joe, meet Gil, he's the suspicious one; and Rollie, who is usually much better humored than he is this evening; and sitting back in the shadows is Timothy—he keeps his own counsel unless he's being paid."

"Which I'm not," came a low bass voice from the shadows.

"And Talia, my fellow thespian. If you want to pick the brains of the marquee players, you'll have to move up to a better establishment. Perhaps a coat and tie would be in order."

Joe acknowledged the hit. He looked like a manual laborer. Which he was, actually.

"Are you a copper, too?" Gil asked.

"No."

"Then what business is it of yours?"

Gil was angry. More so than the others? Or perhaps he just showed his feelings more freely. Noreen was cool as a cucumber. But Joe suspected that was a façade, too.

"Charlie was found at my family home."

They all stared at him, and Joe felt a little proud of himself to be able to stifle this group of emoters.

"Your home?" Talia was the one who broke first. "You're a toff? I thought—" She flinched.

Joe guessed Noreen had just kicked her under the table. Their eyes caught for a brief moment but neither acknowledged it.

"What did you think?" Joe pressed.

"Just . . . that . . . he . . ."

"Must have been found on the street," Rollie finished for her. "Overcome by robbers."

Did they really think that? Hadn't Will told them where Charlie had been found?

Noreen smiled slowly. Amused. He didn't trust her.

"You mean you live in one of those ostentatious lean-tos, and you come drinking down here with us mere mortals?"

"Actually, this is a step up from where I live," Joe said.

"Family throw you out?"

"No, I needed a place to work."

"Work? Lord, what kind of work do you do that you'd give up that life?"

"I invent things."

"How very interesting." Noreen glanced at the others.

"Go on now," Rollie said. "Like what? The telephone?"

"Or maybe one of those moving picture shows," Talia added. "We saw one in New York. Now, that was exciting. I'd like to be a moving picture actress."

"Let the man talk," Timothy said from the shadows, and leaned forward. Not a thug but another young man, clean-cut, with good features, a trim build, and a fairly expensive suit.

"Nothing so glamorous," Joe said, trying to make himself amenable. "Right now, I'm working on a machine to make sugar refining more efficient and another one that makes bags for holding sugar granules."

"Why? Sugar doesn't come in granules."

"But it could. And the granules could be bagged and sold in stores."

"How big would these bags be?" asked Rollie.

"Small enough so that you'll be able to carry it home in a tote with your other groceries."

"Now, that's an invention. Have another and tell us more," Timothy said.

Joe had a feeling that he'd just been played by a cast of very able thespians. They'd gone from combative to friendly in a few sentences. Got him talking about sugar instead of asking them questions.

But did that mean they actually had something to hide? Or that they were just jerking him around for the sport of it?

"Thanks, but I'm already over my limit. I was just hoping that one of you might have remembered something that could help."

"So you can squeal to your copper friend?" Gil asked.

"You can trust him to do the right thing."

"Sure, and what will he want in return?"

"Just the truth." Joe stood. "It's been a pleasure. Good night."

"Sure you don't fancy another round with us, Mr. Edison?"

"Thanks, but I'd best be getting home."

"Fancy that, so should I," Noreen said. "I wouldn't mind having an escort. I don't know how safe the streets of Newport are."

Joe expected the others to protest, but they seemed to have forgotten Joe was there and were talking among themselves.

"My pleasure," Joe said, and offered Noreen his arm.

Deanna thought the evening would never end. They'd all been invited to the Rensselaers' for a dinner party. Deanna didn't really like dinner parties; they never discussed anything interesting and once you were seated you could only talk to the people on either side of you. Tonight Deanna had been stuck between a hard-of-hearing older gentleman and some bashful young man who stuttered each time he tried to say something.

She was relieved when Lionel said it was time to leave. They had barely all gotten situated in the carriage when Gran Gwen let out a huge sigh.

"I declare, that was the most ennui-inducing dinner party I can remember attending."

Mr. Ballard tapped on the roof and the carriage jolted forward. "You didn't enjoy the backstabbing that poor Maude Grantham got?"

"Ordinarily I would. Anyone who wears their morals on their sleeve the way Maude does deserves the occasional setdown. But it's not nearly as fun if she isn't there to receive them."

"Well, I think she's got a lot of nerve passing judgment on everyone, then throwing a theater party for her husband," Laurette said.

"Yes, my dear, that *was* a slip in her usually overly fortified outlook on the world. And she's paying for it now," Mr. Ballard said.

"Oh, Lionel," said Laurette. "Those people never pay for their sins."

"Yes." He smiled fondly at his wife. "It's only the poor who pay."

"And you, who indulge me and my passion for justice."

"A small price to pay, I assure you."

"Are you making fun of me?"

"Never." He took her hand and kissed it. "Well, maybe just a little."

Laurette popped his hand playfully with her fan. He laughed and pulled her into a hug.

Deanna averted her eyes. She'd never seen married couples flirt with each other as the two Ballards did.

"Ahem," Gran Gwen said from the opposite seat, where she was sitting next to Deanna.

Lionel straightened up. "I began your pardon, Gwen . . . Deanna." He spoke contritely but his eyes brimmed with merriment, and for a second Deanna could see Joe as he would be in twenty years. And her heart made a little stutter.

She turned to Gran Gwen. "I don't think I've ever heard you speak in a French accent as you did tonight."

Gwen laughed. "Oh, I only drag it out when I want to put paid to some people's pretensions. And it works like a charm. They'll appropriate our art, our aristocracy, even our cuisine, yet they can never quite trust us. We confuse them. Besides they think we're all immoral opium smokers."

Deanna looked at Gran Gwen, shocked.

Gwen patted her hand. "Of course that last part is completely untrue."

Across from her, Lionel snorted.

"What about that one lady, the crass one, with the unpleasant face? The one who said those cutting things about Charlie and why he was in the conservatory. She practically accused you of murdering the poor man. You didn't speak French to her."

"Mamie Fish? Oh my dear, that's just part of her personality. She insults everyone; some consider it an honor to be insulted by her."

"Well, I wouldn't."

"If you're in her company at all, you will one day be insulted by her. She is notorious for her vituperous remarks. Just let it roll off your back. She doesn't really mean any of it."

"Then why does she say those things? And saying Mrs. Grantham looked more like a bedouin than the men on stage. I can't imagine people would put up with it."

"Well," Laurette said, "I say she can keep her ill humor, but she should do something useful with it."

Lionel smiled indulgently. "You mean she should feed starving children instead of buying expensive birthday presents for her dogs."

"Horrible woman," Laurette said.

"Intelligent woman," her mother countered. She turned to Deanna. "Mamie Fish can barely read or write. I doubt if she even finished third grade. She has no education, no social manners, she's not even nice-looking. Fortunately her husband is rich in the same league of the Astors and Rockefellers and Vanderbilts, but even so, Mamie knows she would never be accepted in society if she tried to be one of them. They would have her head on one of her fourteen-karat-gold plates.

"So she's as outrageous as she can muster. And so far it's worked. I have to give her credit—she'll make herself the leader of society or go out in flames trying."

"Maybe," Lionel said. "But she may have gone too far when she started going about with that supercilious Harry Lehr."

"Oh, I suspect he's planning to ascend on her rising star until he has them all eating out of his hand, the charming little manipulator. I confess I don't like him. Of course, I wouldn't give you a nickel for Ward McAllister, either, but I suppose someone must fill his shoes now that he's dead."

"I thought he was funny," Deanna said.

"Harry? He is, and very clever. And don't worry your head about the likes of Mamie and Harry. But steer clear until you're a little more experienced."

"Is everyone in Newport other than what they show to the world?"

"Most people everywhere, I'm afraid."

"Not us," Deanna persisted. "I mean, you and the Ballards and the Randolphs."

"Only when necessary, my dear. And never to each other."
The carriage came to a stop. "Home already? I declare, the
conversation on the ride home was more interesting than the
entire evening."

Once they were inside, the Ballards said good night.

"I think Deanna and I, too, will make an early night of it.
We don't want to be late for church."

"Church?" Deanna asked.

Lionel, already leading his wife away, stopped and turned
back to his mother-in-law. "I'm sorry, Gwen, but if you expect
Laurette and me to accompany you, just to assuage gossip
about a body being found—"

"I expect you and Laurette to lie abed until all hours of the
day. Deanna and I will go to church."

"To stop gossip?" Deanna ventured.

"Good heavens no," Gwen said. "To stir it up."

Chapter
8

Joe really hoped the fact of him walking down the street with an actress on his arm late on a Saturday night wouldn't make it into the *Town Topics* gossip column. He didn't care about gossip, but he did care what his family thought. He wasn't doing anything scandalous. Didn't really intend to. Though it was tempting.

How was a man to seek his pleasure while remaining honest and respectful—and out of jail? Stupid question. Get married. But he didn't want to get married. Not yet.

Grandmère wouldn't mind his consorting with actresses, but his mother would be upset that he would take advantage of someone who was at the mercy of every stage-door johnny and gigolo.

His family was very liberal in their views about most things. They neither condoned nor feared the prurient eyes of the Comstockians and Parkhurstians. But they drew the line at taking advantage of people who couldn't demand society's protections. Unmarried women of any profession were not to be taken advantage of, and that included prostitutes and madams. Widows in the States didn't have the same freedoms as they did in Europe. So they were taboo, also.

Funny how liberal thinkers and religious zealots almost came to a place of agreement, only for different reasons.

"Penny for you thoughts, Mr. Edison?"

Joe smiled down at Noreen. "I'm thinking that you could just call me Joe."

She slipped her arm a little farther through his and pressed closer to him. "I thought you were only interested in Belle."

What did he say to that? He was interested in Noreen, at least for the moment. But he wouldn't take her back to the workshop and he wouldn't sneak into a boardinghouse. Plus, even if he had the opportunity, he wouldn't . . . He blew out air.

"You're not very talkative. Must use all your energy for other things." She looked up at him, smiling invitingly. But just as his determination wavered, they passed under a streetlight and he saw the glint of something else in her eyes.

He stopped her. Turned her to face him. "You don't fool me, Noreen. You don't want to bed me; you despise me. You are expecting me to use you to try to find out what you know. And I expect you're willing to use me—and yourself—to find out what I know."

The seduction froze on her face. He'd shocked her, but she recovered quickly. "Good-looking and clever, too." She moved closer, this time not seductively, but with a sense of urgency.

"You don't know what you're asking. I can't tell you anything. I don't really know anything. Except that Charlie and Belle were good friends. She wouldn't kill him."

"Not even if they had a lover's quarrel, or if she thought he'd been unfaithful?"

That brought a smile to her lips. "You don't know Charlie." She spoke fondly, as a friend or even a sister might, but not as a jealous lover. The smile that had softened her features was wiped suddenly from her lips. "There may have been someone else."

"Who?"

"I don't know. I can only ask you to please leave it alone. Theater people have to be doubly careful in their private lives. There are people who would love to see us all in jail because of their own depraved imaginings. Looking for Belle will bring more harm than good. And could be dangerous."

"I can't leave it."

She pulled away from him. "Why? What is wrong with the people in this town that you can't let the police do their job? First that woman this afternoon, now you. Both of you looking for Belle, like she was your long-lost friend. Well, you didn't know her."

"What woman?" Joe asked, a sudden dread stealing up his extremities.

"Oh, some young thing . . . quite beautiful in a unique way— dark, rich hair and passionate eyes." She sighed. "Extremely well dressed." Her expression changed to one of delight. "I locked her in the closet."

"What?"

"She was poking her nose around, and the police showed up. She tried to bolt, but I wasn't about to let her go until she told us what she knew. Which was next to nothing. Do you happen to know her?"

"I believe so," Joe said between gritted teeth. "Was she riding a bicycle?"

Noreen trilled a laugh that echoed brightly in the gaslit street. "Yes. Yes, she was. She said she and Belle became friends over dime novels. What a crock."

"No," said Joe. "Unfortunately, it sounds perfectly plausible."

"Well, I'll give you both a bit of advice. Don't mess with an actor. You never know when we're telling the truth. Listen. If I do see Belle, I'll tell her you both are looking for her, as well as the police. Then she can decide if she wants to talk to you."

"But—"

She put her fingers to his lips. "Don't ask me to say more. I've already said more than I should. If it comes back to bite us, then it will be my fault for trusting you, even a little. And please, for her own sake, tell your friend to stay away." She stretched up on tiptoe and kissed him full on the mouth. He responded automatically.

She pulled away. "Now, I really must go upstairs, before Mrs. Calpini gets her broom after you." She started up the steps to the porch, then stopped. "I'm twenty-two years old, Joseph Ballard. I have a five-year-old daughter. Fortunately, my mother is willing to live with us and take care of her while I'm away. I'm much more prudent than I was at seventeen. But sometimes a man makes me wonder what life might have been. It was nice meeting you, Joe. Good night."

She climbed the porch steps and went inside without looking back. Joe stood on the sidewalk for a while longer, then walked slowly back home, trying to separate the facts from the dross and rational thought from his heated blood.

"You look perfectly lovely," Elspeth said, surveying her handiwork the next morning. "Just as a modest young woman should look for Sunday morning at Trinity Church."

Deanna sighed. She didn't mind the dress, a light blue, bird's-eye piqué with a long, pointed basque. It was quite pretty, actually, though the high-pleated dotted swiss of the bodice scratched a bit, and Elspeth had once again laced her too tightly.

"Gloves," Elspeth reminded her.

"I've been to church before."

"My, aren't we being cranky this morning." Elspeth looked at Deanna's reflection in the mirror. "Perhaps it's because you'll be spending hours at church and then luncheon and I'll be picnicking at Easton's Beach."

"Well, I didn't have to get up at five o'clock in order to have church in chapel before I went to work."

"But chapel was only a half hour long."

Deanna screwed up her mouth.

"Oh, it will be fun." Elspeth's eyes widened. "Maybe the preacher will give a sermon on murder. That would be ever so timely."

"I don't think he will," Deanna told her, picking up her gloves. "Not with the Granthams members of his church. I'm sure everyone will be steering clear of the murder of an actor as long as they are there.

"I don't know what Gran Gwen has in mind. I sure hope people don't gossip about the Ballards having a body in their conservatory. You know, how they say, 'Where there's smoke there must be fire.'"

"I know. And Mrs. Ballard is in love with her husband as much as any woman I ever knew of. And him with her."

"They are awfully affectionate, aren't they, even in public, which is kind of strange, but it's nice."

Elspeth nodded. "When they're alone, too. Birdie, she's one of the chambermaids here, says they're just like a couple of—"

"I think that will suffice," Deanna said. "And I hope you aren't going to start saying 'Birdie says' all the time since we banned the 'Orrin says' wisdom of you brother."

"Well, Birdie does say . . ."

"Oh, you provoking creature. Get my hat." Deanna sat at the dressing table while Elspeth fetched her hat from the cupboard.

Elspeth could be provoking, and Deanna's mother was always saying that she let her take too many liberties, but these days Elspeth was the only friend she had. That's what had been so exciting about meeting Amabelle Deeks. Someone near her own age, who liked reading the same novels as Deanna did. And now she had disappeared and was under the suspicion of murder or might even be dead herself.

Deanna sighed. "Think of me, sitting straight backed on those wooden pews while you're splashing in the waves."

"I will, miss. But it won't be all play and no work."

"No, you just enjoy yourself today; you work hard enough the rest of the time."

"This will be fun work. I'll see the other girls I know from town and from service. There's bound to be gossip about what happened night before last."

Deanna shot her a quick look.

"Don't you worry. If anyone comes around from that Colonel Mann's scandal rag looking for juicy morsels, I'll hardly tell him anything. Besides, everybody's already heard about Charlie and how his head was bashed in."

"I'm sure you can add a few gory details."

Elspeth grinned. "Even if I have to make them up. Not to no newspaperman, though. What's our business is our business."

Deanna knew she didn't have to worry about Elspeth in the way most mistresses had to worry about their own servants. Elspeth was true-blue.

"In fact, I know at least one girl who does work for that Mrs. Calpini who owns the boardinghouse where those actor people are staying. She might have heard or seen something."

"You do?" Deanna twisted around to see Elspeth better. "Why didn't you say?"

"I just thought of it. Besides, day workers don't socialize with us that got a permanent position, so I might not even see her. Still, we mostly grew up together so . . ." She shrugged. "Sometimes we flout tradition."

Deanna smiled. She wasn't the only one learning new notions from the Ballard household.

"Some of us who've moved up might act high and mighty, but it just doesn't feel right to me."

"Good for you, Elspeth. We both must try to be more egalitarian."

"I hope that egal-thing doesn't have to do with flying. I also hope Mr. Joe will keep his interest in machines to ones that stay on the ground."

"An automobile, perhaps."

"And don't go too fast."

"A submarine. I don't think they go very fast."

"Nor go under the water. Think what happened to the one in the story we read about in *Frank Reade's Search for the Sea Serpent*."

"Well, maybe not a submarine," Deanna agreed. "Besides, we weren't talking about Mr. Joe, but about your friend who works at the boardinghouse."

"Well, if she's there I'll ask her if she knows anything. And one of the other girls is bound to have heard something."

"Be careful."

Elspeth looked incredulous. "Me, miss? Be careful? I'm not the one going off on that bicycle contraption. I didn't go visiting those actor people and putting myself in harm's way. I'm not the one got locked in a closet 'cause I was being too nosy."

"I knew I shouldn't have told you about the closet."

"You better not keep secrets from me."

"I would never."

There was a knock at the door. Gran Gwen looked in. "Are you ready, my dear?"

"Yes, just as soon as Elspeth ties my hat."

"I'll be waiting downstairs. Enjoy your half day, Elspeth."

Elspeth bobbed a curtsey. "Yes, Madame, thank you."

They took the open carriage to Trinity Church, the oldest Episcopal church in Newport. It was a lovely wooden building with a tall white spire.

Carriages were lined up ahead of them and behind them. Families were walking toward the entrances, pausing only long enough to let a more influential family pass into the church before them.

"It's going to be crowded today," Gran Gwen observed as they waited for the carriage to stop near the front door.

The Ballard pew box was located near the front. The Ballards were an old Newport family, here long before the Vanderbilts, the Wetmores, the Perrys, and their ilk. The box was large enough to contain the entire family as well as a number of guests, though Deanna knew that it wasn't used as often these days as it had been when Mr. Ballard's mother had been alive. His father rarely visited Newport.

Gran Gwen smiled and nodded graciously as they walked down the aisle. Beside her Deanna smiled and nodded, hoping she didn't look half-witted. Try as she might, she never had been able to reach the level of aplomb that her mother hoped for or that seemed to come naturally to her sister, Adelaide.

They arranged themselves in the pew, reached for prayer books and hymnals as the organ—which had to be a hundred years old—played a hymn. They received a few odd looks as people passed. Old lady Stuart, for one, practically stared. Not only was she a stickler for propriety, but rumor had it that she had been her husband's second choice. After Gwen had refused his proposal.

The people of Newport had long memories and held tenaciously to their grudges.

"Ah, the Astors have arrived. Which means Alva and her entourage will most likely be attending services in their private chapel. They'll blame it on Consuelo having the vapors."

"Does she suffer from the vapors?" Deanna asked. She didn't know Consuelo Vanderbilt; they'd never really run in the same circles. Having finally attained society's blessing, the Vanderbilts had quickly risen to lord it over everyone else. Deanna didn't mind. The few times she'd seen Consuelo she appeared as sickly as Adelaide.

"I wouldn't be surprised, but the Vanderbilts and the Astors rarely come to church on the same Sundays. That way they won't have to vie over which family departs immediately on the heels of the pastor—the Astors have the oldest money, but Alva has the clout."

Across the aisle and several boxes away, one pew was conspicuously empty.

"Do you think the Granthams will come?" Deanna whispered from behind her gloved hand.

"But of course," Gran Gwen said, looking over her shoulder. "Even they wouldn't dare not show. And here they are, the Granthams and Edgertons arriving together and presenting a unified front."

Deanna leaned forward slightly to see Judge Grantham, looking portly and pale in a gray suit, seating his wife, who looked extremely formidable that morning in an overly fussy dress and fichu and a black net hat that swept above her head like a sail. Behind them Walter Edgerton guided his wife, Drusilla, to the second pew.

All four of them sat very erect, and Deanna unconsciously adjusted her own posture.

"Really, they should ban Maude's hat from the congregation. Though I suppose it would be impossible not to see the pastor pontificating from his lofty goblet."

It wasn't the first time Gran Gwen had compared the Trinity pulpit to a wine goblet. But it always caught Deanna off guard, and she had to quickly stifle a giggle.

She had to admit the beautiful, but massive, three-tiered structure at the end of the center aisle did resemble a wineglass.

The sermon was not about sin and evil among them, as Elspeth had surmised, but about casting the first stone. Was it a coincidence that the pastor chose that topic for this morning's sermon? Or had he hastily rewritten it after Friday night's murder?

As far as Deanna knew, no one was casting stones at anyone,

though Gran Gwen had warned her to be prepared for a few impertinent looks.

When the service ended, the altar boys snuffed the candles and followed the pastor out the door. The Astors followed, taking their time to stop and speak with various people, while everyone else waited to file out behind them.

Deanna and Gran Gwen had just taken their leave of the pastor when Judge Grantham strode toward them. "My dear friend, how delightful you look this morning." He took Gwen's hand and held it for a moment. "And this must be Deanna; I believe we met the other evening at my birthday party."

Deanna smiled, too tongue-tied to manage anything else. He was a very overwhelming man. Large both in height and girth, not exactly fat, but substantial.

"Delightful party, Samuel. Unfortunate that one of the actors ended up dead in my conservatory."

"Terrible business," he agreed. "I just wanted to let you know that I've been in personal contact with the chief of police to ensure that everything is being done to apprehend the man's murderer. Chief of Police Turner assures me that we'll have no more problems in that direction up at the cottages."

"Indeed."

"I would not be returning to the city this evening, if I weren't certain that you will all be safe." He took Gwen's arm and leaned into her. "Is Lionel keeping in Newport?"

"He returns to New York on this evening's ferry," Gran Gwen said.

"Ah well, I shall see him on the ferry, then."

Deanna became aware of Mrs. Grantham watching them from several yards away. She was standing with her daughter and son-in-law, and all three had stopped their conversation to watch the Judge speak with Gran Gwen.

Gwen also noticed. She smiled slightly and dipped her chin in Maude Grantham's direction.

Mrs. Grantham smiled and dipped her chin to Gran Gwen. Both were equally insincere.

Deanna knew Gran Gwen thought Maude Grantham was a prude and a nitpicker. But Deanna didn't think Mrs. Grantham had reason to be mad at Gran Gwen. She might not like her mode of living or her views on women's rights. But if she was upset that one of the performers at her husband's birthday fete had ended up dead in Gwen's conservatory, she should be thankful that poor Charlie hadn't died in hers. Now, that would be a scandal.

"I believe they're ready for you," Gwen said.

The Judge took in his wife, daughter, and son-in-law with a sweep of his deep-set eyes.

"Quite. Walter and Drusilla feel very bad about what happened, though I've assured them it could happen anywhere. And the cottagers must be supportive of each other in trying times."

"But naturally," Gwen said.

The Judge nodded. "Maude is taking this very poorly. Her nerves, you know. I wouldn't leave her if I didn't have to be in court tomorrow. The poor devil has already been found guilty, now it's up to me to sentence him. But then I shall be returning to Newport hopefully midweek, for a much deserved respite. Perhaps you might drop in on Maude while I'm gone. Just to commiserate, you know."

"But of course," Gwen answered.

"Very good to see you, Gwen." He bowed to her, nodded

to Deanna, and strode back across the grass to where his family waited.

"Did I just promise to visit Maude Grantham?" Gwen asked when he'd returned to his family.

Deanna nodded.

"Oh Lord. And he talked—more likely made demands—on the chief of police. I wonder which poor soul from the acting company the police chief is planning to arrest for murder while the Judge is away."

"Is that what is going to happen? They don't think Amabelle did it?"

"Amabelle, yes, and if they can't find her expeditiously, they'll find someone else." Gwen looked away and quickly transformed her mouth into a smile.

A trio of ladies slowed as they walked past. Then came to a stop.

"Dear Gwen, we're just devastated for you," said the woman Deanna recognized as Gertrude Palmer. "Has anyone figured out what he was doing there?" She cut Deanna a quick sideways look.

A look that made Deanna blush. Surely she didn't think . . .

"Not what you're assuming, dear Gertie." Gwen's eyes glinted with amused malice. "And he wasn't trysting with me, either."

"Oh really, Gwendolyn," said the second lady, and tried to draw the other two away.

"Is that not what you were asking? Which one of the ladies of the house he was rendezvousing with?"

"Certainly not. We came to commiserate, but obviously you are in no need of succor. Come, ladies." They huffed away.

Gwen turned to Deanna. "I know. My behavior was uncalled

for. But really I could just shake these people sometimes. Let's get home and warn Lionel that the Judge will be looking for him tonight. And then hope Cook has something wonderful for luncheon."

They returned to the carriage. The coachman opened the door and let down the step. "On second thought," Gran Gwen said as she arranged her skirts on the seat, "I think it behooves us to make a morning call on Maude Grantham as Samuel asked. Not that she'll be glad to see us." She smiled. "We'll get Laurette to accompany us."

As they drove away, Deanna caught sight of the two actresses she'd met the day before, Noreen and Talia. They were dressed for church and were intently watching the Ballard carriage as it drove away. They must have been at the service, and Deanna hadn't even noticed them. Some detective she was. She wondered if Elspeth would have better luck on her outing at the beach.

Sundays at Bonheur were leisurely, orchestrated for the enjoyment of the family and anyone who wished to call whom the family wished to see. Sunday dinners at the Randolphs' house, no matter whether in New York or Newport, were just as stuffy as all the other meals they shared.

Deanna wondered briefly if her father missed her mother or if he, too, was feeling a bit of freedom. He certainly hadn't raced back to Newport for the weekend like he normally would during the summer season. He had sent a very nice telegram, though.

Deanna changed into her new tea gown for the afternoon.

It was made of green lawn and lace and was designed so that she could manage it herself. It floated around her like a deliciously sinful pleasure as she wafted down the stairs to the parlor.

Her mama would never approve, and Deanna had to admit it did look like a nightgown and just a tiny bit like a costume. But Gran Gwen and Laurette always wore them, and Gran Gwen had ordered it from Worth.

Deanna wished she could wear it all the time.

She swept into the parlor and came to an abrupt halt. Gran Gwen and the Ballards were already there. And so was Joe.

He didn't look any happier than when she'd seen him last. Surely he couldn't still be mad at her just because she had the idea of looking for Amabelle at the yacht on the way home from her—detour from her cycling club.

She gave him a tentative smile, but he didn't smile back.

"Lovely, my dear," Mr. Ballard said as she went to sit on the sofa next to Gran Gwen.

Gran Gwen looked over her head, and Deanna knew she was giving her grandson the evil eye for his bad manners, and good for her. She patted Deanna's hand. "I was just telling Lionel to expect the Judge to accost him on the ferry into the city this evening."

"For my sins," Lionel countered, then waggled his eyebrows at the room like a stage villain.

Laurette slipped her hand in his. "Don't mistake his overtures as friendship. You know he's in the pocket—"

"Yes, my dear. I know, and I don't want that name unleashed in the air in my own home." He sighed. "How did I ever survive without you taking care of me all those long years?"

"I'm more worried about you now," Laurette said. "Knowing his ilk, if the Judge thinks this death can in any way cast aspersions on his family, he'll deflect it to ours."

"And if he doesn't," Gwen said, "there are those who will. That ghastly Gertrude Palmer was fishing and insinuating that poor Charlie, as we know him, must have been to see one of the ladies of the house. I believe I set her straight on that subject." She gave her son-in-law an arch look.

"It isn't funny," Joe exclaimed from behind them.

"Oh, Joseph, what is ailing you these days?"

"Nothing. I beg your pardon."

"I think you and Deanna should take a nice walk down to the beach. It'll do you both a world of good. I think this murder of poor Charlie has upset us all."

A walk with Joe was the last thing Deanna wanted at the moment. A talk with Will would be of more use. But she didn't really have anything to report. And she didn't want to throw suspicion on the theater troupe without real evidence. Though she couldn't imagine why anyone else in Newport would want to kill "poor Charlie."

"Joseph," Laurette said.

Joe stood and bowed slightly to his mother. "Shall we . . . Deanna?"

They walked without speaking until they were almost across the lawn. Deanna wondered if the others were watching them from the window. Was she supposed to find out what was bothering Joe? Is that why Gran Gwen sent them away? Or were they talking about the murder and didn't want her to hear?

"Are you enjoying your walk, or would you rather be relaxing in a linen closet?"

The toe of Deanna's slipper hit a stone and she nearly

tumbled forward. Joe grabbed her elbow, put her back on her feet, and dropped his arm.

"Whatever do you mean?"

He turned on her and grabbed her shoulders, shook her until her teeth rattled. "You stupid little ninny. What did you think you were doing? Lying to Grandmère about going cycling, accosting actresses in the street. Poking your nose into things that don't concern you. Do you know how dangerous that could be?"

Deanna shrugged out of his grip and walked away toward the cliffs. But when she got to the steps down to the beach she stopped. There was no way she was going to ruin her new tea gown because Joe was being so unreasonable. "Did you follow me yesterday?"

Joe hesitated. "No."

"You did. How dare you?"

"Will and I were cycling the same way. I saw you join your group, and we rode on. Obviously, I *should* have followed you, because you didn't stay with the club. Does Grandmère know?"

Deanna shrugged. "Not yet. I was going to tell her, but we had that dinner last night, then she went straight to bed, and then there was church this morning."

He cocked his head like he used to do when he thought she'd done something idiotic.

"Well, I ran into two of the actresses and went back to their boardinghouse with them. I thought they might know something."

"You can't do those kinds of things."

"The same two were at church this morning, but I didn't see them until we were already in the carriage coming home. Don't you think it was strange that they went to our same church?"

"Dee, enough. They don't want you bothering them any-more."

"Oh? How do *you* know?"

"None of your business."

"But—"

"Stay out of it."

"You think you can boss me around like you and Bob always did. Well, guess what, I'm not a child anymore, and you can't."

"You think not? If you can't be trusted, Grandmère will send you to stay with your father in Manhattan and he'll have to tell your mother."

"She wouldn't."

"She'll have no choice. I hope you enjoy living with Aunt Harriett until your mother and Adelaide return to the States."

Sheer panic drove the breath from Deanna's lungs.

"If something were to happen to you, everyone will blame Grandmère and the Ballards. Is that what you want? Is it?"

She could only shake her head, and to her horror, tears sprang to her eyes and rolled down her cheeks.

"Stop it. Don't think you can get your way because of a few tears."

She was trying to stop them. She wanted to tell him he was wrong, but she couldn't get the words out.

"Deanna," he said. "Come on, Dee. Cut it out." He stretched out his hand but she slapped it away.

"Why do you hate me so much?" She turned and ran back to the house, not to the family rooms, or her bedroom, but to the spring house at the far side of the kitchen, where she stood against the cold stone in the dark and sobbed.

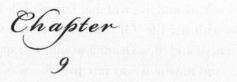

Chapter
9

It was a long time before Deanna had mastery of her emotions. Shaking with cold and hurt, she slipped out of the spring house and crept into the servants' entrance. She managed to get the attention of a footman and asked him to say that she was fine but that she wouldn't be down to dinner.

If he wondered why her face was blotched, her eyes were swollen, and her hair was mussed, he managed not to show it. She crept up the servants' stairs to her own room and locked the door.

She didn't know which made her feel worse: that for some reason Joe hated her; that she was in real danger of being sent to Aunt Harriett; or that her behavior would reflect badly on Gran Gwen and Mr. and Mrs. Ballard—maybe even bring them disgrace.

Though she didn't really understand why. They did much

more outrageous things than Deanna ever did. She just read novels and got locked in a closet.

She was perfectly behaved in public, well, most of the time. And she was useful. Maybe she would just take the ferry to New York and live with her father while she decided what to do with her life. Of course, he would wire her mother in Geneva and then Deanna would be trapped again.

And maybe it was just Joe who was scandalized by her behavior, though she didn't see why. He was the one who had shocked society by going to live with working-class people and doing work where he got his hands dirty.

To the devil with him. She'd just ask Laurette and Gran Gwen right out if they would like her to leave. And then what? She'd cross that bridge when she came to it.

There was a tap at the door.

Deanna's courage failed. She wasn't ready to put it to the test. *Coward*, she told herself. She reluctantly went to the door and opened it.

A maid carrying a dinner tray stepped inside. Deanna's knees nearly gave way in relief. Not Gran Gwen, but cold chicken and pickled peaches.

The maid curtseyed and left the room, quietly closing the door behind her.

The food looked delicious, but when Dee sat down she found she couldn't eat it.

Her stomach was tight, her emotions were in turmoil. She felt like things were closing in on her, society's expectations, her mother's plans for her future, the need to not embarrass the Ballards or bring complete ruin to herself, her ambivalence about what she wanted in life. What choices did she have? Would the choice even be up to her?

She tried to picture herself packing a few things and running away. She couldn't do it. How could she be so cruel to leave like that after all everyone had done for her? And what would happen to Elspeth? She couldn't take her along. How could Deanna support them both? How could she even support herself?

Is that the way Amabelle had run away? Left without a word, or after a fight? Her parents knew where she was, because they'd asked Laurette to look her up. Did they follow her career? Did they ever try to see her? Did they even want her back?

Where was she? Was anyone besides the police even looking for her?

Deanna sat down in front of the dinner tray, cut off a piece of chicken, and chewed slowly.

If she were Amabelle, where would she go? Back to the city? Belle must have an apartment or a room there—did she share it with someone? Had the police looked there? And if she hadn't left Newport, where was she? She had to be staying somewhere.

Deanna cut another piece of chicken. Noreen and Talia might be hiding her somewhere in the boardinghouse. That seemed unlikely, with all the people coming and going. But they might have seen her since Charlie died and were giving her money or food to survive.

It was good to have friends like that. *A family*, she'd almost thought. The actors were like a family. Everyone concerned for one another and comforting one another over Charlie's death.

The star performers were staying at a hotel in town, but Deanna didn't think Amabelle would have gone to them.

From what Belle had said, chorus girls didn't mix with the main players.

Deanna put down her fork. If Deanna had run away, was lost or scared and hiding from the world, she'd want a friend. And she bet Belle could use a friend about now.

So, unladylike behavior or not, an embarrassment to the Ballards or not, she had to find out if Amabelle was still alive. If she was, Deanna would try to help her. And if doing that sent her to Aunt Harriett's, so be it.

J oe thought dinner would never be over. He should have done exactly what Dee had done. Run away and locked himself in his warehouse. That way he might have half a chance of getting some work done. Not that he had much hope for that now.

All winter he'd been working systematically toward two goals: reconfiguring the company's current centrifuge for higher efficiency with accompanying safety features, and completing a prototype bagging machine. He planned to install the prototype in one of R and W's refineries. It would be the first test. Joe would have to spend time in New York. That was fine by him. It's where his work would ultimately be used.

During the winter, there had been the odd setback or two, an occasional instance of vandalism, but nothing like the last few weeks. Since the summer had returned, vandalism increased and the work had slowed to a crawl. It seemed like he was needed everywhere except the warehouse.

His father insisted he accompany his grandmother and Dee to one party after another. His workshop had been attacked no fewer than five times: two window breakings, two arsons, and an attempted break-in. Fortunately, Hiram and his men had been able to thwart all of the attacks.

And to that was added Dee's propensity of landing herself in trouble. When she'd been a child, he'd applauded it. It fascinated him. But he'd expected her to grow out of it. She hadn't. God knows, her mother had done everything she could to argue, upbraid, lambaste, and possibly even beat it out of her, to no avail.

"Well . . ." His grandmother's voice broke into the silence above the pea soup. "Since you've deprived us of one dinner guest, you may at least entertain us with some fascinating banter."

Joe gritted his teeth. Put down his spoon. "I beg your pardon, Grandmère, but Dee deprived us of her charming personality of her own accord. And if I might point out, she is behaving in a way that is the product of your and mama's handiwork."

"You may leave me out of your spats with Deanna," his mother said.

"Mother, it wasn't a spat. I realize you probably don't know what she was doing yesterday afternoon instead of joining her cycling group."

His grandmother patted her lips with her napkin and gave him her full attention.

"Accosting actresses on the street, following them back to their boardinghouse, where she attempted to interrogate them, except for the entrance of the police, when the actors locked her in a linen closet until the police had gone."

Neither his mother nor grandmother even blinked. Joe

glanced to his father, who lowered his head, in fear, shame, or amusement, Joe couldn't begin to guess. Though he imagined the hint of a spasm that rippled across his shoulders was an attempt to stifle laughter.

His father was probably used to behavior like that. It sounded just like something his mother would do. But his mother was happily married for many years to a rich and powerful man. She could withstand a few slurs against her character. Deanna could not. And she seemed to have no idea of what was at stake.

She had stubbornly refused to understand why men could manage their lives one way, that going off to work for them could be a good thing, an exciting thing. But for women, working for a living for most was a drudgery at best, and little more than slavery at worst.

The world was changing; there were a few female doctors, lawyers, even stockbrokers. But for the most part women were given menial jobs while men rose to the higher offices.

If Dee married the right man, with the right amount of social clout, she might, in a few years, get away with the odd suffragette or temperance rally without bringing the wrath of society—and her mother—on her head.

But not now. Staying viably social was not just an amusing pastime for young women. It was a fact of life.

He realized no one was talking; they were all looking at him.

"Will and I were down at a pub last night. He was keeping an eye on the actors. The manager is complaining because they can't work while they're stuck here. He demanded Will find them a place to rehearse."

He saw the glint of interest in his grandmother's eye. "Not here," he added. "After Will left, one of the actresses told me about Dee and warned me that she would be in danger if she continued to investigate."

"What kind of danger?" his mother asked.

"Was it a threat?" Grandmère asked.

Even his father looked up, expectant of an answer.

"Neither. More like she was frightened for Dee and for herself. When I pressed her to explain, she said that I wouldn't understand. And to leave it alone."

"True," said his grandmother. "It is a different world, the theater. But do you think it's more than a lover's quarrel taken to the extreme?"

Joe shrugged. "I have no idea. Amabelle didn't strike me as the kind of girl anyone would be afraid of, merely emotional and silly, but I definitely felt that Noreen was frightened."

"Perhaps she is frightened for Amabelle and afraid that any intervention from outside would be harmful to her?"

"I have no idea," Joe said.

"But I do think you should share that with Will, though I think perhaps you can leave out the part about Deanna being locked in the linen closet." His grandmother's eyes twinkled.

Joe's lip twitched, then he laughed out loud. "Only Dee."

"You may laugh," his mother said, "but Dee is probably in her room crying her eyes out."

"Just because I told her what to do? She's never let that bother her in the past. And someone needs to be thinking about her future."

He was greeted by three silent, serious faces.

"Well, they do."

"I shall go up to her later," his grandmother said. "And I think you should go home. You have committed an unforgivable sin today."

Joe's stomach turned. "Me? What—"

"A man can do many things, Joseph. He may scowl and rail, he may scold and yell; he may even break wind in public and be left unscathed. But when he fails to compliment a lady on her new dress, that is beyond the pale."

Joe knew—thought—she was kidding him. He looked from Grandmère, in her pale aqua tea gown—he'd seen that before—to his mother, wearing a wine-colored tea dress. And though it was a bit too daring for afternoon calls, it was one of his father's favorites.

"The two of you look lovely," Joe said while he tried to make sense of their outrage. "But neither dress is new."

They both continued to look at him.

"I apologize for not complimenting you both sooner. I've had much on my mind. No excuse for bad manners, I realize."

Neither of them moved. Like two Sphinxes from that play, waiting for him to come up with the correct answer. And then enlightenment hit. "Dee?"

His grandmother sighed heavily. "Dee was wearing her new tea gown and it was quite becoming on her. I would say elegant. But did you even notice?"

He hadn't noticed. He'd been so angry.

His mother stood. "It's very chivalrous of you, my dear, to be concerned for Deanna's safety, but not to the degree that you forget to compliment her wardrobe." She glanced at her husband.

He agreed with a dip of his chin.

Surely they were having a joke at his expense.

"And," she continued, "not if your concern pours over into the typical male boorishness of thinking we women can't take care of ourselves."

"I think I've learned by now not to do that."

"I believe I taught him that," his father said, smothering a smile.

Grandmère's eyebrows rose, but his mother's high-handedness was no match for his father's affection. She tightened her lips, but her shoulders shook with a quick silent laugh.

"Yes, yes," Grandmère said. "Chivalry is all fine and good, and I don't relish Deanna putting herself in danger's way any more than you do. However, so far, the worst thing that has happened is she's been locked in a linen closet by a troupe of actors. And you have to admit, she might not have learned a lot from them, but I bet she learned more than Will Hennessey did. Or you, for that matter."

"That's not the point."

"Did you even ask her?"

Joe thought back. He must have, but . . . he hadn't.

"I realize your concerns, but Deanna is not reckless."

"How do you know?"

"She's enjoying her newfound freedom; what's the harm? Riding a bicycle is practically de rigueur among the younger set—they're golfing, swimming, and traveling the world."

"But they don't do detective work, even in an amateurish way. If she gets a reputation for unladylike behavior . . ."

"Joseph." His mother threw her napkin on the table. "I never thought to hear a son of mine—"

"Leave him alone, my dear. He is only concerned for what is best for Deanna. He's not making a moral judgment." Joe's father frowned. "Are you, son?"

"No, of course not."

"There, that's settled, and now I would like to spend the last few minutes of my weekend enjoying the company of my wife."

Joe's mother actually blushed. "I beg your pardon, Lionel. I was on my high horse again. And I beg your pardon, too, Joe." She stood.

"I think we can forgo after-dinner port today," his father said. Joe couldn't agree more.

"If you're planning to return to the workshop and can wait a few minutes, I'll have the carriage drop you off on its way back from the pier." His father followed his mother out of the room.

In three-quarters of an hour, good-byes had been said, and Joe and his father were in the carriage on their way to the ferry.

"I hope you don't mind," Lionel began as the carriage rolled over the cobblestones of the street. "But I wanted to talk to you."

"About?"

"About what's really bothering you these days."

"You mean besides the sugar industry, the vandalisms . . ."

"About Deanna."

Joe took off his hat, pushed his hair back, returned his hat to his head. "I can't get any work done worrying about what trouble she'll get into."

"I see. I don't think Bob would expect you to lose sleep or work time over worrying about his little sister."

There was a strange note in his father's voice. But when Joe looked at him, he was perfectly expressionless.

"It's not about Bob. I care about Dee, I do, but I can't have her disrupting my life all the time."

"Then stay away from her. You don't really have to escort the ladies to their evening festivities. They do quite well without an escort."

"I've tried."

"Well, tell her to stay away from you."

"Father, how can I? And I don't want her to go away, exactly, I just wish . . . I'm not like you. I couldn't sleep knowing Mother was off getting into trouble, possibly being injured. Even if it is for a good cause."

Lionel laughed quietly. "Is that what you think? That your mother leaves and I don't give her another thought until she returns?"

Joe shrugged. "I know you miss her."

"Ha." His father's laugh was so loud and sharp that Joe flinched.

"You're more like me than you realize, son. Do you think it's easy for me to stand by and not beg her not to go, when I'm petrified that she'll get her head bashed in during one of her suffragette marches, or taken to jail and have a feeding tube forced down her throat?

"I know other men think that she rules the roost. They counsel me to put my foot down and keep her at home where she belongs. I could do it. All I have to say is 'Stop doing this.' And she would because she loves me and wants me to be happy, but I wouldn't have her make that sacrifice . . . for the same reasons.

"We sometimes argue but we argue as equals. It's the only kind of marriage either of us wants. Perhaps we are an aberration. But neither of us would stand for an insipid, constrained marriage.

"So if you can't take Deanna's spirit—and Lord, does she have one—you'd better cut her loose. Find yourself a perfectly behaved little wife to have your dinner ready. Or set up a mistress and learn to cook for yourself.

"But love? I think it's already too late for Dee to love a man who would hold her back, and I don't believe that you would love any other kind of woman. Perhaps I'm wrong."

Joe wanted to say that he was wrong. But he couldn't. Joe was afraid it might be too late for him, too.

The carriage drew up to the ferry. "It's up to you, but think about it before you burn any bridges. There's no hurry."

They shook hands, and his father climbed down, but turned back and rested his hand on the carriage door. "Do you want me to speak to her father about taking Dee away for the summer? He can find someone to travel with her to Switzerland, or isn't there an aunt in Boston?"

"No! Sir, I already threatened her with that."

"And?"

"And she asked why I hated her and ran away."

"I see. Well, perhaps we'll give her a little more time?"

Joe nodded.

"Then I'll see you in a few days unless I can persuade your mother to join me in New York. Keep an eye on things here if . . ." He trailed off.

"You think I'm being selfish."

"No. Actually, I didn't finish my sentence because I just saw Judge Grantham's carriage. Gwen said he had something he wanted to discuss with me on the trip." He took a deep breath. "It could be a long ferry ride."

"Surely not to caution you about that actor being killed in the conservatory. His family is the one that brought the troupe here."

"Not to worry. I know how to handle the Judge. Now I must go." He nodded to Joe and tapped the side of the carriage.

As the carriage drove away, Joe leaned out to watch his father stride down the pier to the ferry; tall, straight, a man in control and in love with his wife and life. Then he sat back to enjoy the luxury of the carriage drive to the warehouse.

It was a cool, late afternoon, and for a moment he thought of continuing on to Bonheur. It would be an excellent night for sitting on the lawn listening to the waves while the stars gradually appeared. But he would have to face Dee, and he wasn't ready. His father was right, as he often was. Give it some time.

When he reached Richmond Street, Joe said good night to the coachman, then nodded to the man sitting on a barrel outside the pub—the lookout for the warehouse until dark, when he would be joined by several other large and armed men—and let himself inside.

————◦◦◦⬧◦◦◦————

Deanna was sitting in the embrasure of the window in her room when Elspeth came bustling in. She hadn't bothered to turn on a light. And anyone who did come in would have thought she was asleep.

She was confused and torn between doing what she wanted and doing what she thought might be expected of her. And she felt terribly alone.

She heard the door to the dressing room open, then the dressing room light glowed on.

Deanna sighed.

"Miss Deanna?" Elspeth called quietly. "Miss Deanna, are you here?" She turned on the light.

"Miss Deanna. Where are you?"

Deanna gave up. "Over here by the window."

Elspeth let out a shriek. "Lord, you gave me a turn. What's happened here?"

Getting no answer from Deanna, she marched over and stuck her face close to her mistress's. "What happened to you? What's the matter?"

Deanna sighed. "Nothing."

"Nothing? There's a tray of uneaten food, you look like you've been bawling your eyes out—"

"Ladies don't bawl."

"—Bawling your eyes out. So don't tell me nothing is wrong."

"Joe and I had a fight."

"Oh, is that all. I was afraid somebody had died. Why didn't someone come take this food away? I'll have Cook send up something fresh."

"I'm not hungry."

"Well, if you aren't, I am."

Deanna peered past Elspeth to the clock. "Why are you back so soon?"

"I couldn't wait. I have news. I think." She stopped. "But I'm not going to tell you about it if you don't get rid of that 'poor me' attitude. I think maybe I cracked the case."

Deanna shook her head. "We can't investigate anymore. Belle will just have to manage on her own. If she's even alive."

"What? What's wrong with you? Are you coming down with something?"

"No. Joe says I'm an embarrassment to his family. He hates me."

"He didn't."

"He did. He hates me. And he said if I didn't stop, he was going to make Father send me to Aunt Harriett."

"He wouldn't dare."

"He said he would."

"Did you tell Madame Manon?"

"No. What could she say?"

"She could tell you it was a crock."

Deanna smiled in spite of her mood. "She'd probably say just that, too. But only because she wouldn't want to hurt my feelings."

"Then who am I gonna tell what I learned?"

"No one."

Elspeth gave her a very inappropriate servant-to-mistress look. "You just gonna stop, because Mr. Joseph said to? Cad Metti wouldn't never let anybody tell her what to do."

"That's because she's *your* favorite story detective."

"I don't even think Kate Goelet would, either, though she's not nearly as clever as Cad."

"She is, too. I can't go live with Aunt Harriett; she's worse than Mama."

"Fine. I'll just go get out your corset. You know the one? The really heavy one with all the bones on the inside that poke your ribs? The one your mama made you wear at the Christmas ball and you almost swooned."

"I thought you threw it away."

Elspeth slowly shook her head. "I suppose I'll just call for the trunks and send all your brand-new clothes out to the Sisters of Mercy. Though for the life of me, I don't know what they can do with a lawn tennis outfit, or the new bathing costume, or the split skirt for riding your bicycle. Oh, and you won't need the bicycle, neither.

"Can I give it to Orrin? He'd like a bicycle. Him and Mr. Joseph could join one of those clubs like you belong to . . . though I guess you'll have to unjoin that one."

"That's just what I'm saying. Either I behave or I'll have to give all this up."

"If you behave, you won't be able to wear any of this stuff anyway, because I know your mama won't think one new thing you have is what a proper young lady should have."

"But if I don't give it all up, I'll be in disgrace, probably sent away to a convent or something. And you'll be out of a job. Though I'm sure Gran Gwen would help you find another position."

"I don't want no other position."

Deanna pulled up her knees and hugged them. "What are we going to do?"

Elspeth didn't say anything.

"Cat got your tongue?"

Still she didn't speak.

"You're making your mistress angry."

A minute shrug.

"Okay, I give up. What did you learn today?"

"I went home for lunch and afterward I met some girls from the ward to go to Easton's Beach. A couple of them work at the big houses, like me. We met a few other friends there. We were drinking lemonade and eating tater pie. Midgie O'Sullivan's ma makes the best tater pie, and there was enough for all of us.

"So we got to talking about the goings-on last weekend. And they know that poor Charlie was found dead in the conservatory." She hesitated. "Everybody knows, miss. I didn't tell them that."

"That's all right, Elspeth. I suspect everyone in town knows the details by now."

"Well, pretty much so. They wanted to know everything about it. And you remember once I told you about how when you're a servant you have to gossip some or nobody will trust you?"

"I remember."

"So I told them what it looked like and everything. And Phoebe O'Doul said she heard it was a lover's quarrel and one of the actresses bashed him over the head so she could run off with someone else."

Deanna frowned. "Run off with somebody else? Elspeth. How much of that do you think is sheer fantasy?"

"Oh, most of it, but I haven't gotten to the good part yet."

"Okay, get to it, then, please."

Elspeth frowned. "Nobody knew the name of the actress, so after a while I announced that I knew her name. That got their attention. So I told them, Amabelle Deeks, just as plain as you want, then I said, but her friends call her Belle. That's when Midgie—the one whose mother makes the pies—"

"Yes, I know which one Midgie is."

"She says Deeks ain't no name for an actress. It ought to be more glamorous. And the other girls started thinking about better names. And I broke in and said Deeks was good enough, because Belle was an actress and that was her name. And Midgie laughs and says it's the name for crazy old people. And we're about to come to blows and she says 'cause her little sister does day work for one of them."

"For an old person?"

"Don't be dense, miss. For an old lady named Deeks. Do you think they might be kin, her and that actress?"

"I don't know. Deeks isn't that unusual of a name."

"Well, I think we should find out more."

"I don't know."

"This ain't like you, Miss Deanna."

"Don't say 'ain't,' and I know it. It's just . . ."

Elspeth sat down beside her. "It's just we are at a crossroads, miss."

Deanna nodded. "But which road to take?"

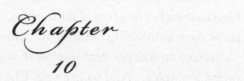

Chapter

10

Sleep didn't come easily to Deanna, and she woke many times in the night; she tossed and turned and tossed.

Should she apologize to the Ballards and stay put? Should she just say she was missing her family and have Elspeth pack her belongings—her considerably pared-down belongings—for New York? She felt sick and alone and she had a responsibility to her family, to the Ballards, and to Elspeth.

She'd tried that excuse when Gran Gwen came to her room a little while later.

"I see," she'd said. "If that's true, I suggest you give it a few more days. It sometimes takes a while to accustom oneself to being away from one's family, especially under circumstances such as these."

Was she being polite, or did she really want Deanna to stay? Deanna couldn't trust herself to know.

"But if it's merely because you argued with Joseph. Well, let me say, you needn't think that Joseph's attitudes reflect those of this family. Young people can be headstrong. That is a good thing. He'll either come round or he won't; that's his choice."

"But am I an embarrassment to my family and yours?"

"He said that?" Gran Gwen laughed with such mirth that Elspeth stuck her head out of the dressing room, where Deanna knew she was listening to the conversation.

"You're an independent woman in training." Gran Gwen raised her voice. "And so are you, Elspeth. Why don't you come out here where you'll be more comfortable?"

Elspeth's head reappeared, her eyes as round as the cheeses at Horn's market. She stepped a few feet into the room.

"Your mistress is one of the bright young women of her class who holds the future for all women. You will do your best to see that she remains safe . . . and well dressed. You may argue with her politely, but be respectful of her decisions."

Elspeth nodded, caught somewhere between a curtsey and a reply. Deanna could tell she thought Gran Gwen was raving mad.

Deanna was wondering about that herself.

"Deanna. You're smart and curious. You must walk a fine line in society and be sure not to cross over it . . . well, not often anyway, and not until you have a developed cachet. You will not put yourself in danger if at all possible. Do you understand?"

Deanna nodded. She knew how Elspeth felt—she couldn't manage to get words out, either.

"And you must have a brilliant Newport season or none of us will ever hear the end of it."

Deanna had gone to bed relieved, but still she tossed in her sleep. She was amazed that Gran Gwen had actually licensed her behavior . . . to a point. But that's not why she stayed awake. She was thinking about Amabelle Deeks and poor Charlie, as he'd come to be called.

She knew it was imperative to find Belle, if she were still alive. Deanna was lucky that she had someone she could trust, but she imagined Belle in hiding somewhere, frightened and alone. Maybe she didn't have the good fortune of having someone she could talk to, who understood her. Her parents might change their minds and forgive her for running away.

But she'd never know unless she was found.

She finally fell asleep in the wee hours; at a crossroads no longer. She would help Belle if she could, and she would become her own woman, and Joe could just like it or lump it.

———◦◦◦)◦(◦◦◦———

B oth Laurette and Gran Gwen were in the breakfast room when Deanna came down the next morning. Deanna was dressed demurely in a visiting gown of peach and yellow muslin. Laurette and Gran Gwen were conservatively dressed as well.

"Good morning," Deanna said, feeling just a little more grown-up and self-assured than she had the night before.

Gran Gwen gave her a warm smile. "Ready to face morning calls?"

"Yes indeed," Deanna said, filling her plate from the sideboard.

"I confess, I'm ready for a little gossip," Gran Gwen said. "There must have been some word about the missing child, Amabelle."

Laurette put down the toast she'd been buttering. "I telephoned her mother yesterday. The police had notified them of Amabelle's disappearance. They're very upset, as you can imagine."

"Are they coming to Newport?"

Laurette, who had just picked up her piece of toast again, put it down. "No. Which I find very odd. What parent wouldn't want to be on hand?"

"Do you know what the rift was about?" Gwen asked.

"No. She just said they hadn't spoken to her in two years."

"Then, why did they ask you to look in on her?" Deanna asked. "Why now?"

"I have no idea. Rosalie, her mother, just said she'd been thinking about her lately."

"But she must be keeping up with her life, or how would she know that she was going to be in Newport?"

"An excellent question," Gran Gwen said.

"I don't know. She wouldn't confide in me. I tried to find out. I thought it might help Will's investigation, and you know how women are more likely to talk to other women than to men, especially one in an official capacity. But I had no luck. I guess I don't have the knack for ferreting out secrets."

"Never mind, dear, you organize brilliantly."

"Thank you, Mama."

⸺∘∘◦)◌(◦∘∘⸺

The first stop on the round of calls was Maude Grantham. The gilded cages, the exotic birds, the fireworks, had all been removed. Only the tents and the stage stood forlorn and empty at the edge of the lawn. This morning the Grantham cottage looked more like a municipal building than a summer retreat.

Though Deanna supposed that was fitting for a judge. The carriage stopped at the front entrance at the center of a shallow loggia that was fronted by four Corinthian columns. They were shown through to the morning parlor, where Maude Grantham sat with her daughter, Drusilla Edgerton.

"Madame Manon, Mrs. Ballard, and Miss Deanna Randolph," the butler announced, and stood aside for the ladies to enter.

"Ah, Gwen, Mrs. Ballard, Miss Randolph. How kind of you to call."

And so it would go all morning, the insipid talk of weather and parties.

But Deanna had never gone visiting with Gran Gwen before.

Gwen bustled ahead of the others. "Oh, my dear, Maude, you must be *bouleversée* over what happened. And the Judge, for such a thing to happen on his birthday, of all days." She *tsk*ed.

Deanna had never heard Gran Gwen *tsk* ever before.

"What were those awful people doing in your house?" Maude countered.

Gwen leaned in conspiratorially. "Well, my dear, the girl's mother was at school in Montreux with Laurette. The Chateau Mont Choisi. Lovely family. But these girls today. Ran away from home, leaving her mother distraught. As a friend, Laurette could only see if she could help bring mother and daughter together again."

Deanna glanced at Laurette, wondering how she was taking this total fabrication. And was shocked to see her looking very demure and smiling slightly, as if to say, *What's another mother to do?*

Deanna thought the actors had nothing over Gran Gwen and Laurette. And she was struck for the first time, blindingly so, as to how façade was all-important to society. She'd known this, of course. But she'd always been looking at it from the inside out; today she was watching it objectively.

"And what do you make of this, Miss Randolph? After what we've been hearing of you, I would think you'd be happy to have a murder right under your nose."

"Mama," Drusilla exclaimed.

Deanna blinked, but kept her aplomb. "I could never be happy of a death, ma'am. A terrible tragedy."

"I wish I had never thought to bring those horrid people here," Drusilla said. "But Papa loves the theater. Edgerton and I thought it would be the perfect gift. Only I couldn't get Gilbert and Sullivan."

They all assured her that it was not her fault.

Deanna felt a little sorry for her. It couldn't be easy being the daughter of the Judge and his wife. She sat ramrod straight on her chair, so close to the edge that one jostle might have sent her to the floor.

None of them really noticed when the door opened and Walter Edgerton strode in, checked, and said, "Ladies."

They all looked up as if caught in something clandestine.

Gran Gwen, of course, recovered first, even more quickly than his mother-in-law or wife.

"Dear Walter, we were just telling Drusilla how much we enjoyed the Judge's birthday fete. Lovely, just lovely," she gushed. "The gardens were transformed into a paradise. So clever, Maude. Where did you find all those exotic birds?"

"Why I . . . well, actually, I had not much to do with the arrangements. Drusilla and Walter offered to arrange it all. I have no fondness for theater, as you must know, but the Judge does enjoy a good play."

"Though perhaps not the caliber we'd hoped for," Walter said.

Drusilla flinched and sat even straighter, if that was possible.

"I was just telling our friends that I was unable to obtain the Gilbert and Sullivan troupe that is touring the States this month and next."

"Yes, well, you did your best on short notice. Though the subject matter left something to be desired."

"Papa enjoyed it greatly; he told me so."

"Yes, dear." Walter Edgerton smiled indulgently at his wife, and Deanna understood what Gran Gwen had told her the night before. She would never marry someone who was as condescending and dismissive of her as Walter Edgerton was with Drusilla.

"I don't agree," Gran Gwen said, jumping into the fray. "Bedouins perhaps were a bit far-fetched, but I'm sure they were Christian bedouins. After all, they could have carried those poor women off to their oasis, or whatever. But they all had a proper marriage in the end."

"Yes," Drusilla said as if it had just occurred to her.

Edgerton bowed slightly. "You're absolutely correct, Mrs. Manon. Being a man, I'm not equipped to see the nuances of the script. Though I do believe it can be said I know my fellow man. And we all know what actors are."

Deanna was sure that Gran Gwen or Laurette would say something, but they both held their peace.

Maude Grantham's smile was growing tighter. "If only those people hadn't wrecked everything by killing someone. Or at least they could have waited until they were back in New York. Despicable creatures."

Gwen nodded sympathetically. "Well, you have the consolation of knowing that it was my conservatory, not yours, that was chosen for the deed."

"Yes, and why was that?" Walter asked.

"I assure you, Walter," Laurette broke in, "none of us have the slightest idea."

"I've heard that you were acquainted with the family of the girl who killed him, this actor."

Deanna started to protest, but caught herself just in time. She was in the company of seasoned sparrers. She would sit back, listen, and learn.

"As far as I've heard," Gwen said, "they haven't charged the girl with any crime. Innocent until proven guilty. I'm sure being a prosecutor, you would agree with that."

Edgerton smiled. He was tall and thin, with a high forehead and light brown hair. He carried himself with a certain elegance, though Deanna couldn't imagine him as the persuasive prosecutor he was known to be.

"Yes, quite. Though I must say, where has she gotten herself off to?"

"I wish they would just find her and let those awful people leave town," Maude mumbled, and reached for her smelling salts. "Their sets and costumes are being stored in our stable. We had to house our horses in town and now they are stuck there, and even though I send the grooms down every day to attend them, I know they aren't receiving the attention they deserve, and it makes going anywhere so inconvenient.

"And those tents and that hideous stage; I'm sure they've ruined the landscaping. It's like living next to a shantytown." She sniffed. "Not that I've ever seen a shantytown."

"I'm sure they are just as anxious to leave as you are to see them go."

"I wish they had never come."

Drusilla made a choking sound. "It's all my fault."

"Nonsense," Laurette said. "And I'm sure they'll be gone

soon. I imagine having to pay for room and board while not working is creating a strain among them. Though, of course, you've so graciously offered to compensate them for their loss of income. That is very generous, Maude, I must say."

Mrs. Grantham merely nodded, giving Laurette that cold half smile she gave everyone. Drusilla was the only one of the three who looked surprised.

"Well," Gwen said, "we must be going. I told Samuel I'd drop in to see how you were getting on. Please, if I can help in any way, don't hesitate to let me know." Gran Gwen stood. Laurette and Deanna stood, and Walter walked them to the door.

"Thank you so much for coming. Mother-in-law has been very upset in the face of this unfortunate event. Poor Drusilla feels responsible, though I've tried to convince her otherwise. The Gilbert and Sullivan players were in Baltimore and couldn't possibly arrive and set up in time for the fete. Good day, ladies."

Edgerton bowed, and the butler showed them out the door.

"Well," Gran Gwen said as soon as the carriage started down the drive. "Poor Drusilla. To give up life with Maude and Samuel to life with Walter is a fate I wouldn't wish on anyone."

"Well, at least they have their own town house in Manhattan," Laurette said. "And only have to live with the Judge and Maude while in Newport."

"They are very odd," Deanna said. "He seemed like he was trying to make his wife feel better, but made her feel worse. And it's strange, but I can't help thinking he was doing it on purpose."

"Very astute," Gwen said.

"I'd bet it was probably more out of habit than done intentionally. Men sometimes have no idea of the damage they can do."

They certainly don't, Deanna thought. Someone should tell that to Joe.

"Why didn't he go back to town with the Judge?" Deanna asked.

"A good question," Gwen said. "I'm sure Drusilla wishes he would."

"I don't know, Mama. She doesn't seem to have a mind of her own. Maybe she sees being with him as better than living at home the full year round," said Laurette. "His attitude toward justice is absolutely medieval. And they say the Judge is grooming him to take over from him when he retires from the bench."

"Well, we might not agree with their opinions, but the one thing you can say about the Judge is that his opinions are his own. Walter, on the other hand, is in danger of becoming a parrot."

"Of Judge Grantham?" Deanna asked.

"The Judge or anyone with the right kind of influence," Gwen said.

"You mean he's dishonest?"

"Not necessarily," Laurette said. "There are judges quite willing to be bribed, but what Mama means is that the law, like religion, can be influenced, and not just by money."

"He's already as pompous as the Judge," Gwen said.

"Gran Gwen, did Mrs. Grantham really give money to help pay for the actors' extra stay?"

"Of course not, my dear, but hopefully I can shame her into doing it." Gran sat back against the squabs of the seat. "I feel absolutely invigorated. On whom shall we call next?"

"Mama, if it's all right with you . . ."

"Yes, Laurette?"

"I think I would like to go home."

"Are you not feeling well?"

"I'm fine, but I feel I should go to Rosalie and explain to her just how dire the situation is. I don't know why she's so stubborn about Amabelle's choices in life. It's odd, but even though actresses do enjoy freedoms that most of us don't, most of them are hardworking, honest, decent people."

"Yes, I was thinking that something needs to be done," Gwen agreed. "The cottagers won't have their lives disrupted for long. If they don't find Amabelle soon, they'll accuse another one of the actors of the murder."

When the carriage stopped at the corner, Gran Gwen said, "Jasper, there's been a change of plan. We'll return home now."

The coachman touched his cap and turned the carriage south.

As soon as they arrived at Bonheur, Laurette went immediately upstairs to summon her maid.

"Shall we sit in the conservatory? It's a sunny day. Or is it too morbid to do so?"

"No," Deanna said. "At least . . . well, we'll have to start sitting in it someday."

"My thoughts exactly."

It was hard not to imagine Charlie Withrop lying on the floor with his head bashed in. Gran Gwen walked right past the place and sat at the far end of the conservatory. Someone, Carlisle probably, had thought to face the chairs out to the sea rather than toward the interior of the room, and Deanna breathed more easily.

"I wonder if we'll see Joseph today," Gwen said.

Deanna didn't care if she ever saw him again.

"I wonder if he's talked to Will about any progress they've made on the case."

"I wouldn't know," Deanna said tightly.

Gran Gwen smiled. "I surmise that Joe has a very deep hole he must climb out of before he's forgiven."

Deanna bit her lip. "Very deep."

Gran Gwen sighed.

Deanna heard movement behind them, and she turned to see Laurette hurrying toward them.

"My diamond pendant earrings are gone."

"Oh Lord. Are you sure you didn't misplace them?"

Laurette pursed her lips at Gwen. "I remember putting them on the top of my jewelry box the night of the Judge's birthday fete. I was going to wear them, but worried about losing them on the lawn. They're the ones Lionel gave me on our first trip to Brazil. And my favorites.

"I crawled on hands and knees, thinking they might have been knocked onto the floor by the chambermaid, but they're gone.

"That little minx, Amabelle, must have taken them. That's why she disappeared so suddenly. Not because a man lay dead in our conservatory but because she had lifted my diamonds. Well, let her just try to hock those around here."

Gwen shook her head. "Really, Laurette, sometimes I'm shocked at your knowledge of slang."

"It's from consorting with the other half, Mama," she said in an exaggeratedly prim voice.

"Cuss like a sailor, is more like it."

Laurette blushed.

"I'm proud of you. I think we should report this to the police."

"I doubt if they can do anything."

"Probably not. But if she did take them and tries to sell

them in Newport, she'll be caught. Everyone knows those earrings."

"How could I ever face poor Rosalie again if the police arrest her daughter for stealing my earrings?"

Gran Gwen smiled sympathetically. "I dare say, it will pale if they arrest her for murdering poor Charlie."

Laurette stood and wrung her hands. It seemed to Deanna they were all coming under the spell of the thespian troupe.

"No, first let me apprise her mother of what is happening. Surely she'll want to return with me. I'll tell Carlisle to have a room prepared for her." She'd begun to pace, oblivious of their presence. "Surely she will come."

She walked to the fireplace and back again. "Mama, I'll take this evening's ferry. Please don't inform the police yet. What if it were Joe instead of Amabelle? Would I want the police called in?" She sat down again. "But what will Lionel think if I don't?"

"Well, my dear, go have your maid be ready to leave for the ferry. This matter can wait until you've talked with Lionel and Rosalie; then send us a telegram with instructions."

"Thank you, Mama. I will do just that. Excuse me." She hurried from the room.

"I suppose you're shocked that we decided not to call in the police," Gran Gwen said to Deanna. "It makes us look just as hypocritical as our fellow cottagers and their insistence on privacy."

"A bit," Deanna agreed. "Laurette knows Will is always discreet."

"It isn't our reputation she's worried about. Rosalie is the one who introduced Laurette to the women's emancipation movement, back in their school days. Her parents were great reformers—and abolitionists. Unfortunately they were killed during the draft riots, trying to save children when the rioters torched the orphan asylum."

"That's terrible."

"Yes. That was only one horrible incident among many in that horrendous war. And it wasn't even on the battlefield." Gran Gwen's expression took on a faraway look, sorrow in her eyes.

Deanna had heard the horrible stories of the war that turned family against family, son against father, brother against brother, but it didn't seem real to her; she couldn't begin to imagine the loss.

"I'd sent Laurette to school in Switzerland several years before." Gwen laughed softly and perhaps a little ruefully. "I hoped to keep her from the fray. Clara and Tom Deeks had done the same with Rosalie. She and Laurette became fast friends. They had much in common."

"She doesn't sound like someone who would cut off her daughter for becoming an actress," Deanna said.

"Things change, people change," Gran Gwen said cryptically. "You never know what people will come to believe in or care for. Now, let's have lunch and go about trying to locate the Mrs. Deeks Elspeth told you about."

 Chapter

11

"**D**ammit," Joe exclaimed, shaking his hand where the wrench had hit his knuckles before falling to the floor. "Why isn't this working?"

Orrin flipped the lever, and the machine whirred to a stop, then he came over to look at the folding mechanism. "Why don't you just have a man stand here and fold the bags as they come down the assembly line?"

Joe scowled at him. "Because, what if he gets behind? What if he knocks the bag over? The bags will keep piling up until they create a backlog, and the whole batch will be unusable. With the folding device, any slowdown or stoppage will be immediately translated to the production line, which will cease moving the filled bags until the problem is rectified." Joe picked the wrench off the floor, noticed the blood oozing from his knuckles.

He needed to clean it up; it wouldn't help for him to get an infection from the dirt or for the oil to be contaminated with blood.

"Damn and damn and damn," he said. "I'll be back."

"Yes, sir," Orrin said, and bent his head to peer into the machine.

"And watch your head while I'm gone."

Orrin nodded. His red hair was parted and combed neatly to each side, his work clothes clean and pressed, which was more than Joe could say for his own. "Uh, Mr. Joe?"

"Yes, Orrin?"

"There's a lady standing in the doorway."

"What?" Joe turned, already feeling exasperation well up inside him. But it wasn't Dee. It was the actress he'd walked home from the pub, Noreen. He pulled a dirty handkerchief from his pocket, wrapped it around his bleeding fingers, and went to meet her.

"I hope you don't mind me bothering you this way."

"Not at all," Joe said. "Though you'll have to forgive me for one moment. A slight accident." He held up his hand, realized the handkerchief was spotted with blood, and dropped it again.

"If you'll have a seat . . ." He pulled out the one straight chair with his good hand. "I won't be but a moment." He crossed quickly to the sink, scrubbed both hands, ignoring the burning and pain. He would like to have washed his face, but it seemed a bit late to pretend that he was anything but a working man in the middle of a workday.

He reached for the peroxide bottle and poured it over the scrapes, gritting his teeth against the sting. Then, one-handed, he rummaged in the miscellany crate until he found a box of gauze and a pair of scissors.

"Bring it over here," Noreen said. "I think that will be easier with an extra pair of hands."

Joe hesitated. He did need another set of hands, and ordinarily he would have enlisted Orrin to tie the bandage. He crossed to the table, pulled out a stool, and sat down.

Noreen cut a piece of gauze and took his hand in hers. Her hand was smooth, warm, and competent. She dabbed at the scrapes, then rolled the remaining gauze around his hand with a light, gentle touch, and Joe found his mind wandering from her nursing skills to her face, the intense eyes, the broad mouth, the full lips.

His breath caught.

"Sorry, did I hurt you?"

"No, not at all."

She smiled. Split the gauze into two ends and tied them together. "There, almost as good as new."

"Thank you. But I don't think you came here to play Florence Nightingale. How may I help you?"

Her mouth tightened. "I'm not sure how to put this. I suppose I will have to trust in your discretion and . . . your rational mind."

Joe blinked. "I always try to be rational."

She smiled slightly. "Can I trust you, Joe?"

"Yes." He said it without thinking, wrapped in the power of her personality. Even as he answered her, a quiet voice reminded him of her warning from only two nights before. Never trust an actor. You never know when they're telling the truth.

She folded her hands, took a slow breath, and focused her eyes on the table before her. Joe wondered if this was an exercise she went through every night before going onstage.

"The others don't know I've come."

Joe nodded. She wanted his discretion, but he couldn't promise until he heard what she had to say.

"We met yesterday to discuss what to do. Most of us live from week to week. We can't afford to not work. Some suggested we offer a few performances rather than sitting and doing nothing to help ourselves."

"And you want my help?"

"I want you to listen."

Joe nodded.

"But others, the majority perhaps, are for packing up and leaving for the city."

"They've been requested to stay put."

"They're frightened, Joe. They—we all—have obligations. If we're not back by tomorrow, the theater will have to return tickets that were bought in advance. Not only will the actors be out of work, but so will all the people that the theater employs. No one is left unscathed.

"Is your police friend Sergeant Hennessey any closer to finding the killer?"

"I'm not privy to that information."

"Aren't you? Or is that your way of saying, 'No, he isn't,' or 'No, I won't tell you.'"

"It's my way of telling you I don't know."

She stood up, walked a little ways from him, then turned back, her hands clasped, beseeching. "We can't go on like this much longer before someone does something stupid. Or takes matters into his own hands."

"What do you mean? Do you know something that will help Will with his investigation?"

"No, no, I don't, but I do know that Edwin is under tremendous pressure. If this isn't solved soon, if they don't release us, he'll lose everything."

"What do you mean? He was paid to bring the company here."

"Yes, but he has contracts with the theater in New York and for a tour after that. We can't be stuck here many more days without the company folding. I'm afraid if his back is against the wall, he will choose one of us to take the fall in order to save the others."

"That's rather coldhearted. The sacrifice of the individual for the common good?"

"If you will."

"And would you all allow that?"

She swallowed convulsively. "Yes."

"A scapegoat."

"Yes, and then pray that there isn't enough evidence, real or—"

"Trumped up?"

"Yes, but not necessarily by Edwin. My guess is the Newport police will welcome a . . . scapegoat . . . and will do what they need to do to convict him."

"Or her?"

Noreen shrugged, smiled slightly. "Perhaps."

"Well, you're mistaken there. Will Hennessey and I go back a long way. He's the most honest man I know."

"And does he control the police department here? A sergeant?"

"No. But he'll fight for the truth, even if the truth is unpopular."

She laughed. "Sorry. I'm not laughing at your friend, it's just for a second you sounded like someone from a melodrama." She sighed. "If it were only so."

"The Judge loves the theater; it was his party that brought you here in the first place. Perhaps he could speak to Will, guarantee your cooperation if you're allowed to return to the city." Even as he said it, Joe knew that it was unlikely. The Judge had a reputation to protect, and even though he might enjoy a play, Joe doubted if he'd be willing to go out on a limb for a troupe of players his daughter hired for his entertainment.

She came back to the table, sat, and leaned toward him. "Why here? If it was one of us, why kill him while we're in Newport? It would be so much easier in the city. People are killed there all the time; many of the murders are never solved. There are so many places to hide a body: an alley, the river. Why here, Joe?"

"And why in our conservatory?" Joe asked.

"Can I assume it has nothing to do with your family?"

"Most definitely."

"Good."

"Could it be because of something that happened after you arrived? Or that had been building and finally pushed the killer over the edge once you all were here?"

"A crime of passion?"

"Or of sheer aggravation."

"What?"

"Nothing, just thinking out loud. Amabelle came to Bonheur, that's my family's home, in the middle of the night. She was seen talking to Charlie on the pier where the yacht party was being held. It's possible that he followed her. I probably shouldn't tell you this, but at this point, nothing can be fully understood until Amabelle is found. Do you know where she is, Noreen?"

Noreen shook her head. "No one does. I was hoping that you might."

"Me? Not likely. And I'd like to keep my family as removed from this as possible."

"One of the actresses and I went to church yesterday. We are religious people, some of us."

Joe nodded. He could see her vacillating about telling her story, and he didn't want to say anything that would make her change her mind.

"We happened to go to Trinity Church—so lovely. We saw your friend there."

Joe looked a question at her.

"The girl who I locked in the closet."

"Ah, Deanna."

She smiled slightly. "Deanna. She was with an older woman."

"My grandmother. Dee is spending the summer with her."

"They were speaking with Judge Grantham."

"They are acquaintances, and we all were guests at his birthday fete, where we attended your performance."

"Yes, that does make sense. You grandmother doesn't like the Judge very much."

"How do you know that?"

Noreen gave a throaty laugh. "Oh, she smiled and did everything that was proper, but little things gave her away. The way she moved, her gestures. Nothing that the ordinary person would notice, but an actor . . . an actor studies human behavior in order to make their parts more realistic."

"I'll be sure to tell her to be more subtle in the future."

Noreen leaned forward and gripped the scissors. "If you care for either of them, tell them to stay away and stop looking for Belle." She seemed to realize she was holding the scissors and dropped them onto the table.

"Why? What does the Judge have to do with all this?"

"Perhaps nothing, but he sits in the pocket of the Society for the Suppression of Vice. And vice is anything that Anthony Comstock says it is. He is the perversity and yet he holds the law. He attacks wherever he can, not just for mailing what he calls 'obscenities' and others call 'information.' But for the way people live, the way they work, the way they love.

"The Judge may love theater, but if Belle has run afoul of the law, he won't think twice about sending her to prison."

"Are you hiding her?" Joe asked. "Because that is illegal. You need to think of your family, too."

"I am. I have two families, my child and mother and the troupe. And I'd turn Belle over to the authorities in order to save both of them."

Noreen stood, and Joe automatically stood with her, but he wasn't ready to let her go. Yet when he started to follow her to the door, she stopped him with a gesture. "You're a good man. I can tell that. Someday, perhaps, in better times, you will show me the inventions that are your passion."

And she was gone. An exit that was over before he realized it had begun. He didn't try to go after her. Why spoil the effect.

<hr />

Learning the address of Mrs. Brunoria Deeks was the easiest part of the excursion. Elspeth merely went to the Fifth Ward and asked where Midgie's sister worked.

"Jones Street off Bellevue, indeed," Gran Gwen said as the carriage turned off the avenue, and mansions gave way to older, smaller houses. "We're practically back at the docks."

The carriage slowed, then came to a stop. The coachman jumped down, but he didn't open the carriage door. "Are you sure you want to go in there, Madame?"

Deanna was sure she didn't want to. The entrance to the property was so overgrown with evergreen bushes and tangling vines that she could see only dark patches of house through the leafy tree branches.

"Not entirely. Please wait for us. Walk the horses if necessary, but try not to roam too far."

"No, ma'am. The horses will be fine. I'll wait here." He held out a hand to help Gran Gwen down, then Deanna.

Gran Gwen pursed her lips. "Hopefully, this is merely an extravagant attempt at privacy."

Deanna swallowed and accompanied her into a dark tunnel and up the walk. Once inside the evergreen battlements, the sun returned, revealing the house and a lawn choked with weeds and browning grass.

The house was a dark, three-storied box except for an octagonal turret at one corner and a wraparound porch filled with dirty, weathered wicker furniture. Tall windows that might have let in sunlight were shuttered over. Two chimneys rose past the steep pitched roof of the attic. Gran Gwen led the way, took a tenuous step on the first tread, tested it, then climbed the steps to the front door.

"Do you think someone actually lives here?" Deanna asked quietly as she followed close behind her.

"If Elspeth's sources are to be believed." Gwen looked for a bell and rang it. Deanna heard it echo down what must have been a long hallway, but no one came to let them in. Gwen rang again. Again the echo sounded hollowly down the hall.

Just as they had decided to give up and were turning to leave, the door opened a few inches.

A young maid in a mobcap stared out at them.

"Good afternoon," Gwen said. "I'm Gwendolyn Manon and this is Miss Randolph. We've come to call on Mrs. Deeks."

The maid was younger than most of the maids Deanna was familiar with. Of course, she knew sculleries started much younger in service than lady's maids. And of course a maid of all work required very little finesse. Just the ability to endure drudgery. Deanna felt a pang of pity for the poor girl.

The maid chewed on her lip. Glanced quickly over her shoulder, then back to Gwen. "I don't know. She don't have visitors, regular like."

"And we're going to remedy that today," Gwen said with uncharacteristic joviality.

"Well, I guess it's okay." The maid bobbed an awkward curtsey.

Gwen scurried Deanna and herself inside before the girl could change her mind.

"Who's there, girl?" a voice screeched from the dark interior of the house.

The maid cast a frightened look at Gwen and Deanna.

"We'll see ourselves in," Gwen said. "Nothing to worry about. You may go about your duties. In there?" Gwen pointed to an archway that led to a dim, shadowy room.

The maid nodded, bobbed another of her awkward curtsies, and Gwen led the way inside.

Deanna stayed as close on her heels as possible, and they entered what must have been a parlor. Very little light made its way through the dirty windows or the stained glass transept. Not only was the room dark, but there were the odors of mold and rot and camphor.

A small lamp was lit in a far corner, and Gwen made her way toward it.

"Brunoria Deeks?" Gwen said in a commanding voice.

Deanna had no idea whom she was addressing; there didn't appear to be anyone else in the room.

"Who's there?"

Deanna stepped back.

"Oh, for heaven's sakes." Gwen groped her way across the room and turned the lamp higher.

"Who's there? Turn that off. Do you want to drive me to the poorhouse?"

This was said at a screech, and Deanna's first response was to cover her ears. She resisted.

"Mrs. Deeks?" Gwen asked.

She got no response.

"Mrs. Deeks," she said loudly.

"Eh?"

The poor old lady was hard of hearing.

Gwen looked around for another lamp and turned it on, too.

From the depths of a Queen Anne wing-backed chair came a fat accusing finger. It wagged and pointed first at Gwen, then at Deanna, where it stayed.

"Gran Gwen?" Deanna squeaked. She'd gotten a glimpse of the woman behind that finger. Corpulent, with thin gray hair covered partially by an old lace cap. Another lamp was lit, and Gwen came to stand in front of the woman who sat there.

The old lady grabbed the arms of the chair and pulled herself forward, the chair creaking under her shifting weight.

"Mrs. Deeks?" Gwen practically yelled the name.

Mrs. Deeks squinted at her and patted the side table until she found a magnifying glass. She held it up toward Gwen and squinted some more, which closed her eyes to mere slits, as her mouth hung open to reveal a set of false teeth.

"Who wants to know?" she yelled.

Gwen glanced at Deanna—this had probably been a wasted effort. The woman couldn't see or hear. And most likely never left the house.

There was the cloying smell of dead roses in the air, maybe emanating from the lady or from a vase somewhere in the darkness. It was hard to make out any of the furniture pieces much less what the shadowed objects were. Deanna had to fight the instinct to put her hand over her nose.

At least there were no cats.

Gwen pulled up a chair and sat on the edge. "I'm Gwendolyn Manon," she yelled into the woman's ear.

"Do I know you?" the old woman yelled back. "Because if I don't . . ." She fumbled by the side of her chair and retrieved a cane with a curved black handle.

Gwen gently but efficiently took it from her hand and balanced it against the arm of her chair.

Deanna was impressed. The old woman barely seemed to know what had happened.

"We're looking for you great-niece, Amabelle Deeks."

"Don't know her. I want my tea."

As she spoke, the maid who had opened the door stepped through the archway, carrying a heavy tea service. It rattled as she fought to hold it upright while looking for a place to put it. Gwen slid a stack of musty magazines from a coffee table and the girl fairly dropped the tea tray onto the table.

"Go away now! This lady will pour!"

The girl curtseyed and walked quickly out of the room. The old woman followed her with her eyes until she was around the corner of the hallway, then she leaned forward to make sure she was really gone.

"Steals my cookies!" She pointed the finger that had greeted them toward a marble-topped étagère. "They are in there. The bottom cabinet!"

Gwen fetched them without blinking. Opened the bottom cupboard door and extracted a large rectangular tin, which she placed on top of a small table at Mrs. Deeks's elbow.

"Shall I open them for you?" Gwen yelled.

"I can hear you just fine. Stop blasting my ear." Mrs. Deeks reached greedily for the tin, pried it open, but instead of taking a cookie or offering it to Gwen and Deanna, she held it toward them. "See! It was practically full two days ago. That maid steals them. Like I don't feed her enough. The hotel sends down my meals and she about starves me, so she can have 'em herself."

Mrs. Deeks looked like she was far from starving.

"And my newspapers. She can't read; I don't know why she's gotta mess up my newspapers. Can't get anybody decent to do for you these days."

It wasn't hard to understand why no one wanted to work for Mrs. Deeks.

"Anything silver or gold she can lay her hands on, it's gone. I'll be a pauper by the time she's finished with me."

"If she's stealing from you, why don't you let her go?" Gwen said in an almost normal voice.

"What?" the old woman yelled. She took a cookie for herself, put the tin back on the table, and replaced the lid. Evidently she was not going to share her cookies or her tea with her guests.

"I told her I was going to tell the police. But I wouldn't let them in. Can't have them tromping all over the carpet."

"You summoned the police on her?"

"No. Didn't have to. They came. The girl was carrying on and crying so, I didn't let 'em in. But if it happens again, I will."

"How long has this been going on?" Gwen asked, cutting a look toward Deanna.

"Since just after she came here. Must be two weeks, two months, three. I don't know; lose track of time, since I never get out."

"Why don't you get out?" Gwen asked.

"Where would I go?"

Gwen suppressed a sigh. "Can you tell me if you've seen Amabelle recently?"

"Don't know her."

"She is your nephew's daughter."

"Him!" She said it as if Gwen had asked her to say a bad word. "I remember. He married that girl, what's her name? Roslyn. Rose something."

"Rosalie."

"Beneath him. A penniless orphan who didn't know how to keep her place."

"They had a daughter."

"Had several. Got no use for any of them. Do they ever come to see me? The devil with them."

She picked up her teacup with a palsied hand.

"I believe Amabelle was the youngest," Gwen persisted.

"The one that ran off to become an actress! Just like her mother. Spends the Deeks fortune and has no loyalty."

"She's appearing this week in Newport with a theatrical troupe."

"Don't want to know about it. Unchristian harlots, every one of them."

"Has she been to visit you?"

"Would have thrown her out if she did. Don't want the likes

of her in my house. I'd send her packing before she knew which way was out."

Gwen stood. "Thank you for your time; enjoy your tea. Deanna, are you ready?"

Deanna nodded; more than ready, she hadn't even bothered to sit. She practically ran for the door and away from that cloying scent and awful old woman.

The maid must have been standing in the foyer, because she met them at the door, looking frightened.

Gwen nodded and smiled at her. "What's your name?"

"Li-Lilbeth, madam."

"Well, Lilbeth, Mrs. Deeks says you're stealing from her."

"Madam. On my oath. I never took nothing of the old lady's. She eats the cookies and forgets she ate them. She misplaces things. I find them and put them back, but she don't remember. Please, madam. I'm not a thief."

"How old are you, Lilbeth?"

The maid didn't answer.

"You know you should be in school, not working for a few pennies from this disagreeable old woman."

Lilbeth hung her head.

"How much does Mrs. Deeks pay you?"

"A dollar fifty a week, ma'am."

"And you sleep at home?"

"I just come in days."

"You promise me you have never stolen from Mrs. Deeks?"

Lilbeth nodded vigorously. "I promise. I never did. I didn't eat her cookies or any of the food what the hotel brought, and I didn't steal anything, not even a penny, I didn't mess with her newspaper or nuthin'. Oh, and I don't want to go to jail."

"You won't go to jail if you're telling the truth."

Lilbeth sketched a fast cross over her chest.

Gwen nodded. "Then you bring your mother around to my house on your day off, and we'll see if something can be arranged for bettering your position in life."

"Me and my ma?"

"Yes, you and your mother. Here's the address." Gwen handed Lilbeth a card. Not her normal visiting card that had only her name on it, but a card of about the same size, complete with address and telephone number.

She reached back into her purse and pulled out a dollar, which she pressed into the girl's hand. The girl's eyes widened, then she bounced on her heels twice, said "Thank you, missus," and ran to open the door.

"Don't forget, Lilbeth. On your next day off."

"Yes, ma'am." The door closed.

"Well, that was a waste," Gwen said as they made their way back to the street. "Unless that was an act to keep us from finding the girl."

"Do you think it could be that? I can't imagine Amabelle staying in that house, but I did wonder when she said the maid was stealing things."

"I don't know, but I really feel we've done enough to help Amabelle Deeks. She'll just have to make the next move."

"If she's still alive."

A breeze ruffled through the tree branches, setting a chill to the air. Deanna looked back at the neglected house. "How can she live in that airless place? I wanted to open every window."

"She's clearly not healthy, and the neglect has made her cantankerous."

"But she's driven everyone away."

"I suppose."

Another breeze ruffled the leaves, stronger this time. "I do believe it's going to rain. Come, I'm for home and a respectable tea."

Deanna couldn't agree more, but she had to look back one more time. Was the old woman watching them from one of those darkened windows? Because Deanna definitely felt something crawling up her spine. But not a sound or a movement came from the old house. Every door and window was sealed—like a tomb, Deanna thought—except for one tiny, forgotten dormer window, raised just enough for the dingy curtains to dance through the opening. A last, forgotten symbol of hope.

Or a flag of surrender.

Deanna shivered.

Gwen took her arm and together they hurried toward the waiting carriage. As soon as the carriage started up, Gwen put her head back and closed her eyes.

"Depressing," she said. "No old person should be left alone to end their life like that. And no young person should start theirs like Lilbeth."

"Will you really help her?"

"But of course, if she and her mother are willing. I lend a hand here and there as I might. Save one or two from working and breeding themselves to an early death."

⚬⚬❧⚬⚬

Laurette's overnight valise was sitting near the front door when Gwen and Deanna arrived home.

"Dear me, I hadn't realized it was so late," Gwen said. "Tea at once, Carlisle, for Miss Deanna, and I'll have a spot of sherry."

"Very well, Madame. Mrs. Ballard is in the parlor at the

moment." The butler bowed and disappeared down the hallway.

Gran Gwen immediately went into the parlor, drawing off her gloves, then unpinning her hat. Deanna didn't know whether to follow or go to her room, so she followed. She was interested if Laurette had found out any more about her missing diamonds.

Laurette was sitting on the settee. Her son was pacing in the space in front of the mantel. Laurette cast an exasperated look to her mother.

"Well, Joseph. What a nice surprise," Gwen said, sailing into the room. "Deanna and I were out for a drive and I do believe there's a storm brewing."

Joe turned, and the storm brewing was in his eyes. Now what was he mad about? Why didn't he just keep himself and his bad mood in the Fifth Ward and leave them alone?

Though it was his house, Deanna reminded herself. Still, why couldn't he just be civil?

"What is going on here?" he asked without a word of greeting. "I come home to find my mother packing, my grand-mother and"—he gestured in Dee's direction—"driving about looking for a thief and possibly a murderer."

"I take it you told him about the diamonds," Gwen said to Laurette, ignoring her grandson completely.

"I was given the third degree," Laurette said, her eyes twinkling at Joe.

"Do you three realize the danger you could be in?"

"Surely it's over for us," Gwen said. "Charlie was killed, and Amabelle must have taken the jewels the first night she was here. And there's the end to our involvement."

"How can you know for sure? Mama, it's time to leave for the ferry. I'll drop you on my way."

"Yes, dear, thank you."

He nodded brusquely. "I'll be waiting at the carriage. I'll be back in time for dinner." He shot a defiant glance at Gwen. "And I'll be staying at Bonheur until my father returns." He strode out of the room, and if the doors at Bonheur hadn't been so heavy, Deanna was sure they would have slammed behind him.

"Oh dear," Gwen said. "What was that all about?"

"Poor thing," Laurette said. "Twice now he's—he and Deanna—have aided Will in an investigation, and he's falling behind in his own work because of it. He's frustrated over some mechanical problem that he hasn't had time to fix. He's worried about the safety of his family. And confused about . . . some other things. Don't be too hard on him while I'm gone."

"Well, if he's going to dash about like a madman the whole time, you'd better make this a very short trip."

Chapter

12

True to his word, Joe was sitting at the table when Deanna entered the breakfast room the next morning. He was drinking coffee and scribbling in a notebook. Gran Gwen was eating toast and reading a folded newspaper. But the first thing that Deanna noticed was . . .

"There are two letters for you, dear." Gran Gwen smiled, a sort of "prepare yourself for battle" kind of smile. Deanna only glanced at the silver salver and its contents before she crossed to the buffet and served herself eggs, ham, and toast. Not that she was hungry anymore.

Knowing a letter from her mother had come drove away all desire to eat, or converse, or think. Better to get it over with.

Carlisle poured her coffee, and Deanna picked up the two letters, one from her mother and another from Adelaide. She'd save that one for last. She opened the one from her mother and scanned the words, looking for the phrase "returning home." Then sighed with relief when she couldn't find it anywhere in the missive. It was just another list of her complaints about the hotel, the food, the doctors, the transportation, the country. It seemed like there was nothing about Geneva that her mother liked.

Deanna thought it sounded wonderful, with its chocolate for breakfast and its clear, cold lakes and quaint houses. The way Adelaide described her few outings under the chaperonage of the institute staff made Deanna want to see it for herself.

She folded the page and reached for the other letter.

Joe stood. "If you ladies will excuse me, I have some work to do. I'll be in the library."

That made Deanna look up. "Aren't you going down to the warehouse?"

"Not this morning. I want to work on some design ideas; working here will be fine."

"Oh." She would have asked him about what he was working on, but he was already striding out of the room, stopping long enough to kiss his grandmother on the cheek, and then he was gone.

"I'm hoping," Gran Gwen said, "that a few days back at Bonheur will make him realize that he can live here and still keep the warehouse without living on the premises."

"I think he likes living down there."

"I do, too. Though I don't see how he could. No hot water, no real tub, the heat an afterthought, an uncomfortable peasant bed, and . . ." She shrugged. "I may be spoiled. But I find nothing about that way of living appealing."

Neither did Deanna.

She nibbled at her toast while she read Adelaide's letter.

"And how do they fare?" Gran Gwen asked when Deanna had finished reading.

"Mama is still complaining, and Adelaide . . ." She paused. "It's strange, but Adelaide sounds like a different person. I guess there was an argument between her doctor and Mama, and the doctor won. But it made Adelaide sick, and he said to her that he would cure her of her mama. What do you think he meant?"

Gran Gwen looked at the ceiling. "I have no idea."

"And she also says she hasn't worn a corset in two weeks. Evidently it is one of the many institute rules." Deanna laughed. "My sister. Can you imagine? And she sounds happy. She also says to please not tell Mama. As if I ever would."

"Good. Maybe the change is just what she needed."

Gwen went back to the newspaper, and Deanna finished her breakfast.

"Hmmph," Gwen said, and slapped the paper on the table.

"Bad news, ma'am?"

"No particular news at all. I suppose it's too early for reportage from Judge Grantham's case. Rather a big to-do I gather.

"He's bound to be returning to Newport as soon as he pronounces sentence. No one wants to be in the city at this time of year. I just hope Will has a suspect to parade in front of him. Quentin said the Judge put it to the new police chief to find the culprit and send the actors back to New York and do it before the regatta next week. What are you planning for today?"

"I thought I would go out to the lawn and sketch a bit this morning unless there's something you'd like me to do."

"Not at all, though you do have to attend some daytime functions or your mother will take you back."

"Well, Vlady and Herbert did mention they were playing tennis later, but then I'd have to invite Ivy Bennett to go with me. She's the only girl I know that will actually run after a ball."

"Runs in the family, I suspect."

"Because her uncle is such a sporty person?"

"That, too. Mainly just wild. Maybe you can convince Joseph to come with you."

"No. I don't want to interrupt his work. I'll be fine." She went upstairs to get her sun hat and art supplies. She did, however, slow down as she passed the library.

Joe was sitting at the desk, shirtsleeves rolled up, forehead resting in one hand as he studied a piece of drawing paper. Her movement must have caught his eye, because he turned, straightened up. "Is there something?"

"No, I just . . . I was just on my way outside to sketch. What are you working on?"

"Well," he said, scrubbing his face, "remember the big wheel they used in the play at the Judge's fete?"

"The one that carried the married couples to heavenly bliss."

"Yeah, that one. Though I think I can put it to better use."

Deanna didn't think heavenly bliss sounded all that bad, but she stepped into the room and went to look over Joe's shoulder at the drawing.

It was a good drawing, Deanna realized. She could tell exactly what it was, a Ferris wheel with two rectangles, one extended at a right angle to the bottom right and another to the top left.

"What does it do?"

"Well, nothing yet. But while I was watching the play, I was thinking about conveyor belts and how much room they require while still needing manpower at each end, plus elevators, so . . ."

Deanna laughed. She couldn't help herself. "Do you even know what the play was about?"

"Sure, some Egyptian stuff."

"So the Ferris wheel would replace the conveyor belt?"

"In some instances. Especially in limited spaces. And this would eliminate the need for an elevator, which would also cut down on inefficiency."

"How?"

He frowned at her. "Are you really interested?"

She nodded. "If I wasn't, I would have gone out the conservatory door and not passed by at all."

He smiled slightly. "So theoretically, the filled bags would move along this shorter belt." He pointed to the bottom right with his pencil point. "Get deposited on the flatbed of the wheel, where they would move counterclockwise to eleven o'clock on the other side, then they would be off-loaded onto another conveyor belt which would take them to be packed in boxes that would eventually be crated and carted to stores or depots or docks.

"It would be a continuous delivery system, consolidating space rather than being divided between conveyor belts and elevators that once unloaded are sent back empty for another load."

"Which wastes time. And how will it be powered?" asked Deanna.

"With electricity, ideally. Though I don't believe the one they used in the play was electrified. I'm hoping to get a closer look." He shrugged. "As long as they're here."

He scribbled something on the drawing. "And if I added gears here and . . ." He trailed off, and Deanna realized he was working out some detail and had forgotten she was even there.

She tiptoed out of the room and went through the conservatory to the lawn. She tried not to look at the place where Charlie had lain as she passed by, but she couldn't repress a shiver at the memory.

What had he been doing here? He must have been looking for Amabelle. Maybe they had planned the robbery together. They'd argued. No one had mentioned finding the earrings, so Amabelle must still have them. But that didn't make sense. She distinctly remembered the blades of grass on his shoes and the grass stains on his trousers. As if he'd knelt—or fallen—or been dragged across the grass. The grass was mown once a week, and even though the landscapers were meticulous about raking the lawn clean afterward, he might have picked up a few blades wet from dew. But that still didn't explain why he was found in the conservatory.

She hurried out into the sunshine and saw that Carlisle had set her camp chair and easel in the shade of a tree. She didn't really feel like sketching, but she opened her pad, set it on the easel, and looked out to sea. Really, how many seascapes and landscapes did she need to draw? She should be doing something.

She took out a pencil and began to sketch, not the waves or the cliffs but the conservatory fireplace. The body sprawled on the carpet in front of it. The grass on the heels of his shoes, the stains on his plaid suit. His face turned to the side as if he were sleeping. But she didn't draw his wounds; it was a sacrilege to destroy such a handsome face.

She hesitated, pencil inches from the page. There was no reason to ruin that face.

Maybe it wasn't about robbery after all, but a personal

vendetta? Someone had mutilated him on purpose, because of anger, jealousy? *A Crime of Passion*. She could see it in her mind's eye. Would Amabelle do something like that?

And so what if she did? No one knew where she was.

Deanna wished she could do something to help find Amabelle Deeks and Laurette's earrings. But it was more than that. She needed to find something useful to do with her life. She'd been willing to give up her childhood flights of fancy, knowing they were just that. Unattainable. She'd resigned herself to marry into society because she thought at least then she would be able to do all the things she wanted to do. But she was quickly learning that was not the case in most marriages.

Even Adelaide, who was the perfect daughter and had until a few weeks ago been engaged and ready to begin her life in society, was now living in an institute in Geneva without her corset.

Joe was inside inventing things to help the industry and the working man—and woman.

And what was she doing? *I'm stuck*, she realized. Stuck and useless. She jabbed her pencil behind her ear and wandered over to the little copse of trees that somehow had managed to withstand decades of storms and winds. She could see the conservatory doors from where she stood. Had Charlie stood in the trees waiting for Amabelle to come out? Or did she signal for him to come in, and then she bashed him over the head?

Or had he been attacked out here, beneath the trees, by some unknown assailant? Someone who followed him to rob him or punish him? Or to punish the Ballards?

Why drag him into the conservatory unless to cast suspicion on Amabelle or the Ballards?

She began searching the ground even though it had been

several days and she knew the servants and the police had gone over it before.

"Dee? What are you doing?"

Deanna let out a squeak and turned around. "Joe, you scared me to pieces. You shouldn't sneak up like that."

"I didn't sneak up. I looked out the window and saw you weren't where you were supposed to be, and I got worried."

Deanna knew she should be grateful that he was concerned, but she just felt . . . cornered. "Thank you, but as you can see, I'm fine."

"You don't look fine, you look sad. Are you missing your family?"

She shook her head. "I was thinking about Amabelle Deeks. Has Will found her yet?"

"No. And he might never. But there's nothing you can do about it. We befriended her, and she took advantage of our goodwill."

"I know, still . . ."

"Well, you can stop worrying about things you can't fix and go change into tennis clothes. We're meeting Vlad and Herbert at the Casino."

"Are we?" She quelled her initial jump of excitement. "What about your work?"

"It'll wait."

"But what about your injured hand?"

"It's my left, and it isn't bad. Do you not want to play tennis today?"

"Yes, of course I do, it's just . . . Did Gran Gwen put you up to this? You don't have to, you know. I'm fine."

"She may have mentioned it. But I could use the exercise, sound mind in a sound body and all that."

"Oh, thank you, Joe."

She practically ran to gather her drawing things and then across the lawn toward the house before she realized Joe wasn't coming. She stopped and turned back to him. He was standing with his hands in his trouser pockets, just watching her.

Then he pulled his hands out and made shooing motions with them and she darted toward the house. She paused at the door just long enough to glance back. Joe was looking at the ground.

Vlady and Herbert were already at the courts when Deanna and Joe arrived. Gran Gwen had insisted on coming with them as chaperone, and they had left her in a comfortable niche in a loggia behind an oval window surrounded by latticework.

"Now, run along. I have my book. And if I stick my head out this opening, I can see you. And really, that's chaperonage good enough for the sticklers of society. Knock the stuffing out of them, my dears. Then invite them to luncheon in the restaurant."

Joe rolled his eyes. "Shall we?"

"Yes, we shall," Deanna said.

"I meant shall we go?"

"I know what you meant."

Vlad and Herbert were lounging against the steps, but straightened up immediately when they saw Deanna and Joe.

"I say, Deanna. You look wonderful."

"Thank you, Herbert." She loved her new outfit, so much lighter weight than her old one and much less restrictive. She might even be able to lunge after a ball. The dress was made of a white and ecru striped dimity with block pleats in the back and smaller pleats across the shirtwaist, with peach cuffs at the wrists. She even had a new white straw boater with matching peach ribbon. She'd drooled over the catalogue picture for months before she finally moved to Gran Gwen's and was able to order it. And it was everything she'd dreamed of.

Vlady gave Joe an appraising look. "How long since you've been on the court, Ballard?"

"A while. Why? Am I out of fashion?"

Deanna thought he looked wonderful in his white flannels. Like the old Joe before he forsook society and went to live with his machines. Actually, all three of them were very handsome and she knew she'd be the envy of every young lady at the Casino today, if any of them bothered to stop gossiping long enough to look out to the courts.

But Deanna didn't care. She was going to play tennis. Really play.

"I'll take Joe," Vlady said. He winked at Deanna. "That way I can keep my eyes on the lovely Deanna."

"And while you do," Herbert said, "Dee and I will trounce you with our superb tennis skills and haute couture." He sketched a bow and ushered Deanna to the near side of the court.

Herbert had improved his game since the last time Deanna had seen him on the court. And they held their own against Vlady and Joe, who was a little rusty. They each took a set and decided to adjourn for luncheon.

⸺◦◦◦)◦(◦◦◦⸺

Joe took the towel from the attendant and dried his face. He was sweating. He wasn't getting the kind of exercise that a man got from sports anymore. He'd feel it tomorrow. He'd almost forgotten how life used to be. To be awakened with a tray of hot coffee. Breakfast made daily and kept warm, tennis at the Casino, luncheon in a restaurant, not at the pub or the food wagon. It was seductive.

Though he could do without dressing for luncheon after a game of tennis. And it was time he got to the reason for so readily agreeing to accompany Dee today. He planned to question Vlady and Herbert, who had both been at the yacht the night Charlie died.

Will was loath to do it, since they'd already gone through questioning before this summer, and he didn't want to push his luck. The cottagers tolerated him because he was well bred and well educated, but they wouldn't tolerate him for long if he kept "harassing" them.

That fell to Joe. "How late did you two stay at Mersey's the other night?" he asked nonchalantly.

Vlad tossed a towel in the bin. "Lord, I don't know. I think I staggered home sometime around four. You, Herbert?"

"'Bout the same, I guess. It was loud and noisy and reeked of tobacco. Ended up talking to Erik Dolan and a couple of fellows out on deck for an hour or so, then I went home."

"We heard you ended up with the body of one of the actors on your parlor floor," Vlady said.

"Conservatory," Joe corrected. "I don't guess either of you saw him that night at the yacht."

Vlad and Herbert looked at each other.

Herbert shook his head. "Wouldn't recognize him if I saw him."

"Nor I," Vlad said, slipping into his jacket. "Besides, I wasn't looking for guys."

"Though I might have seen her," Herbert added.

"Amabelle Deeks?"

"Yes, not that I know her, either. Like I said, I was standing on deck when this young woman runs by. Someone yelled, 'bell.' She stopped and turned around, at which point I realized it might be her name rather than some nautical term. But then she ran down the gangplank, and that's the last I saw of her." He folded his jacket collar over and straightened his tie.

"No fights breaking out at all?"

"Hey," Vlad said, pulling a comb through his hair before tossing it into the waste bin. "We're civilized men."

Joe snagged his jacket off a hook, and the three of them went to join Deanna and Gwen.

"Sorry we couldn't be of more help," Herbert said. "Do you think that actor followed her to Bonheur?"

Joe shrugged. "Or someone followed them both. I don't suppose you noticed that, either?"

"No, sorry," Herbert said as they started down the corridor to the restaurant.

"Well, here's someone who might know," Vlad said. "Mersey. What ho?"

Jacob Mersey had just rounded the corner and came to a stop.

"Great party the other night," Vlady said.

"I aim to please," Mersey said.

"What brings you to the Casino today? I thought you and Dolan were heading to Saratoga for the races."

"Meant to. But I decided to spend a couple more days here. Nice little piece I'd like to enjoy for the moment. If you catch my meaning."

The three nodded. It didn't take much imagination. Mersey was notorious for high living and questionable women.

"I heard you had a bit of excitement at your place, Ballard. Hope it didn't have anything to do with you. Is that why you were looking for a little blonde the next day?"

"One of the actresses' mother is a friend of my mother's. I was staying at the warehouse as usual, but evidently she came during the night, was gone the next morning, having left us a body in the conservatory."

Mersey laughed. "Sorry, old thing, but really. Ah, there's the Casino's manager. I must run. I'm here to persuade him to open the stage for the troupe to rehearse while they await their fate."

"Didn't know you were interested in theater," Joe said.

"I'm not. I'm interested in the lovely Talia. Coryphée extraordinaire and limber as an acrobat. Later." He saluted them and hurried after the manager.

Well, at least they would have a place to rehearse, Joe thought as they sat down to luncheon. Maybe Talia could use her acrobatic talents to persuade Mersey to pay some wages.

⸻◦⊰◦⊱◦⸻

Deanna had a wonderful time, and the luncheon Gran Gwen ordered was superb, but she noticed Joe was rather quiet, and that was disturbing. Did he resent being kept away from his work, even for a morning? One more thing for him to be mad at her for.

After lunch, they left Vlad and Herbert at the door of the Casino and drove south on Bellevue Avenue, then past Jones Street, where old Mrs. Deeks lived her lonely life. Deanna expected that they would let Joe off at the warehouse, but the carriage didn't slow down, and he accompanied them all the way to Bonheur.

"Well, I suppose we'll have to do the grand drive today," Gran Gwen said. "We don't want the town to forget that Deanna is here. But first I must have a nap."

But when they reached Bonheur, Carlisle informed them that Will was waiting for them in the conservatory.

They found him kneeling down at the place where they'd found Charlie's body.

He stood immediately. "Sorry if I overstep."

"Not at all, Will. Do you have news?"

"Not much and none of it good, I'm afraid. I really came to speak to Joe."

Gran Gwen raised an imperious eyebrow.

"And you, of course, if you wouldn't be put off by the subject." He glanced at Deanna.

"I'm sure that Deanna and I can handle it. Shall I call for my vinaigrette?"

Will smiled sheepishly. "I don't think that will be necessary."

"Then please sit down."

They all sat, and it felt to Deanna that things seemed almost normal again. The feeling didn't last for long.

"Walter Edgerton was down at the police station again today, demanding we make an arrest. He doesn't really care who as long as it gets done. His wife and mother-in-law are nagging—you didn't hear it from me. Though I do feel for him, poor fellow. And the Judge will return tonight or tomorrow and expects action. He seems to be taking this personally—not the birthday present he'd hoped for."

"Well," Gwen said, "I don't know why he should complain; the man wasn't found in his conservatory. But that's how these big reformers are. See everything as a slight to themselves."

"I was called in to the chief after he left. He's given me an ultimatum: either find someone to arrest or they're taking me off the case."

"What? They can't do that," Deanna said.

"Unfortunately, they can," Gwen said. "The pressure the cottagers wield is formidable. A word in the right ear, and he'll be dismissed."

"Which means," Joe said, "they're planning on arresting someone who is not a cottager. One of the actors or the crew that came with them," he added, almost to himself.

"Or one of the local lads who hired on," Will said. "A windfall of money one minute, and the next, you get carted off to jail for life. Or hung."

"Will, this is not the time to get bitter," Gran Gwen said. "You simply must find the killer."

Will sighed. "That's why I came out. To look over the scene again, see if there is anything I could have missed. And that cursed girl still hasn't shown up." He rubbed his temples. "I'm stuck for a motive and for a suspect."

Deanna looked at Gran Gwen. Sent her a silent message asking whether they should reveal that Laurette's earrings had gone missing.

Whether she got the message or not, Gwen said, "There's something you should know."

Will closed his eyes. "What is it?"

"We believe the Deeks girl stole Laurette's diamond earrings."

"What? Why didn't you tell me?"

"We only found out yesterday, and Laurette felt torn because Amabelle's mother is a very old and close friend. That's why she went to New York. To consult with Rosalie Deeks. So perhaps a falling-out of thieves?"

"Perhaps," Will said. He looked at Gwen, then to Deanna. "I'm not leaving."

"Actually, I was wondering if it's acceptable to Gran Gwen for you to go over what Miss Deeks said to you the night of the murder. I realize it's been several days, but maybe you've remembered something else since then."

"I remember it. I wrote it down. Elspeth and I have been comparing notes."

Will took out his notebook; his pencil stub looked much smaller. He must have been taking lots of notes. "Okay, just begin again and tell me everything you can remember."

Deanna thought back. Told him how at first Amabelle was timid and frightened, then how she gradually relaxed. "First we discussed our favorite lady detectives in the serials. Then we talked about the theater and being an actress. She wasn't very effusive. She said it was hard work. Actually, it sounded like she didn't much care about acting.

"And I said it must pay well, and she said only for the stars, that the chorus didn't make good money. Then I said she must meet interesting people and . . . handsome men. And she said some handsome, and some not at all.

"Then she kind of got upset again."

"Upset?"

"More like agitated." Deanna paused, trying to remember if there was anything else. "I asked her about her home, and she said she could never go back there."

"Interesting."

"What is? That she won't go home again? Her mother sounds as strict as mine."

Will frowned. "She said she couldn't go home?"

"Yes, then she said she wouldn't. That's right. She couldn't and she wouldn't. Why? And don't say you're not at liberty to tell."

Will wrestled with a smile. "I'm not. But I will anyway, since it will all soon be out of my hands. We interviewed her colleagues. She lives with two of the girls in the chorus. But they say she hardly stays there. She tells them she's staying 'at home.' They think she's lording it over them. Or possibly . . ."

Deanna waited. When it was clear he wasn't going to say more, she said it for him. "Someone is keeping her."

"Dee," Joe said.

"Joe," she mimicked.

"You two, don't begin this nonsense," Gwen warned.

"Yes, Dee. She's most likely being kept. I don't suppose she mentioned any names?"

Dee shook her head. "And I don't think Charlie made enough money to support her, do you?"

"No, I'm almost certain he didn't."

"Well, maybe she's gone there, to her . . . you know."

"Except we don't know where or who or if it's even true. She may be going home, but it's out of my jurisdiction. Hopefully Mrs. Ballard will be able to shed some light on the situation when she returns. Anything else?"

Deanna thought back. "That's all. I told her we would help her, and she said no one could help her. Then Elspeth took her down the hall to the guest room.

"That's the last I saw of her."

"So sometime during the night," Will said, "she managed to steal the earrings. Then she must have gone downstairs to pass the earrings off to Withrop, but why didn't she just go with him?"

"She didn't have any clothes except that gown and cape," Deanna said.

"She stole the earrings while my parents were in the next room," Joe said. "Surely she could have managed a dress or two."

"Or there is a third person," Will said. "Someone who was part of the plan or who took advantage of the situation. It keeps coming back to the acting company. Who better to overhear the two of them making plans involving Bonheur than another actor who decided to go along for the ride?"

"Does that mean you think Amabelle is dead, too?" Deanna asked.

"Dead or with the third person."

"A prisoner?"

"Or she went willingly."

"Or she killed Charlie herself, panicked, and ran." Joe crossed his arms.

"No." Deanna crossed hers. "She couldn't have." Getting no response, she continued. "Because I think somebody killed him outside and dragged his body into the conservatory. Maybe so she would find him."

"And you think this because . . ." Will held his pencil at the ready.

He was taking her seriously. "Because he had dirt and grass on the heels of his shoes and stains on his trousers, like he'd been dragged."

Will broke into an appreciative grin. "That's exactly what I think happened, too."

Deanna heard a low growl. She was pretty sure it was coming from Joe. She turned on him. "You think so, too. I saw you out looking in the grass after I left."

Will let out a laugh. "Not much gets past our Dee."

"But how will we ever find her?"

"We'll find her. I just hope I can find the real culprit before they arrest and execute the wrong person." Will pushed out of his chair.

"Won't you stay for tea?" Gwen asked.

"Thank you, but I have work to do." He stopped at her chair, kissed her cheek. "You understand that I'll have to make inquiries about the diamonds."

Gwen nodded.

"If someone tried to sell or pawn them, it could lead us to the killer."

Chapter
13

"Well, I don't know if Joe is planning to join us for dinner; he seems to have wandered off with Will. But with or without Joe's escort, we must make an appearance at the Schermerhorns' soiree. Anne will never forgive me. We missed her musicale earlier this summer."

Deanna smiled wanly. A soiree was the last thing she felt like tonight. "Will there be music, ma'am?"

"Most likely a string quartet playing in the background. I imagine there will be literary figures and a few artists. William is quite the connoisseur; he has truly good taste. There will be all sorts of people there who might be quite amusing and certainly passionate about their work.

"Not exactly ideal," Gwen said, motioning Deanna into the parlor, "since your mama has already written twice to remind me that the only reason she allowed you to stay at Bonheur was in the hopes that I would find you a suitable husband. I feel we must have something to write about in our next letter to her. There is the Rensselaers' on Thursday. Then the Fishes' ball, but she won't be pleased with them. Oh well, we'll have to do our best.

"So tonight please find someone suitable to assuage her fears that I'm turning you into a terrible example, but don't pay him so much attention that you give some poor soul the wrong impression."

"Ugh," Deanna said.

"Chepstow is a lovely house, grand but not cloyingly so. And the Schermerhorns have a much-to-be-admired art collection. Though I imagine tonight the talk will turn literary, considering the news from England."

"What news?"

"It will probably stay among the men at their port, but if it does erupt in company, just don't pay any attention."

"I don't understand, ma'am. What could it be?"

Gwen sighed. "I suppose forewarned is forearmed. Your mother would skin me alive. But I'm speaking of the trial and sentencing of the playwright Oscar Wilde."

"The one who penned *The Importance of Being Earnest?* The Perrys saw it in London and said they enjoyed it very much."

"Yes. Well, I'm afraid his talent has been overshadowed by his private life."

Deanna waited. There must be some scandal Gran Gwen knew of. It seemed like there were scandals in everyone's households except hers and the Ballards'.

"I suppose you must know. You're bound to see it in the papers. The man was accused of having, um, indecent relations with the Marquis of Queensberry's son. Lord Alfred Douglas."

Deanna waited.

Gwen cleared her throat. "The kind of relations a man usually has with his wife. They've sent him to prison. Ah, here's Carlisle with tea at last. And enough said about Mr. Wilde. Surely no one will bring it up in mixed company."

Carlisle placed tea and cakes, and a decanter of sherry for Gwen, on the tea table.

"Tell Minerva to prepare my bath. And tell Miss Deanna's maid, too. We've had an eventful day; I think we can forgo the drive again this afternoon."

Carlisle bowed. "Yes, Madame."

"Oh, and Carlisle, Joseph is planning to be in residence for a while. If he returns in time for dinner, please let him know that he'll be escorting us to the Schermerhorns' this evening. Have someone lay out his evening kit."

"Yes, Madame."

Carlisle bowed and left the room. Gwen poured Deanna tea and herself a sherry.

She took a sip and looked over the sandwich and cakes tray. "I keep thinking about that old lady and her tin of cookies." She chose a delicate cress sandwich. "Do you think she knows where that wretched girl is?"

"It didn't seem so," Deanna said. "And I can't imagine Amabelle seeking her out for help. I know I wouldn't."

"No. A horrible way to grow old."

"I wonder if her family cast her off?"

"Or just forgot about her. Tragic. Even though she was an annoying old bag." Gwen sighed. "I suppose if I manage to find a better situation for Lilbeth, I'll be responsible for finding her someone more capable, who can do a little dusting and open the drapes occasionally."

It was a short tea, and Joe hadn't returned when Deanna and Gran Gwen repaired upstairs. Deanna wondered where he and Will were and what they were discussing. She didn't like feeling left out.

Elspeth undid her dress and carried it away. Deanna removed the rest of her underthings and climbed into the tub of steaming water. It was long enough to stretch out in and deep enough to come up to her shoulders; marble, carved with fat cupids and grape arbors.

When she'd first come to Bonheur, Deanna had found it a little unsettling to climb naked into the tub in front of the little angel boys, but since they were as naked as she was, she soon accustomed herself to it and now barely noticed them at all.

The water was hot and the oils that Gran Gwen had given Elspeth to use in her baths always left her skin silky. Deanna breathed in and out in slow breaths, scrubbed her skin until it glowed, as she relaxed into a semistupor.

She was practically asleep when Elspeth shook a warmed towel at her and made her get out of the water.

"You'll look like a shriveled prune tonight at the soiree," she said.

Deanna stood and let Elspeth dry her off, then used Elspeth's shoulder to steady herself as she climbed out of the tub.

"I think you oughta have a nice lie-down until dinner," Elspeth said.

And Deanna didn't protest. Between the entertainments and the cycling and the murder, and the visits, she was having a hard time staying the course.

She closed her eyes and didn't wake up until it was time to dress for dinner.

She sat at the dressing table while Elspeth brushed her hair.

"You're ever so quiet tonight, miss."

"I'm thinking."

"About what dress you're going to wear tonight?"

"No. I've already decided to wear the persimmon brocade. Did you hear downstairs if Joe is going this evening?"

"No, miss, is that why you're wearing the persimmon dress? It sets off your hair and complexion perfectly."

"No, it is not. I just wondered. He's being so strange lately. Fun one minute then an ogre the next. I don't understand."

"Orrin says—"

Deanna cut her a look. "I thought you were going to stop saying 'Orrin says.'"

"Sorry, miss, but my brother does say that Mr. Joseph's been having some trouble with part of that machine that's supposed to make paper bags."

Deanna huffed out a sigh. "Is that all?"

"All? Well, it's pretty important to him. And I'd think you could show a little interest, since Orrin says . . ." She glared at her mistress. "Orrin says that his machines are going to save R and W's ars—are going to save the company."

"Well, he has a champion in you."

"And he oughta have one in you, too . . . if you don't mind my saying so."

"Well, I do mind." Deanna rested her elbows on the dressing table. "And I am interested. And I think it's wonderful what he's inventing. But he doesn't care what I think."

Elspeth frowned.

"What is it, Elspeth? Why are you looking like that?"

"I'm not looking like nothing. If you'd be nice to him, he'd be nicer to you."

"I am nice to him. Most of the time."

"Just so long as nobody's nicer to him than you are."

"I don't understand. I *am* nice to him."

"Good, then."

"I wish everything didn't have to be so complicated."

"Ha. Pardon me for not crying. You and me, we've got it made: good food, a nice place to live, a family who loves us. Not everybody gets even close to that."

Deanna thought of Lilbeth, and the obnoxious Mrs. Deeks, and Amabelle, out there somewhere alone, or dead. And Charlie, who would never have a chance to have any kind of a life now. "I'm sorry, Elspeth. I'm being awfully selfish. Forgive me?"

"True-blue, miss. Now, you put on your fine gown and wow all the gentlemen tonight. And when you come home we'll have a nice read." She sounded like everything was back to normal, but Elspeth was frowning when she sent Deanna downstairs.

—∞◦)◉(◦∞—

Chepstow was an Italianate villa with a mansard roof and arched windows. It was so soothing after the extravagance of the Grantham fete and the dinginess of the Deeks house that Deanna was lulled into a calm she knew was deceiving.

Joe had agreed to come with them, and he looked very distinguished even with his bandaged hand. Though he refused to tell everyone that he received the injury in a duel, as Deanna suggested. Really, he'd lost all of his sense of humor recently.

The interior of the house was just as Gwen had described it. There was artwork everywhere, paintings on the walls, statues on tables and in nooks, and smaller items on shelves and in display cases. And yet the rooms didn't seem overstuffed, like some of the huge rooms in many of the newer mansions.

They were, however, overstuffed with the prestigious families of Newport and people Deanna had never seen before. Gwen pointed out artists, poets, musicians, and philosophers of note.

She introduced Deanna to Mrs. Astor, who was rather daunting in her pearl choker as she watched Alva Vanderbilt and her daughter, Consuelo, walk by.

"I see she's let the poor girl out for air, and just when we were all beginning to think she had the child chained to her bed until the duke's arrival," Mrs. Astor said.

Gran Gwen just smiled.

"Will she really have to marry him?" Deanna asked.

"Yes, dear." Mrs. Astor gave her a bored look. "It's what we do."

Gwen bowed and they walked on.

"Not you or Laurette?" Deanna asked.

"Not Laurette," Gwen said, and turned to greet a lanky gentleman with thinning hair and a long thin beard in the German style. And Deanna had no time to ponder whether Gran Gwen had married for love or not.

They were joined by another lady and gentleman, and the man with the beard moved off to another group. Gwen introduced her to person after person who wrote, painted, or was a patron of the arts. It was a delightful, if head-whirling, evening. There were a few young people invited, but not many of her normal crowd, except for Herbert Stanhope, looking unusually distinguished, and Vlady Howe, who had accompanied his mother and was behaving in a very gentlemanly fashion.

Deanna's eyes began to wander, and she saw Joe and Herbert deep in conversation with an older gentleman across the room. She knew they were either talking about the sugar industry or the automobile industry, and she longed to join them.

She wished she knew more people. She could only guess

that would come with time, though she might never be allowed to rub shoulders with such interesting people once her mama was back from Geneva.

She stayed close to Gran Gwen during the evening and absorbed every conversation she could. Everything she heard was fascinating.

"I saw their motion picture demonstration in Paris. I say, the Lumière brothers are way ahead of Edison."

"Perhaps, but he will turn it to good account."

"This fellow Freud in Austria. He's bound to set the medical world on its ear."

"But really, my dear sir, do you actually believe his postulations?"

"Remains to be seen, remains to be seen."

Several men were gathered around a woman dressed in a black tea gown with golden braiding at her neck and sleeves. A poetess whom Deanna had never heard of and with a name that she couldn't pronounce.

"Yes, but you must realize," she said in a thick accent, "words are but a gloss that we agree to understand."

Every group they stopped at was more intriguing than the last. Deanna didn't understand half of what people were discussing, but she was excited by it. She wanted to write down everything, then go back to Bonheur and study every one of the things they mentioned.

"Well, what did he expect?" said a man with a barrel chest and a red sash over his evening wear.

"Come now, sir. Is a man not allowed his private life?"

A loud laughter burst from the group. "Nothing Oscar does is private. He would die of boredom if it were."

"So who do you think will replace Morris Hunt?"

"Thank God he managed to finish The Breakers before he died. Mrs. Alice would have followed him to hell with final instructions."

It was a while before Deanna began to notice that the women were gradually moving into another room. She'd seen several of the girls she knew, and they motioned her over, but she was sure they would just be talking about dresses or Consuelo's duke who would be arriving any day, and really this was all just too fascinating to miss.

After a while Gran Gwen suggested they get some refreshments and sit for a while. Deanna went with her into the second parlor, where they sat down on a settee just vacated by Mrs. Vanderbilt and her daughter. Deanna might have liked to talk to Consuelo, but Consuelo reminded her of Adelaide, so perfectly well bred. She kind of missed her sister and reminded herself to write a letter as soon as she got back to Bonheur.

A footman was there immediately with a tray of wine and lemonade.

"I think it's such a shame," one of the ladies was saying. "No, not about Consuelo. She knows where her duty lies, but about . . ." She leaned forward to the lady sitting in the gossip chair facing them.

The lady across from her snapped her fan. "I hope, Frances, you are not going to mention that abominable playwright—you know the one to whom I refer."

"Oh, him. Certainly not. I was speaking of the dead man found in Gwen's conservatory."

"Oh," the second lady said. She turned to Gwen. "It must have been dreadful."

"Quite." Gwen smiled graciously, but there was an edge that Deanna noticed, that unfortunately the lady did not.

"Why on earth did he come to Bonheur?"

"Not to see me, I assure you," Gwen said.

"Oh, Gwen, you're always so droll. Didn't you take in one of those actresses who was in the play at Judge Grantham's fete?"

"Really, Frances," her friend interrupted. "What a question."

"Well, it is a question," Frances said, her eyebrows raised toward Gwen. "Quite frankly I don't know what Maude was thinking by having that troupe on her property. The Judge may love the theater. Who doesn't? But to give those people free rein of one's property is ridiculous. They say she even allowed the leading ladies and men to use rooms in the house for their dressing rooms."

"I just hope they didn't rob her blind."

They were being so unfair. Deanna started to say so, but the subtle pressure of Gwen's hand against hers silenced her tongue. If her mother had done that—not that her mother would ever have allowed her to listen to the conversation—Deanna would have been angry, but she knew Gran Gwen well enough to know she wasn't trying to stifle Deanna's opinion.

And she was certain of it when Gwen glanced to the lady who was sitting on the second half of the gossip chair, her back to the group and conversing with others.

She turned to Frances, and Deanna recognized Drusilla Edgerton, her face white with mortification or anger, it was hard to tell.

"Frances Dougherty, Mama was gracious enough to let Walter and me plan the fete. It was my idea to hire a theatrical troupe for the evening. And Mama went along with it because she knew my father would enjoy it immensely.

"I take full responsibility for the situation. It was I who

invited the actors inside according to their station as princi-pals. What occurred afterward had absolutely nothing to do with my father's party or my family. So if you feel you must have someone to blame, you should address me."

"Well, really, Drusilla. Don't be so sensitive. You have to admit the whole situation is scandalous."

"I recall you enjoyed the play immensely, isn't that so?" Gwen asked with that same edgy smile.

"Well, really," Frances said. "I was just making an obser-vation." She stood, lifted her chin, and walked away, stopping immediately at another group, who just as immediately all turned to look at Drusilla Edgerton.

Drusilla's lip trembled. But she gave them stare for stare.

"Pay them no mind, my dear. It was a lovely gesture and, after all, the body was found in my conservatory."

"You say that as if it were something to be proud of. Excuse me." She stood and walked away in the opposite direction.

"You were just trying to make her feel better," Deanna consoled Gwen.

"Never mind, my dear. Drusilla, I'm afraid, is one of those women crushed by society rather than fulfilled by it. Let's hope Consuelo has better luck with her duke."

"You mean Drusilla's marriage was arranged with Walter Edgerton?"

"Yes. He was the Judge's protégé. Very ambitious."

"But if Drusilla is unhappy, surely she could tell her father."

"I doubt if Drusilla has ever been truly happy. Some women enjoy their misery."

As the evening went along, Gran Gwen gave her the back-ground of most of the people in the room. She introduced her to society ladies and businessmen, and dropped a few morsels of gossip about most of them. "Only so you understand the context," she told Deanna. Some she declared to be true artists and others, mere charlatans. It seemed Gran Gwen knew everyone.

It was while Gwen was in a lively exchange of ideas with a French painter that Deanna saw Drusilla Edgerton talking with two other ladies. The ladies left and for a moment Drusilla was alone. She was only a few feet away, so Deanna slipped from the conversation to speak to her.

"Hello."

"Oh, Miss Randolph. Lovely evening, isn't it?"

"Yes, isn't it? I . . . I just wanted to say, not to think anyone listens to that gossip about the actors. I thought your fete was excellent."

Drusilla turned a look of derision on her so devoid of comfort that Deanna took a step back. "You know nothing about it." Without another word, she walked away.

"My, my, what did you say to the dreaded Drusilla?"

Deanna started. "Oh, Vlady, you startled me."

"Herbert and I decided we had better come to the rescue before she devoured her prey."

"I felt sorry for her. People said such nasty things about the Judge's party."

"Old cats," Herbert said.

"Yes, and I'm afraid I've made it worse."

"Well, you tried your best," Herbert said.

"Yes, don't give it another thought," Vlady said. "Now, come with us. Mrs. Schermerhorn has convinced the incomparable Miss Kellogg to sing a little Gilbert and Sullivan. What say you to that?"

"I think it sounds infinitely more interesting than being

chastised for trying to be nice." Deanna started to take his arm, but stopped. She turned to Herbert. "Do you think . . . ?"

"It's perfectly respectable," Herbert interpreted, and he offered his arm, easing Vlady out of the way.

Miss Kellogg had just finished a selection from *H.M.S. Pinafore* when Deanna felt someone move up beside her. Thinking it was Joe saying they were ready to leave, she turned and smiled. But it wasn't Joe.

Walter Edgerton stood towering above her, or so it seemed to Deanna. He was smiling, but what he said was anything but friendly. "I hear you've been upsetting my wife."

"No, I—"

"Your mama would certainly not be happy with your behavior if she were to find out what you've been up to."

"But I haven't done anything."

"Don't argue with me, Miss Randolph. My wife's nerves are delicate, I can't have her upset. Please do not continue to insinuate yourself into our family or its affairs."

Mortified, Deanna tried to explain, but he cut her off. "You know the Judge is a very powerful man. He oversees the morals of society. And he can make life difficult for those with questionable lifestyles. Like . . . hmmm . . ." He looked about at the guests. "The Ballards, for instance."

Mortification turned to anger, and she was in danger of telling Mr. Edgerton what she thought of his threats, but Herbert was there, stepping between them. "Sorry to interrupt," he said with his usual insouciance, "but I've come to fetch you as your party is ready to leave."

Mr. Edgerton bowed slightly and walked off.

Herbert drew Deanna's arm through his. And she clung to

it. Her heart was pounding so hard she was afraid it might burst.

"You're trembling. What's afoot?"

"That odious man just threatened me."

"Edgerton? What did you do, applaud too loudly at the G and S?"

"He's upset because these two ladies were questioning the wisdom of hiring a theatrical troupe to entertain at the Judge's party."

"Egad, it must be a slow week in Newport for everyone to be harping on that still. I say ignore him."

"It wasn't just that." They had come to the hallway, and she stopped him to lean closer. "Can I trust you?"

"With your life." He put his free hand over his heart, which would ordinarily be funny, but tonight made her want to cry with appreciation.

"He said if I didn't leave them alone, the Judge could make life difficult for people who—I can't remember exactly what he said—but he implied that the way the Ballards lived was suspect."

"Oh, what sheer . . . balderdash. But I would steer clear of him and his. These righteous sorts don't always have the best aim; liable to hit the innocent by mistake when they're going after crime, or immorality, or whatever they think they're freeing the world from."

"But I didn't do anything."

"Their victims rarely do."

"Do you think he's going around threatening everyone who says anything about the fete?"

"God only knows. He may have picked you out because, one, he doesn't like the Ballards, and, two . . ." He hesitated.

"Two?"

"You're a formidable lady, my dear Deanna."

"Me?"

Herbert grinned. "You. He may feel a wee bit threatened."

"By me?"

"By you. Now, I promised Joe to deposit you at the door. So let us proceed forthwith." He smiled in the way that always brought her a gurgle of laughter, but not tonight. "But, Deanna, I wouldn't bother mentioning any of this to Joe. Gran Gwen will laugh it off, but Joe . . . he might feel he has to confront such accusations to protect his family's name."

Chapter

14

D eanna went straight upstairs when they arrived back at Bonheur. She'd spent the carriage ride home from the soiree waffling between anger and fear that she'd unwittingly set off something that would hurt the Ballards and Gran Gwen. She was caught between wanting to tell them what Edgerton had said to her, and keeping quiet, so Joe wouldn't rush out and do something stupid.

Joe was usually pretty levelheaded, but there were times . . . and lately he'd seemed downright volatile.

She didn't, however, hesitate to blurt out everything she was feeling to Elspeth.

"It was awful," she said as she held the unopened copy of *The Experiences of Loveday Brooke, Lady Detective*, while she sat at the dressing table and Elspeth brushed her hair. "At first the party was nice, the people so interesting, except Joe practically left us at the door and wandered off to talk to everyone but Gran Gwen and me."

"Uh-huh."

"I did meet Mrs. Astor. She's quite frightening. I wouldn't want to get on her bad side. Consuelo was there with her mother, looking like a very tall lamb going to the slaughter. Some of the regular crowd. But the others, oh, Elspeth, it was fascinating—artists and authors and all sorts of interesting guests, and their conversation was exhilarating and probably would have been even better if I'd been familiar with the subjects they were discussing. And it was all so . . . so passionate." She sighed. "Then we sat down with these women, and it was like being in the most boring afternoon visit, at least until the subject turned to the murder.

"Then these women said mean things, you know how they do, like they're being sympathetic but secretly they're gloating over your misfortune. They wondered how the Ballards felt about finding the body of poor Charlie here—but they didn't call him 'poor Charlie,' they called him 'that actor person.' And one of them said something about the Granthams, and Drusilla overheard them. I felt sorry for her, so later I told her not to pay them any mind, and she got mad at me. Me! And I was only trying to be nice."

"Well, then I say let her be unhappy." Elspeth held a clump of hair to work out a tangle. "There are some that just can't be anything other than miserable."

Deanna sighed. "But that's not the worst of it. We were listening to this singer, when Walter Edgerton slips in next to me and tells me to leave his wife alone and that the Judge could make things difficult for the Ballards if I didn't."

The brush stopped. Elspeth scowled at Deanna's reflection in the mirror. "He wouldn't dare."

"Well, that's what he said. I tried to tell him I was just trying to be nice but he wouldn't have any of it. Just told me to *stop insinuating myself into his family*," she finished in her snootiest imitation. "Not that I ever would. Who would want to be a part of that family? Snobbish, opinionated—"

"Powerful," Elspeth finished for her.

"How do you know?"

"Oh, miss, sometimes . . . I told you servants know more than anyone about what goes on in the rich folks' homes. And the Judge is a feared man in the Fifth."

"How can he be? He's a judge in Manhattan."

"But he's got clout. And once he gets his nose bent outta joint over something, you can be sure heads will roll."

"What's he upset about in the Fifth?"

"Our lewd, drunken behavior. Though they never scrimp on the champagne at his house. Not long ago they arrested Molly Adams for desem—desem—handing out . . ." She leaned in close to Deanna and whispered, "Birth control information."

"That's against the law?"

Elspeth nodded seriously. "Smut, Officer Crum called it."

"Oh, Officer Crum can go chase his own tail." No one liked the sergeant who policed the Fifth Ward. Deanna placed the magazine back on the dressing table. "Is it smut?"

Elspeth shrugged. "Maybe, but I'd rather have smut and save my bacon than end up bleeding to death from a back-alley butcher."

Deanna shivered.

Elspeth sighed. "And don't go asking me to explain it to you. People of your class can do better, or they just go to visit their aunties in the country for a few months."

Deanna sucked in her breath.

"Sorry, miss. Did I hurt you?"

"No. It was just talking about aunties. And having gone to see that awful aunt of Amabelle's. What if Amabelle got in trouble with Charlie?"

"And killed him when he tried to stop her from . . . what?" Elspeth asked.

"From telling? From . . . going to her aunt?"

"But she came here, didn't she?"

"But she didn't stay."

"Well, I suppose, but from what you said about the aunt, seems like she wouldn't find any help there."

"No," Deanna agreed. "The old lady said she hadn't seen any of her family and didn't want to see them. Not that she'd be able to. She keeps the rooms so dark. She couldn't even hear them. We had to yell every word. . . . I wonder."

"Uh-oh. When you start wondering, I get to feeling queasy."

"I just keep thinking of that open attic window. It's probably been left open for years."

"Probably. 'Cause a lot of times folks hang their wash up there instead of outside when it rains."

"But there was the stolen food. . . ."

"A servant girl what probably goes home on a full belly. Are we gonna read tonight or not?"

Deanna reached for the book, opened it to the story "The Black Bag Left on the Doorstep."

———◦◦◦❧◦◦◦———

Dreams of pyramids and open windows, Gilbert and Sullivan, and black bags left on doorsteps kept Deanna tossing and turning most of the night, but it was the dream of Joe yelling at her from across the ocean that woke her up.

She lay in bed, blinking. Joe wasn't across the ocean, he was here in Newport. Her mother was in Switzerland. How on earth had Joe and her mother gotten mixed up in her dream? It didn't take her long to figure that out. "Because you're both always telling me what to do."

Elspeth hurried into the room. "Did you call, miss?"

"No, but I suppose I'd better get dressed. There will be more morning calls. It seems Gran Gwen is determined to show me off to Newport."

"It's just because she wants your mother to stop worrying about you. You're not the only one getting letters from her."

"Gran Gwen mentioned she'd written to her."

Elspeth nodded and pulled the covers back.

"I hope she isn't being odious to her and telling her how she should be going on.

"I think I'd better write Mama this morning and give her all the details of my spectacular week, leaving out the murder, the jewel theft, the threats, and the Gothic houses."

Deanna slid her legs over the side of the bed and sat up. "Actually, it has been an exciting week."

Gran Gwen was reading the newspaper at the table in the breakfast room when Deanna came downstairs.

"Good morning, Gran Gwen."

Gwen folded the paper closed and slapped it down on the table. "Feeling better this morning?"

Deanna hesitated as she reached for the chafing dish lid. "Yes. I guess I was a little tired when we came home last night."

"We have been rather burning the candle at both ends lately."

Keeping my mother happy an ocean away.

"It's been wonderful."

Gwen put her cup down. "You sound like you're expecting it to end."

"Oh, I hope not." Deanna really hoped that things would sort themselves out and soon, before her mother came back or Walter Edgerton decided to take his wrath out on Gran Gwen and the Ballards.

"Is there something in the papers that upset you? Nothing about . . ." She trailed off, dreading the gossip that might flow and that Edgerton might use to harm the family. It was reprehensible. None of them had done anything.

"Nothing of any import."

"Where is Joe this morning?"

"He was gone when I came down." She smiled and picked up a folded piece of stationery by her plate. "'Dear Grand-mère. I really must work today.'"

"Good. He's not very much fun lately."

"You'll particularly like this part. 'Please don't let Deanna get into any trouble while I'm gone.'" She chuckled, shook her head, and tossed the note on the tablecloth. "Now I see you're getting upset, but don't. He's a little on his high horse these days, but you have to give men a little room to make themselves appear ridiculous or they end up being like Judge Grantham and the rest of his moralist buddies."

"I don't understand how Judge Grantham can enjoy the theater and champagne and parties and cigars and then be such a puritan."

"Well, he isn't a puritan, but it's politically smart to align himself with the moralists these days. They're geniuses at inducing fear. It makes him appear more like God in the pulpit than a mere man on the bench. Sheer vanity."

"But he does good."

"Of course, mostly. He brings criminals to justice. It's just that sometimes I think he takes his cue as to who should be criminals, from other men who happen to be very powerful."

"More powerful than the Judge?" Deanna asked.

"Much more powerful."

"Elspeth said he had a woman arrested in the Fifth Ward for passing out birth control information. He called it smut."

"I imagine Comstock and his thugs were behind that. They are sanctimonious, small-minded—well, I didn't mean to go off my head about them; the less thought about them the better."

"They couldn't do anything to us, could they?"

"Us? You and me?"

"Or any of the Ballards or Randolphs?"

"Of course not. Who have you been talking to?"

"No one," Deanna assured her. She couldn't tell her about the threats Mr. Edgerton had made. Maybe she had misconstrued them. "I just wondered."

"Well, you shouldn't be spending any time worrying about politics while you should be concentrating on your first season. Wouldn't you like to meet your friends at Bailey's or for shopping? You don't have to stay and entertain me all the time, though I love having you."

Deanna bit her lip. "No, but I thought I would stay here this morning and write letters to Mama and Adelaide; I'm afraid I've been remiss."

"Good. I have some duty calls to make and there's no reason you should have to endure them. Write your letters, we'll have a quiet day, and pick up Joseph during our afternoon drive and bring him back with us to entertain us for the evening."

Deanna dutifully wrote her mother and Adelaide both. News of the parties and the attention she was receiving to her mother. And descriptions of sea bathing and fashion to Adelaide. No mention of murder, actresses, or scandal of any kind.

She was just sealing the second letter when Elspeth, carrying a stack of laundry, came into the dressing room.

"Put that away and then I have an errand that I need you to help me with."

"Yes, miss." It was only a few minutes before Elspeth came back into the room.

"What's the errand?"

"I want you to leave now and walk to this address." She quickly penned Mrs. Deeks's address. "I will meet you there. I wish you had a bicycle, but I haven't seen anyone riding with their maids. And I can't take a carriage because I don't want anyone to know what we're up to."

"And what are we going to do when we get there?"

"You're going to chat up Lilbeth while I sneak inside."

"Lord save us, what do you want to do that for?"

"Because I'm afraid that Mr. Edgerton is going to cause trouble. Amabelle might be dead, might be long gone, but if she's still in town, where better to hide than with a half-blind, practically deaf woman, who blames her maid for the food that's disappearing."

Elspeth's eyes had grown wider as Deanna expounded on her plan.

"It's a long walk, I'm sorry. I'll give you a twenty-minute head start and then I will cycle after you. But don't be obvious that you're waiting for me if you get there first."

D eanna wasted no time changing into her cycling costume. She deliberated about leaving Gran Gwen a note
saying she might miss lunch, as good manners dictated. Good
manners won and she quickly penned an excuse, which wasn't
exactly a lie. She did need to get some stationery, but perhaps
not today. And she and Elspeth would eat in town, if they had
the time.

Elspeth was waiting just off the corner of Bellevue and Jones
Street as instructed. She was trying to look nonchalant while
also staying out of sight by using the foliage to hide herself.
What she lacked in disguise, she made up for in sheer tenacity.
She was frowning at a nanny walking with her young charge,
until the woman took the child's hand and scurried away.

"It's about time, miss," she said as soon as Deanna had
alighted. They walked up the street and crept up to the side
of Mrs. Deeks's home. Deanna pushed the bike into some
shrubbery in case anyone like Will Hennessey happened to
be driving by and came to investigate.

She waited while Elspeth knocked on the servants' entrance
door. It opened almost immediately. "You're running late
today, and the missus—" Lilbeth stopped. "Now, what's this?
What do you want here?"

"I came to see how you're doing. I'm a friend of your sister's;
she said you might need some help."

Lilbeth shook her head. "I do just fine by myself. Not
enough money for two; you'll have to go someplace else."

"Oh," Elspeth said, sliding past her into the kitchen. "I
already have a job. In a big house. Can I have a drink of water?
It's really parching out there."

Deanna listened as Elspeth carried on and her voice grew farther away. Then, with one quick look around, Deanna darted into the house. The kitchen was empty but she could hear the two maids talking from the pantry. "And then I've the wash to gather in . . ."

Deanna hurried across the room and into the hallway. The sudden darkness made her stop and blink several times. Slowly the staircase rose above her. It was a massive carved affair. The runner was worn almost down to the wood. She grabbed hold of the banister and started up stairs. A step creaked. She stopped. No one came. Another creaked and then another.

They all creaked. She'd have to leave it to Elspeth to keep Lilbeth occupied so she wouldn't notice.

At the top of the stairs she paused to have a look around. She couldn't tell if anyone ever came up to the second floor or not. But it smelled musty and dusty, and the wallpaper had started to peel.

She moved down the hallway to where a narrow back staircase led to the attic. Or at least she hoped it did. Listening, she cautiously began the ascent. She stopped completely and put her ear to the narrow door at the top. Not a sound. She was probably wrong, and how foolish she would look if she were caught! But she wouldn't be caught. She turned the doorknob, eased the door open a crack, and peered around the edge of it before stepping inside.

Suddenly she was yanked inside and the door slammed behind her.

She whirled around. An apparition stood before her, an old cricket bat held over her head.

Deanna immediately raised her hand. "No, I just want to talk to you."

"How did you find me?" asked Amabelle Deeks.

"If you'll put that thing down, I'll tell you."

Amabelle frowned at her. "Move back nearer the window so I can see you better."

Deanna stepped back and nearly tripped over something on the floor. Too many detective stories told her it was another murder victim, but it turned out to be a rolled carpet that sent up a cloud of dust in the already dusty air.

"Gran Gwen and I came to visit your aunt Brunoria, hoping that she knew where you were. Really, Belle, we didn't know if you were dead or alive, and everyone is worried."

"Does Aunt Brunoria know I'm here?"

Deanna slowly shook her head. "She's deaf and can't see very well—she hardly turns any of the lights on."

"It's because she's so tightfisted, my father says. She threw him off when he married my mother, and the rest of the family threw her off. Families are awful." She lowered the cricket bat. "So if she didn't know I was here, how did you?"

"Well, the house was shut up like a tomb, every window shade and curtain drawn, except for that little attic window over there. That's what gave me the idea you might be here. It's just what Loveday Brooke would do. I figured it was worth looking into."

Amabelle gave her a weary smile and her shoulders sagged. "It was so stuffy. It made me feel sick."

Now that she'd put down the bat and Deanna got a good look at her, she had to admit Belle didn't look very well. She was pale as a statue, her features were gaunt, and she was wearing some old dress that she must have found in one of the dusty trunks that sat along the walls. It swallowed her figure, which had been pleasingly rounded a few days ago, but now looked like it had lost a few pounds. "Are you getting food and water?"

"After Auntie goes to sleep." Belle smiled slightly. "I sneak downstairs and I steal her cookies and whatever is in the larder. But getting water is harder."

As she said it, she swayed slightly, and Deanna realized that the girl was quite weak.

She caught her and sat her down on a nearby trunk. "You're not well."

"I just need a little water. Could you . . . ?" She motioned to the corner where a pitcher sat on a cluttered crate along with several uneaten cookies. Straight from Mrs. Deeks's cookie tin, Deanna was sure.

It seemed Belle had been trying to make a nest for herself. A pallet on the floor had been covered by an old quilt, and the newspaper lay spread open on it.

"And I suppose you're the one who's responsible for messing up her newspaper every day?"

Belle nodded and chuckled. "I leave the old one by her chair and take the new one. She doesn't know one day from the next, so it doesn't really matter."

Deanna poured water into the cup and handed it to Belle, who drank it all.

"Better?"

Belle nodded.

"I've been portioning it out. She doesn't have running water. Just a cistern and a well. So I have to ration." She handed the cup back to Deanna. "I suppose you want your diamonds back."

"They're not mine, but yes, I do. How dare you steal from people that took you in?"

Belle half shrugged.

"You couldn't sell them around here anyway. Even if they weren't recognized, which they most likely would be, they would be bound to raise suspicion. The police are looking for you everywhere."

"So take them back. They're over there in the handkerchief. Just take them and leave me alone."

"The police aren't going to stop looking for you."

"I told you to take them back. Tell them, oh, I don't know, tell them I'm sorry." She started to cry.

"Belle, I'm not sure you understand. They think you murdered Charlie."

Belle didn't seem to hear her.

"Did you?" And Deanna had a horrible thought. "Amabelle, you do know that Charlie is dead?"

"What?" Belle shook her head. "Charlie? What are you saying? No. He can't be." She looked around the attic as if she thought he might be there. "He was going to meet me. We were going to run away. Run away from it all."

She jumped to her feet but her knees gave way and she fell back onto the trunk. "Charlie? Dead?" She took a breath. "Dead? No, it can't be that." She looked up suddenly. "That must be why he didn't meet me. That's why the police were at the boardinghouse when I got back there. I was afraid to go inside. I thought they were looking for me."

"Oh, Charlie, no." She broke into a keening that Mrs. Deeks might not hear, but Elspeth and Lilbeth certainly would.

Deanna moved closer to Belle. "Hush. You don't want anyone to know you're here, remember?"

"Oh. What am I going to do now?"

Deanna was at a loss. She couldn't very well say *Turn yourself in* and be responsible for Laurette's friend's daughter being sent to prison. "Why don't you tell me what happened?"

"I don't know. He never came."

"Where?" Deanna asked.

"He was supposed to meet me. After the yacht party after . . . Why did we ever—Oh. I have to get out of here. You've got to help me get away."

Deanna was beginning to lose her patience with the girl. "Where was he supposed to meet you?"

"Outside the Ballards' house. I was supposed to ask for shelter, then when the household was abed, I would steal something that we could sell or pawn, and get away. Go out West somewhere.

"I managed to get the earrings from a dressing room while Mr. and Mrs. Ballard were, uh, otherwise engaged." A ghost of a smile, which trembled away. "I went down to meet him, but he never came. I figured he must have gotten scared off, so I came upstairs.

"I knew I could find him the next day at the boardinghouse, but when I heard all the screaming downstairs I knew that Mrs. Ballard had discovered the theft, so I dressed as fast as I could and ran for my life."

"It wasn't the diamonds, Belle. It was Charlie. One of the maids found him, dead, on the floor of the conservatory."

Belle's face twisted. "No-o-o-o. Why didn't he come to me when he was supposed to? I waited on the lawn for at least a half hour. Where was he? Why didn't he come?"

Deanna let her ask her questions; no one would probably ever know what happened that night. Why they missed each other, if Charlie was already dead, or had been killed after she went back inside. Or even who the killer was . . . if it wasn't Belle.

"How did he, was he . . . ?"

Deanna hesitated. There was no reason to tell Belle what he looked like, that beautiful face smashed and bloodied. "Someone hit him over the head. There was nothing anyone could do. They assumed it was you, since you had run away."

"There's no hope for me." And she began to cry in earnest.

"Belle, I have to go. I'm going to tell Sergeant Hennessey that you're here. He's a good man. He'll help find the truth."

Belle grabbed Deanna's arm so tightly that Deanna bit back a cry.

"No."

"Belle, it's the only way."

"You listen. You don't understand. They'll kill me."

"The police? They're not all bad; they'll help."

"No, the police can't help me. If you believe me, you'll get my things from the boardinghouse. Noreen knows which room is mine. Oh, but that won't work. They'll be gone by now. Back to the city. Maybe they took my things with them." She looked down at the old dress she was wearing. Then up to Deanna.

"They haven't left town. The police are making them stay until they finish with their investigation."

"They can't do that. We already missed two performances for this appearance. Monday is dark so, oh, what day is it?"

"Wednesday."

"Wednesday," Belle repeated. She glanced at the pallet where she'd obviously been sleeping. "Wednesday; let me think."

She walked toward the window, turned suddenly. "Could you please help me get my things back? Then I'll leave and you'll never have to see me again."

Deanna didn't bother telling her that it might not be so easy to disappear, but then Deanna had never tried to disappear before. And Amabelle Deeks certainly had.

"Noreen was one of the girls in the dressing tent the other night; she has blondish brown hair and——"

"I know who she is and I doubt if she would give me your things even if I asked."

"She will; tell her it's for Charlie's sake. She'll do it."

It was getting late and Deanna knew she was pushing the limits of what she could expect Elspeth to manage. And then there was the afternoon drive with Gran Gwen. "I'll try, but I won't be able to get back today, and how will I carry it all?"

"It's just one suitcase. We were only supposed to be here two nights."

"But what are you going to do?"

"I'll be okay. Soon. Soon I'll be okay. But please get my things."

"I'll try. I have to go now. Will you be able to get enough water and food until then?"

"Yes, if you'll promise to come tomorrow."

Deanna nodded. She hesitated at the door, but there was really nothing else to say. She left Belle sitting on the trunk, wringing her hands. All that was missing was a villain twirling his mustache, and if Belle could be believed, he was right off-stage waiting to make his entrance.

Chapter
15

Joe stood on what had been the stage of *The Sphinx*. Behind him the wooden dance floor was gone, the birdcages and flowers were gone, the large pieces of scenery had been dismantled and were being stored in the nearby stable. But the stage itself, the roof over it, and the mechanical wheel were still in place.

"So you constructed this exclusively for this performance?" Joe asked, taking a close look at the wheel mechanism.

Obadiah Jenkins sucked on a tooth and nodded. "Ye-ah. Me and the crew came in from Manhattan two days early to get it up and running." Obadiah was a stage carpenter in the theater district. A big guy, clean-shaven, and who recognized something familiar in Joe, another beardless man *who worked with machines*.

"Got my beard caught in a conveyor belt once. Thought it was gonna tear my face off before they got it stopped. As it was, it hurt enough. When the swelling went down, I shaved the damn thing off and I've been shaving every day since."

Joe nodded. Eliminate all the variables, especially when it came to safety.

"I've done one of these before for a production in Manhattan, but my cousin worked on the Chicago one. That was a major undertaking, tons of steel and two hundred and sixty-four feet high. This one? Puny piece of cake."

"But based on the same principle as the big one."

"Hell, same principle as the waterwheel. Wish I had thought it up, the big one, I mean. Then it would be the Jenkins wheel instead of the Ferris wheel carrying loads of people at one time, all of them paying to ride. La-di-da. I'd be a rich man." He shrugged his substantial shoulders. "I'm not complaining. Theater work keeps a roof over my family's head. Pays good enough, for the likes of me, anyway.

"Now, these theater people love their flash—something they and these rich folks have in common. They keep wanting bigger and grander, and Obadiah Jenkins is the person that can put a crew together and get it done." He huffed out air. "'Cept we're stuck here now because young Charlie got himself killed. Told him to stay away from the rich folks. But like a moth to the flame, ya know?"

"I thought he and Amabelle Deeks were engaged."

Obadiah frowned at him. "How do you know any of this? Theater folk don't like other people knowing their business. They have a hard enough time as it is. Work hard, bring a little joy into people's lives, and everybody looks down on 'em."

"Not me." Joe moved closer to the black curtain that hid the inner workings from the audience, and pulled it back to inspect the axle. He really didn't want to talk about Charlie but about the mechanism, but he'd promised Will to keep an ear open. "Did you know Charlie well?"

"Nah. I was just hired on to come oversee this thing. It doesn't have a wheel in the production in Manhattan, just that hydraulic lift thing for the goddess. Now, *she's* a diva.

"I guess the daughter saw this in some other play and insisted on adding one to the show." Obadiah shrugged. "Her nickel. My job security. They just reblocked the wedding scene and the end where they all come back to take a bow.

"We were supposed to take it down the next day, but the police stopped us. I come down once or twice a day to check on everything. You never know when one of these folks will get it in their minds to have a joy ride and then get themselves killed."

"Is the distribution of weight based solely on geometry? Is it counterweighted?"

"A little of both when they're this small," Obadiah said. "Like I said, the waterwheel, or a bicycle wheel."

Joe laughed. "Ah, the glorious wheel."

Obadiah laughed with him. "Once you get it right . . . Ye-ah."

Joe nodded. "Was the 'heavenly chorus' part of the play staged or done that way for technical reasons?"

"Again, a little of both. Gotta stay on your feet on the road. We woulda let them off closer to the ground, but we couldn't make the changeover quick enough. We tried it with only one platform, but the balance was off and it took forever. They woulda been singing all night.

"Then we tried it with two, which worked, only we couldn't let them off on the ground without stranding one couple in the air and stopping the action onstage. So we built a catwalk at one o'clock and they just stepped off to either side as it passed by."

"A lot of coordination," Joe said, gazing up to the flies and the scaffolding to either side of the wheel.

"And rehearsal." Obadiah laughed. "The first time, one of the girls was so panicked she rode around twice before I had to stop the machine and drag her off. Then, at the last rehearsal, someone touched the scrim and the fabric got caught up in the motor, and I thought we'd pull the whole stage down with us. But it went off without a hitch on the night of."

Joe rubbed his chin. "What's the power source?"

"That was a problem. The one in Chicago was run on steam—too loud. I considered electricity. Thought we might rig up a generator, but the smell would have asphyxiated half the audience in this enclosed space. And we didn't have the relays to leach power from the generators running all those little lights in the lawn.

"In a real theater, we would use a counterweights system, but I couldn't do the rigging in this space. In the end we came up with this." He motioned Joe over and threw back a large canvas cloth.

It took Joe a few seconds to understand what he was looking at. He laughed out loud. "The glorious wheel indeed." It was a custom bicycle, held stationery and bolted to a frame. A chain from the back wheel ran over to a system of gears.

"Good thinking," Joe said.

"Think you can make use of this?" Obadiah gestured to the wheel.

"I think so. Only I'll opt for electricity."

They were interrupted by a harsh call, and a man striding toward them.

"Just what are you two doing in here?"

"Edgerton," Joe said.

Walter Edgerton stopped. "Ballard? What are you doing here?" Now his tone was more curious than angry.

"Mr. Jenkins here was kind enough to offer to show me the inner workings of this Ferris wheel."

Edgerton glanced quickly at the wheel. "I wish my wife had been content with dinner and dancing. This is a nightmare. My mother-in-law is beside herself, says every time she looks out the window and sees this, she is afraid she'll have an attack."

"Is she prone to attacks?" Joe asked.

Edgerton rubbed his face. "She's . . . shall we say, she knows what she wants."

Joe nodded shortly. "And what does she want?"

"First, for all this to be taken away. And to send those awful actors back to where they belong. On the streets of New York."

"But I thought the Judge enjoyed the entertainment."

Edgerton's mouth tightened.

"And had the good sense to return to the city once things started falling apart. Leaving me to shore up mama-in-law and Drusilla. Of the two, I don't know who is the more hysterical. Drusilla wringing her hands and whimpering that it was all her fault. Really, the woman could have a career on the stage. Or her mama and her demands.

"Which brings me to . . . She was nearly prostrate after your grandmother and that Randolph girl left."

"Left where?"

"This house, Monday morning. A morning call. Them and a hundred other nosy busybodies. No offense, Ballard."

Joe ground his teeth. "None taken." Busybodies, maybe, but he was pretty sure his grandmother—and Deanna—had ulterior motives.

"I'll speak with them if you like." *In his dreams.* Joe wouldn't dare interfere, but Edgerton didn't need to know that.

"Never mind. It's taken care of." He started to leave. Stopped. "Have they found the killer yet?"

Joe shook his head. "Not that I've heard."

"And the girl?"

"Amabelle? No."

"I'll have to talk to the mayor again. The whole household is upset. Cook burning the dinner, my wife and her mother in hysterics. This is unendurable." He strode away without another word.

"Seems to me," Obadiah said when Edgerton was gone, "the ladies in that house are not the only ones having a fit of the hysterics. He was having a rare set-to when I came in yesterday. They were standing at the open window overlooking the yard."

"Edgerton and his wife?"

"Edgerton and the Judge's wife."

———◦◦◦❋◦◦◦———

Deanna managed to get down the stairs and out the back door before she practically ran into Elspeth.

"Whew, miss. You took your time. Lilbeth is out hanging the laundry. I woulda helped her, but I thought I should keep an eye out for you. Was she there?"

Deanna nodded. "But let's get away from here."

"Let me just say good-bye."

While Elspeth was gone, Deanna fetched her bicycle from the shrubbery.

"Now what are we going to do? Turn her over to the sergeant?"

"No. I promised I wouldn't tell a soul."

"Oh, miss."

"I know. But she was so frightened, I didn't have the heart to turn her in. I also promised I'd go see that odious Noreen and see if I could get Belle's things back. Elspeth, she was wearing some old dress that she must have found in the attic; she looked awful. Like she was sick or something."

"Really pale, like Adelaide gets when she has one of her headaches."

"Hmmph. Maybe she and Charlie were expecting a little package, and that's why they were running away."

"Do you think so? Then why not just get married and make everything proper?"

Elspeth shrugged. "They're actors."

"Were, at least Charlie was."

"So what are we going to do?"

"I'm going back to the boardinghouse to see if Noreen is there and somehow convince her to give me Amabelle's belongings. I'll say her mother wants me to send them home or something."

"What am I going to do?"

It would be so much simpler if Elspeth had her own bicycle. But Deanna was already taking her chances being seen by some gossip as she rode around town. If she and her maid were seen on their bicycles, it was bound to get back to her mother. And her mother would surely foist Aunt Harriett on her. Besides, Elspeth was adamantly opposed to showing her ankles in public.

"You're going to meet me there, but stay out of sight."

Elspeth rolled her eyes. "Where are they staying?"

Deanna told her and off she stomped.

Deanna's mother would say Elspeth was getting above her station, and perhaps she was, but Deanna couldn't imagine having some mealymouthed maid who was always telling on her. It had been the one questionable decision her mother had ever made. But since she'd spent all of her attention on launching Adelaide into society, the choice of her second daughter's maid had been an afterthought. Which was fine by Deanna.

She rode straight to Mrs. Calpini's boardinghouse, but came to an undignified stop when she saw the Black Maria parked in the street outside. As she stood astride her bicycle, the van started up and drove away, leaving a group of people on the lawn and on the porch.

Deanna climbed off her bike and rolled it quickly up the street to the house. The first people she saw were Talia and two other girls, huddled together, their faces masks of fear and apprehension.

Deanna leaned her bike against a tree and hurried to them. "What's happened?"

The women just looked at her.

Deanna looked toward the porch, where Gil, Timothy, and several other men had turned away and were talking among themselves.

"Talia? What's going on?"

"They've arrested Rollie for killing Charlie."

"Rollie?" She remembered him. He'd been the most upset about Charlie being dead, as Deanna recalled. He seemed like a nice man, except being nice didn't stop people from killing.

"Do you know why? Do they have evidence?" If they did, this might exonerate Amabelle. She could come out of hiding, and Deanna wouldn't have to keep her promise to not disclose her whereabouts.

"Evidence?" one of the women shrieked. "They have Rollie. That will be enough."

She burst into tears, followed by Talia and their companion. "Where's Noreen?"

Talia sniffed, looked around. "She was here a minute ago."

Not seeing her, Deanna started for the house. At least maybe she could get Amabelle's clothes so she wouldn't have to face the world wearing a dowdy dress years out of fashion or a white toga and gold cape.

The men had preceded her inside, and when she reached the foyer, there was a yelling match going on between the landlady and a man whom Deanna had met at the theater performance, Edwin Stevens, the company manger. The other players had disappeared.

Deanna took the opportunity to slip upstairs. If she could find Noreen, maybe they could gather Amabelle's possessions before they were noticed by the others.

But once she reached the second floor, she stopped. Two of the doors were closed, two were left wide open as if the occupants had left in a hurry. Talia and Noreen's room? Rollie's? She could imagine the police dragging him forcibly out of the house. Unless Will had drawn that duty; he would have accomplished it with much more finesse.

She heard low voices coming from a room at the end of the hall. She tiptoed toward it. She didn't want to bother the occupants unless it was someone she knew who could help her. Maybe Noreen was there comforting someone.

She stood just outside and leaned forward to peer in the room. Gil and Timothy were sitting on the bed. Gil's arm was around Timothy's shoulders. Timothy's head was bent forward.

As she watched, Gil lifted his head, caressed a piece of hair that had fallen across Timothy's forehead.

It was such an odd gesture of comfort from one man to

another, that Deanna stepped back. Gil looked up. Saw her. He stood up and with two strides, crossed the room to slam the door in her face.

She fled back downstairs to find everyone else standing around Edwin Stevens.

He held up both hands. "Calm. We must stay calm. I can't talk sense into this crazy landlady. I'll have the stage manager call the hotel and book rooms." He shot the fingers of both hands violently through his hair. "Then I will approach the Granthams about paying for this delay. And then I will see about getting Rollie out of jail. But you must stay calm." He lowered his voice. "And very discreet. Now, go collect your things. One day we'll have a good laugh about this over a pint or two."

"Over Charlie, too?" Talia spat out the words.

"No, not over Charlie. But we'll remember the good times. And we'll dance when the real murderer is brought to justice."

"You don't think Rollie did it?"

Stevens hesitated. "I certainly hope not."

They broke up then, Stevens to use the landlady's telephone and the others upstairs to pack. Deanna followed Talia to her room. "Where is Noreen?"

"I don't know. Go away."

"What about her things?"

"I'll pack them. And you better not talk to anyone about what you heard."

Deanna shook her head. What had she heard? A bunch of people trapped in a town where they knew no one, losing money as each day slipped by. Away from their families, angry, grieving for a friend and colleague, and each reacting in their own way. And now, one of them accused of murder.

And yet she couldn't get the image of Gil and Timothy out of her mind. The gentle touch, the concern for a friend.

She shook her thoughts clear. "What about Amabelle's things?"

"Someone will pack them."

"Maybe I should. The lady I'm spending the summer with is a friend of her mother's. I'm sure she would want them."

"Well, you can't have them. How do I know you're not some snitch come in here to make us all look bad?"

"I'm not. I want to help."

"Then bugger off." Talia stepped in front of her, clipping her shoulder hard enough to send Deanna stumbling back.

Things were getting out of hand. It was time to ask for help.

Elspeth was standing across the street, hands on her hips, when Deanna came out of the house. "What's going on over there?" Elspeth said as soon as Deanna reached her.

"Pandemonium." Deanna explained what she knew, though she left out the part about Timothy and Gil. She wasn't sure why, but she just felt like it wasn't something she should share, at least not out on the street.

"I'm afraid we have to make one more stop."

Elspeth slumped. "I near wore off the soles of my shoes running around after you all day."

"I know, I'm sorry. We really should think about getting you a bicycle."

"No, thank you very much. Where are we going next?"

"To the Fifth Ward to see Joe. But on the way we can stop at the grocery and get a soda. I'm parched."

"That's the best idea I've heard all day."

They walked west then south, Deanna pushing her bicycle. Several blocks later they stopped outside the grocery to buy two root beers, and stood drinking them on the walkway with Deanna quickly looking around to make sure no one was watching them. But as soon as the first swallow of cold soda made its way down her throat, she forgot all about what was acceptable for a young lady and guzzled the rest in sheer enjoyment.

They returned the bottles and continued on their way, and within a few minutes they had reached the Fifth Ward.

"I don't think you should be walking in this neighborhood," Elspeth said.

"No one will see me," Deanna assured her. "The cottagers never come here."

"I'm not thinking about them, I'm thinking about your safety."

"Oh," Deanna said, and walked a little faster.

Two blocks later they were standing, unscathed, outside the warehouse where Joe now lived and worked.

It was a brick building and though it looked like it was two stories, there was only one large, cavernous space inside. Joe had partitioned off the area that had formerly been offices and made it into his living quarters, but it was always a shock to see how he lived.

She didn't see his bicycle, but sometimes he kept it inside; thefts were notorious in this section of town. And even though she knew Joe had hired men to watch the premises to repel any possible saboteurs, she didn't know if they would energetically pursue a bicycle thief.

She stood back while Elspeth knocked on the door. It was opened almost immediately by her brother Orrin. "Elspeth. What—Miss Deanna. What are you both doing here?"

"Is that any way to speak to a lady, Orrin?"

Orrin was taller than Elspeth. Both brother and sister

looked very much alike. Pale skin and red hair, that in Orrin's case waved naturally back from his forehead. Deanna had never seen Elspeth's hair unpinned, she now realized. She always wore it in a low bun.

Orrin stepped in front of the slightly open door. "Mr. Joseph ain't here."

"When do you expect him back?"

"I don't know, miss. Soon? I—"

"Whatcha think, leaving my mistress to stand out on the street with a bunch of rowdies? We'll wait for him inside." Elspeth pushed her brother out of the way and opened the door for Deanna to guide her bike in. She had rolled it almost to the middle of the room before she saw the reason Orrin didn't want to let her in.

Noreen Adams sat at the scrubbed table, a cup of tea before her, and looking very much at home.

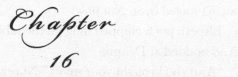

Chapter
16

"Just what is going on here?" Elspeth demanded. Which was a good thing, since Deanna couldn't seem to find her voice. She could only stare. Noreen in Joe's rooms. How long had she been there?

"Well, put my mistress's bicycle somewhere and make her a cup of tea."

Deanna felt the bike lift from her hands. Now she had nothing to hold on to. She could only stare at Noreen and wonder what she was doing in Joe's rooms. And wonder how she could possibly leave without looking like a fool.

She glanced around for Elspeth, but Elspeth had Orrin by the car—not an easy feat since he was a head and a half taller than his sister. She was leading him toward the stove. But Deanna had no intention of sipping tea with Joe's . . . whatever she was while Rollie was being arrested and Amabelle was hiding in an attic fearing for her life.

Though now that she noticed, Noreen didn't look like a

woman with love on her mind; she seemed anxious and maybe afraid. And hadn't Talia said Noreen had been with them a minute before?

"So we meet again," Noreen said in a lofty tone, but Deanna wasn't fooled by it. Not now.

Elspeth put a chipped mug on the table, pulled out a stool. And nodded at Deanna.

"And you brought your maid," Noreen added.

Deanna sat down. Frowned across the table at the actress. "Do you know they just arrested Rollie for Charlie's murder?"

Noreen blinked twice. "Yes, that's why I came, but how did you know he'd been arrested?" she asked, dropping all pretense. "I was going to ask for Joseph's, Mr. Ballard's, help. I know he is acquainted with the sergeant on the case."

Deanna looked around for Orrin; found him and Elspeth standing along the far wall, watching the two seated women. It made Deanna smile inside. "Orrin, where is Joe? Do you know when he's planning to return?"

Orrin pushed away from the wall. Wiped his hands on his trousers. "He's down with one of them theater people looking at some contraption they used in the play. He didn't say when he was coming back. But you know how he is, miss."

Deanna nodded. Joe in the thralls of scientific discovery could forget all time. Should they all trek over to Judge Grantham's cottage and demand entrance?

"But he's been gone for a while now, so I expect he'll be coming along shortly." Orrin looked at the door as if he were expecting—praying?—for Joe to enter.

"It's all right, Orrin. We'll wait, if that's amenable to you."

Orrin cut a look to his sister.

"She's asking if we can stay."

Deanna caught the glint of Noreen's smile before she erased it.

"Oh sure, miss. Though it's kind of a mess right now. We're having a little problem with the delivery system."

Noreen leaned forward across the table. "How do you know about Rollie? Do you know that policeman, too? What did he say?"

In for a penny . . . "I didn't see the police, but I was on my way to the boardinghouse when I saw the police wagon take someone away. Talia said it was Rollie."

"Why were you going there? What business do you have there?" Noreen's voice was suddenly shrill even though she was attempting to keep it calm.

"I was looking for you."

Joe left Obadiah in the pub after having bought him a couple of beers. It was too early for Joe to drink; he had plans for the afternoon's work. But he drank anyway to be polite, and he was feeling slightly light-headed and close to euphoric when he burst into the warehouse.

"Orrin, I've just had a brill—" He stopped in his tracks. Either that second beer had been stronger than he imagined or there were two ladies taking tea in his kitchen, such that it was.

He shook his head to clear it.

They were still there. Deanna and Noreen.

"Mr. Joe! Joseph! Joe!"

Joe held up both hands, one of which was still clutching the piece of paper he'd used to jot down the ideas for a continuous loading-unloading system he'd had during his second beer.

He snatched it down. "What?"

"I didn't know what to do, Mr. Joe."

"It's about time you got here—Miss Deanna having to sit with the likes of her."

"You said you were interested in helping. They've arrested one of our company."

"Joe, I know that Amabelle didn't kill Charlie."

"Well, Rollie didn't kill him, either."

"Well, somebody did. We'll just have to keep looking."

"Are you going to tell him?"

"No, and you had better not say anything, either."

"Mr. Joe, do something."

"Mr. Joseph! Have you been drinking? And here it is, not even two o'clock."

"Two o'clock? Oh no. Elspeth, Gran Gwen will be wondering where we are."

"Yes, miss."

"Joseph, please, Rollie can't stay in jail. He's too, too . . . can't you speak with your police friend?"

"Stop!" Joe held up both hands, though he was more inclined to put them over his ears. "What we need here is some order. First, as much as I'm flattered to have two lovely ladies in my . . . uh . . . parlor." Joe grinned at that. His parlor was the same as his kitchen and dining room, an area framed off from the rest of the warehouse that served as his workshop.

"Joe!"

Dee's exasperated voice brought him back to the seriousness of the situation.

"One at a time, and Orrin, could you put on some coffee? Something tells me I'll need all my wits about me."

"Hmmph," Elspeth said. "I'd better do it. And I'm making it strong, too." She turned away from him, and Joe pulled up the last stool, the one with the uneven legs, and sat down at the table.

"Now, what's happened?"

Both women just looked at him. Only Elspeth clattering pots and crockery at the sink broke the silence.

Joe tried to keep his patience, though he really just wanted to draw up more precise plans for his sketches and start applying them to the bagging machine. If he could work out the logistics, it would unlock dozen of ways to use the mechanism.

"First of all, they've arrested Rollie for murdering poor Charlie," Dee said.

"And who is Rollie?"

"He's one of the actors."

"He's a dear boy who wouldn't hurt anyone. I've even left Letty with him." Noreen turned to Deanna. "Letty's my daughter. She adores him. He adored Charlie, showed him the ropes. He wouldn't hurt him."

"Then why has he been arrested?" Joe asked.

"We have no idea except that—oh, it must be Edwin, he said he'd do anything to get the company back to work. I don't want to think he'd turn in one of his own, but you can't really blame him for trying." Noreen stood suddenly. "I'm going to confront him. I should have done that as soon as they arrested Rollie."

"You were there when the police came?" Joe asked.

"Yes," Noreen said. "As soon as I realized what was happening, I came here. I knew you would have more sway with the police than any of us."

"So how did you get here?" Joe asked Dee.

"I . . ." She glanced at Noreen, and Joe caught the slight movement of Noreen's head. He cut his eyes back to Dee.

"What's going on?"

"Nothing."

"Something. Dee, you're a terrible liar."

"I am not. I mean, I'm not lying."

"Do leave her alone, Joseph. Deanna had come to see me at the boardinghouse and she saw them take Rollie away and came here to tell you. Now, enough talking. We need to act."

"Are you sure you're not already acting?"

Noreen glared at him. "Obviously I was mistaken to take you at your word. I'm sorry to have bothered you." She picked up her purse. Nodded to Orrin, who was just bringing Joe's coffee. "Thank you for the tea. I won't be bothering you again."

Joe groaned. "God spare me from volatile women."

Noreen's step didn't falter as she reached the door.

"Noreen, come back. I'm sorry. Tell me everything." He caught sight of Dee's expression. God only knew what she thought about Noreen and him. "You, too, Dee. My apologies."

Noreen reluctantly returned to the table.

Joe gave one last glance at his sketches and called Orrin over. "Will you please go to the police station and ask Sergeant Hennessey to join us? And ask him to first call Bonheur and tell my grandmother that Dee is with me. For my sins. And I'll bring her home in time for dinner."

"Yes, sir."

"I'll go, too, miss. If that's all right. Keep him from mucking about and wasting time."

"Of course, Elspeth," Deanna said.

"I wouldn't do that," Orrin groused.

"Mucking about," his sister repeated.

Noreen chuckled. "If the situation weren't so dire I would be enjoying the interaction between the two of them. Great character studies."

That got a frown from Orrin *and* Elspeth before she shoved him out the door.

Joe drank his coffee and hoped Will was available and got there soon.

He was in luck. Will stepped in ten minutes later.

If the room had dropped into an uneasy silence while they waited, it erupted again into a babel of voices. Dee's and Noreen's, mainly. Joe just sat back to wait for them to wind down.

Will looked a little nonplussed. Joe offered him the rickety stool and went to drag a crate from the storage room to sit on. This might turn into a long afternoon.

The flow of questions, demands, and wringing of hands cut off immediately when Will reached inside his coat and pulled out his notebook and pencil stub.

"Now, which one of you ladies would like to begin?"

Noreen and Dee looked at each other, and Joe wondered how two women who had barely met and who already disliked each other could so quickly become allies. Some things about women were unfathomable.

While they were waiting, Will said, "I called Gran Gwen. She says she won't ask and to bring the whole lot of us home with you for dinner. I thanked her for myself but I'm on duty, where I'll probably stay until this is over."

"Firstly," Noreen said. Somehow, without speaking, the two women had decided on Noreen taking the lead. "Why did you arrest Rollie?"

Will consulted his notes. "That would be Roland Gibbs."

"Yes."

"I'm not at liberty to say."

Noreen looked taken aback. "Why not? You were at liberty to arrest him. Or can you not tell us because you drew straws and he came up with the short one?"

Will's jaw tightened, but before Joe could intervene, Dee did.

"What she means is do you have real evidence against him, or did someone rat him out?"

Will sputtered. "Dee, really. I mean, Miss Randolph."

Joe thought Dee looked rather proud of herself. He could tell Noreen was impressed at the way Dee had disconcerted Will and was not at all shocked at Dee's use of dime thriller vocabulary.

"Well, I think it's a valid question," Dee said, blushing slightly.

"Please, Sergeant," Noreen said, leaning forward. "Rollie did not kill Charlie. I know he didn't."

"Can you prove this?"

Noreen hesitated, and Joe knew she couldn't.

"No, can you prove he did?" She met Will's eyes. Hers were hard and Joe felt a pang of compassion for her, raising a child on her own, earning her own way, having no one to stick up for her but herself. "I didn't think so. And I'll go one step further. You received an anonymous tip, did you not?"

Will shifted slightly, but the short leg on the stool nearly dumped him onto the floor.

"You did," Noreen said triumphantly. "Well, I can disabuse you of the veracity of that. It was from Edwin Stevens, our company manager."

"And did you see the note?" Will asked.

She hesitated. "No. But I did hear him say he would do anything to get us back to New York."

"I will certainly be talking to Mr. Stevens about this. And do you happen to know the whereabouts of Miss Amabelle Deeks?"

Noreen and Dee avoided looking at each other so completely that Joe knew at once that one if not both of them knew where Belle was.

"She's not dead?" Will asked.

But if Will thought he could fluster Dee, he was wrong. She didn't blink, and Joe couldn't help but be impressed by her discipline, even though he knew it was wrongheaded. She would soon be able to hold her own in any ballroom or dinner party or with a husband. He just hoped she found someone who could respect her and encourage her.

"Ladies," Joe said, "Sergeant Hennessey cannot help Rollie or Belle if you don't confide in him."

This earned him a sardonic look from Noreen. She turned to Will. "Tell me what the anonymous note said."

"I'm not at liberty . . ."

"Then neither am I."

"Nor I," Dee added for good measure.

Will gave her such a look that Joe was afraid he was going to say, "Now listen here, young lady," and that would be such a setdown and such a shame.

Joe stepped in. "Would it compromise your investigation to tell us what the note said?"

Will's Adam's apple worked. Dammit, why didn't he just say yes and be done with it?

But he looked from Noreen to Deanna and back again.

"Shall I guess what it said?"

"No," Will blurted.

"So it *is* that." Noreen looked at Deanna. "They're afraid of sullying your ears with the truth, my dear."

When did Dee become her "my dear"? Joe wondered. And what truth were they talking about?

Dee looked first to Noreen then to him, looking resigned that she would be sent from the room like a naughty child.

"Really, how long are you going to clip this one's wings?" Noreen asked. "Can't you see she's not made for the idle life of drawing rooms and ballrooms? If she isn't given a chance to spread her wings, she *will* fly, like Amabelle, to join the theater, the circus, or much worse. Would you have that?"

"What?" Will said, and drew back on the stool as if seeing better could make him understand what she was getting at.

"We're talking about murder, not about drawing rooms," Joe said in a last desperate effort to keep Dee innocent.

Noreen turned to Deanna. "We're talking, my dear, about men who love men."

―――∞◄█►∞―――

At first Deanna had no idea what Noreen was talking about. Then, as the heat rose to her face, she remembered Oscar Wilde and what Gran Gwen had told her. The trial talked about in whispers; that offhanded conversation at Chepstow. "Oscar never knew how to keep his private life private." The love that dares not speak its name. Gil's touch to Timothy's hair.

She swallowed. "I see." She took a breath. "And were Rollie and . . . and Charlie?" She didn't know what to ask. She wasn't even sure she knew how it worked. She wasn't all that sure of how it worked between married people.

"Not Rollie," Noreen said. "So if the note called him that, they don't know us. And it's just a piece of malicious mischief."

"But Charles Withrop."

Noreen took a deep breath. "He's dead so I don't suppose it matters now. But yes."

"But he was engaged to Belle," Dee said.

"Yes," Noreen said.

Dee didn't ask for elucidation. She'd have to get that from Grandmère as soon as she got home.

"Perhaps we could discuss this further . . . later," Will suggested.

"You can discuss it whenever you please. Right now, I have to make certain my belongings are getting moved to wherever we'll be staying next. And that the mean-spirited Mrs. Calpini hasn't tossed them to the street."

Dee grabbed her wrist. "And—"

"All of my belongings," Noreen told her.

Joe stood. "Why don't we all repair to Bonheur? I'll hire a hack and we'll stop by your boardinghouse on the way. Will can remain on duty and continue his questioning over food."

Will cut a severe look to Noreen. "Before you bother to ask, yes, Miss Adams. I do request your presence. I'll be sure that you get to your new lodgings safely afterward."

Noreen opened her mouth.

"Or you can go to the hotel and you and your group can sit there until we're satisfied that we have the correct killer or find another." Will finished with a slight shrug, which said he didn't much care.

Noreen didn't answer. "Good," Joe said. "Now we can all have a proper dinner. Orrin, you can come, too."

"Thank you, sir," Orrin said from where he'd practically crammed himself into a corner. "But I'll just go on home if that's all right."

"Of course."

"Not me," Elspeth said. "I go with my mistress."

"Naturally," Joe said in his most pompous voice.

"Very well," Will said. "But I'll meet you there."

"And I have my bicycle," Dee said.

"I'll bring it to you tomorrow," Joe said.

"I may need it before then."

"Very well, I'll hire a hack for the three ladies and I'll ride Dee's bicycle to Bonheur."

"Don't let it get scratched," Dee instructed him.

"I won't."

"Very well." Dee smiled smugly.

Joe left to hail a cab. When it arrived at the door of the warehouse, Dee, Elspeth, and Noreen climbed in, and Joe gave the driver directions to Mrs. Calpini's boardinghouse.

"I'm not going to tell your sergeant anything until you tell me where Amabelle is," Noreen said as the cab clattered down the cobbled street.

"Why?" Deanna asked.

Noreen glanced at Elspeth.

"Don't look at me that way," Elspeth said. "I'm true-blue."

"She is," Deanna added.

"I don't think Edwin would accuse Rollie of what the note accuses him of, even to get us out of Newport and back to work."

"You said he would do anything to get them to let you all go."

"But not that. It casts a pall over the whole company, casts aspersions on everyone's personal lives. He wouldn't do that."

"Who would?"

"That's what I don't know. And that's why I think we need to warn Belle. You have to tell me where she is."

"What are you going to warn her about?"

"That they're looking for her—the police."

"She knows that," Deanna said. "That's why she's in hiding." And there was the subject of the diamonds. Though Deanna had remedied that situation. "I think once the killer is caught, Belle will no longer need to hide."

Noreen sighed. "You have no idea."

"Did Charlie love women, too?"

"Possibly, I never discussed either with him. It isn't something you discuss. One is bad manners and the other is illegal."

"Then I don't think you should be discussing things like that now," Elspeth interjected. "Begging your pardon."

"Quite an inappropriate subject for ladies, Elspeth, is it?"

"Yes, miss—Madame." Elspeth beetled her eyes at Noreen. Deanna could tell she didn't approve of the actress.

"Did you mean what you said about me not being fit for a ballroom?" Deanna asked.

"You misheard me. It has nothing to do with whether you are fit or not, though I'm sure you've been a smashing success during the season. What I said and meant was you weren't made for the ballroom. Society doesn't inspire you, challenge you, nor even interest you, does it?"

Deanna didn't answer at first. Her mother would be crushed if she didn't make a good match and take a respected role among her peers. But Noreen was right. After a few short months Deanna had come to realize that she'd never be completely happy discussing menus with Cook or sitting morning after morning listening to the same gossip. "No, actually, it doesn't. But my mother—"

"I know. Look what poor Belle has endured. But to be cast off from one's family is no little sacrifice. I'm lucky that my mother accepted me and Letty back. Of course we aren't in the same class as you and Belle. And quite frankly, I'm glad of it."

The carriage came to a stop.

"Ah, we're here," Noreen said. "I won't be but a minute." She started to alight.

"Shall Elspeth and I come with you? Elspeth is a whiz at packing. And I can help with Belle's things."

"You two stay with the hack and make certain he doesn't leave us stranded. After years in the theater I'm also rather a whiz at packing. I'll only be a moment." Noreen hurried up the walk to the boardinghouse and rang the bell. The door opened and after a fair amount of conversation, the landlady let her inside and shut the door.

Chapter
17

Deanna kept her eye trained on the front door of the boardinghouse. "Elspeth? Does it seem to you like Noreen's taking a long time?"

Elspeth screwed up her face. "Being an actress, she oughta be used to packing her own cases, like she said."

"She may be having to pack Belle's, too."

"Maybe, or maybe she's done a scarper."

"I think I'd just better go in and see."

"Shall I come with you, miss?"

"No, you stay here and make sure the cabbie doesn't leave us."

Deanna climbed down from the cab and walked briskly up the walk to the boardinghouse, where she knocked firmly on the door. It took a while before the door opened and the landlady peered out at her. "You again. What do you want?"

"I was waiting for Noreen."

"Well, you won't find her here."

"Why, I just let her off at this very door."

"So you did and she just left by the back." The landlady laughed, shook her head, and started to close the door. Deanna stuck her foot in it just like Cad Metti would have done. Cad Metti was more Elspeth's style of detective, but desperate times . . .

The landlady looked so surprised that it worked.

"Where are the actors staying now that you kicked them out?"

"Well, I couldn't have murderers staying in my own house, now, could I?"

Deanna didn't give her opinion on innocent until proven guilty, so she merely said, "Where, please?"

"The Ocean House Hotel. That place used to be grand, but it's gone downhill. Don't get the clientele it useta get. Shame, and catering to actors now. What will happen next?"

"Thank you," Deanna said, and hurried back to the cab. "Ocean Hotel," she called to the cabbie, and climbed back inside.

"Scarpered?" Elspeth asked.

Deanna nodded. "I didn't think she would. I thought . . . oh well. At least we know where she's probably gone."

They set off down Bellevue to East Bowery Street, where the expansive Ocean House Hotel sat on the corner on a slight knoll. It was hard not to be impressed with the sheer immensity of the place, with its wide, columned porches, high-pitched roofs, and octagonal pergola.

"You're never going in there by yourself, miss. What if someone were to see you?"

Deanna sighed. "I'm so sick of always being worried about what people will think. You'll have to go and ask which rooms are theirs. But be careful that no one overhears you. We don't want them all 'doing a scarper.'"

"Yes, miss." Elspeth climbed down to the street and glared up at the cabbie. "You just make sure no one accosts my mistress while I'm gone."

"Well, ain't you an educated wench," he said, and settled back to wait.

She was gone and back in a few short minutes. "We're in luck. They're all on the side veranda having a 'meeting.' We can get there without having to go inside." She glared up at the cabbie. "We may be a while. So take a nap."

"I got—"

"My mistress will pay you handsomely if you wait." She shrugged. "Or nothing if you strand us here."

"Hey."

Deanna started to intercede but Elspeth was more than capable of handling the driver.

"Don't put yourselves out." The cabbie pushed his hat forward to shield his eyes and settled back to nap until they returned.

"This way," Elspeth said, avoiding an area crowded with what appeared to be traveling salesmen. She found a second set of steps. "Up here."

The acting troupe seemed to be assembled at the corner of the veranda. There had to be at least twenty-five people all crowded together, rather like cattle corralled by the porch rail. Several actors sat in lounge chairs or shoulder to shoulder on the edges of chaises, others had brought out wooden chairs that had been gathered closely together, while others stood. Though the voices were kept low, Deanna could tell long before they reached them that there was an argument going on. And in the midst of it was Noreen.

She was the first to see Deanna approach, and the group immediately became quiet. One by one they all turned to look at Deanna and Elspeth.

It was daunting, all that theatrical energy directed at her, but Deanna refused to be cowed.

"I wondered how long it would take you to find me," Noreen said, coming forward to meet her. Stop her? Turn her around and send her on her way?

"And you were much quicker than I'd hoped for. That Mrs. Calpini just couldn't keep her mouth shut. Well, no matter. You might as well meet the others."

"This is Deanna Randolph," Noreen announced.

"Some of us have already had the pleasure," Gil said. "What did you tell them that got Rollie arrested?"

"Nothing," Deanna said.

"That's just what I was about to tell you when Deanna made her entrance. There was an anonymous note."

"To the police?"

"None of us would do that."

"I don't believe it."

"It's a fabrication just so they'll have a suspect, and one with no friends in this godforsaken town."

Deanna wanted to tell them it wasn't how things were done here, but she couldn't. She'd heard this same conversation from the people who lived in the Fifth Ward who were servants and tradespeople. In this case, Deanna didn't think the police were protecting any of the rich people, but they might be looking for a scapegoat. Not Will, of course, but there were others . . .

"It accused Rollie of murdering Charlie?"

"Evidently," Noreen told them.

"What reason could they possibly name that would point to Rollie?"

"Not jealousy," Gil said. "He didn't care for Belle by half."

"Not Belle," Noreen said.

"Then what?" Timothy's expression changed as he watched Noreen. "What rot."

"It's vicious."

"And it's untrue."

No one had said it out loud but it seemed that everyone on the veranda knew what they were talking about—even Deanna. And everyone seemed to have the same opinion.

Timothy looked around the troupe. "Who would do such a thing?"

"Right on cue," Noreen said. She was looking past Deanna's shoulder, and Deanna turned to see Edwin Stevens striding toward the group.

"What's going on?" Edwin asked. "They said at the desk you were all out here. Has there been news? Have they let Rollie go?"

Timothy, fists raised, pushed past Noreen to confront him. "Tim, no."

"What the hell?" Edwin said, taking a step backward.

Noreen slipped in front of Timothy and stood between the two men. "Someone sent the police an anonymous letter accusing Rollie of murdering Charlie out of jealousy."

Edwin snorted. "Over Belle? He couldn't stand the girl."

Noreen shook her head. "Something quite different."

"What reason?"

"It doesn't matter what reason," Timothy said. "Was it you?"

Edwin's head snapped toward Timothy. "Me? Are you crazy? Why would I do something like that?"

"Because you said you'd do what you had to in order to get us out of here and back to work," Gil said, stepping next to Timothy.

"You did. We heard you," said another of the actors.

"We did, didn't we?"

"Yes."

They were getting louder, and a uniformed man stepped onto the veranda and looked sternly at the group.

Edwin held up both his hands as if he were warding off a mob. "I can't believe any of you—any of you—could think such a thing of me. I am sorely disheartened." He pressed one hand to his chest and lowered his head.

Deanna couldn't tell if he was acting or was really hurt.

"Then tell us you didn't."

Edwin snapped back to his forceful self. "Of course I didn't. How stupid do you think I am? Decimate my cast so I can take a ragtag group of folks back to the city only to not be able to fill all the roles in the play? Only to have to close the show and let all the employed actors go? Am I an idiot?"

"No, no," they assured him.

He'd won them over; he'd won Deanna over. The only two people who still looked skeptical were Timothy and Noreen.

"Maybe Rollie did kill Charlie and Belle," Talia said.

"Maybe he killed Belle," Gil said. "Lord knows she wasn't very nice to him. But not Charlie."

"He might," Talia said. "If Charlie tried to stop him, and he had to kill Charlie, too."

"Then where's Belle's body?"

"He threw it over the cliff."

"Talia, don't be absurd."

Elspeth rolled her eyes. "They're worse than we are, miss."

"Actors," Deanna said. "It's just like reading *Beadle's Weekly*, only in a play."

"Belle isn't dead," Timothy said.

Speculation stopped in a heartbeat, replaced by shocked silence, as slowly one by one the actors all turned to face Timothy.

Only Deanna and Elspeth exchanged glances of their own.

Elspeth stood on tiptoe and whispered, "I thought she said no one knew where she was."

"Shh." Elspeth was right. Belle had said she'd spoken to no one. To trust no one except Noreen.

"How do you know?" Talia asked. Her voice was more strident than it had been the first day Deanna had met her, and she wondered if the stress were overcoming her.

"I saw her. At least I think it was her."

"Why didn't you say something? Tell the police?" Noreen asked.

"I wasn't sure. And besides, we couldn't very well tell them why we were out at that hour."

"What hour?" Edwin Stevens asked.

Timothy looked at his hands. "It was this morning. Around six; the ferry had just come in from New York. I was . . . I'd been having a drink with some people and . . . the ferry let out, and across the street someone stepped out from a brick alcove. It looked just like Belle, but her head was covered in some babushka and she was wearing an old Mother Hubbard dress. She started toward the crowd, then saw me and rushed away."

He took a breath, blew it out. "That's when I knew it was her. At least I'm pretty sure."

"Did you follow her?"

Timothy shook his head. "I knew Edwin would have my head. Truly, Edwin, the time just slipped away. It was just a few drinks." He looked beseechingly at Stevens.

Stevens just looked back at him, and slowly his face paled with anger. "Have I not warned you about this? I would fire you, but at this point I can't afford to lose anyone else. But . . ." He turned to face the group. "If anyone's actions cause any more damage to the reputation of this company . . .

"I'll tell you all what I've told you before, though sometimes I wonder why I bother. If you're going to make it in the theater, you have to have discipline.

"You can't go about carousing all night and be able to turn in a good performance. You can't drink and drug and go whoring and not have it affect your abilities. Look at the good actors that bad living destroyed." He lowered his voice.

"Look what just happened to Oscar Wilde. Now he's finished."

Deanna saw Timothy flinch, and Talia roused herself to smirk at him.

Noreen shot her a withering look. "And that goes for you women in the chorus, too. And don't look innocent." Her gaze held Talia's, before it broke and encompassed the others. "I know a good number of you were at that party after the performance. You complain that you don't make enough money, but you'll never get out of the chorus by taking up with randy men who will use you and spit you out like rancid milk when they're done with you."

"You should know." It was said barely above a whisper, but Noreen heard it and so did the others.

"You're right, Talia, but I pulled myself back up from the depths to get back to work. I don't plan to lose that, ever again."

Edwin turned on his heel. "And why are we discussing this with strangers about?"

"She's not exactly a stranger, Edwin." Noreen quickly explained how Charlie's body had been found at Bonheur and how Belle had run away, about locking Deanna in the linen closet and finally meeting at Joe's and being questioned by Will. What she didn't tell them was that Deanna knew where Belle was hiding.

"My goodness," Edwin said. "You have been busy. Have you ever thought about becoming an actress?"

"No, she hasn't," Elspeth said. "She's a lady and a detective."

Deanna cut her eyes to Elspeth.

"Well, we read about lady detectives," Elspeth amended. "Sorry, miss."

"Not exactly a fabrication," Noreen said. "And I think she may be able to help us. But we have to level with her."

Deanna was finding it hard to swallow, literally and figuratively. Her? A lady detective? Somehow it didn't seem so exciting an idea now.

"A lady detective, how swell. It sounds just like something out of a dime novel," Gil said.

Any other time Deanna would have enlightened him on the subject. There were several women detectives working at the Pinkerton agency, and many women spies still working even though the Civil War had been over for several decades.

"So how is that going to help us? Blame me or Tim or Talia or any of the others for the murder, because I bet she can't find her needle in her sewing box without her little maid here."

"She knows where Belle is hiding."

All eyes turned to Noreen, then Deanna.

"Where?"

"You have to tell us."

"She could be in danger."

"We'll make her tell."

Deanna began to seriously worry about her own safety.

"Quiet," Noreen said. "I already tried to get her to tell. But now that I've had time to think about it, I don't think she should tell. Not anyone, including us and the police."

"Why?"

"Because if Rollie didn't kill Charlie—and I think we can be assured that he didn't—and Belle didn't kill Charlie—"

"She would never."

"Never," echoed around the group, except for Talia, who remained tight-lipped and frowning daggers at Noreen.

"Then," Noreen continued, "the murderer is still out there. And he—or she—may be planning to kill Belle next. Or even one of us."

Joe turned from the mantel and walked back to the drinks table, a path that he'd been treading for the past twenty minutes. He should have insisted on going with Noreen and Dee in the cab. No telling what they would concoct alone together. "It shouldn't be taking this long to pack up a few belongings and come to Bonheur."

Will sat with a glass of whiskey at his elbow. "Gran Gwen? Is this an inordinate amount of time for a woman to spend packing?"

Gwen shrugged. "She's an actress. I imagine she's had

occasion more than once to throw her things into a case and climb out a hotel window to escape payment. Those tours are notorious for stranding actors in towns miles from anywhere and without a penny to their names."

"Does that mean yes?" Joe asked.

"Really, Joseph, your manners."

"Sorry, Grandmère, but . . ."

"I know, and if you're worried about Dee, I think you and Will should take a carriage and go look for them."

"You're worried, too."

"Not really, but there is possibly a killer loose out there. I would hate to be sitting here sipping sherry when Dee might be in danger. What would I tell her mother?"

"You might make light of this, but I think we should go."

Will was on his feet and they were headed to the door when the sound of a carriage stopped them. Joe hurried to the bay window and looked out. "It's them."

Will returned to his chair and picked up his glass. Joe went back to the mantelpiece and his own glass.

A few minutes later, Noreen and Deanna entered the parlor. Will stood; Joe faced the doorway.

"Sorry we took so long. We dropped Noreen's things off at the hotel on our way."

"Gran Gwen," Deanna said, "this is Noreen Adams."

Gran offered her hand. "Joseph has told me about you. I'm so happy that you've joined us."

Noreen barely hesitated before she extended her own hand. "Thank you, though I'm afraid this business has interfered with your evening at home."

"Nonsense, dinner will be served soon. You don't mind an early dinner, do you, Miss Adams?"

"No, not at all, but you really needn't include me. I've only come at the police sergeant's insistence."

"We're delighted to have you. Aren't we, Deanna?"

"Yes, and besides, I can't wait until after Will's interrogation to eat. I'm starving. I haven't had a thing since breakfast. And I'm sorry I didn't get back in time for luncheon and the afternoon drive, but I've been rather busy."

"I can imagine," Gwen said. "Joseph, pour Deanna and Miss Adams a sherry."

Since Gran Gwen refused to discuss investigations, arrests, or sordid news items at the table—bad for the digestion and a slap in the face to Cook—dinner was an enjoyable affair. Noreen was encouraged to talk about her work and her little girl. Stories of Joe, Will, and Deanna's brother, Bob, growing up on the island were recounted. As well as all the tricks they played on Deanna, incidents which were somewhat embarrassing to her, but the memories made it feel like happier times.

"I can tell they are all very fond of you," Noreen said to Deanna as they repaired upstairs after dinner. "I envy you that."

"Well, we were friends once. Then our fathers, Joe's and mine—decided we should get married. Consolidate the family fortunes."

"And you refused?"

Deanna shook her head. "I didn't have time to. Joe never even asked me, but moved to the Fifth Ward to his warehouse to work on his inventions."

"Oh dear, a humiliation?"

Deanna shrugged. "Only to my mother."

"Ah. Well, if you want him, I wouldn't give up. Men are . . . what am I saying? I have no idea. I made a terrible mess of things. But Joseph has a passion for his work, it's very clear."

"I know. Of that I'm a little jealous."

"Because you think he has no room for you?"

"Oh no. It's because I don't have an all-consuming passion myself."

Noreen broke into her throaty laugh. "I have no doubt that you will find one. Now we had better go back to face the music or they'll think we ran off again."

But when they came downstairs Gran Gwen was sitting alone in the conservatory.

Deanna couldn't repress a shudder as she and Noreen walked down the carpeted flagstone to where she was sitting in a high-back chair.

"Joseph and William are outside. I suspect Will has taken up a pipe and Joseph insisted that he show him the terrain that was searched the other morning. So we're quite at our leisure for a bit. However, they fully intend on talking with you both, which Will said very sternly, so shall I assume you have knowledge they don't and are refusing to tell them?"

"Yes, Gran Gwen." Deanna glanced at Noreen. "At least I do, but I promised not to tell. But I did manage to retrieve these. She pulled out the handkerchief that she had tied the earrings into and untied it before presenting it to Gran Gwen.

"My, my. Where on earth did you find these?" Gwen glanced at Deanna. "Or is that one of the things you promised not to tell?"

"Yes, but she's sorry. She says she was desperate."

Noreen leaned over to see what was in the handkerchief. "They're real?"

"Yes," Gwen said. "And of much sentimental value."

"Oh, Gran Gwen. I'm in such a fix. Will is going to ask me all sorts of questions that I promised not to tell."

Noreen nodded. She looked from Deanna to Gwen. "I don't think any of us realized . . . I still don't understand what happened."

"Neither do we," Will said, striding into the room from the outside. Joe was right behind him.

Deanna noticed that Gran Gwen quickly folded the handkerchief and held it in her lap.

"Well, gentlemen, did you find any elucidating evidence that you missed before?" Gwen asked.

Chapter
18

"No," Will said, sitting down. "Not that I expected to. We made a thorough search that morning. Found nothing then. More of the same tonight."

"You'd expect to find churned-up sod," Deanna added.

Will gave her a tired look. "Have you been mucking about in my crime scene?" He shrugged. "You're correct. I don't think there was a struggle. My theory is, someone sneaked up on the victim when he was standing in the trees. On Saturday morning you could see where heels had been pulled across the lawn. The marks are gone now." He smiled fleetingly at Gran Gwen. "Thanks to the diligence of the Bonheur gardeners."

"Oh, I am sorry, Will," Gwen said. "I didn't think to tell them not to work."

"Not at all. We had finished up there."

"But did you find a murder weapon?" Deanna asked.

Will shook his head. "I shouldn't be discussing this, but

they have a suspect in custody, and they're ready to write off Amabelle Deeks as missing or dead."

"Why? Just because—" Deanna bit off the next words.

"Just because what?"

"Just because she isn't here to defend herself."

"She really needs to do that. Because if she is alive and she's deliberately hiding out, she'll be in big trouble. Might even go to prison."

"Stop it," Noreen snapped.

Deanna held her breath. *Don't tell. Don't tell.*

"Those third-degree tactics don't become you, sergeant."

Will threw up his hands, stood up, and walked halfway across the room. "If you think this is the third degree, you're mightily mistaken. And I'm only trying to help your friend. Pretty soon it's going to be out of my hands. And the powers that be will railroad your friend Rollie right to prison. And they will make certain that a few choice inmates know exactly what he is."

Deanna stopped breathing halfway through his tirade. She'd never, ever, seen Will lose his temper like this before.

"You don't know what you're talking about," said Noreen. "And you're just like the rest, picking out the weakest in the herd and bullying them until they agree to anything you say. All this talk about wanting to help—ha! You just want to save your own—" She clamped a hand over her mouth. Turned to Gran Gwen. "I beg your pardon. I forget myself. Thank you for your hospitality, but I really must end the evening now."

She stood, bowed slightly toward Gwen, and walked toward the archway.

Joe had risen automatically.

Will clapped his hands. Once. Making both Gwen and

Deanna jump. Twice. Three times. Slowly. methodically. Each sound echoing to silence. "Very dramatic."

Noreen had reached the archway; she turned around. "You disgust me!"

Deanna blinked, looked at Will. He looked stunned.

"She's leaving," Joe said.

"Well, see to it that Carlisle has the carriage brought round," Gwen said.

Joe hesitated. Looked at Will, then followed Noreen out.

"I'd better . . ." Deanna hurried after him. She was barely aware of Will beginning to apologize to Gran Gwen.

Noreen was standing in the drive, Joe at her side, both mute.

He gave Deanna an anguished look. "The carriage is coming round from the stable."

Deanna nodded. "We'll be fine."

Joe practically fled back inside.

Deanna didn't know quite what to do. She'd been taught never to show excess emotions, to always be in control, to look the other way when necessary. But this—her heart was pounding, just like she'd actually felt Noreen's anger herself. And her hurt.

Deanna came to stand beside her. "Are you all right?"

Noreen wiped beneath her eyes, neatly using two fingers, and Deanna thought it must be a technique for not messing up stage makeup.

"Noreen?"

Noreen cut her a sideways glance. Took a deep breath. "I got a little carried away. Sometimes that happens, something hits a little place inside that you've neatly hidden away. It makes for good theater but, whew! I'll have to apologize to your sergeant, but not tonight.

"Though I must say, I didn't expect that attitude from him

for some reason. And it gave me a perfect excuse to take over the scene." She turned to Deanna and smiled. "I think you should just go upstairs and not talk to them tonight. It will give me time to see if I can find out anything more from the others. Then you can either warn Belle or turn her in."

"And you?"

"If they drag me screaming from my bed tonight . . ." She smiled, but wanly. "I'll expect you to come pay my bail."

"I will, but I'm going to tell Belle that she has to turn herself in or I will."

The carriage came through the gates and stopped at the entrance.

Noreen climbed in. "Do what you must, and thank Gwendolyn for the lovely dinner. Please tell her I'm very sorry for my bad manners."

"Don't worry, when Joe and I fight, she always says she enjoys a good squabble."

Noreen chuckled, and the carriage drove away.

Deanna turned back to the house. She was confused about what she should do. Was she shielding a murderer? But hadn't they already decided that the killer must have dragged Charlie's body across the lawn to the house? Belle couldn't have done that.

She didn't know how she was to get upstairs without being called out. Joe was probably standing just inside the door, she thought, but he wasn't, and she climbed the stairs without interruption.

As soon as she was in her room, she called for Elspeth.

She was breathing hard when she came into Deanna's room. "I was in the kitchen. What's the matter? Are you ill?"

Deanna shook her head. "There was such a scene."

"Oh, miss. Have you and Mr. Joseph been going tooth and nail again?"

"No. Noreen and Will."

Elspeth's mouth dropped open. "In front of everybody?"

"In the parlor after dinner. She went from charming to outraged in the blink of an eye. She stood there, framed in the archway like a painting, mesmerizing us all . . . *The Wrath of the Valkyrie Queen.*"

"Huh?"

"Then she stormed out and Joe ran after her to call for the carriage. Will just stood there."

"What was she so upset by?"

"I'm not sure. Will kind of threatened her. I've never seen that side of him before."

"Probably because you've never seen him putting the kibosh on anybody."

Deanna shrugged. "I think it really upset her, but by the time I went out to see about her, she'd mostly recovered and acted like it was all an act to disrupt the questioning. She told me to come upstairs instead of going back into the parlor."

"She was working them."

"Yes, but I think part of it was real. Like she . . . I don't know. Like she started out acting and it turned into something else."

"Huh."

Deanna sank into the slipper chair by the window. "I don't know what to do. Noreen said to wait and she'd try to learn more from the others, but I don't know. I'm withholding evidence."

"Well, we don't exactly know that Belle is evidence. You said that she didn't even know poor Charlie was dead."

"So she said."

"She also said she would be okay. Soon. It was like she knew she could get help."

"I hope she wasn't counting on that Rollie fella. She'll have a long wait if she was."

"If she was, what was she doing at the docks? Timothy said he saw her at the docks. He meant the wharf. Where the ferry comes in. Passengers were disembarking. What else is down there?"

"There are some establishments. Maybe she was scrounging for food."

"In the daylight, when hundreds of people are just arriving in town?"

Deanna nibbled on her thumbnail.

"Stop that."

Deanna put her hand down. "Why do you go to the ferry just when it arrives?"

"Maybe she was going to stow away?"

"I think she was meeting someone."

"Well, she didn't meet anybody, 'cause that actor Timothy said she ran when she saw him. Well, he said he *thought* he saw her. And you can't trust what any man who's been out carousing all night sees or says."

"Really," Deanna said. "It seems to me that a lot of men seem to go out carousing more than they stay home."

"I expect not like that Timothy goes out. Maybe Noreen will be able to get more out of him when he doesn't have an audience."

"Because he didn't trust us," Deanna said.

"That, and because I also suspect that he ain't saying anything to anybody about where he was. Not if he doesn't want to end up in the cell next to Rollie."

"Him, too?"

"I don't know. I just know it goes on."

"Here in Newport?"

"In Newport, too."

There was a tap at the door.

Elspeth and Deanna exchanged looks. Elspeth went to answer it.

Gran Gwen stepped into the room. She looked very imperious to Deanna, who got a sick feeling in the pit of her stomach. She stood.

Gwen walked over and sat in the chair Deanna had just left. "Don't leave, Elspeth."

Elspeth, who had tiptoed halfway to the dressing room, stopped and reluctantly came back to stand before her.

"Now, sit down and tell me what you can, and we'll try to get us all out of this mess. Beginning with Noreen. Was that outburst real or feigned?"

Deanna told Gran Gwen what she had told Elspeth.

"Good actors," Gwen said, "can tap into those places of reality; that's what makes them great, and next to impossible to live with. She'll have a good career with a little luck. I wasn't sure."

"What about Will and Joe?"

"Oh, men, they never get these things, especially when they're handled by someone as accomplished as Noreen. Unfortunately, Will is under a lot of pressure."

"But it's only been a few days. He's good at what he does."

"And that's half the problem. He only proceeds on evidence or what can be deducted from the evidence. Facts. His superiors must tread a fine line between law and politics. Sometimes facts and evidence are the last things they are concerned with."

"And Mr. Edgerton is forcing them to arrest somebody?"

"Possibly. Why do you say that?"

"Because he threatened me at the Chepstow party."

"Threatened you? Surely you misunderstood him."

"I hope so. It was very uncomfortable."

"Why didn't you tell me?"

"I'd just tried to say something nice to his wife, to make her feel better after what those women said."

Gwen let out a guffaw of laughter, and Deanna felt the heat flood her cheeks.

"What on earth did you say?"

"That nobody listened to that kind of gossip and I thought their fete was lovely. She told me that I knew nothing about it. And then later Mr. Edgerton came up and told me to stay out of his family's business or he would make life rough for all of you. I've brought disgrace on us all." She just heard Elspeth's snort of derision before she burst into tears.

"Now, dear, you've haven't done a thing wrong. You're just learning how to live in society. Trust me, you are navigating it very well, and you're just beginning to develop the tough skin every lady needs, but won't admit to having, in order to stay on top of the game."

Deanna lifted her head just enough to see Gran Gwen's face.

"I insulted the Judge's daughter, failed to send out even one lure to a potential husband. I've ridden my bicycle against express orders from my mother, and I've lied to the police. Will will probably send me to jail, and then I will be a disgrace."

"I doubt if he will go that far. But I think you must deal with this. So first thing in the morning, we will go to wherever this silly child has been hiding and tell her we're turning her over to the police for her own protection. Then we'll tell Will. He is being pressured by the powers that be and you don't want to see him demoted because of something you didn't do."

Deanna shook her head.

"Good, then after breakfast, we'll take the carriage and go rendezvous with Amabelle Deeks. Now, don't give it another thought. Everything will turn out as it should. Will has left, Joe's working on his drawings, and there's nothing more we can do until tomorrow. Good night, dear. Elspeth."

Elspeth hurried to open the door for her. As soon as she closed it she said, "That Drusilla sounds like a right piece. Not very nice, they say."

"She's unhappy," Deanna said thoughtfully. "And who wouldn't be between her mother and father and her husband. I know I wouldn't want Walter Edgerton for a husband, though I shouldn't say so."

"Maybe he doesn't treat her right."

"He's very upright." Deanna turned around for Elspeth to undo her dress.

"Humph. Those kind are the ones that take a little on the side."

Deanna stepped out of the dress. "To listen to you, one would think that no husbands are faithful to their wives."

Elspeth gave her a look before she slipped a white lace–trimmed nightgown over Deanna's head. While Elspeth carried her gown to the dressing room to hang it up, Deanna sat down at the vanity and scrutinized herself in the mirror. She wondered what people thought when they saw her. What men thought.

Elspeth came out, crossed to the table, and began unpinning Deanna's hair. "I'm not saying this one does. But my ma says when a wife is so sour, her husband looks elsewhere for something sweet." Elspeth raised her eyebrows comically. "Like an actress, maybe."

Deanna raised her eyebrows back at her.

"Well, they're known for their loose morals."

"I know that's what people think," Deanna asked. "But do you think it's true?"

"Strutting about in all sorts of costumes, eating dinner in public restaurants at all hours, walking in the street alone at night; just a step above a professional streetwalker."

"Noreen said they aren't like that. That most are just hard-working people like everyone else. And Noreen certainly isn't like that. Is she?"

"She goes gallivanting around the country and leaves her baby with her mother? Does that sound natural to you?"

"I think it sounds like a necessity of her trade. Besides, they should have been home by now. If Will could just find the killer." Deanna reached for her sketching notebook. "Though I suppose I'm the one—what do they call it?—obstructing the investigation."

She turned the page to the sketch she made of Charlie, lying beneath the palm trees on the marble floor of the conservatory. She'd drawn it just as she had seen it, though she had to admit she left the broken skull a little vague. She even added the clods of dirt and grass on the heels of his shoes.

Her art teacher had told her mother that she had talent and she should send her to Paris to study. Her mother had nixed that, and her teacher had never mentioned it again. But Deanna knew she could reproduce images even after they were gone.

"Belle said she had planned to meet Charlie outside with

whatever she could steal. She went out but he didn't come." She turned the page and quickly sketched a girl standing on the grass.

"Where was he? Was he really late or had he decided not to come at all? No, that doesn't work. He was found in the house. Was he waiting in the trees—afraid to come out?"

She quickly sketched a standing male figure, drew a sweeping line for a tree, and hurriedly shaded the insides so that it hid most of the figure. "Why wouldn't he come out?"

"Chicken?" Elspeth guessed. She finished pulling the pins out of Deanna's hair and placed them in the pin case on the table. She picked up the silver-backed brush and began to brush out the carefully curled tresses.

"Maybe. Maybe he saw someone moving about in the house and decided it was too dangerous. But why not get her attention and have her come to him? *Psst, Belle, over here!*" Deanna said in an urgent whisper. "Why didn't he go to her?"

"I don't know."

"Will said that the theory is, someone dragged him across the lawn to the conservatory. Charlie is a pretty tall guy. Belle wouldn't be able to drag him across the lawn, over the stone patio, and into the conservatory.

"There must have been another person there." She flipped back to the sketch she'd just made, and added a shadowy figure on the other side of the page. "Maybe he couldn't go to her or get her to come to him because he knew he was being watched."

Elspeth sat down and tapped the brush to her chin. "Could have been that Rollie fella they already got in jail."

"But that's only because of the anonymous note. They don't have any proof."

"That we know of," Elspeth said.

Deanna gave her an exasperated look. "Besides, Rollie's half the size of Charlie. If you're going to kill somebody, why not do it in a convenient spot where it's easy to get rid of the body? Not drag it into someone's house and carefully arrange it on the floor of their conservatory. Why would someone do that?"

Elspeth shook her head. "Just plain crazy, I guess." She put the brush away and began braiding Deanna's hair.

"Maybe to leave a message."

"What kind of message, miss?"

"Something the killer left for Belle to see. But why?"

"If you ask me, that's specu—just plain guessing."

"Seems like that's all we have." Deanna picked up the copy of Loveday Brooke, put it down again. "I know one thing. First thing tomorrow we're going to convince Belle to give herself up."

∞•◦◖◗◦•∞

In spite of her resolution, Deanna spent a restless night. Her conscience was bothering her. She knew she was wrong not to confide in Will, and around daybreak her guilt turned into fear as her imagination took off, and she wondered if Belle was in danger or if she would be dead by the time Deanna got to her.

She could hardly wait to make it through breakfast so she could return to the Deeks house and tell Belle her time was up, that she was going to the police to tell them where she was.

But she knew things would not go as planned the moment she stepped into the breakfast room and found Laurette and her husband sitting at the table. Laurette was explaining something to Gwen, but she broke off when Deanna entered the room.

Deanna forced a smile. "I didn't think to see you before tomorrow."

"We just got off the ferry. I couldn't wait another minute to come home. I made Lionel come with me for a long weekend. I had to bribe him." She looked mischievously at her husband, who merely lifted his eyebrows and drank his coffee.

"And, by the way, thank you for . . ." Laurette lifted Gran Gwen's handkerchief holding the diamond earrings, just enough for Deanna to see them.

"Mama says we had to wait for you before we discussed this ghastly situation. Joe was here but his head is filled with cogs and electricity this morning. We sent him to work."

Well, that was one good thing, Deanna thought philosophically. At least she wouldn't have Joe glowering across the table at her and demanding she tell him where Belle was hiding. Still, she was anxious to get away.

"Any news to report?"

Deanna looked at Gwen.

"Things are progressing slowly," Gwen said.

"I heard that from the Judge himself."

"Oh?" Gwen put down her fork. "When did you see him?"

"As luck would have it, he was on the same ferry as us. He evidently had meant to return the day before, but work interfered and he ended up with us."

"Again," added her husband.

"Poor Lionel was forced to endure two ferry rides in one week with him. But we couldn't very well cut him."

"We read about his sentence in the newspaper," Gwen said. "Imprisonment for a poor half-wit. He didn't hurt anyone."

"So the defense lawyer said, according to the Judge. But

the jury brought back a guilty verdict and he had no choice but to abide by it, also according to the Judge."

"With twelve years' imprisonment or the insane asylum," Gwen said. "That's criminal."

Deanna forced bits of her breakfast down. She felt bad for the poor man, but wanted to get started. Unfortunately, she had already committed too many sins against etiquette as it was, to be rude this morning.

"If you ask me," Lionel said, "these reformists push their zeal into a kind of perversion."

"The Judge is bad enough, but that son-in-law . . ." Gwen said.

"Well, Edgerton knows what side his bread is buttered on. Though I'm not sure he practices all he preaches. But it's a difficult position, hanging on to someone else's coattails. So much so that he comes across as being even more moralistic than Grantham."

"Well," said Laurette, "I did find out something that probably has no bearing on the murder, but it does help explain the bad feelings between Rosalie and her daughter."

"Because she became an actress," Deanna said.

"Not at all. It's because she was not content to work hard and live within her means as an actress. Miss Amabelle Deeks took a lover and evidently a fairly rich one."

"Charlie?" Deanna said. "He can't be making that much more than she is."

"Well, it could be, I suppose, if he also happens to be independently wealthy. Whoever it is has set her up in an apartment on Fifth Avenue. It isn't public knowledge. Rosalie is mortified, of course. Her husband was furious. Is that any help to your investigation, Dee?"

"Mine? I'm not—" But she was.

"Well, someone should. We had a late supper with the Judge last night on the ferry. He is not happy with the way things are going. He's planning on going to the chief of police today and . . ." She lowered her voice. "He wants that girl found.

"He feels it besmirches his character to have his name associated with murder. And when I pointed out to him the murder actually took place at Bonheur, he had the gall to say, 'Thank God.'

"I told him we would call on Maude and Drusilla this morning, Mama. I hope you don't mind, but he's going to be putting a flea in the police department's ear all morning. And he's worried about her nerves."

Gwen snorted and put her napkin down. "Deanna and I had plans this morning. But perhaps we should divide and conquer."

Deanna frowned but said, "Certainly."

"I'm going to the reading room," Lionel announced, "where I will be the only one actually reading the papers, since I didn't get to read for the last two days because someone got to them before I did and made a complete mess of them." He smiled at his wife. "And where I won't be bothered until I come home in time for tea, a brief nap with my wife before dinner, and the Rensselaer ball."

Deanna had forgotten the ball. And she was already as tired as a post. If she wanted to get a nap in before dressing tonight, she'd better get a move on.

"I have a few errands I have to run," she said, looking directly at Gran Gwen.

Gwen didn't miss a beat. "Then take Elspeth with you. I'll have Carlisle bring the carriage around."

Deanna had wanted to take her bicycle because it was easier, faster, and she didn't have to worry about what the driver might think, but she needed Elspeth.

"I've been thinking about teaching Elspeth to ride a bicycle," Deanna said as she got up from the table. "Do you think that would be too avant-garde?"

"Certainly not," Laurette said. "Just think how much freedom you would have, and you could take your maid as chaperone. You could set a new trend."

"And send her mother into a spasm," Gwen reminded them.

"Exactly," Laurette said, and took a bite of toast.

Chapter

19

By the time the carriage came for Deanna and Elspeth twenty minutes later, Deanna was wild with worry.

She dismissed the coachman at the corner of Mrs. Deeks's street, though he tried to convince her to let him wait at the door.

They compromised by promising to meet him back at the corner in a half an hour.

They strolled down the opposite side of the street with Elspeth carrying a large shopping bag with a change of clothes from Deanna's wardrobe, some bread and cheese, and an old copy of *Beadle's*.

Elspeth kept reminding Deanna to look like a lady out taking the air, until Deanna wanted to pinch her. But finally they passed the house. A quick look around to make sure no one was about, and they quickly crossed the street and ducked past the shrubbery to the kitchen door.

Elspeth peered in the window next to the door and shook

her head. She turned the doorknob and the door wouldn't open. They walked around to the back, but the windows were too high to see in. Fortunately a milk box was sitting on the back stoop. Elspeth and Deanna dragged it over to the window.

They both straightened up and looked at each other across the milk box.

"Maybe it took two people to drag poor Charlie to the conservatory," Deanna said.

"That's what I was thinking." Elspeth climbed on the box, cupped her hands, and looked in. Jumped down and shook her head. "I don't see anybody. What if Lilbeth isn't here?"

"We have to get in that attic. I can't stand it any longer. I'm already in so much trouble."

Elspeth nodded and climbed back onto the milk box. She pushed at the window but it didn't budge; jumped down, and they dragged the box back to the porch.

"Now what?" Elspeth asked.

"I'm thinking."

"Well, think fast."

"We'll have to knock on the front door and hope she lets us in."

"And say what? *Sorry, but we need to search your attic for your niece, who we think might be a murderer?* It'd give the old girl a heart attack."

"No, I'll say I've come for a visit, and while I'm distracting her, you sneak past me and unlock the kitchen door. I'll meet you there as soon as I can get away."

"Oh, miss, you might give *me* the heart attack."

They walked around to the front door.

And froze when a carriage rattled past.

Elspeth tugged at Deanna's elbow. "Act natural."

Deanna nodded. They were virtually breaking into someone's house to abet a wanted person, and she was supposed to act natural. The mind boggled. "Let's get this over with."

She walked up the steps, motioned Elspeth to stand to the side out of sight, then rang the bell.

She was greeted with total silence. She tried again.

"Maybe it's broken," Elspeth said.

"It worked the other day." The door opened a crack. Mrs. Deeks's wrinkled face peered out at Deanna.

"What do you want?" She squinted her eyes in an effort to see better.

"I came to visit with you. I was here a few days ago with Gwendolyn Manon."

"Aha, the people looking for the little harlot."

Deanna bit her tongue. "Yes."

"Well, I haven't seen her."

"Well, I just came to visit. I thought you might like some company."

"Can't give you tea, the girl isn't here. Can't depend on servants these days, always taking off when you need 'em."

Deanna thought if Mrs. Deeks were a little nicer her servants might stay longer, but she didn't say so.

"You can come in and get my tin of cookies out. I can't manage the latch. Then you can take yourself off."

"I'd be happy to." Deanna glanced at Elspeth, who nodded, and Deanna stepped inside.

"Be sure to shut the door."

"I will. You just have a seat and I'll get your cookies." She slowly started to close the door while the old lady made her way into the parlor.

Deanna stuck her hand out and motioned to Elspeth, who slipped through the door. Deanna put a finger to her lips.

Elspeth gave her a look and melted into the shadows.

Deanna joined Mrs. Deeks in the parlor, took the cookies out of the cupboard, and lifted the lid.

She grabbed two greedily. "Do you know how to make tea?"

"Why no," Deanna said. She'd never been called on to make tea before.

"You girls, what do I hire you for?"

"I'm not your servant, Mrs. Deeks. I came for a visit."

"Well, I don't want any visitors. Take yourself off."

Thank you. Deanna could hardly hide her impatience to leave, though she doubted Mrs. Deeks could see that.

"But I'll keep the cookies." The old woman wrapped her arm around the tin.

"Well, do enjoy them. I'll see myself out. Good day." Deanna was sure she looked like a jack-in-the-box, popping up and down in a curtsey as she hurried to the door before Mrs. Deeks changed her mind.

A minute later she was at the back door. Elspeth let her in. "Hurry," Deanna said. "She's eating cookies, but she might decide to make a cup of tea. She asked me if I knew how."

"Ha," Elspeth said, remembering to whisper.

"You can show me later—let's go." Deanna led the way, peeking around the door to make sure no Mrs. Deeks awaited them in the hall. They silently sped to the back of the house and up the servants' staircase. Deanna was out of breath by the time they reached the attic door. She knocked. "Amabelle, it's Deanna."

Amabelle didn't come to the door.

"Belle, let me in."

Still no answer. Deanna turned the knob. Elspeth's smaller hand closed over the top of hers. "I'd better go in first, miss."

"Nonsense, she isn't dangerous." Deanna started to enter, but stopped. "But thank you, Elspeth." She stepped inside with Elspeth on her heels.

The attic was empty. Of people, anyway. The boxes and trunks stood mutely around the room, the pallet Belle had made for herself was gone, the table where Deanna had found the earrings was pushed back under the eave. The window was closed. There was no sign of anyone having been there.

"She's gone," Deanna said.

"Are you sure? Maybe she's exploring the house—she must be that bored—or using the facilities."

Deanna shook her head. "She had it fixed up like a sitting room, and she's put everything back."

"Do you think the coppers got her?"

"Maybe. But wouldn't Mrs. Deeks have said something if they descended on her house and dragged her grand-niece out to the police wagon?"

"I don't know. She thought you were the maid." Elspeth was obviously trying to hide a grin.

"Go on and laugh, but you're teaching me to make tea when this is all over. I never thought about it before, but I can't cook a thing. All those lessons in deportment and French and Italian and music and painting; the closest they come to telling you how to live is how to plan menus and give orders to the cook."

"Miss Deanna, could you please stop philo-philosophizing and take care of the problem at hand?"

"Sorry. Let's see. She must have left of her own will. If the police took her, they wouldn't have bothered to clean the room.

She didn't want anyone to know that she'd been here." Deanna looked around the room as if the answer lay in the dusty castoffs.

It didn't.

"Let's get out of here. I'll think better when I'm not petrified of getting caught."

"Good idea," Elspeth said. "And this time I will lead the way. I'm much better at sneaking around than you. And not because I sneak around on you. It's from playing with my brothers and sisters."

Elspeth marched across the floor and out the door, down the stairs. Deanna stopped only long enough to close the door, then followed closely behind her. Elspeth stopped at the second floor, listened. Motioned for Deanna to follow.

They were just reaching the first floor and were moving quickly but quietly toward the kitchen, when there was a banging at the front door. Both girls froze, then Elspeth yanked Deanna into the butler's pantry. She put her fingers to her lips, pointed to the floor. She wanted Deanna to stay put. Deanna nodded.

Elspeth peered around the kitchen door, looked both ways, then hurried across the room to stand on tiptoe and look out the window. She made a frantic motion for Deanna to come. By the time Deanna reached her, she had the back door open and was looking back and forth. Then she pulled Deanna out the door, pausing only long enough to close it, and they sprinted across the lawn to the safety of the shrubbery.

They watched from the bushes, eyes and ears alert. It was the police. They had found out about Mrs. Deeks. And they were too late.

"Do you see Will Hennessey?" Deanna asked, craning her neck around the bushes.

"No. What are we going to do? They might arrest us."

Deanna thought they might, too. She was in such hot water. "We have to get farther away," Deanna said. She looked around. "Maybe we can cut through to the next street."

"Somebody will see us and have us arrested for trespassing," Elspeth said.

"Do you have a better idea?"

"No."

They moved along the shrubbery until they got to the next property line. One of the houses was fenced in by a wrought-iron railing, the other was open.

"Act like we belong here," Deanna said.

She walked ahead, Elspeth a couple of paces behind her, at a slow stroll. It was the hardest thing Deanna could remember doing.

They managed to reach the far street without mishap.

"If anyone stops us now, it will be their word against ours." Deanna grabbed Elspeth's elbow and they hurried to the corner, hoping that the carriage would be nearby.

"There it is. Bless Jasper, he deserves a medal."

"He'd probably rather have a big tip," Elspeth huffed, following after her.

"Which he shall get," Deanna said. She stopped below the coachman. "Jasper, I have a few errands to run. Do you know if they were planning to use the carriage this afternoon?"

"I don't know, miss. But I'm sure they wouldn't mind you doing your errands. There are other carriages."

"Thank you. Next stop is the Ocean Hotel."

Jasper's eyes widened slightly at that, but he merely said, "Yes, miss."

They arrived at the hotel a few minutes later only to be told that Noreen Adams was out, in fact all the actors were out. And they would be checking out the next day.

"They're leaving?" Deanna asked the concierge.

"Yes, miss."

"Thank you."

"You might check at the Casino, miss. That's where they've been rehearsing."

"I will." She hurried down the hotel steps, Elspeth right behind. "The Casino, please, Jasper. We've not a minute to spare."

"Why are we in such a rush, miss?" Elspeth asked, holding on to the edge of the carriage as it sped away.

"If they're really leaving tomorrow, it can only mean one of two things: That they've cleared Rollie's name and have another suspect in custody. Or they're leaving Rollie as the scapegoat."

"Do you think the police found Miss Belle?"

"No, I don't, but it's time she stops hiding and tells them what she knows."

It took eons before Jasper pulled up in front of the Casino.

"We may be a while."

"Yes, miss."

Deanna went straight to the entrance of the theater. When she tried the door she was surprised to find it unlocked. She and Elspeth slipped inside, careful not to make a sound. Crossed the foyer and slipped into the auditorium. The house-lights were lit, but no one seemed to notice when they sat in the back row.

"It's beautiful, miss."

"You've never been?"

Elspeth shook her head.

Deanna looked around, trying to see it through Elspeth's

eyes, and it was impressive, all gilt-edged ivory with a sky blue ceiling dotted with gold stars.

But today she had no use for the theater's magic. She had to find Amabelle Deeks and turn her in to Will.

The actors were onstage, but wearing their normal clothes. A piano had been pulled off to the side, and a man was accompanying a trio of singers in what Deanna recognized as "Three Little Maids from School."

They must be presenting Gilbert and Sullivan when they returned to New York. *Tomorrow*, she thought. Had Belle returned to the fold? Were they hiding her now?

Edwin Stevens stood at the front of the stage, moving the members of the trio around like pawns on a chessboard. One of the singers was Talia, but Deanna didn't see Noreen anywhere.

She looked around the audience. Several of the actors were sitting in the first rows, watching the rehearsal. Deanna perused the backs of their heads and decided Noreen wasn't among them.

She might be backstage, but Deanna wasn't even sure how one found the backstage. The door opened behind them, and she turned to see Jacob Mersey come in and stand at the head of the aisle.

Elspeth tugged at Deanna's sleeve. "Who is that?"

"The man who owns the yacht where the party was held. The one Belle escaped from."

Elspeth nodded wisely. "He looks like a villain," she whispered.

In the uneven light, he did look a bit sinister, tall with dark, lank hair and a drooping mustache. A perfect villain from a melodrama. Deanna knew he was a reprobate from Gran Gwen. And that he used women ignominiously from Laurette.

He was looking toward the stage but suddenly turned toward Deanna and Elspeth. Deanna and Elspeth slipped down in their seats. They barely breathed as he walked past them down the aisle toward the stage.

He paused briefly and looked over the row of actors, then turned and went through a door on the left side of the stage.

Deanna and Elspeth exchanged looks. Elspeth started to get up. Deanna stopped her. "Stay here in case I miss Noreen while I'm backstage. If she starts to leave, tell her to wait for me."

Elspeth shook her head.

"I'll be fine," Deanna whispered.

Elspeth gave her the evil eye.

"Promise." She tiptoed down the side aisle of the theater, found the door Mersey had used, and pushed her way in. She was in a hallway that ran down the side of the stage. Several doors led off from it, and Deanna surmised these were dressing rooms.

She walked slowly by each one until she heard voices. One was Mersey's, and he sounded very angry.

Deanna crept forward to hear better, staying close to one of the long velvet curtains that edged the stage. She could see Mersey's back as he stood at the door of one of the dressing rooms.

"Where is she? One of you must know."

No sound. Deanna wondered whom he was speaking to; possibly Noreen, since she hadn't seen her in the auditorium or onstage.

"We don't know."

That sounded like Timothy.

"And furthermore, we don't appreciate you bursting in here and making threats." Gil's voice.

"That little minx is causing me a huge amount of trouble. And if you don't tell me where she is, I'm going to pass that trouble along to you."

"We don't know where she is."

Deanna allowed herself to breathe. That was Noreen's voice. "In fact, we think she's dead. Killed by whomever killed Charlie."

"By your friend in jail?"

"Perhaps."

Deanna expected to hear Gil's and Timothy's hot denials, but no one said a word.

"I don't envy him if that's true," Mersey said. Mersey almost sounded frightened himself.

It was a gruesome thought. Rollie, a murderer; he would face execution if found guilty. But Belle wasn't dead. At least she hadn't been yesterday.

"If you see her, tell her I have a message for her. He reached into his breast pocket, leaned over out of Deanna's sight. Was he giving them a card?

"Sure thing," Gil said.

Mersey turned and strode back the way he'd come. Deanna just had time to press into the curtain before he passed. She stuck her head out, then walked into the dressing room. She reached the door just as Noreen was about to shut it.

"Where did you come from?" Noreen asked.

Deanna pulled her into the hallway. "From Mrs. Deeks's house. Belle is gone. And the police were arriving just as I was leaving. I barely got out in time. I was hoping she came here."

Noreen shook her head.

"Are you sure? Because she really needs to come forward and tell us what she knows."

"Maybe Belle really did kill him." Timothy stood in the doorway, looking angry and tragically handsome. The others stood around him, their faces forming a human nimbus. *St. Timothy, the Martyr.*

"Either way," Deanna said. "We need to find her."

"Well, you'll have to find her on your own, then. We're leaving in the morning," Timothy said. He stepped outside, moving the others back, and shut the door.

"What? The police are letting you leave? Have they closed the case?"

"Evidently they feel Rollie is a good enough suspect and they're letting us go. The crew is over at the fete theater, packing up costumes and sets to carry down to the ferry to Warwick in the morning. We'll all go by train to Manhattan."

"What about Belle?"

"Hang Belle," Noreen said. "She's the reason we're in this mess. And she won't even show up to do her part. An acting company is a family. You are loyal to the others and you have to depend on each other in order to be successful."

"And everyone feels Belle has betrayed them?"

Noreen nodded. "And is letting Rollie take the fall for something he didn't do."

Deanna was beginning to feel the same way. Belle had seemed truly frightened, but could be in a safe haven by now if she'd only stayed put like she'd promised.

Why had she run? And where was she?

"So I guess this is good-bye, not the way I would have preferred but . . . but I'll be glad to get home to my child. Tell your friend Joseph that it was a pleasure to meet him."

She smiled slightly, then opened the dressing room door and

went inside. The click of the door closing told Deanna she could expect no more help from Noreen or any of the other actors.

Deanna turned reluctantly away, and right into Elspeth.

"Let's go, miss. Miss Noreen's right. That Deeks girl has done a scarper. She didn't care enough about the others to face the music. I say we let her go."

Deanna nodded slowly. She didn't want to give up. Her own behavior had been reprehensible. She should have told Will where Belle was hiding the minute she found out.

Then Rollie wouldn't be in jail, deserted by his friends and fellow actors. And it was most likely too late to do anything but accept the responsibility for what had happened.

"Come on, I guess I'd better find Will and confess." She opened the door to the auditorium and started up the aisle.

Elspeth ran after her. "He won't arrest you, will he?"

Deanna shrugged. "I hope not." She kept walking. If she didn't stop, she wouldn't be tempted to go to Bonheur and try to forget the whole thing. She didn't slow down until she reached the foyer, then stepped outside to the street.

"Maybe we shouldn't tell him right yet, miss. I mean, how are we even gonna find him?"

"We'll just go down to the station and ask to see him."

"Do you even know where the police station is? What if he isn't there?"

"Well, Jasper will know, and you know, don't you?"

"You're not going down to that station with all the riffraff and thieves. And that's that." Elspeth stamped her foot to drive her point home. "You'll create such a scandal. Your mother will be very displeased."

She'd be more than that, thought Deanna. She'd probably

send Deanna to some kind of sanitarium in Switzerland—and leave her there forever.

"Well, we can't just stand here in the street. That *will* create a scandal. Ugh."

Elspeth nodded. "I wouldn't mind some lunch, and I'm sure Jasper would agree. We'd best go to Bonheur and let them call over to the station."

Deanna hesitated. She just wanted to get it over with. And she didn't want everyone at Bonheur to know. "No, I need to do this now."

"Maybe you could tell Mr. Joe and he could tell the sergeant."

"Joe will be even angrier than Will. I'd rather face Will."

"I think we should go ask Mr. Joe what to do . . . even if he does yell at you. At least he might give us some dinner."

Chapter

20

Orrin had been acting oddly all morning. They'd stopped for lunch and he'd hardly said a word.

Joe asked if he was feeling well. He said he was fine. So they finished lunch and went back to work.

They settled back into the familiar rhythm of inventor and apprentice. Joe giving instructions, or thinking out loud, with Orrin listening and learning and making astute observations.

But as the afternoon wore on, Orrin seemed more distracted than ever, and agitated. They were measuring the angle they would need to add the automatic delivery system to the actual conveyor belt. Orrin was usually excited about new projects, but today he seemed distant.

"Orrin, is something wrong?"

Orrin just frowned, his eyebrows dipping toward his nose.

"Is it because I've been staying nights at Bonheur?" Joe dropped the tape and wrote some calculation in his notebook.

"Are you worried about the equipment? Hiram and the men have been doing a good job of policing the place."

"No, sir, it's not that."

"Then what is it?"

Orrin sighed, stretched his neck.

Screwing up his courage, Joe thought. But for what? God forbid he was about to lose an apprentice.

"It might be none of my business, and you can tell me so, you can even fire me, but my sister takes good care of Miss Deanna and she cares an awful lot about her."

"Yes. I know. They're very close." Elspeth had become the friend Deanna should be seeking among her own class, but Joe could understand that. It was like Orrin and Will and him. Especially since he'd decided to devote his life to his machines, he'd found it harder and harder to relate to his own peers.

"Is there a problem between Elspeth and Miss Deanna?"

"No, sir, but Elspeth—and me, too—don't want to see Miss Deanna hurt."

Joe put down his notebook. Looked at Orrin. What was the man getting at? "Nor does anyone," he said.

"No, sir."

"So what is the problem?"

"Well, sir, I'll just come right out and say it."

"Please do."

"You ain't playing Miss Deanna false, are you, sir?"

"Playing—? What on earth are you talking about?"

"With that actress person, the one they call Noreen."

Enlightenment dawned. "No, of course not." Though the thought had briefly crossed his mind. It's not like he and Deanna were engaged. Or even planning to be. Joseph was not interested in marrying anyone.

Orrin was watching him intently.

"No, Orrin, even though Dee isn't really my girl, I'm not playing her or anyone else false. I'm not carrying on with Noreen. She's an interesting lady, but mainly she is a part of the case that Will"—*and Deanna*—"is involved in. That's why you've seen her here. And you may see her again, but it means nothing. Nothing has, um, occurred."

"That's all right, then." Orrin's face lightened, and Joe was looking at the old Orrin. "What do you want to measure next?" he asked, and picked up the end of the tape.

It took Joe a second to get back to normal. Is that what everyone thought?

They worked in silence for the next half hour, only speaking to call out a number or move to a new position. It felt good to be back at work, but even now, Dee was on his mind. He'd left the house before she'd come down this morning. Surely now that his parents were back, his mother would keep her from running off half-cocked.

What was he thinking? As far as Joe could tell, his mother lived in a permanent state of half-cocked.

Maybe she could at least get Dee to confide the whereabouts of Amabelle Deeks.

He heard footsteps across the warehouse floor and looked up to see Will striding toward him.

Joe grimaced. Whenever Will dropped in unexpectedly, Joe's first reaction was always *What's wrong?* Usually there was nothing amiss, and Will was just stopping by for a friendly visit. Still, Joe could never stop that first visceral reaction.

He put down his tools and went to meet him.

"You on the job or is this a social visit?"

"Neither, actually. As predicted, I was taken off the case. Sort of."

"Sort of? How can you be taken off a case sort of?"

"Judge Grantham has returned, and he and Edgerton were down at the station. Together they disparaged the department in general and me specifically for not doing more to clear up the murder. Edgerton was demanding that we charge Roland Gibbs and start trial proceedings, though we don't have a whit of evidence against him. The Judge was demanding we 'Find that girl and bring her to justice.' Lord, they can't even agree as to whom they want charged.

"They both lambasted us for not searching the aunt's house. Threatened to go there themselves."

"The aunt?"

"A Mrs. Deeks, great-aunt living like a recluse over on Jones Street. We knew about her. We went twice and talked to both the servant girl and to the aunt. The old lady is absolutely potty and swore she wouldn't let the 'little harlot' in the house; the maid swore there was no one in the house but the two of them."

"And you believed her?"

"The aunt was adamant, and I know the maid's family. She wouldn't lie to me. So this morning the new team and the captain himself laid siege to the old lady's house, with a warrant written by the Judge, to search the place."

"And?"

"According to the word on the street, they made a hash of it, found nothing, and frightened the old lady, who has threatened to bring charges against several of the officers."

Joe laughed. "Typical. Well, since it's out of your hands, pour yourself some coffee; the newspaper's on the table. I just need a few minutes to finish up these measurements."

"That's where the 'sort of' comes in."

"Ah. *Caveat legatus.*"

"In spades. The Judge has asked for me personally to find Amabelle Deeks. Ergo, I'm here playing least in sight. Lord, these cottagers and their demands."

"I don't suppose there's any way I can help?"

"I could use that cup of coffee if you haven't burnt it to ashes."

"Can't guarantee that, but you're welcome to it. Then I'll take you for a pint and some dinner."

"What? It's a little early for you to knock off work, isn't it?"

"Yes, but we're at a good stopping place, and I'll come back later and finish up."

When Joe came out to the front a few minutes later, Will was sitting at the table, a steaming cup of coffee at his elbow and the newspaper spread out before him.

"Ready?" Joe asked.

Will nodded, folded the newspaper once.

"Leave it," Joe said. "I'll clean up later."

"What's your hurry?" Will asked, plunking the paper on the table and picking up his hat.

"I'm hungry and I thought we'd go down to Bonheur. The food's better than the pub, and I just want to make sure Deanna is staying out of trouble."

"You're not her nursemaid."

"I'm well aware of that."

"She'll resent you for it."

"I'm well aware of that, too."

"Then what are you going to do?"

"I'm still undecided. We can discuss it over a whiskey and Cook's excellent food."

——◦◦◦)◘(◦◦◦——

The carriage came to a stop in front of Joe's warehouse on Richmond Street. Jasper jumped down and opened the carriage door, but instead of handing Deanna down, he stood, blocking her way.

"Begging your pardon, miss, but I'm not sure the mistress would want you visiting here," he said.

"Yes, thank you, Jasper, but it's something I must do. You may go back to Bonheur now. I'm sure Mr. Joseph will see us home."

He didn't move, but looked toward Elspeth as if he expected her to support him.

She didn't.

"Then I'll just make sure Mr. Joseph is in." He strode over to the door and knocked. Waited, then turned to Deanna. "No one is at home, miss."

Any other time Deanna would have been tempted to giggle at the idea of Joe "at home" in this derelict building standing among other derelict buildings. But today she was just impatient.

"They're probably working and can't hear you. Please try again."

He knocked, knocked again, and finally the door opened. Orrin stood frowning out at the coachman.

"Where is your master?"

Orrin frowned more fiercely. "Gone to dinner."

"Oh good," Deanna said. "Elspeth and I are starving." She climbed down from the carriage before Jasper could try to dissuade her. Elspeth climbed down after her.

Deanna smiled at the coachman. "Thank you so much,

Jasper. I'm sure you must be wanting your dinner, too. Will you be so good to tell Carlisle that I won't be back for a while?"

"But, miss," Orrin began.

"You hush up," Elspeth told him.

"Thank you, Jasper."

"Yes, miss." He climbed up on the box and with a last look at the group standing in the doorway, he clucked to the horse and drove away.

"Well?" Elspeth gave her brother an exasperated look. "Where are your manners?"

Orrin jumped as if someone had goosed him. He stepped back. "But Mr. Joseph ain't here."

"Isn't," Elspeth said. "Now will you please go to the pub and tell Mr. Joseph that my mistress is here, and will he please bring her something to eat—and me, too—as we haven't had any lunch or tea."

"Have you eaten, Orrin?" Deanna asked.

"Yes, miss."

"So go," Elspeth said.

Orrin frowned at Elspeth, nodded jerkily to Deanna. "Lock the door and don't open it unless you know it's me or Mr. Joe. There's bad 'uns all around here and men that want to steal what Mr. Joe does, or destroy it—"

"Orrin," Elspeth said, drawing out his name like Deanna realized she used to do to her own brother, Bob, and suddenly she missed him sorely.

Orrin pulled his leather apron off and hung it on a peg. Took his cap off another peg and left. Elspeth locked the door behind him.

"That sugar man still after Mr. Joseph's inventions?" Elspeth asked, pulling a chair out for Deanna to sit on.

"Yes. He's ruthless, but Joe will prevail. I know he will."

Elspeth found some tea; managed to put water on to boil after experimenting with the knobs of the Acme oven that Joe had modified over the winter. Deanna picked up the newspaper that was lying on the table and opened it to the society page.

There was mention of the Chepstow party, naming a few of the more well-known dignitaries. Several paragraphs on the Grantham fete, with descriptions of the décor and the women's finery. A column on a baseball game, something Deanna had never been to, and an article that interested her immensely, about the cycling rally taking place in Newport. The regatta was coming from Manhattan, the first boats had already arrived. The season was in full swing.

She heard the teakettle whistle and was dimly aware of Elspeth bringing things to the table. She was beginning to wonder what was taking Orrin so long. The pub was, she imagined, the one catercornered to the warehouse. He should be back by now.

"Elspeth, look out the window and see if you see them coming."

Elspeth looked out, and Deanna noticed for the first time that the windows were now fitted with iron bars. *Like a jail*, Deanna thought. Was Joe in danger living and working here?

"No, miss, I don't. Oh, there he is." She went to the door and opened it.

"I told you not to open—"

"I saw you coming. Where's Mr. Joseph?"

"He weren't there. But the landlord gave me some bread and cheese. He placed the package he'd been holding on the table. "Said if you wanted something hot, they got beef and carrots and potatoes and he'll send a girl over with it, if you want."

Deanna shook her head. "This will be great. We don't really have time to eat a proper meal. But please thank him for me the next time you see him."

"Yes, miss."

Elspeth brought a cracked teapot over and an equally disreputable mug.

"Where else could he have gone?" she asked Orrin.

"I don't know, miss. There's several decent pubs in the neighborhood. Do you want me to check them?"

"Well, how long does he usually stay gone?" Deanna asked as she folded the newspaper and started to hand it to Elspeth.

"Well, he usually doesn't go out until we knock off work, and I go home, so I don't rightly know. But if he goes out in the afternoon he usually comes back within a half hour or so."

Elspeth arranged the teapot and packet of cheese and bread on the table, found two plates and a large knife. She arranged the plates and reached for the newspaper that Deanna was holding out to her. But Deanna suddenly pulled it back.

"Elspeth, get yourself and Orrin a mug and sit down, both of you. I'm not the Queen. And I think . . . ." She unfolded the paper and looked at it.

"What?" asked Elspeth as she hurried to bring two more mugs to the table. She pulled a stool over, sat, and began cutting slices of cheese and bread. "What do you think, miss?"

Orrin stood a little ways off. "I'll have a bit of tea if you please, miss, but I'll stand."

"But what do you think?" Elspeth asked impatiently.

"I think we better find Belle Deeks before someone else does."

⟞⟝⟞

"Good afternoon, Carlisle. Where is everyone?" Joe asked, stepping into the foyer at Bonheur.

"Mr. and Mrs. Ballard and Madame Manon are on the terrace having cocktails."

"And Miss Deanna?"

"She and her maid are still out."

Joe's breath hitched. "Shopping?" In his dreams; Deanna didn't really like to shop.

"I couldn't say, sir. She's been gone most of the day. She took the carriage. Jasper drove them."

"Ah," Joe said, feeling slightly mollified. Jasper wouldn't let them get into trouble.

"We'll join the others on the terrace. Could you ask Cook if she's willing to feed two weary, hungry souls? Nothing fancy. Just filling. Sergeant Hennessey has had a trying day and no food."

"Very good, sir." He went off toward the back of the house, and Joe and Will went through the second parlor and onto the stone terrace.

There was a light breeze blowing, and Grandmère had wrapped a flowing scarf around her hair and shoulders, the tips of the scarf lifting with each breeze.

His father saw him and stood. "Joe, come join us. Is this a professional or a social call, Hennessey?"

"Social," Will said.

"Then have a seat and a drink. You find us a trio of idlers this evening. Something we don't often experience in this household."

Joe was glad to see his father so relaxed and his mother so attentive. He was sorry that he would even have to bring up something that might disturb that mood.

"You look pensive, Joseph," his grandmother said.

"Do you know where Dee is?"

"She took the carriage."

"Do you know what she is up to?"

"My guess is she's gone to fetch that tiresome Amabelle Deeks and make her turn herself in, or is fraternizing with the actors with whom she seems smitten."

"And you let her go? Do you realize the Deeks girl could be a murderess?"

"I sent Jasper with her. He'll keep an eye on them."

"Is that why you've come?" She included Will in the question.

"Joe just took pity and offered to feed me."

"Is Cook preparing something?"

"Yes," Joe said. "But there have been some developments we thought you would want to know."

"Do tell."

Will told them about Judge Grantham and Edgerton coming to headquarters to demand conflicting actions by the police. How Will had been dismissed and then approached privately by the Judge.

"I knew as soon as the Judge returned he would start pushing his not-inconsiderable weight around," Laurette said. "He just can't seem to keep his fingers out of everyone else's pie. And now his shadow, Edgerton, is going his own way? No wonder you're hiding out."

Joe took a drink from the tray that had appeared at his side, nodded to the footman, who then moved on to Will. "Mother, tell Will what you learned while you were in the city."

"About Amabelle and her family or the other?" asked his mother, and took a sip of her drink.

"All of it."

She had to wait, since at that moment Carlisle returned with a footman carrying a tray of food, which he set down on the butler's table that Carlisle then moved closer to Will and Joe.

When the food was served and the servants had departed, Laurette said, "Well, I have a little news that might or might not be helpful. It turns out that the reason the family has cut off communication with Amabelle is not that she ran away to become an actress—Rosalie isn't narrow-minded—but because, not content to just do that, the silly girl began living the high life and is abiding in an evidently swank apartment paid for by a gentleman whose identity is unknown."

"That could be anyone," Will said. "And how does Charlie Withrop fit into that scenario?"

"I have no idea," Joe said. "But I thought it might help. It seems like I can't stay out of this investigation."

"I'm sorry," Will said. "But it doesn't seem that I'm able to make any progress on my own."

"It's because you only have half the information," Gwen said.

"Half?" Will said, surprised.

"It isn't your fault, dear, but let us all face facts. You cannot police the cottagers all by yourself. And as long as none of them—except perhaps us—will cooperate with any of the police, except you, because you are an educated man from a good family, and then only begrudgingly, you will never be able to gain all the cooperation you need to solve crimes. I bet you haven't even been allowed back into the Grantham grounds or the fete theater, have you?"

Will shook his head. "But I don't know what we could learn there."

"Perhaps nothing, but that is where these people spent most of their time that night . . . except for the orgy afterward."

Joe started to protest that it wasn't an orgy but decided not to bother. It may have turned into an orgy after he left.

"It was Dee who approached the actors and who gained Noreen's trust."

Joe didn't mention his interactions with Noreen, either.

"She found Amabelle Deeks."

Joe and Will both stared at her. "You know where she is? Dee refused to tell."

"She promised the girl not to tell a soul. The girl was afraid for her life."

"That's impeding an investigation," Will said.

"Which is not necessarily a bad thing," Gwen told him. "Your force has already arrested one person with absolutely no evidence, you said that yourself."

Will shut his mouth. No one said another word.

And into that silence, Joe's father asked, "Why here?"

"What do you mean, sir?" Joe asked him.

"Why kill poor Charlie in Newport? It would seem to me to be much easier to murder and dispose of a body in New York City than in a Newport family conservatory."

"An argument started before they arrived which came to a head here?" Joe ventured.

"And the killer came with the troupe?" Will said.

"Or the killer followed them here," Laurette suggested.

"Or was already here," said Joe.

"Tell me," Will said. "Do any of you know why the Granthams hired this particular troupe?"

"I have no idea," Gwen said. "Though I confess it was not a play I would have thought Maude or Drusilla would approve of."

"And yet, we heard that it was Drusilla who insisted on it," Lionel said. "Would she go against her mother or her husband because she knew her father would like it?"

"Neither would hold sway if she thought her father would like it," Laurette said. "Which he obviously did. Did you see him, Mama? He sat rapt for the entire hour. I guess you can't completely despise a man who supports the theater."

"Depends on his reasons, my dear."

Laurette stared at her husband. "And do you know what those reasons might be if not for the play?"

"God, no. I was just thinking of what Joe said about Jacob Mersey's yacht party and Edgerton being there."

"But I only saw him on our arrival. I didn't see him again. I assumed he left. But Mersey was paying marked attention to several of the girls. Later he said he was interested in Talia, hired the Casino theater for them to rehearse in while they were stranded here."

"How did you learn—oh, never mind." Will sat back in his seat, dejected.

"Mersey mentioned Talia, but he's been known to court more than one lady at a time. He could have been interested in Amabelle."

"I would think Mersey too indigent to kill someone over a woman . . . or two." Lionel trailed off.

"Edgerton threatened Deanna the other night at Chepstow," Gwen added.

"What?"

"Calm down, Joseph. I believe he told her to stay away from his family. He was merely reminding her of her place in society . . . she is young and her place is tenuous."

"What could she possibly have done to cause his censure?"

"Tried to be nice to his wife. Which I could have told her was wasted energy. Drusilla is as sour as they come."

"She's had good practice from that draconian mother of hers," Lionel said.

"Yes, Maude does tend toward the dour," Gwen said. "Now, let the boys eat in peace for a moment."

Joe found that he was no longer hungry. He was also concerned about Dee. She didn't seem to realize how easy it was to find yourself in a situation you weren't able to handle. It was bad enough in the ballroom, but in questions of the law and her own safety . . .

They had just finished eating when Carlisle reappeared. "I thought you might want to know. Jasper has returned with the carriage."

"Did he bring the girls with him?" Gwen asked, a tinge of concern in her voice.

"No, Madame. He said he left them off at Mr. Joseph's warehouse, and to tell you they would get him to bring them back to Bonheur."

Joe and Will were both on their feet before he'd finished his sentence.

"Carlisle, please have the stable send round my curricle."

"Yes, sir."

"Now, Joseph, don't go off half-cocked," said Gwen. "What do you aim to do?"

"I'm going to fetch Dee and Elspeth and bring them here, where you will watch them and make sure they don't try to leave again. Then Will and I are going to pay a visit on the Judge."

Chapter

21

"I am such a fool. Look at this paper." Deanna spread out the newspaper and opened it to the local news page. "What do you see?"

Elspeth leaned over to look; even Orrin moved closer. "Articles about what's happening in Newport this week."

"And what else?"

Elspeth shrugged. Looked at Orrin.

"Just the train and ferry schedules."

"Exactly. The day I found Belle she had been reading the newspaper. She joked about how she stole it each night and rearranged the pages to confuse her aunt before she returned it.

"I thought she was looking at the society news to see what they said about the Grantham fete and the play. But what if that wasn't why she was reading that page? What if she was looking at ferry schedules?"

Both O'Larens looked at her, and she realized they were expecting her to know the answer.

"We know, or at least are pretty sure, she actually went to the docks. Timothy—one of the actors—said he thought he saw her at the wharf," Deanna explained to Orrin. "She was wearing an old dress that she found stored in a old trunk in the attic."

"You think she was going to make her escape?" Orrin asked, getting into the spirit of the investigation.

"Wearing a disguise," Elspeth added.

"Possibly," Deanna said, trying to rein in their imaginations. "Except she didn't have any money. But the last time I saw her, she said she would be fine, soon. I really think she was planning to meet someone getting off the ferry. Except Timothy thwarted her attempt. He called her name and she ran."

"Maybe she met him someplace else," Elspeth said.

"Or her," countered Orrin. "It coulda been a her."

"Or her, though I think we can agree that it would probably be a he."

Orrin huffed out a sigh.

"Because when the Ballards went to town, they found out that Belle had a, um, protector."

Orrin looked blank.

"She means an old geezer that keeps a woman for his own pleasures."

"Elspeth." Orrin blushed. It colored his whole face and neck.

"Well, not necessarily old," Deanna said. "It could be someone young and rich. Or even just well-to-do."

"But I thought she and poor Charlie were engaged to get married."

"Well, there seems to be some confusion about that. But let's hold off on Charlie for a moment."

"Okay, the mystery man, then," Elspeth said. "How did she know he was coming?"

"She might have wrote him a note," Orrin said.

"Or sent him a telegram," Elspeth said.

"Possibly," Deanna said. "But someone might see her mailing it. And how would she get a stamp? And what if the person who read it threw it away? And someone else found it. Would you ever do something like that, Elspeth?"

Elspeth thought, then shook her head. "No, because we read detective stories and know better."

"Belle reads them, too. She wouldn't do anything that might leave a clue."

"Except an open window." Elspeth grinned.

"Except an open window." Had there been other clues Deanna had missed? Had Belle found the person who she said would take care of her? *Soon*, she'd said. Because she knew he would be coming to Newport. But people came to Newport every day. And if he had already arrived, they would be long gone.

Deanna shook the newspaper out to its full size. "Next to the ferry schedules, they always announce the people who are arriving each week. Only the society people, but . . ." She ran her finger down the list. "Dr. and Mrs. Seward Webb, Mr. Carry, Miss Florence Cole, Mr. C. Morrison, Judge Samuel Grantham." Deanna smiled. "Wouldn't that be a kick?"

"Not him, miss."

"Probably not." She shoved the paper away. "It probably doesn't matter at this point. If she did rendezvous with someone, it's probably too late to catch them. Except . . . where would they go? Not back on the ferry with her dressed like the witch from a fairy tale—or a Greek goddess. She'll need

clothes to get on the ferry. Actually, she'll need clothes wherever she goes."

"And Noreen has her clothes," Elspeth said.

"And the troupe is leaving tomorrow and she'll be stuck."
Deanna stood, took a pace around the room. Looked out the
window for Joe. No sign of him.

"Do you think she knows?" Elspeth asked.

"Let me think." Deanna came back to the table, sat down.
"She may not know when they're leaving, but they'll have to
leave sometime. So where would you go to make sure they
don't leave without you?"

Two blank faces looked back at her. "They're no longer at
the boardinghouse; she won't know where they are staying.
And even if she did, they'd never let her inside dressed the way
she is. They'd think she was a beggar in those clothes . . . and
something worse if she wore her costume.

"Oh, how could I be so dim-witted?" She turned to Elspeth.
"Where would she go if she wanted to make sure she wasn't
left behind?"

Elspeth shook her head.

"To the scene of Judge Grantham's fete. All the sets and
costumes are stored there. Mrs. Grantham was complaining
about what an eyesore they were."

"Oh, miss. That would be a perfect place to hide."

"And with all the costumes, she might even find something
to wear that will look presentable. Or at least find a crate to
stow away in."

Deanna stood.

"Miss, you're not going there?" Orrin said.

"Of course—how else will we find her?"

"But, miss, they will never let you prowl around their lawn."

"We're not going to tell them."

"You'll be arrested for trespassing or worse," Orrin said. "At least wait for Mr. Joe to return."

"No, we won't, and we can't wait for Joe. I have to make Belle turn herself in. It's my fault the police don't have her now and the reason why Rollie's in jail."

"It isn't your fault. You were just trying to help," Elspeth said.

"But I made a mess of it. I promised her, but I should have told. Now I want to fix it if I can. I'm selfish. I know. I made a simple mistake, but how will I explain that if Belle is gone and Rollie is on trial for murder?"

"Oh criminy, miss. Come on, then."

The sun was setting when Joe stopped the curricle in front of his warehouse. He tossed the reins to Will to hold and jumped down. Orrin opened the door immediately.

"Where have you been, Mr. Joe? I looked in the pub and everywhere."

"We went to Bonheur. Are Miss Deanna and Elspeth still here?"

"How did you know they were here?"

"The coachman told me. Are they still here?" He started to go inside.

"No, sir, you just missed them."

"Are they going to Bonheur?"

"No, sir, Miss Deanna said she couldn't wait any longer, and they were going to . . ." He bit his lip. "She said she thinks she knows where Belle is hiding and it's all her fault."

"Where?" Joe had to concentrate not to grab his apprentice by the shoulders and shake him.

"At Judge Grantham's."

"Grantham's?"

"That's what she said."

"And she thinks Belle is at Judge Grantham's?"

"I'm not sure. She just said something about the ferry and clothes, I couldn't follow it all."

"The ferry and clothes? Are you sure?"

Orrin nodded. "She just said that if you got back to follow her to the fete. And to bring the sergeant."

"How did they go?"

"Made me hire them a hack. I knew you wouldn't like it, but . . ."

"That's okay; it's sometimes difficult to say no to a lady."

"And to my sister, sir."

"I can believe it. How long ago did they leave?"

"Maybe twenty minutes."

"Okay. Why don't you lock up and go on home? We won't be doing any more work for tonight."

"Yes, sir. You'll take care of them, Mr. Joe."

"I will." Joe climbed back in the curricle and turned the horses around. "What do you think they're doing?" Will yelled over the rattle of the carriage.

"Hopefully not confronting Judge Grantham about anything. Not at this hour. Not with the whole family at home. What the hell does she think she's doing?"

Deanna took Elspeth by the wrist and pulled her through the trees at the edge of the Grantham property. The sun was setting, painting the sky red and orange and leaving everything before it in silhouette.

They made their way across the lawn, Deanna acutely aware of the lights coming from the Judge's mansion. The whole family must be home, and they were the last people Deanna wanted to see tonight.

She hadn't thought far enough ahead to how she would get Belle out to the street once she found her—if she found her.

But a terrible suspicion had been darting around her head, concerning Belle's rich and powerful patron and exactly how powerful he was.

They slowed down as they drew closer to the remains of the theater. Anyone who had been working here during the day had gone, and everything was eerily quiet. The canopied walkway to the stage was now missing, with hardly any evidence that it had ever swept across the lawn to the theater.

Deanna kept scanning the area, listening for the slightest sound, and could hear only Elspeth breathing in her ear.

The ballroom and canopied ceiling over the floor had been removed. Only the stage was standing, a curtain drawn across the front, the quickly constructed wooden roof still covering whatever sets remained.

Behind the stage the wooden walkway ran between the stage and the tents. They were still standing, but tied up tight.

"Come on," she whispered to Elspeth, who seemed to be getting more difficult to pull along.

"Where are we?" she breathed back.

"It's backstage, and these are where the dressing rooms and storage rooms are. On that side is the back wall of the stage. That huge round thing sticking out is part of the Ferris wheel I told you about. The one that took the couples to wedded bliss."

She stopped at the first tent. It took a few long moments for the two of them to untie the knots and climb inside.

"We should have brought a torch," Deanna said, blinking against the dark interior.

"Except that everyone would know we're here."

"True." Deanna moved forward, looking around boxes and platforms, turning in all directions as she went.

"Belle?" she whispered. Then louder. "Belle. Come out. It's me, Deanna. I need to talk to you."

She turned and found Elspeth treading on her toes. They both let out involuntary squeaks and shushed each other at the same time.

"Let's try the next tent."

They groped their way back to the tent flap and stepped onto the walk. They tied the flap back and moved on to the next one.

"What's this one?" Elspeth asked as they untied the flap.

"I'm not sure." Deanna pulled back the flap and stepped inside. Elspeth moved quickly behind her. Elspeth screeched, and Deanna stepped back into her. She was standing on the same level as a giant mouth gaping open.

"Wh-what is it?" Elspeth stuttered behind her.

Deanna took a deep breath. "It's only the Sphinx. It's like a big tomb, but it's only papier-mâché. Belle?" They got no answer in that tent or the next, which appeared to be the costume tent, judging by the stacks of huge theater crates packed and ready to be carried to the wharf the next morning.

They searched the dressing rooms, men's and women's, and found nothing but the empty dressing tables, the rows of lights still lining the tops, but giving no light. A few pieces of trash, but nothing more.

"She's not here," Elspeth said.

"Certainly looks like it." Deanna sighed. "And I was so sure she would come here. Now what are we going to do?"

"Get ourselves out of here before someone comes." Elspeth pulled Deanna toward the open flap.

Someone was already here. Deanna heard voices. She thrust Elspeth to the side and stood near the opening of the tent, listening. The voices were muffled. She peered around the edge of the tent opening. No one was in sight.

She motioned Elspeth to go out, then turned to hastily retie the tent.

Then she heard a familiar woman's voice.

It was coming from the other side of the theater.

"Stop. Don't come any closer."

Deanna and Elspeth exchanged looks.

They'd found Amabelle Deeks.

D eanna grabbed Elspeth's arm and they both stood still, trying to hear. But all was silent. Deanna could see light coming from the stage between the chinks in the wooden walls. They must be on the stage. She motioned for Elspeth to follow her. They passed the wheel and tiptoed across the wooden walkway to the entrance to backstage and peeked in.

Crates were stacked everywhere, some only half-filled. Pieces of scenery were lined up like soldiers. The whole space was a warren of boxes, crates, and stage pieces. It stood to reason that everything would be stored back here; it was the only space that had a wooden roof.

Deanna could hear Belle talking, but she couldn't see who the other person was. She needed to get closer. Carefully she stretched out her hand and touched the splintered rattan of a large basket. Using it to guide herself, she crept forward,

Elspeth clasping her sleeve and staying close. Her foot hit something metal, one of the rings that Deanna thought must be part of the fireworks display that had blazed across the lawn. She barely caught it before it fell and took the others with it.

She could see a light ahead. Someone must have lit a lantern.

"Did you bring them?"

"Yes, yes." A man's voice.

A shadow moved across the floor. Deanna dove behind a crate marked FIREWORKS, dragging Elspeth with her. When she looked out, the shadow had moved on.

"Why, Belle? Why are you doing this?"

Deanna and Elspeth exchanged looks. What was Belle doing? They had to find a way to see. And hope Joe and Will would get here before Belle got away.

"Protecting myself like you said I should."

A sound like an animal cry. It gave Deanna the shivers, and it didn't come from Belle.

Deanna moved slowly along the crates until she found an opening just large enough to see through if she climbed onto one of the smaller boxes. But as she reached for something to hold on to, her elbow hit the edge of a smaller box. It had been pushed just far enough onto the crate to keep it from falling. It went sliding over the edge.

Right into Elspeth's arms. Elspeth's cheeks puffed out as she breathed out. She put the box on the floor, then she looked into it. Shook her head and climbed up behind Deanna.

"Did you hear that?" asked the man.

"No. What? Don't try to distract me. Put the clothes and the money in that valise."

"Belle, why are you doing this? Charlie and I were always good to you. Why did you have to kill him? Why? I don't understand."

"Me? Liar. I didn't kill him, you did. I know you did. And you said you loved him." Belle finished with a drawn-out keen that finally fell to silence.

Deanna couldn't see what was happening. She hiked up her skirts and shimmied out to where she could lie across the top of the crates and look down on the scene. Elspeth wedged herself in next to Deanna, and the two of them lay side by side looking out of the narrow opening.

Two people were lit against a black curtain; one of them, a plump pretty actress, held a tiny pistol, a derringer, in her hand. She was pointing it at a large barrel-chested man with wisps of white hair that crisscrossed his pink scalp.

Just like characters in a melodrama. *A modern melodrama*, Deanna thought, *where the damsel overpowers the villain with her pistol.*

"Me?" The man turned slightly and she recognized him.

Judge Grantham.

"I didn't kill Charlie," he said. "Oh, that I had never met you. What is this trick, Belle? Do you think you can blackmail me? Is that it? Don't I always give you what you want? Why would I ever kill either of you?"

"Because we were going to leave you."

"Leave? No, you weren't. Charlie never would have left. He enjoyed the rich life. He loved me."

"We were, and you found out and killed him."

"You don't know what you're talking about, Belle. I was at home with my family after my birthday fete. You're being hysterical."

The gun bobbled in Belle's hand, which was shaking badly.

The Judge stepped toward her.

"Don't. Don't come any closer," Belle cried.

"Is this an act, Belle? Are you trying to cast aspersions on me, to protect yourself? Because let me tell you, my girl. I'll see you hanged."

"I didn't kill him. Don't threaten me." Belle was indeed becoming more and more hysterical.

"Then who did?" the Judge asked in a voice quickly losing its control.

Where were Joe and Will? If they were off wining and dining, she would never forgive them.

"I'm afraid I did."

Deanna's head swiveled toward the new voice. He was standing in the shadows so she couldn't see his face, but she recognized his voice. The same bitter edge as when he'd threaten her at the Chepstow soiree. Walter Edgerton.

Elspeth frowned at Deanna, and Deanna realized Elspeth had no idea who these people were. She'd just have to wait to find out. Things were moving too fast for explanations, and the slightest noise would betray their presence.

She had a momentary idea to send Elspeth to find Joe and Will, but by the time she even found a cab, this scene would most likely be over.

Edgerton finally stepped into the light and Belle turned her pistol on him.

He was holding a larger one.

"You killed Charlie?" Belle asked, her voice shaky. "Why?"

"To stop you both from destroying a good man and me with him."

"That's why he didn't meet me? He was there, but he was already dead? Why couldn't you just let us go?"

The Judge swayed. "Walter? Walter, tell me this isn't true. Murder? Was that necessary?"

"Unfortunately, Sam, yes. Your conduct made it necessary. But it didn't work out quite how I planned. I had to drag the little pervert's body inside, thinking that this piece would surely be blamed."

Belle sobbed. "You're despicable."

"I do what is necessary to protect the Judge's good name and rid the country of prostitutes and perverts."

"I'm not a prostitute and Charlie wasn't a pervert; you're the sick, twisted one."

Edgerton turned on the Judge. "No, *he* is." His anger and swagger seemed to die in the same instant. "Why did you do it? I looked up to you. Modeled my life after yours. You were my mentor and patron. How could you sell me out like this? You old hypocrite."

The Judge hung his head, the energy drained from him, and Deanna was afraid he might faint dead away.

"You leave him alone," Belle cried. "You're an evil, vicious man. Not even a man. An animal."

"Shut up."

The Judge ran a hand over his face. "You didn't have to kill the boy."

"Yes, I did. You left me no choice. You were going to ruin everything."

"I'll send you to prison."

"You wouldn't dare." Edgerton laughed shrilly, and Deanna was afraid a bit hysterically. "And risk me telling all about you and your filthy libertine ways."

"I'll call the police myself. I don't care what happens to me."

"You'll keep your head. Parkhurst and your friends at the Society for the Prevention of Crime would love that. Their champion tried in the courts as a pervert himself. You'll be ruined and the whole family with you. They'll never be able to hold their heads up in public, their peers and friends will despise them."

"I don't care!" With a howl, the Judge lunged at the younger man. The revolver went off with an earsplitting explosion.

The Judge staggered, stood long enough to look Edgerton in the eye, then, grabbing his stomach, he toppled forward.

Belle screamed.

Deanna's ears were echoing, but she was paralyzed in place.

Belle dropped to her knees beside the older man and turned him over.

"Oh, Judge. I'll call for a doctor."

He shook his head slightly. "No use in that."

She took his hand. "You were good to me. I know that."

Deanna had to pull herself forward to see his face.

"I did love you, my dear. In my own way."

"I know. Just not in the way you loved Charlie."

The Judge's eyes closed.

Edgerton moved forward, his face a mask of shock. "Why did you do that, you stupid old man? Now what am I supposed to do?"

He turned on Belle so fast that Deanna had to scramble back not to be seen.

"Who's up there?" Edgerton demanded.

Deanna and Elspeth froze, so close that their noses almost touched.

Slowly, they crawled back down the crates.

"Come out now or she dies."

Deanna grabbed Elspeth. "Go for help," she whispered.

"Come out or I'll shoot her. I have nothing to lose."

"Go get help," Deanna whispered.

"I'm not leaving you."

"Go, that's an order."

Elspeth shook her head.

"Now!" Edgerton's voice had reached a voluble panic.

Elspeth stepped down. Came back holding a handful of Roman candles from the box they'd knocked over.

"We don't have matches."

"Yeah, we do." Elspeth smiled, though it was more like a grimace, and patted her skirt pocket. "Cad Metti," she whispered, citing her favorite sleuth. "A good detective always comes prepared."

She disappeared into the shadows.

Deanna stepped away from the boxes to give Elspeth time to escape.

Edgerton whirled around. Stopped dead, his revolver pointing somewhere off to the side. He wasn't very good at this holdup business. Of course he didn't have to be that good. It was the gun and the bullet that did all the work.

He shot his free hand through his pomaded hair.

"Come out here." He began to back up as Deanna moved forward. Aiming the gun first at Belle then Deanna, back and forth, back and forth. It was hypnotizing.

"What the hell am I supposed to do?" he whined. "This is the damn Judge's fault. Now I'll have to kill both of you, it just isn't fair."

A loud whistle, then a resounding boom exploded from outside.

"What the—what was that?"

Another of the same.

Holding the revolver aimed between the two women, he backed up and peered out the curtain. Deanna could see only smoke, but she hoped like crazy that the sky was lit up and somebody would be coming to see what was going on.

Joe had just stepped out of the carriage at the door of the Grantham cottage when the sky lit up with fireworks. "What the hell?"

"Looks like someone is celebrating," Will said.

"I hardly see what the Granthams have to celebrate." Joe turned back to the door. And knocked.

The butler, white faced and grim, opened the door almost immediately. He saw Will behind Joe, and his face drained even whiter.

"Is Judge Grantham at home?" Joe asked when it became clear he had no intention of letting them in the house.

Maude Grantham came running out of the parlor. "Samuel, what on earth is going on?"

She checked when she saw Joe and Will. "Where is the Judge? What is he doing?"

"We came to see him, ma'am," Joe said. "Is he not here?"

Maude looked around. "He was here but he had to go out."

"Oh, do you know where he went?"

She shook her head in jagged little jerks.

"The reading room, perhaps?"

"I don't know."

Another blast went off.

"Can someone please stop that noise? My nerves. My head.

Who is doing that?" She saw Will. "Would you please do your job and get rid of whoever is making that racket?"

She put her hand to her temple and tottered back into the parlor.

Joe turned to the butler. "Miss Randolph isn't visiting here, is she?"

"No, sir, no one has visited since this morning."

"Thank you."

He and Will walked back outside. "I'm getting a bad feeling about this," he said.

"So am I. Let's check it out." Will started off toward the theater at a jog.

They were two-thirds of the way there when Joe saw who was causing the cacophony.

"That's Elspeth," he said, and ran to meet her.

She ran toward them. "He's got them, Miss Deanna and Belle. Behind that curtain. He has a gun. Help her, sir."

Joe and Will began to run, Will only trailing slightly behind as he reached inside his jacket for his revolver.

At the curtain, they stopped; sidled along until they got to the proscenium. Then Joe pulled it back slightly and looked inside. Walter Edgerton's back was to him, facing Deanna and Amabelle Deeks, who stood just in front of the Ferris wheel as if they were ready to hand over their tickets.

Bad analogy, Joe.

Edgerton must have a gun aimed at them, because they both were holding very still.

Dee's eyes widened slightly as she saw him, but that was the only reaction she had.

Joe felt Will move in beside him, his revolver trained on Edgerton.

"Edgerton!" Will called.

Edgerton turned. At the same time Dee stepped back into darkness and vanished from the stage.

"Hold it right there," Will called.

Instead, Edgerton whirled around and with a giant leap, grabbed Belle, locking an arm around her and holding her as a shield.

"Back off and I won't hurt her." Edgerton stepped back, dragging Belle with him.

"If he makes a break for it, I'll shoot if I can get a clean target," Will said.

There was a pop and the sounds of gears interlocking.

Edgerton looked around, clearly panicking. As he dragged Belle back, Belle suddenly went limp. Edgerton staggered under her dead weight. And Joe smiled in spite of his racing adrenaline. She hadn't fainted, she was making it impossible for him to escape. He couldn't drag her dead weight fast enough to get away. He would have to let her go and then Will would shoot.

Joe heard a creak and saw the wheel jerk slightly.

Edgerton continued to back away, bringing him closer to the wheel. One final step back and the wheel came to life. Belle threw herself against him. His grip loosened ever so slightly, but she took the opportunity to jab him in the ribs and stomp on his foot. He howled, staggered, and fell backward on his butt. His arms splayed outward; his hand hit the edge of the apparatus, and the gun flew from his hand.

Belle ran toward Will. And Walter Edgerton was miraculously lifted above the ground by the giant Ferris wheel. But unlike the pairs of lovers from the play, Edgerton would not be going to marital bliss—he'd be going to jail.

Will ran forward and pulled Belle to safety. Then Joe led

them around to the back walk to pick up Edgerton when he came down to earth.

And he found what he knew he would find: Dee pedaling as fast as she could. She and Belle had somehow colluded while being held at gunpoint.

He let her keep at it until he saw Edgerton's feet pull up on the platform as he lowered to the ground.

"He's going to make a break for it," he called to Will.

Will merely nodded. He had it covered.

"You can stop now, Dee!" Joe called.

She looked up, her eyes wide, the sweat beading on her forehead. And Joe smiled. What a girl. He could kill her. But right now he was just glad to see her alive.

Will hauled Edgerton off the wheel's platform when it was still several feet from the ground.

Will handcuffed him and dragged him back to the stage, where Belle stood over a recumbent figure. Joe knew it was Judge Grantham before he even saw the body.

"He killed Charlie and he killed the Judge," Belle cried. "And he tried to kill Dee and me, too."

"Ridiculous," Edgerton said. "She killed Charlie and Judge Grantham. I was just trying to hold her for the police."

"This is going to be a mess," Will said.

Joe shrugged. "You weren't on duty. You were merely visiting with friends and stumbled over the murder. No one can fault you for that, or blame you for overstepping into their territory."

Will cracked a laugh. "I pray that it will be that simple. I'm sure Mr. Edgerton here will have a whole fabricated, but plausible, explanation by the time we take him to the station."

He was surly and unrepentant. And he'd probably go free.

Dee and Elspeth had come back to the stage. "Mr. Edgerton did kill Charlie. Elspeth, Belle, and I heard him confess and we all saw him shoot Judge Grantham."

"Lies!" Edgerton yelled from behind them. "It's a conspiracy. You can't believe anything this one tells you." He lifted his chin toward Belle.

"But we can believe everything the other two tell us," Will said, and smiled.

The fireworks had attracted a crowd, though not as far as Joe could tell, anyone from the house. He wondered how much they were aware of, if they would stand by their husbands for better or for worse. If it would even come to that.

Judge Grantham had enough favors owed to escape the scandal, and Joe still wasn't sure what exactly it was, except that it involved Charlie and Belle. But he could guess. And he also could guess that the Judge's righteous cronies would find a way to save his reputation. They had too much to lose to let him, even in death, bring them down.

But Edgerton? Would they save him in order to preen him as the Judge's replacement? Or would they just look the other way, pretend they didn't know him. Let him swing for murder.

Will managed to find two police officers in the crowd and sent them off to fetch a police wagon. And also to send for the medical examiner.

Joe thought about asking Will if it would be all right to take Deanna and Elspeth home, but he didn't have the heart to leave Will alone with the mob.

Dee, Belle, and Elspeth stood off to one side like three avenging angels, three very tired avenging angels.

Joe went to stand by Dee. "It shouldn't be too much lon-ger now."

Deanna gave him a half smile.

"How did you know how to run the wheel?" he asked.

"You explained it the day you were working at Bonheur."

"I did?"

"Yes, you did," she said patiently.

"And you understood it?"

Deanna looked to the ceiling and back to Joe. "Pull a lever, ride a bicycle? I should think so."

They stood waiting until Will came over to them. "Good work, girls. But I really wish you had consulted with me first."

"We tried to," Deanna said. "I had gone to tell Belle that I was turning her in and give her a chance to do it herself. But she was gone, so Elspeth and I went looking for Joe to tell you, but you two were off dining somewhere and we couldn't wait."

"Well, don't make a habit of it," Will said sternly.

Joe could tell he wasn't really angry and so could Dee and Elspeth.

"I'm sorry," Belle said, and batted her eyelashes at Will. Really, the girl was a piece of work. "I was afraid the killer was after me."

"Uh-huh."

"And she was right," Deanna told him.

"Hmm." Will turned to Elspeth. "Are you the one who set off the clarion call?"

Elspeth lifted her chin at him. He towered over her so it didn't have much effect. "If you mean," she said, "was I the one that set off the fireworks, the answer is yes."

"How did you manage it?"

"We always set off Roman candles on the holidays, the ones

here are just bigger. Besides, I had these." Elspeth pulled a bag from her pocket and opened the drawstring. She fumbled inside and finally held up a small rectangular box.

"Matches?" Will asked. "You carry matches?"

Elspeth grinned at Deanna. "A good lady's maid always comes prepared."

Chapter
23

"Well, the Rensselaers will just have to wait for our presence tonight," Gwen said, taking a glass of sherry from the tray Carlisle was holding out to her.

Joe had just come downstairs bathed, shaved, and dressed in evening wear. "I suspect Will Hennessey will be around to question us." He took a whiskey from Carlisle. Dee hadn't come back downstairs.

"Do you really think Dee will be up for a ball? She must be exhausted."

"I completely agree," Lionel said. "Perhaps we should all stay home this evening. Catching killers is daunting work."

"And not to be encouraged," Joe said.

"Oh, Joseph. You can hardly stop her doing what she will," Laurette added. "If her mother couldn't do it, I don't imagine you will have better success."

Joe swirled the liquid around in his glass. "I don't want to do anything like that. But really, she can't go around overcoming villains, and hiding in theaters, and breaking into people's houses."

"Oh, can't she just." Gwen leaned back and laughed delightedly.

"It is not something to be taken lightly."

"No, it isn't," his father said, giving his mother-in-law a quelling look, which she ignored. "It's a great responsibility accepting the way another person lives." He glanced at his wife. "It takes great fortitude."

"And good cigars and whiskey," Laurette said, getting up from the chaise and coming to give Lionel a kiss on the forehead before sitting on the arm of his chair.

"I've been a great burden to your father."

"A great challenge," he corrected her. "And a delight." And the smile he gave her made Joe look away.

"What will happen to Edgerton?" his mother asked.

"I suppose we'll have to wait for Will. I'm sure he's still with the family, who, by the way, didn't even come out of the house during all the ruckus. Not even after the butler was summoned and sent back to the house with a message for Mrs. Grantham."

"Maude's no dummy," Gwen said. "A cold fish, but not without a brain. I'm sure she won't make an appearance without a cadre of lawyers. And as for Drusilla." Gwen shuddered.

"They'll weather the scandal, of course," she continued. "People like that always do. But it's ironic, is it not, that Walter did everything in his power including murder to prevent the Judge's actions from becoming a scandal, and he became the scandal instead." Her expression changed and she looked past the others to the doorway where Deanna had just entered.

"She doesn't look tired at all," Gwen said in an underbreath. "She rather looks . . ."

Amazing, thought Joe. *She looks amazing.* She was dressed in a light blue gown that seemed to shimmer as she moved through the light. With a décolleté lower than her mother—and Joe, for that matter—would allow her to wear in public. Because somehow there was a figure beneath that dress he hadn't quite been aware of before, and white translucent skin lifting gently with every breath. He took a gulp of whiskey.

She didn't look tired at all, she looked ready to take Newport by storm. Confident, calm, and a little flushed. Her dark hair was pulled back from high cheekbones and was dressed with silver ribbons. And she took his breath away.

Joe looked up to see his father watching him.

Lionel shook his head slightly, obviously amused, and looked away.

"Come in, my dear," Grandmère said.

Dee swept into the room. Was this the same girl who was pedaling like a madwoman, dripping sweat to bring down a killer just hours before?

Joe stood. "Would you—" He cleared his throat. "Would you care for a sherry?"

She turned a brilliant smile on him. "Yes, thank you."

He had left her an hour ago with her face smudged with dirt, her hair flying every which way, and her dress a wrinkled mess. Maybe he'd fallen asleep over his whiskey and this was a dream.

But she took the glass he offered, her glove touching his bare hand.

"Are you up to a ball tonight, my dear?" Gwen asked.

"Oh yes, I feel quite invigorated."

Joe's mother smiled. His father looked resigned, and Gwen beamed on her protégée.

Deanna sat down next to Gwen. "Do you think the police will let Belle leave with the other actors in the morning?"

They all looked at Lionel.

"I'm no barrister but I imagine they will. They have her address in the city, though I'm sure she won't be staying there for long, once Maude Grantham finds out the Judge was paying for it. To know her husband was keeping a mistress would be humiliating enough, but that he was keeping a mistress merely as a conduit to Charlie . . . I hope Belle has the good sense to stay away from the woman."

Deanna nodded. "Is it wrong to feel a little sorry for the Judge? I mean, I know he was an awful man, but he loved Charlie. It seems to me he should be punished for all the other stuff, like sending people to prison for doing the same thing he was doing. But not for doing it."

"I wouldn't worry about the Judge," Gwen said. "He had his cake and ate it, too, while he was living."

"Mama," Laurette said.

"And the world will never know him for anything but as the mouthpiece for all those closed-minded, self-styled moralists. Moral, my foot, passing judgment on people, making it illegal for women to practice birth control so they can feed the children they already have, for what a husband and wife do in their own houses, for—"

"Mama!" exclaimed Laurette. "We all know how you feel."

"Yes, well. Don't worry about the Judge, Deanna. It will all be hushed up. Even if Walter starts blabbing, they'll just say he's vindictive—or mad. And it will go worse for him in court."

"Will Elspeth and I have to testify in court?" Deanna asked, growing slightly pale.

"Heavens no," Gwen said. "They won't even ask, because

they know that your papa will never allow it. But it won't come to that."

"It will probably never get to court," Lionel said. "They'll send Walter off to a sanitarium for a while, saying the stress of work unbalanced his mind." Lionel snorted. "It's the way of the world, my dear."

"He tried to convince Will that Belle killed the Judge and Charlie, too."

"He can try. But I think the Grantham lawyers would rather sacrifice one son-in-law than have the Judge's reputation besmirched by what might come out in court."

"It isn't fair," Deanna said.

"No, it isn't," Lionel said.

"That's why it's important to put your energies into things that can be changed," Laurette said.

"Mother," Joe said.

"Ah, I hear the carriage," Gwen said. "Shall we go?"

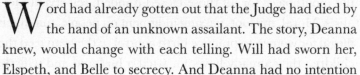

Word had already gotten out that the Judge had died by the hand of an unknown assailant. The story, Deanna knew, would change with each telling. Will had sworn her, Elspeth, and Belle to secrecy. And Deanna had no intention of letting it be known that she had anything to do with the matter.

Strange as it seemed, she was still more frightened of her mother's opinion than she was of a murderer holding a pistol.

She danced almost every dance, twice with Herbert, who was full of plans for his trip to Germany and the fledgling automobile industry there. She even waltzed with Joe, who was particularly quiet. She thought he might still be angry with her for her "escapades," as he thought of them. But he danced well, and it helped keep the images of the Judge and Edgerton at bay.

They left the ball fairly early, and the sway of the carriage lulled Deanna into a blissful place close to sleep, but when the carriage stopped at Bonheur, all the events of earlier in the evening came racing back. It left her agitated and anxious.

Lionel and Laurette went upstairs.

Gwen waited for Deanna, but Deanna stopped at the bottom of the stair. "Do you think I might sit out on the terrace for a bit?"

"Of course, my dear. Joseph, will you accompany Deanna for a stroll out in the garden? You can trust him, Deanna, to behave like a gentleman."

"Do you mind, Joe? I'd just like to be outside in the air for a while."

"It would be my pleasure."

Gran Gwen took a shawl from the sofa and put it around Deanna's shoulders. "Don't stay out too long. We have another busy day tomorrow."

Deanna walked out the back of the house, Joe silent beside her. There was a breeze off the ocean, and she pulled the shawl around her shoulders.

"Too cold?" Joe asked.

"No. It's clearing out my cobwebs."

Joe smiled. "You used to always say that."

"That's because it does. There's so much about the world I don't understand, Joe."

"I think no one ever understands everything. You'll learn what you need to learn."

They walked on down toward the cliffs, stood by the steps down to the Bonheur beach. Watched the waves churn into foam at the bottom.

Joe moved closer. "Deanna, there's something I want to say."

She wanted to say *Not now*, but best to get it over with. She lifted her chin.

He took a breath. "I love you, Dee, but I can't be worried about you all the time. I can't concentrate on my work when I don't know what you'll get into next. I have to stay focused on making the machinery more efficient. That's the most important thing if we want to stay competitive, hell, if we want to stay in business at all. Do you understand?"

Deanna nodded, but she wasn't hearing much of what he had said. She'd gotten stuck on the "I love you, Dee" part.

"My father says I'll get used to it, but I don't think I will. I worry about you."

Deanna broke out of her haze. "Well, don't. I don't want you to worry about me and I don't want to take time away from your machines, they're your passion. But I won't give up my passion, either . . . as soon as I find out what my passion is."

"Ah, Dee. You could be a grand lady. You have all the makings and the energy and cleverness that your sister lacks."

"I don't believe that's the life for me, Joe."

"No, I'm afraid that it isn't, either. But you should try."

"I have tried. I've spent months going to balls and buying new clothes and it's been delightful, well, about half of it has been delightful. As to the rest . . . it was wasted time. My best friend is my maid."

"You just need to take the time to find girls with your own interests."

"Like your mother?"

"No, not like my mother."

"Your mother goes to balls, she's invited to soirees and all the rest, and yet she has her work to fulfill her."

"Yes, but that's because . . ."

"She's married to a rich and important man?"

Joe laughed. "Only partly so. The rest is because of her sheer captivating personality."

J oe led her toward a bench that sat at the cliff's edge. He and Bob and Dee and sometimes Will had sat here years before making up stories as the days wore on. Now Bob was dead. Will was downtown wrapping up a murder investigation. Just he and Dee sat here in the dark. The wind was brisk, and he put his arm protectively along the back of the bench. She settled comfortably against him.

They sat looking at the night sky, as the clouds scudded across the stars. The waves hushed on the beach in the inlet below their feet. The moon lay low on the horizon. It was a quiet time, a peaceful time, something Joe thought they both needed.

"You know, Dee. I don't come out here much anymore. It's nice sitting here like we used to. These days it just seems like all I do is work. But it's important work. And it's up to me. Did you ever stop to wonder what comes next?

"I didn't realize until tonight how much you—I don't know— have grown to be a woman.

"We make a pretty good team, don't you think? We get along okay, most of the time. You actually listen to me natter on about my inventions, and I think you understand what I'm talking about. And you'll find your own calling. I have no doubt about that.

"I don't know, there just seem to be so many ifs. I guess, all in all, we might be good together. It's not the life you've been raised to enjoy, and you've probably figured out by now, I don't want to go back to that life. But we could make this work. What I mean is . . . well, hell, Dee. What do you think?"

Dee sighed.

"Do you think we should try to make a go of it together?"

Dee sighed again.

"Is that a yes, or a no, or a maybe? Dee?"

He looked down at her, her head resting on his shoulder. Her eyes were closed.

He laughed quietly. He'd be sitting out there a long time if he waited for an answer. His intrepid, sometimes infuriating, detective had fallen asleep.

Author's Note

The Gilded Age was a time of colossal riches, conspicuous consumption, and outrageous expenditures. Wealth was something to show to the world. Money became the standard by which society was judged. The Knickerbockers, the old moneyed families of New York, were forced to accept the "new rich," those who made their fortunes in shipping, oil, railroads, and manufacturing, into their ballrooms and social clubs.

What these newcomers lacked in taste they made up for in extravagance. And ruthlessness.

But it wasn't just among the social elite that change was happening. And it was happening fast. Jobs opened up for middle and working class men and women. Education was mandatory so many young men, no longer content to become day laborers, farmers, or dock workers, migrated to the city to become clerks and office workers and partake of city life. Young women, once destined to be servants or laundresses, were accepted into colleges, found employment as typewriters (the term for those who did the typing), store clerks, and bookkeepers.

Jobs once only open to men had new female competition. But as is often the case, the more things changed the more they remained the same. And still haven't changed today. Women might work alongside men but they weren't paid as much.

One of the few places a woman could earn as much as and often more than her male counterpart, was in the theater. Talented actresses and singers were in great demand. Retired actresses became managers, opened their own theaters, took companies "on the road." And though they were disrespected by the "genteel" classes, especially the women, many were hardworking, moral people.

The rich were known to invite entire casts to perform for their guests in Newport, building theaters for the performance on the grounds of their "cottages," while the Manhattan theater remained dark, and losing money, during their absence.

Of course the double standard was very much alive and so while the divas might be entertained with a glass of champagne on the veranda after the performance, there was nothing unusual about some of the lesser actresses picking up a little extra work down on the yachts of the rich husbands of Newport.

On the following day, life went back to normal with the men retiring with their cigars to the Newport Reading Room. The society women taking their daily carriage rides or shopping in one of the boutiques along Bellevue Avenue. The actors, after too little sleep, piling onto the train or steamer to return to the city, to spend their days in rehearsal and their evenings in performance.

Others were moving into the twentieth century and they were moving there together. It wouldn't be too odd to see Laurette Ballard standing side by side with a working-class woman as they marched for contraception, and to meet again protesting for the right to vote. Strict societal lines continued to break down.

Inventions made life at home easier. Sewing machines, tele-phones, ovens, and carpet cleaners, not to mention the flush toilet, left more leisure time available to all classes and women joined in the craze for sports: tennis, golf, yachting, riding.

Even the most respected ladies could be seen riding a bicy-cle. Fashionable split skirt cycling outfits were all the rage. Female cycling clubs were formed. But as usual, there was a huge outcry against this sport. Doctors, still mostly male at this time—though that was rapidly changing also— warned of dire injuries that bumping over the road could incur.

Of course, what they really feared is exactly what hap-pened. Once the "weaker sex" tasted a bit of transportational freedom, they weren't content to stop there. In another year, the automobile became the only way to travel.

While the rich still invited a select few into their inner circle for an evening's fun, the rest of the country began "going out." Pubs and boardwalks, fairs and circuses, moving pictures and museums, baseball and horse races.

In 1891, the first Ferris wheel appeared at the Chicago World's Fair and though it was dismantled, other Ferris wheels appeared making the circuits of watering holes and fairs.

And as with any time of great change there was a huge backlash of fear and anger. In the same year that Alfred Nobel set aside his estate to establish the Nobel Peace Prize, French captain Alfred Dreyfuss was falsely accused and convicted of treason. Oscar Wilde was convicted and sentenced to two years in prison for homosexuality, just months before the first US Open Golf Tournament and four months before the first American auto race.

1895 was a transformative year and the reason I chose to begin the Newport Gilded Age mysteries during the time.

There was no turning back, the "modern" man and "modern" woman were on the ascent.

And I like to think of Joe and Deanna leading the way.

For more about life in Newport during the Gilded Age, go to shelleyfreydont.com.

Shelley Freydont is the author of several mystery series, including the Newport Gilded Age Mysteries (beginning with *A Gilded Grave*), the Celebration Bay Mysteries, and the mysteries featuring Lindy Haggerty and Katie McDonald. She is also the author of several novels under the name Shelley Noble, and her books have been translated into eleven languages. Visit her online at shelleyfreydont.com.